Killer Vintage

KILLER VINTAGE

A West Texas Wine Thriller

Eric D. Sanchez

BROWN BOOKS
PUBLISHING GROUP

This is a work of fiction. Any similarity to real persons, living or dead, is coincidental and not intended by the author.

Killer Vintage: A West Texas Wine Thriller

Brown Books Publishing Group
Dallas, TX/New York, NY
www.BrownBooks.com
(972) 381-0009

A New Era in Publishing®

Publisher's Cataloging-In-Publication Data

Names: Sanchez, Eric D., author.
Title: Killer vintage : a West Texas wine thriller / Eric D. Sanchez.
Description: Dallas, TX ; New York, NY : Brown Books Publishing Group, [2025]
Identifiers: LCCN: 2025936830 | ISBN: 9781612547275 (paperback) | 9781612547282 (ePub)
Subjects: LCSH: Young men--Texas, West--Fiction. | Tour guides (Persons)--Texas, West--Fiction. | Wineries--Texas, West--Fiction. | Missing persons--Fiction. | Drug enforcement agents--Fiction. | Lubbock (Tex.)--Fiction. | LCGFT: Thrillers (Fiction) | BISAC: FICTION / Thrillers / Suspense. | FICTION / Literary. | FICTION / Coming of Age.
Classification: LCC: PS3619.A5169 K55 2025 | DDC: 813/.6--dc23

ISBN 978-1-61254-727-5
EISBN 978-1-61254-728-2
LCCN 2025936830

Printed in Canada
10 9 8 7 6 5 4 3 2 1

Author photo courtesy of Jennifer Polito.

For more information or to contact the author, please go to www.KillerVintageBook.com.

To Stacey, Braxton and Charlotte—
"I love y'all this much!" (my arms outstretched)

Things are not always as they seem . . .

—Attributed to Phaedrus

Prologue

Monday, June 13, 1994
11:54 p.m. CDT
US Highway 87, six miles north of Tahoka, Texas

Riding in the passenger side of the Freightliner, the man known to some as Bill Masterson adjusted his gaze on the side-view mirror. Masterson saw no headlights, and the only vehicle behind the Freightliner was several hundred yards behind them. Ahead, the road was empty, with the occasional white road reflector embedded in US HWY 87 beaming back with the Freightliner's headlights. The bright lights of Lubbock, which were close to fifteen miles to the north, offered the only other signs of life.

Five minutes later, as the Freightliner passed the green-colored exit sign that announced County Road 7600, Armando, Masterson's driver, engaged the Jake Brake on the truck. With a muffled backfire, the truck slowed from its sixty-five-miles-per-hour pace.

8 8 8

Behind the truck, El Paso DEA Senior Special Agent Traegar Jackson, who had been following the Freightliner since it pulled away from the *taquería* in Big Spring, Texas, made sure that his vehicle remained completely anonymous on the road. Following a large truck like this during the day was easy, especially with more cars and traffic. However, this time of night, with hardly any traffic, a lone Chevy Tahoe following a freight truck would be easier to spot. Several times, Jackson had put almost half a mile between his car and the Freightliner.

As he saw the bright red brake lights, he noted the upcoming exit and began to slow down his vehicle until he eventually pulled his Tahoe to a crawl on the side of the highway, several hundred feet from the exit ramp.

Driving slowly and waiting patiently, the Freightliner's right turn signal came on as the truck turned right on CR 7600 and headed east. The truck drove past the Town & Country convenience store on the southeast corner of CR 7600 and HWY 87.

Jackson depressed the gas pedal on his Tahoe and followed the Freightliner.

Just over two thousand feet later, the Freightliner approached South Plains Cellars and pulled onto a small, caliche-paved road. Jackson decided to drive past the turning Freightliner and continue east before doubling back. He immediately began to scan for a concealed area off the county road to continue his surveillance.

Armando brought the rig to a complete halt in front of an eight-foot chain-link gate. All the lights at South Plains Cellars were off except for two. Dust clouds from the rocky road reflected off the Freightliner's lights and the wheels grinded to a halt. The first light shone from the ground up on the left side of the road and lit up a sign with the South Plains Cellars winery logo and its large, stenciled letters: GRAPE DELIVERIES ONLY—PREPARE TO BE CRUSHED! Masterson always smiled when he saw this sign. Good to know that some people in business had a sense of humor.

Another light emitted from the top of a ten-foot pole from the same side of the caliche road. This light was brighter and helped illuminate a larger area, specifically for the camera, whose red light and lens stared directly at the two passengers in the Freightliner. Masterson looked at his watch, which displayed 12:00 a.m.

"Right on time, Armando. Nicely done."

"Gracias, Señor Bill. Easy drive."

The man on the other end of the camera looked at the image of the two gentlemen sitting in the cab of the Freightliner and spoke into a microphone. "Come in," he said.

Outside, his voice rang from a loudspeaker.

Slowly, the roller wheels on the eight-foot-tall gate slid on a steel rail embedded across the caliche road from right to left, allowing the Freightliner truck to drive onto the winery's crush pad, parking next to the winery's crusher and destemmer machine. Armando depressed the Freightliner's clutch, moved the transmission from first gear to neutral, killed the engine, pulled the emergency brake, opened the driver's side door and hopped out of the cab. Masterson opened his passenger door, grabbed a midsized, empty blue duffel bag, and exited as well.

Before Armando and Masterson reached the giant garage door, it suddenly opened, and bright halogen lights inside the winery caused Masterson and Armando to temporarily shield their eyes. A figure stood in the middle as the garage door opened.

"Ah, Señor Bill, always on time. Good to see you, amigo."

"You too, Hector. Hey, give me and Armando a moment, we've got to take a piss. Here are the keys." Masterson tossed a set of keys to Hector, who grabbed them smartly midair.

"No problem. Boys, let's get started!"

Hector clapped his hands, and four gentlemen sprang from behind him, three of them holding two large four-inch hoses about forty feet in length, and the other man, just ahead of the others, grabbed the keys from Hector's hand and approached the Freightliner's stainless steel tanker.

The man walked to the very back of the tank, quickly identified the valve and subsequent lock. He inserted the brass key into the lock and removed the lock and valve cover. The other men quickly connected the hose to the open valve and secured the hose connection to a wine tank, deep inside the winery. The first man then scaled to the top of the stainless steel tanker truck, using the small ladder. At the center hatch, he turned the large wing nut, cracked open the top lid, and rested it on one of the exposed folded bolts. He walked across the top of the tanker, moved down the back ladder, placed his hand on a large turn valve and waited.

"I'm ready, Mr. Hector."

Hector then barked, "Is tank four ready?"

Three seconds later, a voice in the winery replied, "Tank four ready, Mr. Hector."

Hector pointed his finger to the man with his hand on the stainless steel tanker's valve and spoke. "Open it, now."

The man turned the valve open, and gravity took over. The grape juice mixture, along with dissolved cornstarch, moved quickly from the tanker into the four-inch hose. Once the mixture reached the end of the first forty feet of hose, another man turned on a switch to an aluminum nitrile single double-diaphragm pump, which used compressed air to contract and expand the diaphragms. This in turn caused the grape juice to move quickly from the tanker to the large five-hundred-gallon stainless steel tank, with a large number "4" stenciled in black on the side. With the pneumatic pump maxed at thirty-five gallons per minute, Hector and his team would off-load this tanker's close to two hundred and fifty gallons in just under eight minutes.

⌸⌸⌸

In the darkness, behind a large and low-hanging cottonwood tree, well-shielded by the summer foliage, Jackson snapped his twenty-fourth picture—the last frame left in his camera roll. With his targets less than three hundred feet away, he used a smaller lens for his Nikon FM2/T. The bright halogen lights emitting from inside the winery and on the winery's crush pad offered the perfect amount of lighting for his photographs.

Realizing he had reached the end of his roll of film, Jackson pressed a release button on the right side of the camera, unfolded a small crank on top of the camera, and turned the crank counterclockwise, which spun the exposed film safely into the film canister. Reaching into his film bag in the front driver's seat, he grabbed a new roll of Fuji 1000-speed film, with his handwritten initials "TJ" in black Sharpie ink.

Jackson was a perfectionist when it came to documentation. While other DEA agents on his team used the more readily available Kodak film, Jackson preferred Fuji.

Jackson placed the new Fuji film canister into the back of the camera too quickly, and it bumped awkwardly off the camera's left interior and dropped to the ground. The canister bounced twice on the ground and rolled underneath his parked Tahoe. Jackson swore to himself. He didn't have time to grab his flashlight and search for the Fuji film canister. Instead, he grabbed a fresh roll from his camera bag. He breathed slowly to calm his nerves. After a few seconds, he deliberately and slowly loaded a fresh roll into the camera, advanced the roll three clicks, and then went back to snapping pictures.

Shortly before and after passing the Freightliner on County Road 7600, Jackson had driven another quarter mile east down the road, before turning around. He'd killed his headlights on his Tahoe and pulled off the side of road, using a patch of extremely tall Johnson grass as cover. He waited for the rig to pull into the winery and onto the crush pad. With his headlights still off, Jackson slowly drove a few hundred feet and parked near the home of South Plains Cellars' closest neighbor, an abandoned farmstead lined with cottonwoods.

With no pay phone in the immediate vicinity to relay his position to El Paso DEA headquarters, Jackson went to his shaky backup plan. He reached over to the backseat and retrieved his DynaTAC Motorola portable cellular telephone, model 8000X. Weighing two and a half pounds and ten inches in length, the DynaTAC Motorola portable cellular telephone was a monster. The telephone companies started rolling out 2G cellular phone service to major U.S. cities in '92—and El Paso had it, finally.

Jackson crossed his fingers that this service had finally arrived in Lubbock.

After confirming reception and dial tone, a relieved Jackson called the dedicated messaging service used by El Paso Division DEA agents in the field for after-hour updates. He quickly left his name, location and a short voice message. His fellow agent on the case, Brian Harris, would hear Jackson's message first thing in the morning.

The farmstead he parked closely nearby looked like the perfect cover. He'd have to find out in the morning what its status was. It offered an excellent vantage point to watch the action at the winery's crush pad.

When the last of the grape juice exited the thousand-liter stainless steel tanker, Masterson walked up to Hector and shook his hand.

"Pleasure doing business with you, Hector."

"You too, Señor Bill." Hector then reached into his pocket and pulled out a small, portable walkie-talkie.

"Mister Sáenz. We are all good here. All product received."

In less than a minute, Jaime Sáenz arrived with a black briefcase and walked over to Hector and Masterson, who were standing near an elevated concrete tank pad, supporting the now half-filled wine tank number four. Jaime Sáenz placed the black briefcase on the concrete tank pad and removed the clasps on both ends of it. It sprang open. Looking back at Bill Masterson was his familiar and most favorite founding father, Benjamin Franklin, along with 9,999 exact-looking friends. Masterson picked up the first stack with his left hand and used his right thumb to flip through all of the hundred-dollar bills.

A gust of wind blew a low-hanging, leaf-covered cottonwood branch where Jackson was standing with his camera. He brushed the limb aside and continued snapping his pictures in the darkness. Jackson grinned. All his photographs, plus what he just witnessed, would be more than enough for the DEA to move his investigation forward. The only sounds Jackson heard were the familiar clicks of his camera and the faint sounds of sporadic vehicle traffic driving up and down US HWY 87, well over a third of a mile away. Suddenly, a distinctive and audible metal click broke the moderate silence. Immediately following the click, a flashlight broke the surrounding darkness.

With his camera in his left hand, Jackson slowly turned around and saw two men standing a few feet behind him. A larger and more muscular man facing Jackson's right pointed a modified Beretta 92 nine-millimeter-caliber handgun directly at his head. Attached to the automatic pistol was a slightly larger suppressor screwed to the end of the gun's muzzle. The older man, bald, wearing glasses above a large black mustache, pointed the flashlight and spoke with a thick Mexican accent.

"Señor, why are you taking pictures of that winery?"

Jackson did not respond but quickly took in the situation. With his left hand holding the Nikon camera, his right was free and could easily grab his Glock 17 nine-millimeter pistol attached to his belt holster on his left hip. As if sensing Jackson's thoughts, the older man spoke again.

"By the time you reach for your gun, my friend, you will be dead. Now please, place your camera on the ground, slowly take out your gun from your holster, put it on the ground, and take two steps back."

To emphasize the older man's point, the stronger man moved closer to Jackson, with the Beretta and its silencer now only inches from his cranium. Jackson swore to himself and did as he was told, placing his camera and gun on the ground in front of him and stepping back a few paces.

"You have no idea the kind of trouble you're bringing down," Traegar said. "Best you walk away and pretend like you never saw me."

"That will not be possible," the older man said.

The older man then extended his right leg toward the Nikon camera and gun and kicked them to his right, where they skidded and bounced off the matted, red caliche, clay ground surface, away from Jackson's reach.

"That camera is worth over a thousand dollars. I'd appreciate it if you could show a little more respect to one of the finest pieces of photographic technology on the market today."

"You telling me I am not respectful? Is that what you are saying?" said the older man.

Traegar said nothing, only glaring back at the old man.

"Roberto, teach this man some manners."

With his bulging and muscular arms extended, Roberto responded by quickly pointing his Beretta toward Jackson's right kneecap and squeezing the trigger. The muted report of the gun sounded like a rock hitting the side of a car. Jackson collapsed to the ground and screamed in agony.

The older man spoke again.

"Now that I have your attention, I will ask my question again. Why are you taking pictures of that winery?"

The pain searing through Jackson's knee was almost unbearable. Grasping it with both hands, blood began to seep through his fingers. Jackson spoke in a belligerent tone.

"It's none of your fucking business *why* I'm taking pictures of that winery."

The older man frowned. He leaned toward Jackson and spoke in low tone. "There are some things that must be kept secret at any cost. Do you know how we do that?"

Jackson struggled to speak, but finally responded: "You will regret this."

The older man ignored him. He stepped back several feet from Jackson, lowered his head, and spoke softly.

"This is how," he said in a low voice. "Now, Robert."

Roberto pointed the gun at Jackson's forehead and squeezed the trigger. Jackson saw a small flash of light, heard a distinctive *pop!*—and then darkness.

Jackson's body fell lifelessly to the ground.

1

Tuesday, June 7, 1994
8:57 a.m. CDT
Lubbock, Texas

Bud Garza placed his lightweight Ping golf bag with grasshopper extenders a few yards away from the tee box and grabbed his driver, preparing to tee off. Bud's fraternity brother, Doug Webster, looked aimlessly about the sunbaked golf course. Bud, extremely busy with classes during spring term, hadn't seen Doug much since early in the year. They were finally making up for lost time now, but also playing a "goodbye" round of golf, as Doug, who had finally graduated, would soon be leaving Lubbock for good.

"Shadow Groves, my ass," said Doug. "You know, in about twenty years, this course will finally live up to its name." He wiped a bead of sweat from his neck with a sports towel and sighed.

Shadow Groves Golf Course, located in the northwest section of Lubbock, Texas, was only a few years old. The young Chinese elm trees that lined the fairways were still supported by guy wires and wooded one-by-four stakes to secure the saplings against the harsh winds of West Texas.

"Not sure what you expect," Bud answered. "This *is* Lubbock, after all. Amazing that there're any trees at all."

"I expect a place to live up to its name!"

"You know, for being such a man of the world, it shocks me that it took you six years to get that business degree."

"Took my time, Bud. Besides, the old man didn't have a spot for me at the company until this year. Another week, and I'll be set."

"Doug, you graduated almost three weeks ago. Why are you still hanging in Lubbock?"

Bud lifted his head and then lowered it, taking a practice-swing driver.

"Well, like I said. I won't start working for my dad until next week. And I'm having a good time where I'm working now."

"Current job? Why is this the first time I'm hearing about you even *having* a job? Where the hell are you working?"

"South Plains Cellars."

"You mean that fancy winery south of town?"

"Yep, that's the one."

"Well, other than giving you more of an excuse to drink during the day, what are you doing out there?"

"I'm a tour guide. I've been doing it all summer. I get paid five-fifty an hour, and you're right, when the opportunity presents itself, I do get a few drinks of wine during the day. But you got to play it cool. I lead tours, show people how they make wine, and then at the end of the tour, we taste through some wines."

"And you get paid *real* money to do this?" joked Bud.

"It's a pretty cool gig. You have to do other stuff, like cleaning glasses, folding shirts, replacing wine displays with new bottles, take out the trash, sweep a little—but that's pretty much it. Oh, and every now and then, the owners will have dinner at night catered in for guests, and they'll ask us if we can help out serving wine. That's about as hard as it gets."

"Nice gig," replied Bud. He took one more practice swing with his knock-off-named Big Bertha–style driver. He approached his ball, swung his club, and with that familiar *clink* sound, shot his ball down the fairway. He gazed after it. Good. Only a slight fade.

Suddenly, something Doug said previously didn't make sense.

"Doug, what do you mean by *owners*? I thought the bank owned that place. Wasn't there a big thing a while back about it going under?"

Bud recalled the newspaper article he read in the *Lubbock Avalanche Journal* about the bankruptcy and receivership of South Plains Cellars by Tanrock Capital Bank. He was himself a business major and prided himself on keeping up with local doings. Besides, the *Lubbock Avalanche Journal* printed the business news and the sports news—his true passion—in the same section of the newspaper.

"The bank doesn't own them; they just loaned the money to the new owners who run the winery now. Here, let me hit my ball."

Doug stepped up and swung his driver, and his golf ball flew straight down the fairway. He bent down to pick up his broken wooded tee and continued to recount his experience.

"Seems that when they built South Plains Cellars about five years ago, they raised almost all the money from the folks in Lubbock and the surrounding counties. They sold company shares at a thousand bucks a piece. These same folks already knew about the success that Pheasant Ridge and Llano Estacado Winery were having, especially when Llano got that Double Gold Medal at the San Francisco International Wine Competition back in the mid-eighties. They figured if Llano Estacado was having all this success making wine in West Texas, why not build a new winery and give the people of Lubbock a chance to own a piece of it as well."

"You seem to know an awful lot about wine, Doug."

"Hazards of my new occupation."

"So what went wrong?"

"Well, they ended up raising close to six million dollars. In turn, they spent close to five million on the winery itself. You should see it, Bud, it's *palatial.* It's got a huge cedar-lined room where they store and age the wine barrels, all this stainless steel state-of-the-art wine-making equipment, marble columns from Italy, imported staccato fixtures, expensive French barrels. It's amazing."

"You really are a tour guide. All right, it's a nice winery. But what went wrong? Why did they file for bankruptcy?"

"So, when the winery opened its doors in 1989, they about sold all the wine they had on hand. If you ask people, most of the wine sold was to some of the same folks in Lubbock who owned shares of the winery. Everyone wanted to have a bottle and a piece of those first vintages made at South Plains Cellars. Some bought it as a memento; others just wanted to have gifts they could give at Christmas and brag to their outta-town friends and family that this wine came from a winery that they partially owned."

"Wait a minute. So, how do you know the South Plains Cellars' inner workings? That can't be on the tour guide agenda."

"Remember how I told you they occasionally have wine dinners at the winery?"

"Yeah."

"Well, sometimes when they are having these wine dinners, they invite employees of Tanrock Capital Bank to fill in the empty seats."

"And?"

"Let's just say when a seat-filler is a cute bank loan officer, and she gets a bit tipsy, she won't stop talking."

"Got it." Bud smirked.

"Let me tell you, this cute one I met last month was a chatterbox. Even . . . er, in the boudoir, if you know what I mean."

"I get the picture. I'm amazed you could concentrate enough to listen."

"Hey, if talking loans and investment is what gets a smokeshow like that going, I'm all for it."

"I suppose."

"Anyway, she couldn't stop talking about the bank, the winery and all of the financial problems they had a few years ago."

"Financial problems?"

"Around August or September of 1992, the winery ran out of money and couldn't pay their growers. No grapes. No wine."

"What happened?"

"Well, those grape growers got mad. You know, all of 'em are cotton farmers and they ain't used to people not paying 'em. When they gin the hundreds of acres of cotton they just harvested, they get paid at the co-op, albeit several years later. When they showed up with bins of grapes and the winery didn't have any money to pay 'em, they got pissed. It got really bad. Liens against the winery, lawsuits, even physical threats. I think Jennifer said the police got called to the winery to settle things down between them and some growers."

"*Jennifer?* Oh wait . . . the cute loan officer?"

"Right. Jennifer . . . something or other."

"I see. This was a very close relationship, obviously."

"So, last month, mostly out of curiosity, I did some research in the library stacks on campus about the wine business and wine operations. Most of the information I read was based on wineries in California. Seems that the wine industry and wineries have two major business obstacles. First, you got to have a shit-ton of money to invest in storing all that the wine before it gets sold. The second issue is that your main ingredient is grapes. A winery is almost wholly dependent on the weather and what Mother Nature deals you. You can have years where there's a bunch of high-quality grapes and other years where there's not. So, when the winery temporarily closed its doors in '92, the same bank that owned the note took 'em over. According to Jennifer, there was a group of new owners that were able to raise more money, and now they're trying to turn it around."

"You just might make a businessman yet."

Bud was impressed, but he should have expected as much from his friend. Doug, despite his good-old-boy demeanor, was no dummy, and he had a curious mind. That was why they were friends. Doug also had a deep-seated desire not to let down his father, whom he secretly revered.

"So where is the winery getting its grapes?" Bud asked. "Especially since, as you mentioned—or, excuse me, 'Jennifer something-or-other' mentioned—it got messy."

"The bank folks found out that some of the same growers who got screwed in '92 had loans with Tanrock Capital Bank for land and farm equipment. The bank officials worked with the new ownership group and smoothed things over with several of those growers. The bank then cut them a break on a few of their loan notes if they would start selling grapes to South Plains Cellars again."

"Did it work?"

"The winery is back in business and making wine, that's for sure."

"Sounds like you had a lot of free time on your hands."

"Bud, it's not like we are all that busy working. It's a winery . . . in West Texas. . . . Look around, Bud, there's not that many people living out here, let alone deciding to spend some time visiting a winery in the middle of West Texas. Monday through Thursday, I'm lucky if I do two or three tours a day. Once I clean all the glasses, hang up all the shirts and clothing, pull up bottles on the display, sweep up, I just kind of hang around."

"So, what do you do?"

"I go in the back, talk with the wine maker. I talk to the cellar rats. I ask questions. I read *Wine Spectator* magazines."

"What's a 'cellar rat'?"

"A cellar rat is a slang wine industry term for 'cellar worker.' They work as assistants to the winemaker, helping pump wine from tank to tank, cleaning out barrels, assisting with bottling, and crushing grapes. They do all the hard, dirty grunt work of making wine."

"And you're giving that all up to work like a slave for your old man probably for decades before he gives you any real responsibility?"

Doug laughed nervously. Bud knew his quip had not been that far from the truth. Or at least what Doug feared was the truth.

Then a happier thought occurred to Doug.

"You know, Bud, *you* should apply for my job when I leave the week after next. You just told me before we teed off that you're not liking your lifeguarding job. You should look at working as a tour guide instead. I bet I could get you an interview lined up super quick."

"I don't know shit about wine."

"Hey, neither did I. I'm just an old Army hick from Kilgore, Texas, remember?" Doug was getting enthusiastic at the prospect of sharing his job with a fellow fraternity brother.

"Look, the winery has a bunch of training videotapes and other information about wine. And you've got that total recall memory thing going, Bud."

"Eidetic. And it doesn't really work like that."

"Doesn't matter. All you do is memorize the tour-guide speech and you are in. If anyone asks you a question you don't know, just tell them that you will ask the winemaker and get back to them. Nine times out of ten, the person who asked that same question will completely forget about it."

Bud thought for a moment about his future potential career move in the wine industry. "And you get paid every two weeks?"

"Yep, that's the way it goes."

Bud smiled, and while his immediate thought was his next approach shot, Doug's idea scratched at the back of his mind. Despite the lifeguarding, his school expenses had left him more or less broke by the end of the term.

Now he faced a summer term of expenses. His parents did what they could to help, but he needed to put food on the table now.

He'd need to update his résumé, that was for sure.

But working an easy and interesting gig while he got his bearings wasn't such a bad idea. Besides, where else could you actually drink on the job and get paid for it?

No, not a bad idea at all.

2

Wednesday, June 8, 1994
7:21 p.m. CDT
Rio Grande River, near Solis campsite, Big Bend National Park

The scrub brush, cottonwoods and mesquite trees draped over a river of brownish water that burbled quietly above a shallow sandy bottom and eased its way south. Usually, the river was swollen during this time of year, but the heavy May and June rains had not come with their normal intensity this season.

Juan Perez breathed a sigh of relief. Swimming was not his best skill in life and lifting his fifty-kilogram backpack above his shoulders would be much harder work.

As the trailhead stopped at the river, Juan looked across it. He scanned the other side, looking for his marker. In the background, the Chisos Mountains stood tall, marking the southern beginnings of the vast Rocky Mountains range. Focusing on the landscape closer in, his eyes quickly caught the target. There it was, a bright yellow flag, tied to a rusty metal pole, about twenty yards up along the shore, nested between two large cottonwoods.

His instructor told him to position himself directly south of the marker, and from there, he could easily walk across the river, with the water being no higher than his shins. If it had been a normal rainy season, Juan would have had to find another crossing point.

Juan adjusted his backpack on his shoulders; he scanned upstream and downstream, looking for any sign of hikers, *gringo touristas* in rafts or canoes, or any presence of U.S. *federales*. With no one in sight within miles, Juan looked at his compass and moved along the riverbank until the needle pointed north toward the marker. He then cautiously walked in the riverbed toward the yellow-flag marker.

Surprisingly, he made it across the river with relative ease. The cool waters of the Rio Grande felt good on his swollen feet. But this was just the beginning. He had only walked about fifteen kilometers, with many more kilometers ahead.

Juan crossed the river, ascended the raised riverbank, and approached the rusty pole with the yellow marker. He noticed a metallic shine on the ground below his feet. He brushed away the loose mesquite and cottonwood leaves and branches, exposing a large one-by-one-meter metal door, which was buried in the river shoreline. With a twist of the latch, the metal door creaked and revealed its contents.

Inside the waterproof metal locker, there was an olive-drab Coleman pup tent, eight canteens of water, two pairs of dry socks, a flashlight with a red filter lens, and various food packets. Juan immediately opened one of the canteens and drained the entire contents. The June weather this day in the northern Mexican state of Coahuila had hit a high of 41 Celsius, 106 Fahrenheit, and the temperature was finally dropping.

After assembling the tent, Juan unzipped its entry flap and moved the contents of the metal box inside his new home for the evening. With only the heavy backpack left to store, he sat down and untied his wet shoes and then peeled off his even more wet socks. He carefully arranged the socks on top of his tent to dry and placed his shoes just outside and near one of the tent's poles. His moist and shriveled feet felt cool as a breeze snaked its way up the riverbank.

As he heaved his backpack into the tent, he crawled inside. He raised the zipper up around the entire tent entryway, and he laid his weary body to rest. A minute later, Juan Perez was fast asleep.

3

Thursday, June 9, 1994
7:04 a.m. CDT
Marfa, Texas

One hundred and forty-four miles north and west of Juan's impromptu campsite, a man was still asleep in his black Chevrolet Tahoe, the only car parked on the southeast side of the Presidio County Courthouse on the corner of East Lincoln Street and Highland Street. The morning sunrise, already ten minutes in progress, crested over the single-story buildings in downtown Marfa, Texas, and the cloudless sky allowed the bright light to penetrate the darkness in the man's vehicle. Across the street, the sun's rays bounced off the three-story courthouse and illuminated the pink stucco, covering the quarried local brick and stone used to build the impressive edifice. The building's tall, white rotunda dominated the little city, as it had one hundred and seven years ago when it was first constructed.

He woke from his five-hour sleep, eyes opened and adjusted to the light surrounding him. He glanced at his watch and quickly looked west down East Lincoln Street. The green garbage truck was still parked in the last place where he saw it pull up about seven hours ago. Not wanting to lose sight of his target but answering the biological need pressing his body, the man quickly exited his vehicle, walked across the street, approached the nearby building of the Presidio County Jail, and opened the glass entry door. The only person in the reception area was a young man, a deputy, with the name J. SMITH on his Presidio County police uniform.

"Did you sleep in your car all night?" inquired the young man.

"Yeah. That's the downside of stakeouts. Do you mind keeping an eye on that green garbage truck for me? I've gotta take a piss."

"No worries. At this time of day, the only cars I see are yours and his."

He walked through the reception area and made a beeline to the jail's restroom. A few minutes later, he emerged. When he arrived back at the reception area, he glanced through the glass door, noticing the green garbage truck was still parked.

"Any place I can get a quick bite to eat?"

"There's a Waffle House just off San Antonio Street, a few blocks east of South Highlands Avenue. You've got plenty of time and the service should be quick. The church crowd won't hit that spot for a few hours."

"Please call the Waffle House right away if you see anybody approach that vehicle." The man's thumb pointed toward the direction of the green garbage truck. As he left, he spun around and asked the deputy a question.

"Did you want anything?"

"All-Star Marfa Special would be great, eggs scrambled," the smiling deputy replied.

"You got it."

The man walked across the street, jumped into his Tahoe, and drove off quickly.

The deputy stretched his arms and yawned. His eight-hour night shift was almost over. Sometimes weekend duty was not so bad. Not only was he assisting in an active investigation, but he was also going to get a free breakfast to boot, all courtesy of the federal government.

4

Friday, June 10, 1994
9:20 a.m. CDT
Lubbock, TX

"Turn off US 87 and take the CR 7600 exit. Turn left and head east on CR 7600. You will see the winery on your right. You can't miss it."

Doug's directions had been spot on. Bud turned into the entrance slowly and his jaw dropped.

The South Plains Cellars entrance was flanked by large elm trees on either side, reminiscent of an antebellum Southern plantation. Beyond the elms were rows and rows of green vineyards, their vines clustered with green bunches of grapes. These rows looked carefully manicured and stretched from the entrance of the winery to FM 7600. There were acres and acres of them, too, maybe twenty or thirty. The winery's taupe-colored front facade looked like an old Spanish mission, with large wooden doors guarding the entrance. Above the doors was a large Spanish-style belfry, with a large bronze bell. The large parking lot surrounded a circle garden, with Knock Out rose bushes around the edges, and a four-tier water fountain in the middle. On the winery's left and right sides, pergolas extended outwards, supported with taupe Doric columns.

Bud circled the parking lot two times, trying to take it all in, then parked his Explorer in the space designated for visitors. As he sauntered toward the winery, a movie scene popped into Bud's head:

"Welcome to Toad Hall," quipped Skip, Rob Lowe's character from the 1983 movie *Class.*

"I have never seen such a vulgar display of wealth in my entire life. How do I get one?" replied Jonathan, played by Andrew McCarthy.

"Well you can do what we did. Bootlegging bought the place."

"Bootlegging?"

"Uh-huh, before Gramps went legit."

The winery's outdoor landscaping was amazing. No weeds, and the winery grounds were immaculate. Small rock pebbles served as the landscaping base, with flowers and bushes all carefully groomed. Bud felt as if he were walking on the set of a *Southern Living* magazine house photography shoot.

He grabbed the large wooden handle of the winery's "grand entrance" door and had to use considerable effort to open it. He stepped inside and was taken aback yet again.

Inside the grand tasting room, Bud noticed smaller Doric columns surrounding the room and foyer entrance. Above hung a large wrought-iron chandelier suspended from the top of what looked to be a twenty-foot-high ceiling, with artificial lighting that imitated the sun, shining through small-paned windows. The granite-slated floor encompassed the entire tasting room, comprised of three-by-three-foot granite slabs, interlaced with smaller-sized ceramic tiles.

To the right was a long granite stone bar, supported with stone of various dark hues. Behind the bar, multiple wine bottles were stored inside wall-mounted diamond-shaped storage bins, with wine bottles lining the black granite shelf. To Bud's left, there were stone statues, wine barrels, and merchandise—T-shirts, polo knits, caps, etc. All of it was tastefully displayed amongst the smaller case displays of wine, coupled with wooded racks filled with wine themselves.

White tablecloths adorned the wine barrels, each with bowls filled with wine-tasting crackers, two wrought-iron black chairs bookending each barrel. Urns of various sizes filled the tasting room, giving it a pleasant and friendly feel. Bud stood in amazement.

"Impressive, isn't it?" a voice spoke behind Bud's back.

Against his slight surprise, Bud reluctantly tore his gaze away from the surroundings and turned toward the voice. "I'll say. This place is amazing."

A hand stuck out toward Bud. "I'm Jerry Campbell. You must be Bud Garza. Doug told me quite a bit about you."

Bud extended his hand and shook Campbell's, whose firm grip matched the strength of Bud's.

"Nice to meet you, sir," replied Bud.

"Yes, nice to meet you, Bud." He led Bud toward a side door. "Why don't you step into my office, and we can get the interview started?"

The door led immediately to an office, and Bud sat down in one of the guest chairs in front of Campbell's desk.

"So, what do you think of the place?"

"It's amazing."

Campbell sat in his office chair across from Bud. "Yes, it's definitely one of the better places to work in this area."

Campbell wasted no time and peppered Bud with standard interview questions, which Bud answered to his best ability. After about five minutes of this, Campbell abruptly stood up and said, "Okay, that's enough. When can you start?"

"I mean . . . Don't you want to look at my résumé?" Bud was still holding the manila folder in his hand.

"Nope."

"Uh, I've got tell my boss at Northridge Country Club. If I can swing it, can I start this Monday? If that works for you."

"Perfect." Campbell extended his hand and Bud shook in return.

"Looks like we're getting another Sigma guy that works here."

"Doug Webster told you, didn't he?"

"Indeed. And Doug is not the only Sigma brother that works here. Steve Worthington works here as well."

Holy moly—*oh shit*. "Steve Worthington?" Bud couldn't believe his bad luck. Steve Worthington, infamous for being one of the biggest assholes Sigma had ever seen. He'd almost been kicked out of the fraternity on multiple occasions, only to be saved by his father and some mysterious alumni connections. Worthington these days was held up as an example of what *not* to be as a Sigma brother.

What was worse, Bud had been there and witnessed it all. He'd practically had a front row seat.

Jerry Campbell paused before replying. "Yes, Steve has been with us for almost three years. How well do you know Steve?"

Bud snapped back to attention. "Uh. Pretty well. We used to be roommates a few years ago."

"Great." Campbell sized up Bud with his eyes, then said, "You know, you guys look a lot alike. You could pass for brothers, or cousins for sure. Same build and same height."

"Yeah, we're . . . not related," said Bud. "At all."

Campbell glanced at his work-desk calendar and looked for Worthington's name.

"Anyway, Steve is off today and through the weekend, but he'll be here this Wednesday and he can help train you. And Doug's last day is the Sunday after next, so he should be able to get you started. Plus, we also have two more tour guides, Jason Rector and Jill Hatten, both of whom will be good resources as well."

Bud smiled as best he could at the news. "Great."

5

Friday, June 10, 1994
9:33 a.m. CDT
Lubbock, Texas

Steve Worthington was late. He slammed his fist on the wheel of his white 1994 Bavarian Motor Works 325i convertible and let out a storm of curses as he sped toward the airport. The car's Blaupunkt audio system was blaring out Jesus Jones's two-year-old hit, "Right Here, Right Now."

Right here, right now, I need to be someplace else, Worthington thought.

He shook his head and looked at his Rolex: 9:33 a.m. His Southwest Airlines flight was scheduled to leave at 10:10 a.m. He barreled his BMW past the Lubbock International Airport entry signs and swerved in the opposite lane, barely missing the black Ford F-150 pickup truck that was driving at a normal speed in front of him. Thank goodness there was barely any traffic, unlike the continuing traffic nightmare of his hometown of Austin, Texas.

Worthington brought his car to a full stop in the airport parking lot. He grabbed his Reebok athletic bag from the back passenger seat, quickly opened the driver's side front door, slung the strap over his shoulder and stepped out of his car. He reached back in the car and carefully grabbed the oversized sixty-four-ounce 7-Eleven Double Gulp beverage cup, filled to the top, secured with a plastic lid and straw from the front passenger seat. Only then did he close and lock the driver's side door with the car key.

Worthington ran inside the airport entrance and directly to the Southwest Airlines counter with no customers.

"Finally, a break!" muttered Worthington to himself. He quickly looked at his watch, which read nine forty-two.

The Southwest agent greeted Worthington with a warm smile. "Hi, welcome to Southwest Airlines. How can I help you, darling?"

"Yeah, I'm on Southwest Airlines number nineteen," Worthington said half out of breath as he placed the 7-Eleven cup on the counter and fished his wallet from his bag.

He presented his identification to the gate agent, who was already checking on the flight.

"Looks like your flight is on time." The woman frowned. "Do you have any luggage to check?"

"Nope."

"If you hustle you should still make it, honey." The agent punched in Worthington's information while he breathed a sigh of relief.

The woman smiled at him again and reached below her terminal to retrieve the boarding pass. Worthington nodded, grabbed the pass, then his cup, and ran toward the airport security entrance.

The security line was only a few people deep when Worthington arrived. He quickly threw his bag on the security table and held his boarding pass in one hand while holding on to his cup in the other. Then he placed his mouth over the straw, pursing his lips around it.

"Thirsty?" inquired the very overweight security agent standing in front of him. The man seemed too fat to even fit through a metal detector.

Worthington looked back and grinned. "Yeah, running late, too."

"What kind of sandals are those?" inquired the Transportation agent, with a quizzical look on his face as he stared at Worthington's feet.

"Birkenstocks."

"They look . . . comfortable . . ." muttered the agent. "Never seen anything like 'em, though."

Worthington shrugged and handed his boarding pass to the security agent, who seemed to struggle with every breath he took.

The agent glanced at his pass and said, "Have a safe flight. Looks like you are gate four." Worthington held his cup with his lips pursed around the straw as if still drinking and walked through the security metal detector quickly.

"Thanks," he said

He grabbed his bag off the metal rollers, threw it over his shoulder and ran over to gate 4.

The gate 4 agent smiled as Worthington approached. Not as old as the agent at the counter, this one was much younger and better looking. She looked at the ticket and said, "You just made it."

She examined his boarding pass and shook her head. "Too bad an A-lister like yourself wasn't here earlier. I think all we have left are center seats."

"Yeah. Running late today."

The gate agent handed Worthington a teal-colored plastic boarding pass emblazed with the numbers 97 in black at the top. "You look familiar. Have we met before?"

Worthington lied again. "Probably. I've been flying to Austin quite a bit. My mother is not doing too well."

"Oh, I'm sorry to hear that, honey. Hope she gets to feeling better."

Worthington walked over to the entrance of the Jetway.

"What's that you're drinking?"

Worthington froze. Nobody has ever asked him that before, especially at the airport. Worthington pondered for a second.

"What did you ask?" replied Worthington.

"I said, what are you drinking? You must be thirsty. We hardly see people with such big drinking cups boarding the plane."

Worthington gathered his thoughts. He didn't actually like soda. He blurted the worst-tasting one he could conjure. "Mr. Pibb."

"Oh." The gate agent shrugged. "Who drinks that when you can drink Dr. Pepper?"

"Yeah, I know," Worthington replied numbly. "It was all they had left."

"Well, have a good day and thank you for flying Southwest." The gate agent extended her empty right hand and Worthington returned the teal-colored plastic boarding pass and entered the Jetway ramp.

Marching down the ramp, he looked again at his watch. 10:05. He'd just made it. As he entered the Boeing 737, he pursed his lips around the straw again and pretended to drink his fictional Mr. Pibb as he walked down the plane's passenger aisle full of flyers. He scanned the airplane and stared toward its tail end. On the very last row, he a saw an older man sitting on the aisle seat with no one else in the center or window seat. Perfect.

The older passenger got up as Worthington nodded toward the empty window seat. He squeezed through the row, placing his Reebok bag under the window seat in front of him while still holding on to his cup. He latched his seat belt and took another draw off the cup and straw.

Whew.

Now he could finally relax. He couldn't remember how many flights he had taken over the past year to Austin. Thirty? Forty? Too many to count. It didn't matter. On every trip he scored two thousand dollars from his employer in Austin.

"It's all that and a bag of chips," whispered Worthington to himself as Southwest Flight 19 pulled out from the Jetway.

6

Friday, June 10, 1994
9:40 a.m. CDT
Lubbock, Texas

Campbell reached into his office desk and handed Bud a large black binder.

"This is our training manual for new tour guides. When you get home, start memorizing these bullet points about the winery—you'll be expected to talk about them when you give your tour. Now, don't get intimidated by all the information. I don't expect you to give your first tour by yourself anytime soon. For the next couple weeks, you will accompany Doug while he's still here, along with Worthington, Jill or Jason in an observational capacity only. You'll quickly discover as you identify different parts of the winery, the visual recognition will prompt your brain to remember what each part does." Bud opened the large binder and started to thumb through the new orientation guide.

"In the back is a videotape cassette. You have access to a VCR, right?"

Bud nodded.

"Good. That tape cassette comes from the Wine Institute of California. This is the same training tape that many wineries in Napa and Sonoma, California, use to train their winery tour guides. It will take you through the basics of each major wine-grape varietal, Cabernet Sauvignon, Chardonnay, Merlot, Sauvignon Blanc, and a few others. What they smell like, their taste profile, and even suggested foods to pair with each wine. There's even commentary and interviews from André Tchelistcheff and Robert Mondavi."

Campbell paused. "Do you know who André Tchelistcheff or Robert Mondavi are, Bud?"

Bud had no clue who either of the gentlemen were, other than they had something to do with wine.

"I'm afraid I've never heard of 'em."

Campbell tilted his head. *Finally, a new tour guide who doesn't bullshit me.*

"Look, Bud, no worries, you will quickly find out. Make sure you watch this training tape at least two times, even more if you like."

"Okay. Will do."

Campbell stood up and walked around his desk. "Good. Let me show you around. Best pay attention. I'm going to give you the 'official' South Plains Cellars tour. Now, you don't have to memorize everything I say today. All the information I'm going to give you is in the training manual."

Bud stood up and prepared to follow Campbell.

"Now, Bud, our busiest times are Thursdays through Sundays. As the number three tourist attraction in Lubbock, Texas, next to the Buddy Holly Museum and Llano Estacado Winery, we average anywhere from twelve to sixteen tours a day during those days. Like today, along with Tuesdays and Wednesdays, we may conduct only two to four tours per day.

"As our guests arrive, let them make their way to here, this large stone table, with our guest book. Be sure and greet each guest with a smile and state, 'Welcome to South Plains Cellars. Is there something we can do for you?' Never say, 'Is there something we can *help* you with.' Saying the word *help* implies to our guests that they are unable to do something by themselves and makes them uncomfortable. That is exactly the opposite of what we want here."

Bud engaged his memory—which was remarkable, if not quite as marvelous as Doug had implied—and it seemed Campbell had noticed the look of attention on his face.

"So, you've greeted our guest or guests and nine times out of ten, they will request a tour. We run our tours every thirty minutes, so before you approach our guests, look at the clock and the tour guide logbook so you know in advance when the next tour will start." Campbell looked at his watch and lifted his head up. "Let's pretend we're ready to do a tour now. We will walk over to this door, which opens to the side patio portico and the crush pad. Be sure and hold this door open until all the guests walk through the doors." Campbell pushed open the patio doors and smiled. Bud followed Campbell outside.

"Everyone, my name is Jerry Campbell, and we want to welcome you to South Plains Cellars, the premier winery of Texas. South Plains Cellars was founded in 1988, due to the initial success of other pioneer West Texas wineries like Llano Estacado Winery and Pheasant Ridge. So, you may ask, why West Texas, and why is it a good place to grow grapes and make wine? As you may know, here in this part of West Texas, we're at three thousand five hundred feet in elevation. This part of the state only receives around nineteen inches of rain per year. However, in this semiarid region, we get hot days and cool nights, which promote vigorous growth for our wine grapes here. Wine grapes like drastic diurnal swings, which promotes flavor and development. Wine grapes do not need as much water as other crops, like all the cotton fields you see around us."

Campbell extended his hand and swept it in a large 180-degree rotation. Other than the winery in front and the estate vineyard in the back, acres upon acres of cotton fields surrounded the winery. Bud had once heard that almost twenty-five percent of the United States's total cotton production came from this area of the South Plains.

"Now, as you may have seen on your drive up, we are proud owners of twenty acres of our estate vineyards surrounding and in the back of the winery. Mostly planted to Cabernet Sauvignon, we also have a few blocks of Cabernet Franc, Merlot, Malbec and Petit Verdot, which are the five noble grapes that make the famous red wines of Bordeaux.

"So unlike grapes from California, Oregon and Washington, which are harvested in September and early October, our grapes in West Texas reach maturity in late July and August, due to the heat in this area. The first grapes to make it to the winery are the white wine-grape varietals, like Sauvignon Blanc, Chardonnay, Chenin Blanc, Riesling and Muscat Canelli. As the harvest continues, the red wine grapes still on the vines go through what we call 'veraison,' the changing of grape skin color from green to purple. Upon veraison and at the right sugar levels, or 'brix,' in the wine grapes, our red wine grapes arrive at the winery. These include grapes like Cabernet Sauvignon, Merlot and Zinfandel."

Campbell walked over to the winery's crush pad, which consisted of a large concrete pad, with a support truss, cables and pulleys. Below the support truss rested an enormous stainless steel bin with a large auger screw inside.

Attached to the right side of the bin was a large stainless steel tube exposing another auger screw inside and raised at a 45-degree angle ten feet above Bud's head. Buttressed at the end of the stainless steel tube was a large chute at the top, with blue painted letters spelling out the word DEMOISY. From there, a stainless steel chute continued upward to two much larger machines, cylindrical in nature, painted in dull light yellow with the word WILLMES stamped in black color on the side.

"Almost all of our wine grapes are harvested at night and arrive in the very small hours of the morning. Once the truck carrying our grapes stops at the weigh station and the weight of the grapes is determined"—Campbell pointed to the very small building adjacent to the crush pad—"the truck of grapes pulls up here. Our wine cellar workers then hoist each half-ton bin of grapes and dump them into this receiving bin, which, by the means of this auger screw, move the grapes into our elevated crusher-destemmer machine. That machine removes almost all the grape stems, leaves, etcetera, leaving only grape juice, skins, seeds and pulp, or what we call 'must.'"

Bud tried to imagine the process, but found he couldn't quite get his mind around the whole thing yet. He badly wanted to see this machine in action. Must be awesome to watch, he thought.

"From there, it depends if the grapes are meant to become red wine or white wine," Campbell continued. "Let say, for example, that the grapes are for a white wine, like Chardonnay. Once the Chardonnay grapes leave the crusher-destemmer, the must moves into either one of these large pneumatic presses. Each of these German-made presses can hold up to twelve tons of grapes. Once the press is filled, a giant bag inside inflates with air and softly presses the must with a pressure of up to about almost two atmospheres, or thirty pounds per square inch. The grapes' juice is then extracted from the must, where it gets pumped into one of the many stainless steel fermentation tanks in our winery.

"Now let's say we are making a red wine, like Cabernet Sauvignon. Once the grapes leave the crusher-destemmer, the must is pumped directly into our stainless steel tanks, and we inoculate them with yeast to start the fermentation process. More on that later. Are there any questions so far?"

Campbell's presentation had been so engrossing that Bud almost looked around for a show of hands. Campbell smiled and continued. "No? Not very curious today. Want to get to the good stuff, I see. Let's continue our tour, and please follow me into our red wine room."

Campbell pressed a large green button on the winery wall next to the crush pad and immediately next to a large garage door. In a flash, the garage door opened. Bud walked through the giant threshold and into the winery itself. Appearing in front of him was an elevated concrete pad, about two feet high at the front and rising slightly higher toward the middle, supporting multiple, very large stainless steel tanks. The tanks were neatly arranged in rows, with stainless steel elevated catwalks between them and a maze of pipes above each tank. The front of each tank stated the exact gallon capacity, clearly marked below the stamped word of the manufacturer: MUELLER, ST. LOUIS, MISSOURI. While each tank varied in size, every tank's midsection had dimples around the entire circumference. Campbell pressed another green button, this time on the inside of the winery. The large garage door quickly closed.

"These are our fermentation tanks and where we make our red wine. Once the must arrives in this room, our winemaking team starts the red-wine-making process. We add yeast and immediately the must or juice begins to ferment. For those who remember high school biology, remember that the natural byproducts of fermentation are three things: heat, alcohol, and carbon dioxide. You will notice the large fans above my head, which help ventilate the toxic carbon dioxide from the winery." Campbell pointed to the fans installed in the ceiling at different sections of the winery.

Campbell stopped and surveyed his surroundings, again pretending he had a large group of tourists. "Now remember what I said on the crush pad about how white wine and red wine are made differently? And how grapes for red wines avoid the German-made press on the crush pad and are pumped directly into any one of these stainless steel tanks?"

Bud felt a little silly but answered as if he were a tourist. "Yes."

Without acknowledging Bud directly, Campbell continued. "Well once the must for red wine is pumped into, say, this tank, the winemaker adds the yeast and the fermentation process starts. As the yeast converts the sugars into heat, alcohol, and carbon-dioxide, that same carbon dioxide pushes the grape skins to the top of the tank. To extract the red color for a red wine, the juice must be in contact with the skins. We then attach a pump to one of these pipes here and 'pump over' the juice from the bottom of the tank to the top. A good analogy is the process of making coffee, where hot water percolates over coffee grounds and creates the hot brew. This is a very similar process where the juice percolates through the skins, obtaining the right amount of color, flavor, and tannins. Many times, our winemaking team will perform multiple pump-overs each day until the wine is ready."

Bud listened and watched with fascination both the process and Campbell's passionate delivery.

"Once the winemaker deems that a red wine is ready, the team will use one of these same pipes and pump the red wine into another empty stainless steel tank. We then pull up this smaller bin"—Campbell pointed to a small stainless steel bin, with a much smaller auger screw resting inside at the bottom of the bin—"and park the bin right here." Campbell pointed to the front and bottom of the Mueller tank. "Now, you will notice this larger, round door on the side of the tank. One of our cellar workers will open this door, climb inside the tank, and start to shovel the skins, seeds and remaining grape material out and into this smaller bin. Since there is still wine captured in this material, we will pump it back into the press to get more wine. Once all the material is removed, the tank is cleaned and sterilized for a new batch of must. Are there any questions?"

Bud moved his head from side to side, taking it all in. Surprisingly, he had yet to see any of the cellar workers. It was just him and Campbell in the vast room.

"No questions? All right, let's walk over here and over to where our white wines are made."

Campbell walked over to another giant garage door, this one covered on the front with large, clear plastic straps each about a foot wide and hanging vertically from the top of the door to the floor. Bud felt a temperature drop before approaching the straps. Campbell pressed another green button, and another giant garage door opened as quickly as the other; he moved to the middle of the row of plastic straps. Grabbing the middle strap, he pulled it along with the other straps on the right side, allowing Bud to walk through the door.

Bud shivered and instinctively grabbed his upper arms to alleviate the drop in temperature. Campbell leaned near and said with a wink, "This is the best part of the tour in July and August."

Campbell stepped back in front of Bud and resumed his tour.

"Once the yeast has consumed almost all the sugar in the juice for a white wine, our winemaker determines when to stop the fermentation process. Sweet white wines like Muscat Canelli, Riesling and Gewürztraminer don't take as long to ferment as do dry white wines like Chardonnay and Sauvignon Blanc. So, to stop the fermentation process, our winemaking team turns on these propylene jackets."

Campbell immediately slapped his hand on the dimpled section of a large tank. "Inside these jackets is propylene glycol, a refrigerant which drops the temperature inside the tank quickly to just about thirty-two degrees Fahrenheit. That causes the yeast to die and halts the fermentation."

Campbell pointed to one of the two pipes sticking out about six inches from the side of each tank, and less than two feet above the bottom of the tank.

"We pump the fermented white wine to another empty tank from this 'rack valve,' leaving behind the dead yeast and any other grape material that has fallen to the bottom. We call this process 'racking wine.'

"Now, you will notice the cooler temperature in our white-wine-making room. Almost all our tanks are empty as 'crush'—that's when mature grapes arrive at the winery—is less than a few weeks away. We have just a few tanks filled with wine, which will be bottled soon. You may notice that tank here."

Campbell pointed to a large ten-thousand-gallon tank, which had a thick layer of ice around it, covering up the dimple coolant jackets. "That is finished wine waiting to be bottled. Since we do not want that wine to start fermenting again, we keep the temperature low, and the wine inoculated with nitrogen gas to keep it from oxygen exposure."

Bud stood again in amazement. He's never seen a ten-thousand-gallon tank, let alone four other ten-thousand-gallon tanks. This part of the winery was an immense cavern of space; the ceiling had to be seventy feet high. There were other tanks of different sizes, and true to what Campbell stated, all of the tanks were empty, with their large bottom doors open and ajar. These wine tanks also had adjoining stainless steel catwalks, as well as a crisscross section of pipes of different lengths and gauge size.

Bud had also noticed a small, green-lit digital temperature indicator on the giant tank. The display read thirty-two degrees.

"You can see by the number of tanks in our white wine room that South Plains Cellars prides itself on its white wine production," Campbell continued. "And soon you will be able to taste our top-selling wine, Regal de Cabernet. The large tank with the ice around it, waiting to be bottled, holds just over four thousand cases of Regal. And if there are no questions, we can now proceed to our bottling room."

At the end of the immense white wine room, Campbell led Bud to another giant garage door, with more clear plastic straps hanging vertically from the top of the threshold. Campbell pressed the green button and the garage opened quickly; he parted the plastic straps again and led Bud into a hallway. On the left, Bud noticed windows, and a large rectangular room housing a bottling line and various equipment staged a different section of the bottling room. Bud noticed how the bottling line track snaked in a serpentine nature, with curves here and there. He noticed the manufacturer's name, written in Italian, but failed to recognize the name, let alone try to pronounce it.

"Now, this is our bottling line, all state-of-the-art equipment from Italy. Behind the bottling room is our winemaker's laboratory. While you can't see the lab directly, it does adjoin the bottling room through that gray door and is considered the 'nerve center' of all our winemaking here at South Plains Cellars."

Bud noticed the simple gray windowless door with the words Winery Lab stenciled in bold black letters near the top.

"As you can see up front, our bottling line, fully staffed, can bottle up to sixty bottles of wine per minute. The entire bottling process starts from left to right, through these windows. Now, once the wine is ready to be bottled, our workers will unpack the cardboard boxes of empty wine bottles, then flip the boxes upside down so the bottles sit right side up. The bottles then make their way to the first machine on the left, that large circle machine. The machine performs sterilization and blasts nitrogen air in the bottle. From there, the empty bottles head toward the bottler, which elevates each empty bottle against the machine's one of twenty nozzles. As each wine bottle presses a nozzle, wine is dispensed into each bottle. From there, the full bottles of wine reach the corking machine, which, with another spurt of nitrogen gas, creates a vacuum and inserts a cork into the bottle.

"Next, the bottles move along that straight part of the bottle track. Here we have several workers that place foil capsules on top of each bottle. After they've been placed, the bottles then reach that machine"—Campbell pointed to a tall, black stainless steel machine—"which compresses the foil capsules firmly on the top of the bottle. After that, the bottle line turns right and goes to this large machine in front, which automatically places adhesive-backed labels, both front and back, on each bottle of wine. After that, the fully bottled and labeled wines are then shifted there"—he nodded in the direction—"where several workers will carefully place each bottle in the same empty boxes over there"—he nodded helpfully again—"where the whole process started. Each cardboard box holds twelve bottles each, and from there they're placed on wood pallets and shipped to our distributors in Texas. If there are no questions, then let's continue down this hallway to our 'little barrel' room."

Campbell walked in front of Bud as they exited the hallway with the bottle room and approached two massive French doors, lined with cedar and small glass windows. The strong aroma of freshly milled cedar hit Bud's nose like a hammer to his face.

Bud finally couldn't help but ask a question. "How tall are these doors?"

Without missing a beat, Jerry Campbell smiled at Bud and quickly blurted out, "As we walk through these *twelve*-foot-tall doors, our 'little barrel room' awaits." He opened the doors and Bud stood in awe again at what was in front of him.

The cavernous space made Bud feel very small. While the barrel room was not as large as the massive white wine room, the room was just as tall ceiling-wise and well-decorated. Each of the large room's four walls were lined with cedar-wood planks, with the rough side protruding in a vertical but tasteful fashion. On both the left and back side of this "little barrel room" were stacks upon stacks of sixty-gallon barrels, eight barrels high. On each barrel, Bud made out some of the words burned into the barrelheads, along with black spray-painted numbers, such as "60." Other words he was seeing for the first time, words such as *tonnellerie*, along with proper names like Nevers, Vosges, Allier and Limousine. Preceding each wall of barrels by a few feet were stanchions connected by red velvet ropes for keeping the more curious tourist from approaching the barrels too closely.

In the middle of this "little" room, hoisted into the ceiling high above Bud's head, was a magnificent wrought iron chandelier, close to ten feet in diameter, with small, black fleurs-de-lis surrounding each of the twelve large candles. The chandelier sat suspended in the ceiling, with a large iron chain that was looped to the side. Bud followed the iron chain to a hoist-and-pulley system, which obviously raised or lowered the giant chandelier.

Bud's eyes led to each corner of the room, where he saw elevated two-by-three-foot Kenwood speakers, which were currently broadcasting Frank Sinatra's "Luck Be a Lady" at a low volume. The smell of cedar, along with wine from the barrels, was strong and distinctive, but still pleasant.

"Welcome to our 'little barrel room,'" Campbell properly introduced, "and as you can see, there is nothing little about it. You are currently standing in the largest winery barrel room in the state of Texas—and one of the best decorated. The walls are freshly lined with cedar, and on the left and back walls you will see our barrels. The one with the rubber stoppers over the bungholes are aging both our red and white wines."

Bud giggled to himself, immediately thinking of *Beavis and Butthead* and how each character laughed compulsively after saying the word "bung-hole," one of their favorites. Obviously, the cartoon show had not hit Jerry Campbell's radar screen and he continued, pointing to the barrels with dark red stripes painted in between their metal hoops.

"These are our barrels of reserve wines, which are only available for sale at the winery. The majority of barrels on the left side and back of the wall are empty and will be prepared for the upcoming crush in a few months.

"You will notice several of the barrels have different French names like Vosges, Allier, Nevers, and Limousine." Campbell pronounced Vosges, *vohsz*, Allier as *aye-yah*, Nevers as *nah-var* and Limousine as *leemo-sahn*. "These are forest regions in France where the most expensive French white oak trees are grown, harvested, milled and aged. In the early 1800s, when Napoleon Bonaparte ruled France, he envisioned a giant French fleet of wooden navy ships to compete with the British Navy. Once these giant oak forests became mature, close to a hundred years, the wood did go to building and fulfilling Napoleon's dream of a giant French Navy. However, the advent of iron dreadnaughts and steel battleships in the late 1890s quickly put wood battleships on the endangered list. The good news for us in the wine business, the same old, well-aged wood in these forests is now used for barrel production."

"The other barrels are American white oak, which comes from the forests of Missouri, Kentucky, Ohio, and a few other states in the surrounding Ohio Valley. American oak imparts pronounced scents of vanilla and other toasty oak characteristics, while French oak imparts aromatics of exotic fruits and spices. American oak barrels cost us around three hundred to three hundred fifty U.S. dollars a barrel, while the French oak barrels can cost almost three times as much, well over nine hundred U.S. dollars a barrel.

"Barrel production is basically the same in France as it is in America, except that in France, the French barrel makers, or *tonnellerie*, split the oak trees to create the barrel staves, since French white oak is less dense than American white oak. American barrel makers will mill the oak staves with a saw, and there is less waste wood as a result, as opposed to the French method. Each barrel producer will harvest very old trees, some at a minimum of fifty years and some up to a hundred years old. The French forests I mentioned earlier will impart subtle and different aromatics to each of our wines. However, over time, each of these barrels will lose its flavor. Much like a tea bag, if you brew a cup of tea with boiling hot water and you use that same tea bag over and over, the tea bag will cease to impart its flavors, aromas, and taste. Therefore, each of these barrels provides a finite time where we can extract flavor, aromatics, and taste profile to our wines." Campbell curled the right side of his face to direct a reassuring smile and subtle wink at Bud. "But don't worry, we take pride in ourselves and our barrel program here at South Plains Cellars. Every year, our winemaker orders fresh and new French and American oak barrels for our winery."

Campbell drew his gaze back ahead. "Finally, each of you may notice the two small letters at the top of each barrel. Some barrels have the letters LT, some have MT, while others have HT stamped on the barrelheads. Each of the two letters refers to the barrels' toast on their insides. LT means light toast, MT means medium toast, and HT means heavy toast. So, what do we mean when we say 'toast'?"

Campbell turned around and pointed at the back wall toward a display next to the French doors featuring different oak staves, charred at different levels of heat intensity. Below each oak stave, words described the level of toasting and process. The visual medium made it immediately much easier for Bud to comprehend.

"You will see the photograph on the left side of the exposed barrel staves showing a barrel maker with a half-constructed barrel and spinning the barrel on top of a flame of fire. The longer the barrel maker keeps the barrel over the flames, the more the sugars inside the wood caramelize and impart stronger aromatics and flavor. Once the barrel maker is pleased with the level of toast, he will use thick cable ties wrapped around the barrel to secure the other end with a metal hoop. The barrelheads are secured, and the barrel is ready to be shipped and used for wine production.

"Now, if there are no questions about our 'little barrel room' and barrel production, then let's go through these doors here for the best part of the tour, the tasting." Campbell smiled and opened another set of French doors, which were the normal height of eight feet.

Campbell and Bud arrived back where they both started, in the winery's tasting room. To Bud's left was the winery bar, with its long marble countertop and slated rock stacked underneath. Behind the bar and built into the back wall were wooden X-frame wine storage racks. Beneath the X-frames stood tiny display porticos, featuring each of the wines sold at South Plains Cellars. On the ceiling above, tiny halogen lights spotlighted several wines. At both ends of the bar were two giant ceramic vases. In the middle of the bar, a silver bin held a clutch full of what looked like oyster crackers, but rounder and whiter in color. Across from the bar stood well-aligned case stacks of South Plains Cellars wines, with the top cardboard case cut in a diagonal fashion on the sides to better feature each wine for sale. Behind the case stacks of wine were clothing racks of men's and women's polo shirts, caps and other clothing accessories, plus other knickknacks, all bearing the South Plains Cellars logo, or "SPC" emblem.

While Bud was taking this all in, Campbell stepped behind the bar, reached to its lower counter, grabbed two Riedel wineglasses, and placed the glasses on the bar.

"All right, Bud, this is how we want your tour to run. And like I said, don't feel intimidated by all the information I just spilled out. That same tour took me several weeks to memorize. And remember that you'll be on as many tours as you can for the next two weeks, on an observation basis only. Before we taste through all our wines, what questions do you have for me?"

Bud froze and his eyes widened. "We are tasting all of these wines?"

"Yeah, better now than later."

Suddenly, the back door to the bar opened and a young man bellowed out a question.

"Jerry, where the hell's all the citric acid? How do you expect me to clean and sterilize all these wineglasses from Sunday? We must have had close to twenty tours yesterday. Did Jill forget to refill the bin *again*?"

Campbell turned his attention to the interrupting worker. "Jason, just go into the back and get one of the bags—the corner of the white wine room, near the walk-in cooler. Use the dolly; those bags of citric are heavy."

Campbell then turned his attention to Bud. "Before you go, I'd like you to meet our new tour guide, Bud Garza. Bud, this is Jason Rector."

Bud and Jason shook hands, Jason's a bit limp, but firm enough.

"Wow, that's a helluva handshake you got there," Jason commented, wincing with a slight touch of pain.

Bud smiled. "Thanks. My parents tell me I sometimes shake hands too strongly. I've got to work on it. Guess I'm nervous since this is my first day."

"No worries. So, you're the new guy, huh? Doug told me a little bit about you. Are you a Sigma?"

"Yep. Doug pledged a year before me."

"Cool. Did Jerry give you his tour yet?"

"Oh yeah, we did," Campbell interrupted. "We are just about to start tasting our wines."

Jason smiled. "That's the best part of the tour. Be sure and spit after tasting each one. There is more alcohol in those wines than those beers you throw back at Sigma parties."

Bud immediately sensed Jason was not in a fraternity, let alone a fan of them. It was something Bud was well used to hearing on campus.

Jason retreated to the confines of the kitchen and the storage room to get the dolly truck. Campbell spoke next.

"Okay, where are we?"

"Getting ready to taste a bunch of wines," Bud confirmed, pausing to look at his watch before continuing: ". . . at ten twenty-four in the morning."

Suddenly, the tasting room's wall-mounted phone rang and Campbell walked over, picked up the phone's receiver, and spoke.

"South Plains Cellars, what can we do for you today?"

Campbell listened to the voice on the other end. After about fifteen seconds, he replied, "Of course, Hank, see you in a few minutes." Campbell placed the phone back in its cradle.

"Looks like my meeting with our general manager is at ten thirty a.m., not eleven thirty." Campbell looked at Bud. "We'll have to do the tasting part early Monday morning, nine a.m. sharp."

Bud smiled. "Great, I'll see you then."

Bud then followed Campbell to his office and retrieved the large black binder filled with training material and the videocassette tape. The two men shook hands again and Bud, feeling a bit overwhelmed, exited the palatial winery.

On the other hand, he thought, it was a job where you got to drink wine. A lot of wine, apparently.

"Two more days of being a lifeguard. I can handle that."

7

Sunday, June 12, 1994
11:14 a.m. CDT
Lubbock, Texas

Glancing across the water, Bud's eyes focused on the bodies in the pool. The glare of the West Texas sun hit the pool's surface, causing the reflection to subtly dance across the aqua blue waves. *Just four kids so far . . .* Bud knew more would arrive, as it was only a few minutes after 10:30 a.m. With an anticipated record-high temperature in the forecast, it would only be a matter of time before the pool would be teeming with more kids, looking for a cool respite from the summer heat. Pearl Jam's "Even Flow" played from the club's pool bar. Yet another band from Seattle hitting the big time, Bud thought. Something must be in the water up there.

As Bud turned his head, he scanned the entire pool, quickly counting kids to make sure all heads were above water. He slightly adjusted the Oakley sunglasses perched on his nose and made another visual pass. The biggest myth of drowning was that people scream for help. In fact, it was quite the opposite. Potential drowning victims are more often so panicked that they fail to make a sound, which was even more likely if the drowning victim was a small child. What was more, plenty of people drown in a pool only a few feet from the pool deck.

Bud shifted his weight slightly in the lifeguard chair, adjusted his sunglasses again, and continued scanning the pool, his head moving left to right. His thoughts drifted to the conversation the prior night with his fraternity friends at a bar near where they all went to college.

"I'm telling you right now, that is a known fact," exclaimed Kenneth, who beamed with his newfound theory on relationships. He picked up a chip from the nacho platter they all were sharing and twirled it around as if it held hidden secrets.

"Interesting theory, Ken. I'm sure if Sigmund Freud were still alive, he could probably argue a point or two otherwise," cracked Bud. Bud and Kenneth had been good friends since they both pledged the same fraternity in 1991. He took a swig of Miller Lite from his sixteen-ounce glass mug and savored his favorite refreshment.

"So, I heard Doug say you got a job replacing him as a tour guide at South Plains Cellars?" said Kenneth.

"Damn, that was fast. How did you know?"

"I bumped into Doug at the Town & Country off Fourth Street. He was getting a can of Copenhagen, and I was getting some gas."

"Well, it's true. I start on Monday. That place is amazing."

"So you're leaving all the señoritas in the bikinis at Northridge?" Alejandro was surprised and shook his head in disbelief.

"Yep. I'm done lifeguarding. It's a great pool, but it's mostly young kids and more than half of them don't know how to swim. When I was back home, I think I saved maybe two or three kids in a summer. Now that I'm up here in the Hub for summer school, I've rescued five to six kids the past two *weeks*."

"Bud," said Kenneth, "you are in West Texas. Geographically speaking, not as many lakes or swimming pools as back home."

"Yeah, you're right."

Alejandro, in a seemingly important point to make, raised a finger, then quickly finished chewing his chip and swallowed. "Screw that, Bud. Don't tell me you don't like checking all that hot ass at Northridge. After our golf coach is done riding our ass on the practice range, I can't tell you how many times we get a chance to walk by the pool on the way back to our cars, and we see nothing but beautiful señoritas all around that entire pool."

Kenneth guzzled down the last of his beer in his glass, with his hand slightly raised, index finger pointing toward Alejandro. "You know, Bud, Chi-Chi Rodríguez here brings up a good point."

And so it went long into the evening.

Sitting in his elevated lifeguard chair, Bud collected his thoughts to the scene in front of him, then twirled his whistle on his fingers. He couldn't say exactly why yet, but his lifeguard instincts were buzzing. Then something caught his eye.

8 8 8

Elise Broadbent was excited when her mom informed her that today was swim day. Her mother had just bought her a new swimsuit and while four-year-old Elise didn't know how to swim yet, she was excited. When they arrived, Elise ran straight toward the shallow splash pool, but playing in the splash pool was only fun for a short while.

After she dropped off Elise at the splash pool, Sally had made a beeline straight to the outdoor bar. A recent divorcée, Sally Johnson wanted to get a Bloody Mary quickly in her hand. Raising a child as a single parent was truly more work than she'd anticipated, even though Sally had a comfortable living with her husband's monthly alimony payments. And the argument Sally just had with her ex on the phone that morning did not make things better. She caught the bartender's eye and spoke to her familiar acquaintance.

"Jocie, how are you?"

"I'm good, Sally, thanks for asking. A Bloody?"

"You read my mind."

"Your favorite lifeguard is working today." Jocie motioned her head toward Bud Garza sitting in his elevated guard stand.

Sally glanced at the handsome lifeguard, flipped her hair out of her face to obtain a better view of Bud, and sported a mischievous grin.

"He's about as tasty as this Bloody Mary I'm about to have."

Jocie smiled and began building Sally's morning cocktail.

8 8 8

A few minutes later, Elise got bored. Grabbing her small beach ball, she left the small splash pool and wandered to the main pool and looked around. *This* was the place to be, Sally thought, where the big kids and adults were jumping in the pool and splashing each other while laughing and playing games. This was where a great time was to be had.

Elise clutched the beach ball tight, walked closer and closer to the pool, small step by small step, and smiled. Taking it all in was mesmerizing. Why did her mommy not want her here? Daddy had said the same thing, but he wasn't here for some reason. Mommy kept saying that Daddy was working more and was only around on the weekends. She hoped that would end soon and he'd be around to snuggle her for bedtime again.

Suddenly, the small beach ball Elise was carrying popped out of her hands and landed in the large pool, near the edge. Bending over the edge, Elise tried to retrieve her ball.

Losing her balance, Elise fell sideways into the pool.

Immediately, Elise's head popped up, just above the water. Panicked, she realized she could not stand on the bottom of the pool. She began moving her arms and kicking her feet in a compressed fashion, but it was no use. The water was coming in from all sides and she started coughing as it raced into her mouth. She tried to scream but no words or sounds came out.

Suddenly, there were two loud whistles, followed by a large splash of water that came over her head. Elise's little body shifted as the water level suddenly rose. Two hands clutched under her armpit around her torso, raised her head and chest slightly above the water line, and then quickly dragged her over to the edge of the pool. By the time Elise coughed again, she was hoisted above the edge of the pool deck and placed bottom first on the deck. A boy lifeguard pulled himself out of the water next to her. Elise could not hold back her tears and burst out crying.

Bud leaned down on one knee, stood Elise up and spoke softly in her ear. "It's okay, little darling. It's all right. It's over."

Bud's whistle blast had caused everyone to stop what they were doing, go silent and stare at Bud and Elise. Sally suddenly heard only her voice in mid-conversation with one of her club girlfriends at the bar. She, like the others, turned her head in the direction everyone else was looking.

Odd. The little girl by the pool had on Elise's flowery swimsuit. She was standing in between the hands of a kneeling lifeguard.

Oh no.

"Elise!" Sally raced over to her child and the lifeguard.

Bud immediately noticed a woman racing over and turned Elise's body in the direction of what was obviously her mother. Bud kept trying to calm the girl down and whispered in her ears, "Here is your mom, sweetie. She will take care of you."

Sally almost slipped twice on the pool deck, running over to her daughter.

"Elise! Oh, my God, are you okay?"

Elise cried as Bud handed her little body over to Sally. Elise recognized her mother and started to wail and cry even louder, "Mommy!"

Sally bent down and embraced Elise and began speaking. "It's okay, Elise. Mommy is here. Mommy is here."

As the girl's cries started to subside, Sally noticed the very handsome and fit lifeguard standing in front of her. She pulled back her hair over her forehead and smiled.

"Thank you so much. You saved my daughter's life."

With his slight Texas accent, Bud replied, "No problem, ma'am, it's my job."

Bud continued, "She was only in the water for a few seconds. Probably more scared than anything. She'll be fine."

Sally continued to look at Bud, noticing his his square jaw, wavy brown hair, broad shoulders, cut muscles and six-pack abs. A few more seconds passed and an awkward silence between the two began to grow. Embarrassed, Sally shrugged her shoulders and came to her senses.

"Is there anything I can do for you for saving my daughter?"

"All good, ma'am. Like I said, it's my job." Bud flashed a grin and started walking toward his lifeguard stand.

"What's your name?" Sally questioned.

"Bud Garza, ma'am."

"I'm Sally Broadbent. Wait, I mean Sally Johnson. My name is Sally Johnson." She felt now even more embarrassed. Sally looked down and could see Elise clinging to her thigh and still softly sobbing.

"Nice to meet you, Sally Johnson." Bud smiled again.

"You said your last name was Garza?"

"Yes."

"You don't look like a Garza." Sally cringed, wishing her words to return to her mouth and stay there.

Bud winked and brushed the skin on his right forearm with his left hand. "A little more cream in the coffee."

"Oh, I'm so sorry, I shouldn't have said that. I'm not a racist or anything like that." Sally cringed again and her face flushed red, with more embarrassment.

"No worries, Sally. You're not the first person to say that. No offense taken." Bud had dealt with his Hispanic surname not matching his skin tone and the stereotypes men and women like him get his whole life. It was easier to laugh off the comment than to take any offense.

"Thank you again." Embarrassed, Sally picked up Elise in her arms and walked away.

Bud quickly scaled back up the lifeguard-stand ladder and settled into the chair. He looked at his watch. The TAG Heuer, a high school graduation gift from his folks (but picked out by his sister), displayed 11:32 a.m. Just three more hours of work and he would be done lifeguarding.

8

Sunday, June 12, 1994
6:04 p.m. CDT
Lubbock, Texas

Bud dropped his Ping golf bag in the back of his 1992 Black Ford Explorer, jumped in the front seat, cranked up the ignition and as the engine fired up, opened the center console. His hand descended inside and grabbed a well-worn tape cassette case, with the faded words NEW ORDER—SUBSTANCE on the spine in black letters. The song listings on each side of the clear cassette were mostly worn off, but Bud knew them by heart. Soon, "Bizarre Love Triangle" cranked through the speakers as Bud drove home.

Twelve minutes later, Bud bounded up the apartment complex stair to 4E, sighed in relief as he entered his unit, and put his golf bag in the corner of the living room.

After a shower, he rewound his VCR he'd set to record *SportsCenter* on ESPN, which he was hooked on, and which also helped him keep up with the latest in sports—common fodder in conversations with his fellow Sigma fraternity brothers. He pressed play and the faces of the hosts Dan Patrick and Keith Olbermann flashed onto the screen.

Bud then looked at his watch: 6:54 p.m. Damn. Well, he could be a few minutes late and put up with a little harassment. He picked out a purple polo shirt with a Ralph Lauren logo and put on a new pair of cargo shorts his sister had bought him out of pity after seeing his worn-out high-riding pair of shorts his mother had bought him sometime in the 1980s. Then he kicked on his Teva sandals—his own recent discovery—and was ready to go.

Bud loved these sandals, probably one of the most comfortable shoes he'd ever purchased; he'd even seen a few guys on the golf course wearing Teva golf sandals with metal spikes.

After a three-minute walk up the street, Bud arrived at his favorite watering hole, Conference Café. There was already a line about twelve people deep to get in the door. Bud was in no hurry and waited for his turn. The line was filled entirely with college students, almost all of them enrolling in school for the summer session. A large man with arms as big as Bud's thighs guarded the door, halfway sitting on the topside of a small stool that was completely dwarfed by his body.

"Well, look at those fancy shorts—you got enough pockets, Bud?" cracked Geno.

Bud smiled, bent his head slightly down and shook it side to side. "You never know when you may need an extra pocket or two." Bud reached for his wallet to fish out his Texas driver's license.

"Keep that pretty-boy ID in your wallet, Bud. We know who you are." Geno smiled and clicked his counter.

"Thanks, Geno."

Bud entered Conference Café to the sound of Ace of Base's "The Sign" blaring over the elevated speakers in the restaurant. The place was packed, all the tables were occupied and the large bar to his right was filled with students waiting to order drinks.

After walking through the front door, Bud glanced at one of his two favorite pictures hanging in the bar and restaurant. One was a large photograph of Major League Baseball pitcher Nolan Ryan, the all-time leader in strikeouts—5,714, Bud recalled—and no-hitters (the number 7 flashed across his brain).

In the photo Ryan was wearing a Texas Rangers uniform, blood on his jersey. Although Bud had missed watching the September 8, 1990, game, he'd seen the highlight. Kansas City Royal Bo Jackson chopped a hard ground-ball liner straight at Nolan's face. Ryan was able to make the throw to first and get the out, despite Jackson's lighting speed. The ball, however, broke open Ryan's lip.

The picture to the right was another photo of Nolan Ryan, this one taken three years later. It featured a forty-six-year-old Ryan with a headlock around twenty-six-year-old Chicago White Sox Robin Ventura, after he charged Nolan Ryan on the mound.

Conference Café was the most popular restaurant bar in Lubbock, especially for the college crowd. Started by three graduate students from Texas Tech, they opened the restaurant by mortgaging their automobiles and through an infusion of investment capital from the trio's parents. While the sports bar restaurant trend had already begun on the East and West coasts, it had been unheard of in Lubbock, Texas, and they had a hit.

From its grand opening, Conference Café had become "the place" to drink and eat at Texas Tech. Bud immediately liked it, and that it was three blocks from his apartment made it even more appealing. Soon, it became his only watering hole.

"Bud, over here!" shouted Alejandro.

Bud headed over and grabbed the table's only empty chair. "Shit, the place is packed tonight."

"It's the NBA finals. Game three. The Rockets and Knicks are knotted up at one game each. Battle of the game's two great centers, Olajuwon and Ewing," coolly explained Kenneth.

"I hope Olajuwon gets revenge on Ewing for that NCAA Championship back in '84," added Alejandro. "And that Houston finally gets its first championship. We've been waiting for that."

"Shit, your *city* had its shot last year," retorted Kenneth, "but those Oilers spit the bit against Buffalo. I'm still amazed how a defense allows thirty-two points in the *second* half."

"Doesn't matter," said Bud. "Cowboys would've still beaten 'em in the Super Bowl." Kenneth smiled and he and Bud did a quick high five.

Alejandro shrugged. "The only reason Dallas won those two Super Bowls was because Minnesota gave 'em all those draft picks for Herschel Walker. Crazy decision." Alejandro smiled ironically, sure he was about to get their goat—and he wasn't mistaken. "But we're talking round ball now. And my team didn't lose almost seventy games this season."

Bud and Kenneth nodded glumly. Their favorite NBA team, the Dallas Mavericks, were still reigning supreme as the league's cellar dweller.

"We need a new owner. And a new GM and a new coach," muttered Kenneth.

Alejandro, his point made, decided to let them off the hook. "Hey, how about this scenery? It is *muy bueno, caballeros*," he said with a grin.

Bud and Kenneth scanned the restaurant. “Most definitely,” Kenneth replied.

Bud zeroed in on a group of women, their table full of half-drunk bottles of Zima, with generous amounts of cherry grenadine added.

“What is it with Zima? It’s just clear malt liquor. Not even real beer.”

Bud looked at the full pitcher of Miller Lite on the table, sighed with relief and poured himself a glass.

Interlocking all his fingers and extending his arms palms outward, Bud stretched out and spoke, “All right, time for some trivia, gentlemen. Who’s our waitress?”

“Who do you think? Cheryl.”

Bud smiled. Not only was Cheryl very easy on the eyes, but she was also a very good server, with a knack for great hospitality. She was a natural beauty who wore hardly any makeup, and she had thick, sandy-blond hair, which was fashioned in either a baseball cap or ponytail.

“I like your shorts,” said a familiar voice from behind Bud.

Bud turned around and saw her. He blushed slightly, immediately stood up and gave her a big embrace. Bud enjoyed giving Cheryl hugs.

“Hey, Cheryl. Y’all are busy tonight,” Bud commented, charming Cheryl with his smile.

Cheryl smiled back and replied, “And we’re short two girls. I guess they’re watching the game somewhere else tonight.”

“Do you need a box?”

“You read my mind.” Bud had already dug out his Texas driver’s license and handed it to Cheryl.

“Let me get y’all another pitcher of beer, too.” Cheryl winked and quickly left for the bar.

Bud watched her walk away, keeping his eyes on Cheryl’s posterior.

Kenneth said, “She’s got a nice ass, that’s for sure.”

“Best in the place,” added Alejandro.

Bud nodded in affirmation.

“Why don’t you ask her out, Bud? She obviously digs you.”

“I don’t know. Cheryl is such a good waitress and takes great care of us. What if we did go on a date and things didn’t work out? Then I came in here and . . . it might not be the same.”

Both Alejandro and Kenneth nodded in agreement. "You speak truth, Kemosabe," Kenneth put in.

Cheryl Truett approached the waitstaff stand at the bar and placed her order for Bud's table. Johanna, another waitress at Conference Café, leaned into Cheryl's ear. "Looks like your favorite guy is here tonight."

Cheryl's eyes lit up and she mischievously smiled. "Yes. And those pecs of his are here, too."

"I really like those new cute shorts he's wearing. What do you call those things?"

"Cargo, or something like that."

"He likes you, Cheryl; all of us girls here know it. You should ask him out."

"Maybe." Cheryl smiled as she tucked a small white box under her left arm, grabbed the pitcher of Miller Lite from the bartender with her right hand, and headed back over to Bud's table.

"Here you go, Bud." She grinned and began to lower to the table the small box that featured a black QWERTY keyboard, tiny green backlit LED screen, and small, black rubber antennae. "And another pitcher of Miller Lite." Cheryl's dexterity was smooth and polished, as both the white box and pitcher of beer came to rest gracefully on the table.

"Great—thanks, Cheryl." Bud immediately handed Cheryl the empty pitcher and she walked quickly over to the next table.

Bud thought the setup ingenious. Bars and restaurants like Conference Café were setting up television screens that posted trivia questions. With satellite-based technology similar to what was being used for television broadcasts, players in the establishments would play against each other, along with other bars scattered throughout the United States, under team names, or "playmakers." Playmakers would answer Trivial Pursuit–style questions that were displayed on the dedicated TV screens scattered throughout the bar. Fifteen random trivia questions were doled out in three rounds, five questions per round. The quicker you answered the question, the more points each playmaker would receive. A question displayed on the screen, and as time began to expire, the screen would offer clues to the answer, thereby eliminating potential answers. However, as more clues were given, playmakers would receive fewer and fewer points.

At the end of each game, the team names of winning playmakers at each location would display, showing first place, second place and so on. Afterwards, the top score at an establishment would be compared to other high scores in bars scattered across the country. The highest Bud ever saw was 14,550 points, which was almost unheard of since the most possible points a playmaker could earn was 15,000 points.

On a whim, Bud suggested the playmaker name "Jerky" for his team after a group of prank-calling comedians from Queens, New York, that he and his friends had discovered through several pirated tape cassettes—it seemed like Alejandro had brought them in one night, maybe—and they all immediately loved them. The comedic routines of The Jerky Boys were silly but hilarious, especially their prank telephone calls with different-sounding characters and impersonations. The "Egyptian Magician" was Bud's favorite.

"Okay: where are we with the game?" Bud asked as he rubbed his hands together.

Kenneth looked up at the television screen, "Looks like two more questions for this round."

They all considered Question 14.

Which food item is used in the production of dynamite?

Four possible answers appeared below the question.

Rice

Potato

Coconut

Peanuts

"It's Peanuts. Number four," said Bud.

As the seconds counted down, each possible answer disappeared, followed by hints to the possible answer on the TV screen, until one answer remained: Peanuts.

Answer: One of the world's favorite snack foods is also an ingredient in the production of dynamite. Peanuts, like all plant products, contain oil. The oil is extracted from peanuts, and it is used in the process of making glycerol, one of the main ingredients in nitroglycerin. Dynamite is basically a mix of nitroglycerin and diatomaceous earth or other organic materials such as clay or sawdust.

"Shit, Bud. How do you know this stuff?" questioned Alejandro.

"Don't know. I just do," grinned Bud.

The screen now displayed Question 15:

The equivalent of the United States White House, what colorful residence is home to the president of South Korea?

Red House

Yellow House

Blue House

Orange House

"Orange House," said Kenneth with some conviction.

Bud smiled wryly but shook his head. "I think it's the Blue House, my brother," he said. "Pretty sure."

Kenneth made a menacing fake frown for a moment, then smiled. "Then we'd better go with Blue House, hadn't we?"

"Yep," Alejando said. "And that Bud Garza memory."

A possible answer disappeared from the screen and the last answer remained: Blue House. The TV screen then displayed more information about the correct answer.

Cheong Wa Dae, which means "pavilion of blue tiles," is also known as the Blue House, the executive office and official residence of the president of South Korea.

"Well I heard they were *gonna* call it the Orange House until they saw those blue tiles," quipped Kenneth. Bud smiled and turned his attention to the other television screens showing the basketball game.

Alejandro shouted, "Come on, Houston!"

9

Sunday evening, June 12, 1994
9:58 p.m. CDT
Austin, Texas

When the Houston Rockets and the New York Knicks started their third quarter, with the Rockets up by seven, 45–38, Steve Worthington was 387 miles away, watching the game at Stubb's BBQ off Austin's East Eighth Street. He ordered his fourth Crown Royal Canadian whiskey. By his side was a very attractive redhead. The live band was on break and the voice of that Irish girl singer for the Cranberries kept asking, "Do you have to let it linger? Do you have to? . . ."

Two days before crashing at a high school friend's house off Highland Avenue and West Sixth and a Half Street near downtown Austin (and spending his time thoroughly enjoying the area's nightlife), Worthington found himself under the ground-transportation sign at Robert Mueller Municipal Airport in the early afternoon. A red Nissan pickup pulled up. Worthington walked up to the right side of the pickup truck, threw his Reebok bag in the back, opened the passenger door, all while still cradling his 7-Eleven cup.

"Where are we going?" Worthington queried.

"The Driskill."

"Nice. What did I do to deserve that place? Y'all usually stick me in that shitty La Quinta off Third Street."

"Seems the old man is showing some appreciation for your fiftieth delivery," replied the driver.

"Cool."

Worthington glanced over to his driver. He had close-cropped brown hair and was wearing a well-worn burnt orange University of Texas baseball cap, a dingy, faded black Chris Sexton concert T-shirt, and a pair of khaki shorts.

The drive from Mueller Airport to the Driskill Hotel was short with no more conversation between Worthington and his driver, with whom Worthington was instructed long before to limit his conversations. The less said, the better.

After losing his first fortune from supporting the wrong side in the Civil War with furnishing the Confederate army with cattle and beef, Jesse Lincoln Driskill rebuilt his ranching and cattle empire in the early 1870s, with ranches in South Texas, Kansas and the Dakotas. He moved his family to Austin, which at the time was the westernmost and largest city in Texas. With seven thousand five hundred dollars, Jesse purchased an entire city block, and his luxury hotel opened in 1886, aptly named the Driskill. Unfortunately for Jesse Driskill, in 1888, a late freeze in the Dakotas killed over three thousand head of his cattle, and he was forced to sell his prized hotel and died a broken man, suffering a fatal stroke in May of 1890.

Just over a hundred years later, Steve Worthington's nameless driver pulled his Nissan pickup up to the palatial Driskill. The driver threw the transmission in park, then picked up the sixty-four-ounce 7-Eleven cup from the center console, carefully pulled out the straw, and pried open the lid to peer inside.

After his careful visual examination of its contents, he placed the lid back on the cup.

"We good?" inquired Worthington.

"We are good." The driver leaned over in Worthington's direction and unlocked the glove box. From inside, he grabbed a white bank money envelope inside and handed it to Worthington.

Worthington felt the thickness of the envelope and quickly opened its seal, running his finger across the top. He pulled the money out and quickly thumbed through twenty hundred-dollar bills and one twenty-dollar bill.

"My flight is tomorrow at twelve thirty p.m. Say eleven a.m.?" said Worthington.

"No can do. That is what the extra twenty is for. Get yourself a cab."

Worthington grumbled silently to himself, *The old man puts me up at the Driskill, but has me get a cab tomorrow?*

Worthington opened the passenger door, stepped on the curb, stuffed the envelope in his front shorts pocket and leaned in the back to grab his Reebok athletic bag.

"Later," said Worthington as he closed the passenger door.

The red Nissan truck drove away, and a Driskill valet approached Worthington.

"Welcome to the Driskill, sir. May I take your bag?"

"I got it," Worthington replied curtly.

He walked into the lobby and up to the front desk. A young and incredibly attractive redheaded woman smiled. "Welcome to the Driskill, sir. What is the name the reservation is under?"

"Steve Worthington."

"Nice to meet you, Steve. My name is Christine. May I have your driver's license?" Christine immediately started typing on her monochrome IBM computer terminal. Worthington handed her his license.

Christine paused. "Yes, here it is. Mr. Worthington, you are staying on the fourth floor in the Cattle Baron Suite . . . very nice." She looked up at Worthington again and grinned, then continued, "And it looks like your room is already paid along with a one-hundred-dollar room credit for any incidentals."

Christine finished her typing and handed Worthington his license along with his room key. "Thank you for staying with us, Mr. Worthington, and if there is anything else you need, again my name is Christine. The elevators to your room are down the hall and to the left." Christine brushed her red hair back with her hand, winked and smiled at Worthington once more.

Worthington smiled back, saying, "Thanks," before pausing briefly to glance at her name tag again. "Christine, I need a wake-up call for my room as well, say nine a.m.?"

"Of course," Christine quickly typed on the computer's keyboard. "Is there anything else?"

Worthington leaned slightly forward to Christine and lowered his voice. "What time does your shift end?"

With a blush and a smile on her face, Christine tilted her head a bit, looked to her left and right, and then whispered back, “Seven p.m. Why do you ask?” Her smile grew wider on her face.

“How about we meet at Stubb’s BBQ for dinner and a few drinks? It’s only six blocks down the street.”

“Maybe. . .” Christine smiled softly and brushed her red hair back again.

Worthington flashed a boyish grin and confidently spoke, “Great. I’ll see you there at seven.”

He immediately turned around, grabbed his bag, and walked toward the elevators, glancing at the large clock above the elevator doors.

The clock read 4:15 p.m. It was game three of the NBA finals tonight and he had some serious cash to burn in the live music capital of Texas, with a better than even chance a hot redhead might be along for the ride.

10

Monday, June 13, 1994
4:30 a.m. CDT
Solis campsite, Big Bend National Park

Juan Perez suddenly woke up inside his tent. He looked at his Casio watch, depressing the small LUZ button on the top right of the device. The time showed 10:31 p.m. Exhausted from his early morning hike and the haze of twelve hours' sleep, he turned on a small flashlight with a red lens filter. Juan opened his map again to review his upcoming journey. According to the map, he was about one kilometer downstream from the Big Bend National Park campground named Solis. Nestled on the bank of the Rio Grande River between the Mariscal Mountain range of Big Bend and the Sierra de San Vicente range of the Ocampo Protected Area of the state of Coahuila, Mexico, Solis was a popular embarkation point for gringo tourists and riverboating enthusiasts who off-loaded canoes and rafts for a gentle downstream journey on the Rio Grande to the much larger campsite of Rio Grande Village.

Once the gringos arrived at Rio Grande Village, they might venture to the Mexican side, visiting the isolated town of Boquillas del Carmen. Juan knew this firsthand, as he had assisted with the boat crossings across the Rio Grande of gringos looking to dine at the small town's taco stands, purchase inexpensive Mexican beer, and buy bottes of non-import-taxed Kahlúa coffee liqueur.

Tourists arrived to cross the Rio Grande into Mexico, paying a nominal crossing fee of two U.S. dollars. Donkeys provided transportation for the short two-kilometer distance to Boquillas del Carmen, a town of less than two hundred souls. As easy as the gringos moved back and forth across the river due to the absence of any United States or Mexican immigration officials at the border crossing, it was just as easy for Juan to cross the border, looking for a better way of life in *los Estados Unidos*.

However, once crossing the river into *los Estados*, almost all these undocumented and illegal immigrants faced the daunting challenge of making the ninety-mile journey to either Marfa, Alpine or Marathon, Texas, the closest towns to Big Bend National Park. From there, they faced another sixty-mile journey to Fort Stockton, Texas. Once in Fort Stockton and with its access to US Interstate 10, it was another three-hundred-plus miles to the major city of San Antonio and even a longer journey to the cities of Dallas/Fort Worth or Houston, where jobs and opportunities for work were available in abundance.

Once Juan reached the age of ten, he began working odd jobs in the city of Palau, Mexico, providing all his money he earned to help support his family. He dropped out of school by the time he reached fifteen and continued to get various jobs in as far north as Boquillas to as far south as Sabinas. When Juan reached the age of twenty, he found work as a donkey handler for the *gringo touristas* who crossed into the town of Boquillas. One day, a well-dressed *gringo tourista* caught his attention. Juan's English-speaking skills were not that great, but he understood well enough, and spoke better English than his fellow donkey handlers.

The gringo's name was "Bill," and after a few initial pleasantries, he discovered that Bill spoke better Spanish, or at least more correct Spanish, than Juan himself. Once Juan finished his work that day, Bill invited him for a beer at Boquillas's biggest bar, *El Loro*, or The Parrot. Thirsty from working in the sun all day, Juan eagerly accepted the offer.

Bill didn't let Juan talk much. He asked questions of Juan, true: when he was born, how many siblings he had, who his parents were, and the various jobs that Juan worked at until his present career as a donkey wrangler.

Six rounds of beers later, Bill leaned forward and lowered his voice.

"How would you like to make more money in a few days than what you would earn wrangling donkeys back and forth from the river to here for over a year?"

Juan's eyes opened at the opportunity.

"And once you are done with the job, you will be in the heart of West Texas, with the opportunity to find better work and money anywhere in the state."

The thought of crossing the border into *los Estados Unidos* had crossed Juan's mind many times; however, the high fees that *coyotes* charged to bring his countrymen or other immigrants illegally into the heartland of the U.S. from Central America were beyond Juan's reach.

Bill continued. "All you have to do is meet me here next week."

Bill pulled a map from his front pocket, unfolded it, and moved away a few of the empty beer bottles from the aluminum table that had a Corona beer logo across its surface. He pointed to a very tiny village, Altares, twenty-five kilometers from Boquillas.

"Once you meet me here—five a.m.—you will be given a backpack. It's a bit heavy, close to fifty kilos, but you look strong enough to carry it. Then follow these instructions— carefully, and word for word."

Bill paused for emphasis, making sure he had Juan's attention. He did.

"The bag is sealed with a metal clip and tag for a reason. Under no circumstances are you to break open the metal clip and seal. If you do, the deal is off."

Bill then pulled out another piece of paper with instructions written in Spanish. He then verbally recited each step to Juan. If Juan followed each of these steps, upon completion of his journey and delivery he would receive a thousand U.S. dollars in cash. In addition, he would receive secure transportation to Fort Stockton, Texas, with no fears of being picked up by the U.S. *federales* along the way, and provided construction job opportunities, including contacts and addresses from Houston to Dallas/Fort Worth.

"So, what am I carrying?" inquired Juan.

Bill looked into Juan's eyes and replied, "That's better not discussed."

Juan immediately knew that he would be moving drugs across the border. He had a friend, Carlos, who lived in his village and was in the same line of work. But he was hauling large bags of marijuana in a boat across the Rio Grande at night, and none of the large bags weighed as much as fifty kilos.

"That's the deal, Juan. Spend a few days hiking north across the deserts of Chihuahua and Coahuila, Mexico, and into Big Bend National Park, where you will have plenty of food supplies and water. From there, if you follow instructions, you will be transported to the heart of West Texas, with access to any major city in the state, along with one thousand U.S. dollars. Along with the work contacts I provide, you can start a better life."

Juan thought for a moment. As much as he would miss his family and the few friends he had in Coahuila, Mexico, he would not miss the hot days or the stubborn donkeys of Boquillas. The one thousand U.S. dollars was more than he would make herding donkeys for well over a year.

With a silent nod of his head, Juan grinned with a smile and replied, "See you next week."

That meeting with "Bill" seemed like weeks ago as Juan unzipped his tent for the last time, grabbed his red-filtered flashlight, turned on the switch and looked for a nearby tree to stand behind and relieve the immense pressure from his bladder.

Juan returned to his tent and quickly disassembled it, rolling it up in his small carry bag. He grabbed the remaining canteens of water and the last of his food, a red apple. He then attached the tent bag to the top of his backpack, along with the canteens. He dug in his pocket and found the map, which showed that he was about two kilometers from Rio Grande Village. He then fished out his Spanish-written instructions for Day Three:

> *Make sure you arrive at the Rio Grande Village camping market by 7 a.m. and no later. If you arrive early, wait outside, at the back of the market building, near the trash bins. A green trash truck will be there with the driver inside the cab. Talk to no one else except the driver. Ask him only this question—"Can I get a lift to Fort Stockton?" From there, the driver will take your backpack and give you further instructions. Again, talk to no one except the driver.*

Juan tucked the instructions into his pocket and looked at the map again. The trailhead hiking route to Rio Grande Village was about thirty meters from his present campsite. He leaned over, hoisted the very heavy backpack on his shoulders, and started his journey.

Approaching Rio Grande Village camping sites along the river thirty-five minutes later, Juan could hear the early morning sounds of campers waking up: coffee pots clanking, mild, soft conversation, and even a yawn or two of people greeting a new day. He looked down at his watch. The time was 6:38 a.m. Juan started walking faster.

As the trailhead ended on the edges of the campsite, Juan walked across the paved highway of US Route 385 in Big Bend National Park; the Rio Grande Village camping market was one kilometer away.

A few minutes later Juan spotted the large, green trash truck, which was parked exactly where Masterson stated. He looked at his watch again: 6:54 a.m. He'd just made it. Juan never realized how hard it was to carry a fifty-kilogram load a distance of thirty-three kilometers.

Juan walked right up to the driver's side cab of the trash truck with the words BREWSTER COUNTY WASTE MANAGEMENT emblazed across the driver's door. The window was rolled down.

Trying to catch his breath, Juan spoke: "I need a lift to Fort Stockton."

Immediately the cab door opened, and the driver jumped out to the dusty ground.

"Follow me and say nothing."

With the bright light of the sunrise shining in his eyes, Juan could not make out the driver's face from the time his feet hit the ground. All he could now see was the backside of the driver and his khaki pants, olive green short-sleeve T-shirt, black boots and a dark black baseball cap. Once the driver reached the back of the trash truck, his right hand extended toward a small control box near the truck's bumper. He flipped open the control box's metal cover and grasped a small black knob and pulled it down. Juan could hear the hydraulic hoses of the trash truck pushing fluid before a large door began to open in an upward arc on the truck's right side. He was shocked at what he saw next.

In 1977, when the green painted Mack R-Model/Leach 2-R Packmaster garbage truck rolled out of the Mack manufacturing plant in Lower Macungie Township, Pennsylvania, its original delivery location was destined to the dusty city and oil boom town of Big Spring, Texas. The arrival of this brand-new Packmaster, along with four subsequent sister garbage trucks off the assembly line, hit the front-page section of the *Big Spring Herald*, whose readership was currently enjoying the explosions in the oil refinery business and in other related energy sectors involving oil development, pipelines and various petroleum product support services. Times were good in Big Spring, as this small town in Howard County, Texas, was hitting new records of employment and new home and school construction, both feeding the buoyant and ever-rising population.

By 1983, however, six years after the oil bust, the city of Big Spring was on the verge of bankruptcy. Facing funding shortages, it decided to mortgage off a few of its assets, including one six-year-old green Packmaster garbage truck.

The winning bid of twenty cents on the dollar (made by a crafty city manager who knew how to stretch a city's capital-improvement budget) went to the city of El Paso, which needed to replace its aging fleet of garbage trucks. Nine years later, a city employee parked the Packmaster garbage truck near the border of Ciudad Juárez, Mexico, and El Paso, Texas, to quickly run into his favorite *taquería* shop for an early breakfast. When the driver picked up his bag of breakfast tacos, he exited the restaurant and, to his surprise, the Packmaster was gone. El Paso police later determined it was stolen by a gang of Mexican car thieves and driven across the border.

The gang members quickly sold the truck to a *gringo caballero* named "Bill" for five thousand U.S. dollars. Masterson, in turn, drove the truck to a body shop on the outskirts of Juárez and refitted the truck with a completely new interior that provided enough space to conceal ten passengers and still leave ample room for storage—all while maintaining the original rear-loader design and function.

Juan blinked his eyes again as the large door on the truck's right side opened completely, revealing seven people inside, and all his native countrymen. Each man blinked their eyes rapidly, as their pupils adjusted to the sudden entrance of the light of the sunrise.

After briefly processing the scene before him, Juan heaved his backpack into the storage space near the front of the cab on his right.

"Get in, no questions, and be quiet," the driver spoke in a stern voice.

Juan paused. "Who are they?"

"You thought you were the only one? Ha! Get in, now."

Juan quickly climbed inside the truck and found an open seat next to one of the men. Before he could sit down on the chair, the large side door closed. Five seconds later, Juan heard the Packmaster engine turn over, the gears shifting the transmission, and then he felt the movement of truck.

11

Monday, June 13, 1994
9 a.m. CDT
Austin, Texas

The telephone rang promptly as instructed in Worthington's hotel suite. After six consecutive rings, there was movement on the bed. Lying naked on his back, still under the bed covers and comforter, Worthington reached his left arm over to the bedside desk, knocking the lamp slightly as he reached for the phone's receiver. After the seventh ring, Worthington lifted the receiver off the phone's cradle and brought the earpiece to his ear.

A man's voice said, "Good morning, Mr. Worthington. This is your nine a.m. wake-up call. Have a good day."

Worthington groggily replied, "Thanks," and placed the receiver back in the cradle. His head was throbbing.

A woman's hand moved up Worthington's left side and began caressing his chest. A voice came from under the covers, "What time is your flight?"

"Twelve-thirty."

"And what airline?"

Worthington yawned while scratching the hair on his head. "Southwest."

"You know, you could always catch a later flight back to Lubbock."

"And why would I do that?"

"Because I don't have to work today."

Christine's head appeared from under the covers, while her hand moved down Worthington's chest to below his waist. "And because I love morning sex, and from what I have in my hand, it looks like you do as well."

With a grin on his face, Worthington rolled over and softly pressed his chest on top of Christine's. He'd promised his girlfriend Tracey he would be back in Lubbock around 1:30 p.m. and then spend the rest of the day with her at Buffalo Springs Lake. However, a more pressing matter had arrived to throw those plans out the window.

Worthington softly kissed Christine on the neck, just below her right ear, and replied, "I can always catch a later flight." Christine threw back her neck and closed her eyes.

Fifteen minutes later Worthington walked to the shower in the suite and turned on the hot-water valve. Christine remained in bed, still enjoying the fluttering climax that enveloped her body. *Now that was some great sex.* As she rolled around on the bed in her ecstasy, she carefully avoided the moisture spots on the fitted sheet. Christine had several lovers in her young life, but she never had one that lasted *that* long in bed.

Ten minutes later, Worthington stepped out of the shower and dried his body off with the thick knapped towels. With one towel wrapped around his torso, he used another towel to dry his hair. Worthington approached the bed and walked over to his athletic bag. Christine watched him intently as he began to dress.

Christine flicked back her red hair and smiled. "I can give you a lift to the airport, if you want."

Worthington looked uninterested but responded, "Sure, that will work."

"Or you could stay longer if you want," whispered Christine from beneath the bed covers.

"Christine, we had sex four times already, you've gotta give me a break so I can get my strength back."

"Okay, fine." With her lower lip protruding in a frown, Christine got out of bed and walked over to the bathroom.

Worthington watched Christine's nude body move with a sultry gait across the hotel room. His eyes followed her backside intently as she entered the hotel suite bathroom.

Fifteen minutes later and fully dressed, Christine brushed her red hair in front of the vanity stand, trying to freshen up from the previous night and morning's activity.

Staring at the mirror, she spoke cheerfully. "Did you want some breakfast? I know a great spot—"

"Not hungry," Worthington cut her off. "Besides, I've got to get to the airport and see if I can get another flight, remember?"

Christine finished brushing her hair and replied, "That's right." Disappointment rang in the tone of her voice.

"Are you ready?" Worthington queried impatiently.

"Yes." Christine finished applying a touch of lip gloss. Worthington grabbed his athletic bag and swung it over his shoulder.

The young couple exited Cattle Baron Suite and walked toward the elevator. Worthington pressed the down arrow button.

"So, how often do you come to Austin?"

Worthington's eyes were focused upward on the digital numbers, indicating the elevator's progress from the bottom floor.

He carefully chose his words. "Quite a bit."

"And when do you think you will be back?"

"A couple weeks, I think." In fact, Worthington knew his schedule like clockwork. Last week, his employer had asked him if he could start flying every week, instead of twice a month. Business was growing fast.

The elevator doors opened and an older-looking gentlemen stepped out. Worthington and Christine stepped aside and entered the empty elevator. Once inside the old-fashioned Otis-manufactured elevator car, Worthington pressed the lobby button again and the doors closed. Christine turned and immediately pounced on Worthington, kissing him passionately. Worthington returned her advances, moving his hand and caressing Christine's thighs.

As the elevator reached the lobby floor, and before its door opened, Christine violently pushed Worthington away and brushed her hair with her hand and straightened her blouse. She then quickly pressed the number four and turned to Worthington. "Stay here while I go and get my car."

". . . What?" a baffled Worthington replied.

"Because my manager is on duty, and we can't be seen walking out at the same time."

"Really?"

"Yes. Really. Now have a nice trip back to the fourth floor and I will see you out front in a few minutes. I'll be in the red Mazda Miata."

After Worthington finished his second descent to the lobby floor, he walked over to the registration table and fished out the hotel key in his pocket.

Dropping off his key at the front desk, Worthington walked over to the entrance of the Driskill and immediately noticed the red Mazda Miata convertible parked up front.

Worthington approached the convertible and Christine Daughtry leaned over to open the passenger door. He noticed Christine was not wearing her bra, and her large, ample bosom almost fell out of her shirt with its top three buttons undone. Christine's plan worked as she caught Worthington staring at her chest, and she quickly replied with an innocent statement, "Oh, my gosh, excuse me." She made a show of retracting her hand to cover her blouse.

Worthington smiled. "No need to be excused." He threw his Reebok bag in the back seat. "It's not every day you get a car door opened up that way."

Christine snorted a loud laugh and leaned over to kiss Worthington again, finishing her kiss by slightly tugging on his lower lip with her teeth.

"Let's get you to the airport."

12

Monday, June 13, 1994
11:32 a.m. CDT
Eastern city limits of Fort Stockton, Texas

The Packmaster finally pulled to a stop. Juan heard the hiss of hydraulic fluid and the right-side door opened.

"Welcome to Fort Stockton, Texas, men. Grab your bag and get out!" barked the driver.

Juan grabbed his heavy backpack and was the first to step out of the Packmaster. The other mules quickly followed suit and gathered close to each other, not sure what was coming next. Most of the mules, like Juan, struggled with the weight of each of their backpacks. Juan stood and surveyed his surroundings.

Hugging the southeastern beginnings of the Rocky Mountains off US Interstate 10 in deep West Texas sat Fort Stockton. Founded in January 1859 as a military post to protect travelers and commerce freight using the Butterfield Overland Mail route, Fort Stockton became the headquarters for the African American troops of the Ninth United States Cavalry after the Civil War. Tough and well-disciplined, the Buffalo Soldiers became a crack regiment with a hard-fighting reputation, relentlessly repelling Apache Indian raids in the territory and quickly receiving praise for their bravery and stamina amidst the region's harsh weather conditions. After the Apache wars ended in the mid-1880s, settlers, ranchers, farmers, and merchants moved into Fort Stockton, Texas, helping to create a community of trade for the surrounding smaller communities scattered deep in the swale of West Texas.

Despite Fort Stockton's historical significance as a hub of commerce in West Texas, Juan found himself in a darker place, abiding perhaps by the same free market demands of trading products, however those products being of the illegal drug trade that had plagued this area since the late 1970s.

"From Fort Stockton, you can travel anywhere in the United States," he recalled Masterson stating.

With the vast semiarid plains of West Texas surrounding him, the only sign of life in this desolate part of town was a large building, with white-painted sheet-metal sides and a tin roof. No other structure was visible for miles. Several open-bed Ford and Chevy pickup trucks were parked on the right side of the building, with men inside their cabs. On the left side of the building sat a parked Freightliner tractor trailer, but Juan could not see the trailer.

"Get in a single-file line right here," yelled the driver.

The mules lined up, each bearing the weight of over a hundred pounds of drugs. Then they followed the driver with labored balance as he led the group into the building. Since Juan was the first in line, he could see the driver fish into his pocket and retrieve a very small black box with two buttons. The driver pressed one of the buttons and the building's garage door opened.

"Follow me inside." The driver walked into the garage first, with the line of mules following in close step.

Once inside the large building, Juan quickly noticed an elevated, large stainless steel hopper in the back, with wooden stairs leading to the hopper's top. Parked below the stainless steel hopper was a stainless steel tanker. To the left of the tanker truck, Juan could see the same Freightliner rig he saw outside, a large garage door already open immediately above it. Other than the elevated platform, the hopper, the truck and the trailer, there was nothing else in the building other than a half-filled trash can that looked like it had not been emptied in months. Juan and the other mules stepped inside the building. The men who were in the parked pickup trucks followed behind them and ultimately positioned themselves in front of the mules to the right of the driver.

"You," the driver commanded, pointing directly at Juan, "follow me up these steps."

Juan walked toward the wooden steps, struggling with the heavy load on his back. Once atop the platform, Juan stood next to the hopper, which led into the open hatch of the tank trailer. Juan's nose twitched as he smelled something sweet, but with a medicinal component, emanating from the tanker.

"Place your bag here."

Juan lowered the heavy bag on the platform. The driver then fished out a pair of wire clippers and cut the metal clip securing the bag's heavy-duty zippers. He then unzipped the top of the bag.

"Reach inside, grab those packages and toss them into the hopper. Now."

Juan followed the instructions and knelt over the bag. The first package he grabbed was wrapped in what felt like wax paper with small ridges. Upon further inspection, the wrapper was light tan in color and looked just like a corn husk. Juan studied the package further, but then the driver barked at him.

"Stop looking at them and get them inside the hopper."

Juan glared back at the driver and started moving faster, unloading each of the packages and tossing them into the hopper. He could hear the splashes of each package as it entered the belly of the tanker. As Juan continued, he noticed the driver now had a small silver device, which he clicked every time Juan tossed in a package.

After fishing out the last package, Juan stood up and faced the driver, who spoke again.

"Fifty. Good. Walk back down and get in the back of the line with the others."

Juan again followed his instructions as the driver motioned to the next mule to meet him at the top of the stairs and the platform. Each mule performed the same task as Juan. When the remaining mule threw in the last package, the driver clicked five hundred on his handheld counter, then adjusted his baseball cap and followed the last mule down the stairs.

The driver then walked over to the driver's side of the Freightliner and waited. From behind the Freightliner another man appeared. Juan immediately recognized the man who called himself "Bill." Bill slowly approached the group of mules and spoke.

"Gentlemen, I want to congratulate each of you. You each followed my instructions and have successfully arrived in the United States, where you will now have the opportunity for a better life."

The driver then reappeared, this time carrying a black briefcase, and stood next to Bill's left side. Both men approached Juan and stopped. The driver opened the briefcase and inside Juan saw more *gringo dólares* than he had ever seen in his life. The same went for all the other mules, a few gasping at the sight.

"Now, our agreement was one thousand dollars U.S. for each of you. As I give you each your money, you have a decision to make. This group of gentlemen behind us are heading to Houston, Texas. There is a huge demand for construction, and from the looks of it, each of you should be able to handle the work."

Bill paused and then spoke again. "This will be the last time we speak, and you are to not speak to anyone about this. Or how you arrived in the United States, or anything that happened here today."

Bill then handed Juan and the other mules each an empty paper bag. The driver then handed each a stack of rubber-banded United States currency, with various denominations of one-dollar bills all the way to hundred-dollar bills. Juan pulled out the hundred-dollar bill and smiled back at the grinning picture of Benjamin Franklin, who, unlike Washington, Lincoln, Hamilton, Jackson, or Grant, was apparently the only happy founding father. After the last mule received their money, the driver closed the briefcase and handed it back to Bill. The two then parted ways, the driver walking back to his Packmaster, Bill walking to the Freightliner and hopping into the cab's passenger side. Juan and the other mules watched both leave the building. A man from one of the pickup trucks spoke next.

"Friends, welcome to the United States. Now, head over to the trucks and hop in the back. It's a long ride to Houston."

Juan and the mules walked outside of the building and chose from the two pickup trucks, with Juan picking the Ford. He climbed in back, relieved to see sleeping bags stored in the truck's bed. As the last mules climbed in the trucks, and the driver started the ignition of the Ford, Juan turned back and watched the Freightliner roar to life, slowly pulling away from the building as it towed the large stainless steel tanker behind it. Juan hunkered down, deep inside the Ford's bed, and crawled into the sleeping bag. He was asleep in minutes.

Unbeknownst to Bill, the *coyotes*, Juan, and the other mules, a man stood undetected, with a pair of Nikon Aculon 160X by 70X binoculars mounted on a small tripod. Perched on an elevated rock outcropping on the side of a small mountain, well over half a mile away from the former dairy warehouse, he watched the entire production, starting with the arrival of the green Packmaster garbage truck. Even from such a distance, the powerful magnification of his binoculars produced images in detail. He could even make out the dates and colors of the small, rectangular Texas automobile license plate registration stickers.

As the last pickup truck left, followed by the Freightliner down the caliche road toward Interstate 10, Traegar Jackson took a moment to wipe the sweat from his forehead before furiously scribbling the Freightliner's license plate number and registration-sticker details in his notebook. He had already made the same notes on the other vehicles, along with the green garbage truck.

Close to his tripod with the high-powered binoculars, Jackson's Nikon FM2/T, armored with a titanium shell and mounted with a high-powered telescopic lens, sat on the hood of his black-colored 1992 Chevrolet Tahoe. He'd already snapped four rolls of Fuji film, capturing pictures of all the participants. As the Freightliner left his field of vision, he quickly collapsed the tripod, placed the binoculars in the carrying case, and removed the Nikon off the hood of his Tahoe and placed it in the front seat. With all the surveillance packed away, the man inserted his keys in the ignition and fired up the SUV. He dropped the automatic transmission handle hard to "D" and slammed on the gas pedal. The Freightliner had a two-mile head start.

An hour and fourteen minutes later, Jackson had followed the Freightliner from Fort Stockton to Monahans, before finally arriving in Odessa at a Love's Travel Stop just west of the city limits. Keeping his distance, the man parked his Tahoe at the furthest gas pump and walked toward a bank of four Western Electric–manufactured Southwestern Bell pay phones. He removed the receiver from the cradle and inserted a quarter in the top left of the phone. After an audible click, the man listened for a dial tone, pressed a ten-digit number, and waited to speak.

After three rings, there was an audible click followed by two words brusquely emitted from the pay phone's receiver.

"Harris here."

The man spoke. "It's Traegar."

"What ya got?" replied an excited Harris.

"A bunch. Right now, I'm following a Freightliner tanker truck with Texas license plate"—Jackson paused and cradled the receiver in the crook of his neck, raised his left shoulder, grabbed his notepad with right hand and then read off the information in his notebook—"L, Lima, F, Foxtrot, D, Delta, eight two six. I repeat: Lima-Foxtrot-Delta-eight-two-six. Let me take a piss and I'll call you back in about ten minutes."

Harris quickly wrote down the license plate numbers on his notepad.

After quickly scribbling in his notepad, Harris hung up his office phone, stood up from his desk and walked toward the bathroom. The name Brian Harris Special Agent in Charge was stenciled in the glass window of his office door, just above the words Drug Enforcement Agency, El Paso Division, Intelligence Center.

13

Monday, June 13, 1994
11:41 a.m. MDT
Biggs Army Airfield, Fort Bliss, El Paso, Texas

Most people trace the United States government's anti-drug efforts to the end of the Civil War. With the invention of the all-glass hypodermic syringe in 1851, the administration of morphine to wounded soldiers became quicker and easier to ease the injuries of battle. However, many wounded veterans became addicted. From the end of the Civil War until early 1914, easily obtained over-the-counter medicines and cough syrups routinely contained morphine, cocaine, and heroin. All these medicines boasted claims of curing insomnia, hysteria, bronchitis, tuberculosis, menstrual cramps and even the ability to soothe irritable babies. Doctors at the time prescribed these dangerous "elixirs" as wonder cures, ignorant to the strong and addictive properties of opiates and stimulants these medicines contained.

With the passage of the Harrison Narcotics Act in December 1914, the United States created a law that regulated and taxed the distribution of opiates and coca. Doctors could still prescribe narcotics to patients but could not do the same for addicts, since addiction at that time was not considered a disease. Subsequent legislative acts followed that tried to curb the use of narcotics and other drugs, including the Marihuana Tax Act of 1937, which addressed the taxation of marijuana. Thirty years later the act was ruled unconstitutional by the U.S. Supreme Court, as the law violated the Fifth Amendment (self-incrimination) in the case *Leary v. United States.*

Two years later Congress addressed the Fifth Amendment issue and passed the Controlled Substances Act in 1970. The original enforcement agency in charge of executing the act was the Bureau of Narcotics and Dangerous Drugs (BNDD), which in 1973 President Nixon changed to the Drug Enforcement Administration (DEA). Ten years later, under the Reagan administration in the 1980s, the DEA's budget grew by leaps and bounds. As the "War on Drugs" hit the media outlets of television and newspapers and the attention of Americans across the country, the DEA's efforts to curtail drug smuggling in the United States expanded. Pressure increased from the top down as the DEA began to bust drug operations from Columbia, Venezuela, Panama and Mexico. Rumors of drug interdiction efforts with the help of the CIA and U.S. military special forces circulated at that time and continue to this day.

In response the media coverage of the "War on Drugs," the National Narcotics Leadership Act passed in 1988, which spawned the Office of National Drug Control Policy (ONDCP). Five years later, President Clinton elevated the "drug czar" to a cabinet-level position.

With a now well-depleted bladder, Brian Harris returned to his office. Nine minutes later, his office phone rang.

"Harris."

"Traegar."

Harris clicked his ballpoint pen and started writing notes while Jackson spoke.

14

Monday, June 13, 1994
9:57 a.m. CDT
Lubbock, Texas

Campbell slightly elevated the Riedel wineglass before him by the stem, his eyes fixed on the red wine inside. He angled the glass above the marble countertop to his left. Immediately below and resting on top of the counter was a flat sheet of white paper.

"Before we begin, how do we pronounce 'Riedel' again?"

Bud replied, "Ree-dle, like needle."

"Very good, Bud. Correct pronunciation is very important, especially in this business." Campbell turned his attention back to the wine in his glass.

"This wine is our 1992 Cabernet Sauvignon. Now keep in mind, Bud, of the five senses our body uses daily: seeing, hearing, touching, tasting and smelling—we use our nose the least. It's going to take time for those nostrils of yours to determine the aromatics. Take this wine here; as I smell this wine, I'm getting hints of blackberry, currants, a touch of cigar box, tobacco and a slight presence of cassis."

Bud listened in astonishment to Campbell's aromatic descriptors. He didn't smell anything like what Campbell rattled off.

Campbell smiled. "Don't worry, Bud, I've been tasting wine for years. Plus, I have the back label of this wine almost memorized. Go ahead and read it."

Saying nothing and still trying to glean what the hell "cassis" was, Bud spun around the bottle of Cabernet Sauvignon and veered at the back wine label.

On the High Plains of Texas, the cool nights and sunny days allow our Cabernet Sauvignon to fully ripen. After our winemaker hand-picks the best lots available to us from various growers in the region, we age this wine in selected barrels of new French and American oak for up to eighteen months. This gives our wine its pleasant aromatics, including hints of blackberry, currants, a touch of cigar box, tobacco, and a slight presence of cassis. We recommend this fine wine with steaks, pork, robust Italian fare, and even dark chocolate. We know you will enjoy the experience.

Campbell noticed as Bud finished reading the back, "Almost word for word, am I right?"

"Spot on."

"Yes, Bud, when in doubt, always read the back label. And Bud, don't worry about tasting wine this early. According to Drew, the morning is the best time to taste wine."

"Who is Drew?"

"How could I forget about Drew Dalton?" Campbell shrugged. "He is our award-winning winemaker here at South Plains Cellars. In your training manual, you'll see Drew's bio and how he came to work here. Originally from California, went to college at UC Berkley, then studied at UC Davis. He made a name for himself working at a few blue-chip wineries in Napa, California. We were very lucky to hire him several years ago. He's the same gentleman who created our best-selling wine . . ."

Campbell paused, giving Bud a sidelong glance. "And which is what wine again, Bud?"

Bud smiled. "Regal de Cabernet."

Campbell grinned and looked at his watch. "Nicely done. Okay, we've been tasting for just under an hour. That should do it for your first wine-tasting training. The tasting room opens up in just a minute or two. In the meantime, bring your training book, along with the Wine Institute of California training tape, and follow me."

Bud picked up his large black binder and followed Campbell through the cedar-lined cellar room, through the large doors, past the bottling room and into the white wine room. Campbell made a hard right, and once he reached the end of the white wine room, a stainless steel metal staircase appeared on his right. Campbell ascended the stairs and stopped at a closed wooden door. Campbell opened the door and walked inside South Plains Cellars' only conference room, which overlooked the large white wine production room. One wall featured floor-to-ceiling windows, which gave any occupant of the room a broad view of multiple, large stainless steel fermentation tanks. The room itself was ornately decorated, with the finest leather office chairs and a mahogany-finished conference table. The conference room had two telephones and an audio/video cart in the corner, complete with a television and videocassette player. On the back wall was a full wet bar, complete with under-hanging wineglass racks, positioned under the rarely used cabinets.

"I want you to spend the next three hours here, reviewing your training manual and watching the Wine Institute of California training tape at least once. At one o'clock, you can call it a day. Be sure and punch your time card before you leave. Don't forget to purchase *Wine for Dummies* and keep the receipt. I'll make sure you're reimbursed. Doug's last day is this Sunday, so I want you to spend as much time with him as you can. Remember: if you get asked a question that you don't know the answer to?"

"Let me ask the winemaker after we finish, and I will get back to you," replied Bud.

"There you go. I will see you Wednesday, June fifteenth, at ten a.m. sharp. Dress appropriately."

15

Monday, June 13, 1994
2:48 p.m. CDT
Big Spring, Texas

Bill Masterson took a bite of his second chorizo, egg and cheese taco and gazed outside through the only clean window in what many locals considered the best *taquería* in town. A small bit of grease and fresh melted butter dripped from his taco onto his aluminum foil wrapper resting on the dining table. Bill gazed outside to the view of his surroundings.

The *taquería*'s parking lot only had a few cars, as the busy lunchtime crowd already left several hours ago. At the far end of the parking lot, a black Chevrolet Tahoe was parked, with a man reading a book and eating a familiar-looking taco. Other than Bill, his driver and the man in the black SUV, no other customers were around.

Finishing their late lunch, both he and Armando went outside to the rig and jumped into the cab. Each had their own cramped bed in the back. Another hour-and-thirty-minute drive remained to arrive at their destination, though he was not expected for another nine hours. Bill knew the routine. Getting close to eight hours of sleep was important to him, and he kept that schedule as diligently as he could.

From inside his Tahoe, Agent Traegar Jackson watched the two men hop into the Freightliner's cab and close the passenger doors. He wrapped up his taco's foil wrapper in a ball, tossed it into an empty white paper bag, and grabbed his notebook. He wrote down a few notes and scribbled down the time. The man then grabbed his paperback book and started to read again.

Removing his Resistol 20X straw cowboy hat and crawling into his small bed in the back of the rig, Bill laughed to himself, reflecting on the millions of dollars' worth of opium just a few feet away from him and Armando. No one would even begin to think that the grape juice and water mixture was filled with the highest-grade Mexican mountain highlands opium from the states of Durango and Sinaloa, specifically the poppy-growing regions of Guadalupe y Calvo, Badiraguato and Tamazula de Gordiano, of the famed "Golden Triangle." Bill grinned as he remembered his first meeting with a man named Gustavo del Victorio Herrencia, or "El Astuto," the Crafty One, a fast-rising drug lord within the Sinaloa cartel.

"Ah, Señor Bill Masterson, *mucho gusto!*" A pleasure.

El Astuto stood a few inches shorter than Bill, and sported a well-manicured mustache and short, black hair, with slight curls on the ends. His white shirt and blue jeans looked brand-new.

With his right hand Bill removed his gray Stetson hat perched on his head, quickly switched the hat to his left hand, and shook El Astuto's hand, exercising the same ancient Western greeting ritual of mankind for hundreds of years.

"Let me ask you this. Do you know much about wine?"

"Red wine goes with steak and white wine goes with fish or chicken. That's about it."

"I will tell you, Bill, as a poor boy from Sinaloa, Mexico, I never knew anything about wine, expect for Sundays at our local *iglesia*. When we developed this operation a few years ago, I learned quite a bit. Follow me."

El Astuto led Bill to a large Chippendale table, upon which rested a detailed map of the United States and Northern Mexico. Next to the map was a stainless steel bowl and what looked like a large corn-husk-wrapped tamale on a plate.

"Señor Bill, you are fortunate where you live, and I will tell you why." El Astuto slapped his right hand on the map, covering Big Bend National Park and the surrounding mountains and plains of West Texas. Removing his right hand, El Astuto then moved a few steps to his left and pointed to Southern California, homing in on the surrounding area just south of San Diego.

"We can only move our product in this same manner here south of California and your homeland of West *Tejas*. There is a city north of San

Diego called Temecula. There are many wineries located just west of there." El Astuto then paused, stepped away from the middle of the table and moved toward the large bowl and the tamale. "Let me show you something, my friend."

Bill walked over to the bowl and peered inside, seeing nothing but clear liquid, which emitted a faint, fruity scent. Bill thought it smelled like grape juice. El Astuto then picked up the tamale and dropped it in the bowl. The clear liquid began to react with the tamale, bubbling around the corn-husk packaging, which soon disappeared. A dark, olive green cube of raw, pure Mexican opium floated in the mixture, but slowly broke apart and dissolved. In a few minutes, the clear liquid was now a light green. Bill stood in amazement, saying nothing. El Astuto then spoke.

"I don't know how it works exactly, which is why I paid for one of the best biochemistry researchers in all of Mexico. He figured out a way to take our product and dissolve it in—of all things—grape juice and water. He did so in such a way that it can't be detected unless the samples were taken to a sophisticated lab. More importantly, he then created a process of extracting the opium from the grape juice mixture that is as clean as a baby's behind. The wrapping paper is special-processed cornstarch, based on corn husks right here in Mexico, which harmlessly dissolve into the juice and water. The extraction process removes everything but our product, which is the finest from Mexico. It cost me over five million gringo dollars, but that biochemistry doctor now has a large injection of funds for his new company at Investigación Biomédica y Científica Incorporada."

El Astuto pointed again to Southern California on the map. "Now here in Southern California, our tanker trucks get pulled over all the time at the San Ysidro checkpoint in San Diego, since the *federales* spend more time, money and manpower trying to stop us, along with several of my other *hermanos* in our business. More than ninety thousand people cross this border point every day. We tend to lose one truck for every twenty trips, and every time it's because our drivers are either speeding, have an outstanding warrant from the gringos, or forgot to bring their forged identity papers.

"You, my friend, will have no problem. Instead of hundreds of thousands of people living here"—El Astuto pointed and swirled his finger in a small circle around Southern California—"you know how many people live over here." He then pointed and swirled his finger again toward West Texas. "It is more like just a few hundred, scattered over hundreds of miles.

"This new NATFA agreement your countrymen made with mine, it will triple our smuggling operations across the other ports of entry, from California, Arizona, New Mexico and your home state."

Bill thought for a moment, then spoke. "Excuse me for asking, Señor Astuto. Aren't grapes a seasonal product? What do you do when the grape harvests are done here in fall?"

"That is where your operation will make more money than our Southern California operation. As you know, there is a *very large* winery in your home state located in Fort Stockton, *Tejas*, called Sierra Madera Winery. A group of legitimate French businessmen bought the winery a few years ago, and instead of letting the winemaking equipment sit idle for eight months of the year, they started making wine from bulk wine grapes from Chile, Argentina and even Australia. Grapes from those countries get harvested in the months of February and March.

"We purchase the leftover juice not used to make wine. Our French amigos think we are shipping the leftover juice for brandy production in Mexico. And more importantly, they don't ask any questions. That is where you come in. Once you've recruited your mules and they make it across the border, our team will pick them up in one of our several retrofitted garbage trucks and drive them to an abandoned dairy ranch, just east of Fort Stockton."

El Astuto then pulled out a large, detailed map of Texas from under the United States map, and he placed and flattened it on top. He pointed his finger to a red X, just to the right of Fort Stockton. "The property is far enough off the highway and the town, where we can work virtually undetected. Once our product is off-loaded in the dairy warehouse and deposited in the belly of the tanker truck, you will drive here." El Astuto pointed his finger to another red X on the map, just south of the city of Lubbock. "You will need to arrive no later than midnight and not before. Our people there will then off-load the tanker. You will then repeat the process all over again."

El Astuto looked up and shouted, "Señor Santiago Zavala! Come here, my friend."

A short, bald, bespectacled older gentleman emerged from behind a group of El Astuto's men and walked through the armed guards, who parted respectfully. He smiled slightly and extended his hand. His large, black mustache covered his entire front lip, while the remaining sides of his mostly black hair had flecks of gray intermingled.

"Señor Santiago Zavala, meet Señor Bill Masterson from Texas."

Bill extended his hand and the men shook. The older man replied, "*Mucho gusto*, Señor Bill."

El Astuto picked up where he left off. "It is Santiago Zavala's winery where you will ensure our product arrives safely. He also runs my entire operation in Texas."

El Astuto paused and patted his hand on the back of Zavala in appreciation.

"And since this is our best product, you will make about two trips per month. Zavala's accounting team tells me that our larger cocaine and marijuana operations move much more volume, but they are not as profitable as our opium."

Bill nodded again.

"With limited delivery times, this will give you more time to recruit the mules you will need to move our product across the border. Don't focus on the popular border-crossing sites of El Paso, Del Rio or Eagle Pass, Texas. Too many *federales*. Instead, I want you to focus on the towns in the Mexican states of Chihuahua and Coahuila, and from villages in Ojinaga in the north to San José Las Piedras in the south and up to Boquillas del Carmen."

El Astuto pointed his finger again, this time tracing the Rio Grande River as it moved southeast from Fort Hancock toward Big Bend National Park, then turned northeast and then began to curve again south toward Del Rio. "There are very many shallow parts of the Rio Grande along this area. The mules can easily walk across the river into *los Estados Unidos*, except during the rainy season in May and June. That is the easy part." El Astuto then paused.

"The hard part is getting these mules food and water so they can continue to make the two-to-three-day trek to a collection and extraction point. Your other job is to make sure the mules know where they can rest, eat, drink and sleep once they arrive at the park. Be sure and keep these locations discreet, but well-supplied. Each backpack the mules will carry holds fifty kilos of opium, which you know, my friend, is very heavy. Be sure to recruit accordingly."

"Every load you move, I will pay you one million U.S. dollars. You can pay your mules as much as you want, but I would keep the amount reasonable. Remember, the biggest recruitment tool you have is the desire that many of my poor countrymen have of making it into *los Estados Unidos* and starting a new life. You should have no problem with recruiting. Bueno?"

El Astuto extended his right hand and firmly shook Bill's.

"Señor Astuto, you have a deal."

16

Monday, June 13, 1994
5:59 p.m. CDT
South Plains Cellars

Jerry Campbell opened a glass door to the EdgeStar 27 wine refrigerator behind the tasting-room bar. He noted the fridge thermometer in passing. It was keeping the thirty-six bottles inside under a temperature of fifty-eight degrees. He grabbed a bottle of what many considered the best wine made at South Plains Cellars, the 1990 Nathan Vineyards Reserve Cabernet Sauvignon.

South Plains Cellars had received some great press on the wine, nabbing gold medals in multiple wine-tasting competitions, earning along the way an elusive *Wine Spectator* rating of ninety-three points, something unheard of in the world of Texas-made wines, especially red wine. The wine may never have been made if it had not been for a mis-shipment of two barrels by the winery's barrel supplier and a young wine grape grower who listened to some valuable advice.

With the wine refrigerator's glass door open, Campbell pulled the bottle of the 1990 Nathan Vineyards Reserve Cabernet Sauvignon. The high-shouldered bottle was heavy, with glass thicker than the other wine bottles South Plains Cellars used in its winery production. Campbell leaned over to the other side of the tasting bar and grabbed two clean glasses. He walked to the barrel room and made his way to the winery lab, located behind the bottling room.

Holding the bottle of wine, along with two wineglasses with his left hand, Campbell punched a five-digit code into a keypad with his right. The door buzzed; its release then signaled by an audible click from its locking mechanism. Campbell reached down to the stainless steel door handle and pulled the door open.

Painted white, the room contained an array of laboratory equipment seen in most wineries across the country. Scattered across one side of the semicircular desktop that wrapped around the room were pH meters, refractometers, hydrometers, thermometers, test kits, and laboratory measuring tools such as beakers, burettes, cylinders, flasks, and pipettes.

On the other side of the lab was stationed more expensive equipment, such as an electric ebulliometer, used to accurately calculate the boiling point of liquids by measuring the temperature of the vapor-liquid equilibrium either isothermally or isobarically; and a Sulfilyser, which quickly measures free and total sulfur dioxide, or SO_2—a compound used a preservative for wine. Campbell had no clue how to use any of this sophisticated equipment and never bothered to ask.

A man sat on a stool with his back to Campbell in front of the Sulfilyser, which was shaped like a short rectangular tower that rose from the edge of a circular base (on which sat a small, short, enclosed bottle of what looked like a sample of pink-colored wine) and tapered at the top. He manipulated a small, flexible hose that ended an inch or two above the circular base, just above the bottle, and rose up the face of the tower, wrapping over the top of it and securing somewhere on its back. Out of the Sulfilyser's side extended another short hose with a round bulbous end. The man turned the machine on and began to squeeze the bulb on the end of the short hose.

Campbell knew Drew Dalton was enveloped in his work, so he walked to the small workstation/desktop island in the middle of the laboratory. He moved a few papers aside and cleared a spot for the bottle of wine and two Riedel glasses. Campbell then realized his mistake: forgetting to grab a wine opener in the tasting room. With his back still turned, Drew Dalton spoke up.

"Left top drawer, under the large burette and the three beakers of Regal de Cabernet wine."

"Thanks, Drew. How did you know?"

"Jerry, you are creature of habit. Almost every time you come back here to drink a bottle with me, you forget to bring a corkscrew."

Campbell laughed to himself and walked over to the drawer. Meanwhile, Dalton made a few notes on the notepad next to the Sulfilyser and turned the machine off. Dalton then spun around on his stool, raised both of his hands to the sides of his head against which he began to rub his fingers in circles, and muttered, "More fucking Regal de Cabernet."

Campbell caught Dalton's words and sympathized, "I know you hate making it, Drew, but it's our cash cow right now. We can hardly keep that wine in stock, in both the tasting room *and* the market. One of my tour guides suggested pairing the wine with Pedro's Tamales. And you know what, the kid was right."

"Pedro's Tamales? With Regal de Cabernet? I never thought of that before. Who made that suggestion?"

"Jason Rector. He's got a pretty good palate."

"Good for him. I've got to try that *interesting* culinary pairing."

"Interesting pairing, that's for sure. Like I said, I know you hate making it, but you make it well."

"Yeah, I know. But there are days when I miss making good *red* wines." Dalton noticed the bottle of 1990 Nathan Vineyards Reserve Cabernet Sauvignon in front of him and picked it up. "Like this guy right here. Man, this was a fun one to make."

"It put us on the map," Campbell added.

"So, what do I owe the pleasure of drinking *this wine* with you this evening? You know, Hank would shit a brick if he saw us back here drinking this."

"I'm going to write it down as breakage. I'll bury in the inventory reporting next week and Hank won't even notice. May I?" Campbell extended his empty right hand.

Dalton handed the bottle back to Campbell, who quickly removed the lead capsule with a swift cut of the corkscrew's small, serrated knife, exposing a small circle of cork on the business end of the bottle. He inserted the steel-worm corkscrew into the cork, all the way to the handle.

"Man, this is a long fucking cork." Campbell struggled to extract the nearly two-and-a-half-inch-long cork.

"You can thank Hank for that brilliant idea. I wanted a standard one-and-a-half-inch cork, but he wanted to mimic Chuck Wagner's Caymus Special Select Cabernet Sauvignon cork closure."

After and audible pop, Campbell began to unscrew the long cork with the corkscrew. He immediately poured a small sample of wine into Dalton's glass and stepped aside. Dalton picked up the Riedel glass and swirled its single ounce of wine. The aromatics of rich blueberry, cassis, dark rich chocolate and cedar filled the wineglass. Dalton took a sip and swirled the wine in his mouth. "Oh yeah, this wine is just hitting its stride. A killer vintage that is still young, but *damn* good."

Campbell provided his glass a generous six-ounce pour and topped off Dalton's glass with the same amount.

Campbell raised his glass. "Cheers, Drew."

Dalton raised his glass and clanked his off Campbell's. "Cheers, Jerry. I needed this today."

Dalton swirled the glass again and took a larger drink. He let the wine bounce around his palate, and a flood of memories from fall of 1991 arrived.

17

November 1991
South Plains Cellars
Lubbock, Texas

Each of the fifty-five American oak barrels of the 1990 Cabernet Sauvignon were placed on the floor of the barrel room, resting on metal barrel racks in four long rows.

Drew Dalton tasted each barrel. He muttered to himself. Each Cabernet Sauvignon wine barrel tasted the same, with a base of aromatics of blueberry and crème de cassis but also expressing aromatics of a varying degree of intensity of vegetative flavor, with hints of green pepper, olive, sage and other dried herbs. The green smells were a specific aromatic compound called methoxypyrazine, often called "pyrazines" for short. Typically, this compound was found in Bordeaux varietals like Cabernet Sauvignon, Sauvignon Blanc, Cabernet Franc, Merlot and Malbec. For hundreds of years, winemakers never knew exactly why some Bordeaux varietals would smell green and others would not. Research in the late 1970s and early 1980s discovered that pyrazines could be reduced or virtually eliminated with more vineyard management. By controlling the growth of the leafy parts of the vines, wine-grape growers could influence the aromatics of the grapes. In other words, wine-grape growers needed to prune their vines more efficiently and even "drop fruit," which meant a vineyard owner would prematurely cut a few grape clusters from each vine.

Drew Dalton made several attempts to instruct his West Texas wine-grape growers under contract of the basic vineyard management skills on how to prune each of their vines according to varietal. Unfortunately for Dalton, most of the grape growers ignored most of the information. Growing cotton was too imbedded in these old West Texas farmers, albeit new to grape growing.

Of course, after every harvest, each of Dalton's growers would appreciate the up to two thousand dollars per ton offer—depending on the grape varietal—they each received when the grapes rolled into the winery. Plus, growers received their money upon delivery, as opposed to spending the year or longer waiting for payment from the cotton gin co-ops. From a revenue-per-acreage standpoint, wine grapes by far outperformed dryland and irrigated cotton.

At the end of one of Dalton's seminars, he noticed one young farmer, Mark Nathan, who seemed to hang on to Dalton's every word, scribbling notes as fast as possible in his small black-and-white composition book. After the seminar, Mark Nathan personally thanked Dalton for his time and valuable information. Dalton's hand was swallowed up by Mark's large paw when they exchanged pleasantries.

As Dalton tasted each Cabernet Sauvignon barrel, nothing stood out in terms of high quality. On every barrelhead Dalton noted each grape grower's name and vineyard name, if one was designated. He sighed as he reached the last four barrels and removed the rubber stopper in the fourth-to-last barrel's bunghole. Dalton inserted his large, glass pipette and held it still in his right hand. Physics forced the wine inside the barrel into the pipette as the pressure inside the glass tube reached equilibrium. Dalton then placed his right thumb on the small opening at the top of the pipette and held it firm. He raised the other end of the pipette to a small tasting glass, held in Dalton's left hand. He released his right thumb and gravity took over, moving the wine from inside the pipette out the other end and into his wineglass.

Dalton quickly replaced his right thumb to stop the flow of liquid and placed the pipette back in the barrel's bunghole, released his right thumb, then slowly pulled the empty glass tube from the barrel. Dalton proceeded to smell and taste the wine, applying the same fifteen steps he used previously. This included observing the appearance of the wine in terms of its clarity, intensity and color. He also smelled for condition, intensity, aroma characteristics and development. He then tasted the wine on his palate, evaluating sweetness, acidity, tannin, alcohol, body, flavor intensity, flavor characteristics and finish. In the end, he wrote down a few notes, giving his overall assessment of the quality of the wine. Dalton found himself stunned. He immediately peered over to the barrelhead and read the words Nathan Vineyard, Cabernet Sauvignon, 1990.

Dalton repeated the same process with the pipette and got the same results. He had not tasted red wine of this quality since his intern days at Joseph Phelps Vineyards in St. Helena, California. Cheerfully, Dalton used a red Sharpie to mark this barrel with the letters "RSV," the acronym indicating the word *reserve*.

Dalton then looked at the three remaining barrels, all of which were from Nathan Vineyards. Like a kid in a candy store, Dalton moved quickly to taste the next barrel. While this wine tasted exactly like the previous barrel, its aromas were more intense, in a good way, and indicative of a barrel with a heavy toast, or charring of the barrel on the inside. There were also more exotic spices in the aromatics. Something was different; this wine tasted even better than the first Nathan barrel.

Dalton put down his wineglass and empty pipette on top of the second Nathan barrel and looked at the barrelhead, visually comparing it with the first Nathan barrel. Same *tonnellerie* barrel manufacturer, Seguin Moreau; both from Napa, California, both stamped with a MT brand, indicating a medium toast.

"What's different?" Dalton muttered to himself. "Both barrels should be American oak . . . Wait a minute . . ." Dalton then saw something out of place.

The first Nathan Vineyard barrelhead had smaller stamped letters of AO, MO, and US, indicating abbreviations for American Oak, Missouri, United States. But the second barrel had no such stamp. In fact, the barrel had no stamp indicating the origin at all. Dalton looked closer at the second Nathan barrel, closely examining the edges of the barrelhead. Tracing his finger around the circumference of the barrelhead, Dalton noticed the very small letters qp followed by the initials o.n.f.

"What the hell is "QP O.N.F.?"

Then, his now-dusty graduate wine training at UC Davis kicked in. Dalton remembered that QP stood for *Quercus petraea*, the Latin genus and species name for French Sessile oak. And then he remembered the initials

O.N.F. indicated the National Forests Office, where the tallest oak trees exclusively come from the French national forests, located almost dead center in the country of France. Dalton smiled. He was looking at a wine barrel about four times more expensive than his other fifty-plus American Oak, or *Quercus alba*, wood barrels. He couldn't believe his luck.

Dalton then tasted the last two remaining barrels. The third barrel tasted like the first one, and the fourth and last barrel tasted like the second. Dalton then looked at the third and fourth barrelheads and noticed the same difference. The fourth barrel had the same small initials QP O.N.F., and it also sported a MT stamp.

Then a thought popped into Dalton's head. He marked the third barrel with the red letters "RSV," and then he made a mark of "RSV+" on barrels two and four. Dalton raced back to his lab and retrieved three 1000-milliliter graduated cylinders. He took his pipette and removed two hundred milliliters from the first non-Nathan barrel. He then did the same for the first Nathan barrel marked "RSV," and then for the "RSV+" barrel. He carefully carried all three back to the lab and began the blending process, using forty-milliliter samples from each graduated cylinder. After several blending ratios, Dalton hit the mark with his fifth attempt. An equal amount of each of the four Nathan Vineyards barrels, along with a small blend from one of the non-Nathan Vineyards barrels, turned out to be the best blend.

Dalton grabbed a pencil and did some quick math. Each sixty-gallon wine barrel held close to twenty to twenty-two nine-liter cases. With all four barrels from Nathan Vineyards, plus two of the best-tasting barrels from the remaining 1990 Cabernet Sauvignon vintage, Dalton had anywhere between 120 to 132 nine-liter wine cases, each case containing twelve 750-milliliter bottles. Better yet, Dalton could easily convince South Plains Cellars' general manager, Hank Evans, to purchase special four-pound, heavy-glass bottles, with a high shoulder and a deep punt, the indented bottom of a wine bottle. With this wine's quality, Dalton bet he could convince Evans to offer this special wine in three-pack wood cases. The winery could easily sell this wine at three times the price of South Plains Cellars' Cabernet Sauvignon.

Dalton did some more quick math. Close to 132 nine-liter cases would yield just over fifteen hundred bottles, or just over five hundred three-pack wood boxes. With a three-times mark-up, Dalton could easily make the winery an extra sixty-five thousand dollars.

When the 1990 Nathan Vineyards Reserve Cabernet Sauvignon was released by South Plains Cellars in the spring of 1992, it was an instant hit that was followed by a swell of positive press. The Cellars's three Texas wholesalers clambered for more as the wine quickly sold out in restaurants and fine-wine shops across Texas, especially after it was given the point rating of "93" by *Wine Spectator* when it hit the shelves in June—a first for any Texas-made red wine. With the 100-point rating system applied by well-regarded wine magazines such as the *Spectator*, *Wine Enthusiast*, and *The Wine Advocate*, any wine earning a score of "90" or higher will usually sell quickly off the shelves.

Hank Evans wisely held back a hundred of the three-packs at the winery, marked them for sale at the winery only and then doubled the price of the wine again.

That was only good news for South Plains Cellars in 1992. In the following months, a severe crash-crunch hit the winery. Almost everything came toppling down.

18

July 1992
South Plains Cellars

Drew Dalton hated those dark days during the second half of the 1992 harvest. Hank Evans was nowhere to be seen at the winery then, using the excuse of having to spend time at various banks across the South Plains and West Texas trying to raise capital to purchase red grapes for the 1992 harvest and keep the winery afloat. That left only Dalton and a few cellar workers to deal with grape growers arriving to South Plains Cellars with bins full of grapes and leaving angry.

At first, the 1992 harvest went smoothly. White wine grapes like Riesling, Gewürztraminer, Sauvignon Blanc, Chenin Blanc and Chardonnay rolled in initially, which is typical for white grapes as they reach maturity faster than reds.

After the third week of harvest in mid-July 1992, Mark Nathan, Dalton's best grape grower under contract, arrived at the weigh station next to South Plains Cellars' crush pad at around 7:14 a.m. In the twenty-four-foot gooseneck flatbed trailer of his 1989 Ford F350 Dually were twenty-two Buckhorn half-ton wine grape bins constructed of structural foam made out of high-density industrial-grade polymer—with ridges and reinforcement adding seventy pounds to their weight, respectively—that could hold up to nine hundred pounds. At the bottom of each bin were two large rectangular gaps that made them ideal for being removed or loaded by a forklift as needed. Stackable bins like these were commonplace in the valleys of wine and fruit industry in California; however, in West Texas, they were still a curiosity.

The bins in Mark Nathan's trailer held the first red grapes of the season, Cabernet Sauvignon.

Mark drove his truck and trailer over the concrete-covered weigh station pad. Then he hopped out of his truck, detached the trailer, and hopped back in to drive to the small building that housed the weigh station measuring equipment, where he hopped out again and walked inside.

"Where is Drew?" barked Mark, before recognizing the man in front of him. "Gaspar, is that you?"

Gaspar Ramirez, a recent cellar worker hired from Pheasant Ridge Winery, replied in a heavy Spanish accent, "Hey, Señor Mark. Yeah, it's me. I leave Pheasant Ridge a few months ago. Señor Drew offer me more money to come here." Gaspar looked concerned. He'd never seen Mark Nathan this angry. "What is wrong, Señor Mark?"

"South Plains Cellars is what's wrong!" Mark looked around inside the small building. "Where the hell is Drew?"

"I last see him ten minutes ago, going to one of the holding tanks inside the winery."

Mark Nathan stormed out of the small weigh station building and marched toward the large, open garage on the crush pad. Mark's large frame was atypical for a farmer in the area. Built like a Mack truck, his huge barrel chest and sizable arms were a large presence to anyone. Donning a new Stetson 7X straw cowboy hat; a dusty white short-sleeve button-down; a pair of Wrangler jeans supported with a leather belt adorned with a well-worn large silver buckle with the words NFR Champion, Bull Riding, 1985, on it; and a pair of custom-made M.L. Leddy's rhino-skin boots from Fort Worth, Texas. Mark Nathan was a well-dressed West Texas cowboy who you did not mess with when angry.

"Drew, where the hell are you?" bellowed Mark.

After several calls, a smiling head popped up over the elevated crusher-destemmer. "Mark, what's up?" Dalton considered Mark Nathan one of his best growers under contract.

Mark walked to the bottom of the ladder to the elevated crusher-destemmer and stared straight up at Drew Dalton, standing eight feet above Mark.

"Do you know what this is?" barked Mark, holding up a fluttering piece of paper.

Dalton, noting the angry tone, decided to not reply with a smartass comment and instead quickly scaled down the stainless steel ladder.

"I asked you a question. Do you know what this is?" Mark's anger grew.

Trying to calm down his friend, Dalton lowered his voice. "Mark, it's a check we wrote you about three weeks ago for your five tons of Sauvignon Blanc."

"No, it's a *fucking* piece of bouncing rubber!"

Bewildered and shocked, Dalton meekly asked Mark, "May I see it?"

Dalton felt a sinking feeling in his gut. This was not good.

"Here, you can have it. And you can shove it up Hank Evans's ass! Where the hell is he?"

"Mark, I can take care of this. Let me get ahold of Hank and see what happened. This has to be a mistake."

"What about the other checks you wrote me last week and the one from the other day? If y'all don't have enough to cover the $6,276 for my five tons of Sauvignon Blanc grapes from three weeks ago, how am I going to believe you have enough to cover what I already brought you, let alone my best Cabernet Sauvignon grapes sitting on that weigh station?"

Dalton saw that his present situation was deteriorating, fast. "Mark, let me get ahold of Hank and I will get to the bottom of this. We will get you paid."

Mark held the bounced check in his large right hand and then pointed his finger toward Dalton's chest. "I call bullshit. And you want to know why? I got three phone calls yesterday. Do you want to know who called me?" Mark raised his left hand in a fist and slowly raised three fingers. "Jackson Smith, Robert Duncan and Stanley McMaker. They are all holding the same *fucking* pieces of rubber that I have!"

Dalton said nothing and just stood silent.

"You remember that grape symposium you held a few years ago? Well, I was the only one that listened. You know how much fruit I dropped this year, and the year before that, and the year before that, so I could bring you and this winery some quality grapes?"

Dalton nodded his head slowly.

"Do you know how much fruit Jackson, Robert and Stanley dropped?" Mark made a zero with his left finger and thumb. "*Fucking* zero. And how do you and that sumbitch Hank Evans repay me? You can't even pay me for my white wine grapes!"

There was a pause, as the only noise on the crush pad was the sounding of the pumping equipment.

Not aware of the drama outside, Gaspar poked his head in. "All done, Señor Mark."

Mark turned his attention to Gaspar. "How many tons, Gaspar?" he yelled.

Gaspar removed a small notepad from the left breast pocket of his plaid, flannel button-down shirt. He turned to the last written page. Keeping his head down and focusing on his written calculations, he spoke. "Let's see, Señor Mark. Gross weight 27,786 pounds. Your trailer weigh 6,200 pounds and bins are seventy pounds each, times twenty grape bins for a total of 1,540 pounds." Gaspar checked his numbers for a second time. "I show 20,046 pounds, or just over ten tons of grapes, Señor Mark," Gaspar said. "If I may say, Señor Mark, these are the best-looking Cabernet grapes I've ever seen this season so far."

With this comment Gaspar closed his notebook and inserted it smoothly back into his breast pocket. He then headed over to the crush pad where there was parked a propane-fueled internal combustion cushion-tire four-wheel Hyster forklift. He jumped in the lone driver's seat and fired up the ignition.

"Good. About what I expected, Gaspar. Please leave my trailer where it is and do not off-load any of my grapes with that forklift. Keep 'em there!"

Confused, Gaspar replied and turned off the ignition. "Why, Señor Mark? The weather start to get warm soon. Weatherman on TV says it will be *muy caliente* today."

Mark then turned to Dalton. His temper had faded, and he spoke in a cooler tone. "Drew, with just over ten tons of some of the best Cabernet Sauvignon grapes in West Texas, and based on what I sold you last year, I'd say that I'm your best grower for that varietal at this winery. Am I right?"

Dalton stood in silence. He nodded. Mark Nathan was by far his best wine grape grower under contract.

Mark walked into the red wine room and headed to the wall-mounted phone beside the green door button. He selected the button for speaker phone and a dial tone opened. He punched ten digits on the phone's keypad. After five rings, a voice crackled from the receiver.

"This is George Broyles."

"George, it's Mark Nathan. How are things at Llano?"

"Just crushing grapes. You know, working eighteen hours a day, pissing off the wife because I'm never home. To what do I owe the pleasure?"

"Just thinkin' 'bout ya."

"You were? Well, let me ask, you wouldn't by chance have any of those great Cab Sauv grapes left on your field? You know I've been trying to get you to start selling me those grapes for the past few years, instead of to that Haight-Ashbury-loving Cal Bear down at South Plains."

"Well, wouldn't you know it, George, but I'm standing right here at South Plains Cellars, with that same Haight-Ashbury-loving Cal Bear. Say hello, Drew."

With shoulders shrugged, Dalton spoke into the phone's speaker receiver, "Hey, George."

"Hey, Drew, sorry about that. Just busting your chops."

"It's cool, George. I'm not sure if Cal Poly commuter-college grads like yourself can spell the word 'wine.'"

"Ha! You're probably right about that."

Even though winemakers are competitors, friendships amongst winemakers in the industry are long and deep if for no other reason than that you never knew if one day you would be asking another winemaker for a job.

A long pause split the friendly banter, and then an unamused Mark continued, looking at Dalton. "Well, aren't you going to tell George the good news?"

Dalton looked at Gaspar and then looked at Mark. He knew what he had to say next.

"George, I need some help here. I've got about ten tons of Mark's Cab Sauv sitting here on my weight station."

"And . . ." prompted Mark.

Dalton spun his story. "Look, George, I think Hank is going to spin down our Cab Sauv business. I know, it doesn't sound right, but he made the decision yesterday. Any way you can take these Cab Sauv grapes off our hands? You know Mark Nathan is one of the best on the High Plains."

There was a pause and a soft click.

Then: "Are you shitting me?" George's voice suddenly boomed with up-close clarity, indicating he'd turned off his own speaker phone and was holding the handset directly against his face. "You're offering me *all* of Mark Nathan's Cab Sauv grapes?"

Dalton paused and then replied, "Yes, you can have 'em all. Down to the last berry."

George quickly replied. "Holy shit!"

Mark and Dalton traded looks, Mark's indicating an authoritative mixture of resentment and relief, Dalton's a tinge of shame.

"I'm sorry to hear that things didn't work out with you and Mark, but man, this is great. Thanks for the business, Mark. Hell yes, I will take 'em. We just off-loaded eight tons of Merlot. Our team wasn't expecting another load for another two hours. I'll get 'em ready."

"George, I will see you in about fifteen minutes." Mark placed the phone's receiver back into the cradle and ended the call.

On the other end, George Broyles hung up his phone and gathered his thoughts. What the fuck was going on at South Plains Cellars? Ten tons of Nathan Vineyards Cabernet Sauvignon? During crush, a general manager didn't just decide at the last minute he was not buying any Cabernet Sauvignon.

Thirty minutes later, several empty refrigerator tanker trucks rolled from Wilmington Warehouses in Lubbock and Amarillo and headed toward Llano Estacado Winery. George temporarily off-loaded as much of Llano Estacado's finished wine as he could into the refrigerator tanker trucks to free up tank space for not only Mark Nathan's grapes, but any other wine grape grower in the Texas High Plains Appellation Viticultural Area that held original contracts with South Plains Cellars. With more grapes than anticipated coming in for this harvest, he just hoped he had enough tank space and refrigerated tank trucks to hold all his contracted juice, plus the grapes originally destined to South Plains Cellars.

When the phone call with George ended, Nathan didn't say goodbye to Drew Dalton. He marched over to his Ford pickup truck and drove toward the front of his gooseneck trailer. After backing up to the front of the trailer, he silently attached it to his truck and drove away.

Dalton ran immediately to the winery lab to call Hank Evans. Evans picked up after a couple of rings.

"Hank, it's Drew. What the *fuck* happened with Mark Nathan's check for his Sauvignon Blanc grapes from three weeks ago? He just marched in here with his load of Cab Sauv grapes and found out the check we wrote him for his Sauv Blanc *bounced*. I mean, are all the checks we wrote—"

Hank cut him off. "Drew, let me speak. Yes, I know Mark Nathan's check bounced. Along with everyone else we wrote a check to this past month."

Dumbfounded, Dalton slumped into his office chair. "What happened?"

"We ran out of money. I've been looking at our books since late last night and checked every entry twice. I just finished an emergency meeting with our board of directors ten minutes ago. Hang on a minute."

Hank Evans was forty-three years old, married with two kids in college, and a wife with an expensive shopping habit. He brushed his hand through what little hair he had left on his head and leaned back in his own office chair.

"Listen, I need some more time to get ahead of this. I'm getting ready to leave for Tanrock Capital Bank right now to see if we can get an emergency loan to cover our payroll and the essentials. What I need you to do is lock the gate to the weigh station and start calling our growers. They can either do two things: give us one-hundred-and-eighty-day terms for their grapes, or they can sell 'em to Llano Estacado or Pheasant Ridge. I already called Campbell, and he is closing the doors to the tasting room. There may be some flare-ups over the next few days."

"Flare-ups? You want to talk about flare-ups? I thought that cowboy Mark Nathan was going to kick my ass right here on the crush pad. The man used to ride bulls for a living! I've never seen him that mad. He also told me that our other grape growers know their checks bounced as well."

Evans frowned. When he was an assistant general manager at a North Coast California winery, growers had more options and more notice if a contracted winery failed to pay for a load of incoming grapes during harvest. The sudden lack of cash on hand caught him completely off guard.

"Drew, I need your help. The next few days may get ugly. I'm going to call the police and make them aware of the situation."

"The *police?*" Dalton almost screamed into the phone, then looked around, realizing how loud he spoke.

"Don't shout it to the world, Drew. Yes, the police. Based on what you told me and how ugly it got with Mark Nathan, God only knows what our other growers will do. Look, make sure the gates are locked. Wind down whatever juice you have left in the crush equipment and shut down the crush pad. I doubt these guys are going to accept one-hundred-and-eighty-day terms for their grapes. Get Gaspar and the rest of your team inside the winery and keep 'em busy. Make sure when they leave for home that all of you *go together* when you leave the winery. The same goes when they come to work in the morning. Make sure you keep the team together and close." Evans paused.

"Hank, what happened?" Drew probed. "A winery just doesn't run out of cash. We are a publicly held company, for Christ's sake. I don't need to remind you that almost all our stockholders are people in *this* community."

Evans listened to Dalton's frustrated tone and responded, "Drew, I don't have time to get into specifics. Please do as I say. I promise I will give you more information. I'm going to be on the road for the next few days. I don't know how well it will go here at Tanrock. I plan to visit as many banks as possible from here to Amarillo to see what we can borrow over the next week. If we can't get any more money, we will probably have to file chapter eleven."

"Chapter eleven? Are you kidding me?"

For a few seconds, neither spoke as Dalton waited for a response, and Evans searched for one.

"Look, Drew," Evans finally said, looking at his watch, "I gotta go. Please do as I say."

Dalton's heart sank. "Okay, Hank. I will. Keep me informed."

Dalton slowly put the phone receiver back in its cradle, then tried to breathe deeply to still the sense of horror racing through him. After several minutes, he managed to control his breathing.

Okay, he thought. Let's start by locking the gates.

19

Monday, June 13, 1994
6:23 p.m. CDT
South Plains Cellars

"Man, that felt like years ago. Those were some dark days, Drew." Campbell just finished his first glass of wine and reached to pour himself more.

"Yeah. And if that wasn't bad enough, that next month us getting kicked in the nuts and finding out that there isn't a Santa Claus again." Dalton swirled the wine in his glass and took a big gulp.

Campbell didn't reply to Dalton's comment. He knew exactly what Dalton meant. This was not the place or time to discuss *that*.

Drew Dalton, who had already pounded two more glasses of wine to Campbell's one, grabbed the bottle and poured the rest. "I *fucking* hate it here, Jerry."

"You know what we signed up for back then. The winery went bankrupt. You and I were super close to losing both of our jobs that week. We both have families to provide for, we couldn't walk away. What goes on here now is nobody's business. That is what we agreed to do."

Dalton stood up, a little wobbly. "That's bullshit and you know it."

"Is it bullshit, Drew? You have a job, just like me. And we are getting paid *five times* what we used to earn. Do you think if you go back to California, or somewhere new like Washington or Oregon, that you're going to find a job that pays a winemaker what you earn now?"

Dalton sneered at Evans's comment and began to pace around the winery lab with glass in hand, saying nothing. Campbell's unpleasant but truthful logic made sense.

"Look, we both *fucking* hate working here."

"These guys aren't going to just let us leave, you know that. Why do you think they installed all this security? You know how many times I've wanted to punch that keypad outside this door into the wall. They're not going to *let* us leave, Jerry. You know that."

Frustrated, Dalton put down his wineglass and sat on the stool in front of the Sulfilyser, crossing his arms.

Campbell noticed his friend's nonverbal defensive posture. "Drew, keep doing your job, just like me. The money we both earn keeps our wives and kids very happy. Our wives fly to Dallas together and go weekday shopping at Neiman Marcus and NorthPark Mall, for Christ's sake. How many times have they done that now?"

Dalton snorted and half laughed. "Too many."

"Exactly. Now get home, man. You look exhausted."

Dalton stood up and walked to the door. Campbell opened the door for his friend and watched as he cleared the entrance. Campbell then looked at the security camera in the corner of the ceiling and placed his right forefinger on the winery laboratory wall and clicked the light switch to OFF.

20

Monday, June 13, 1994
6:37 p.m. CDT
Conference Café, Lubbock, Texas

Bud entered the doors of Conference Café and joined Kenneth and Alejandro at the table from last night. They exchanged the normal high fives and Bud sat in his usual chair.

"Gentlemen, I just finished my first official wine tasting this morning at South Plains Cellars."

"This morning? Kinda early to get your drink on," replied Kenneth.

"Attakid, gettin' started early with the new gig, huh?" Alejandro smiled and raised his glass of beer.

Bud surveyed the restaurant, which was nowhere near as full as it was the prior night. Sting's "If I Ever Lose My Faith In You" issued from the ceiling-mounted speakers at a much lower volume than the night before.

"Wanna beer, stranger?"

Bud immediately recognized the voice and turned to find a smiling Cheryl Truett managing a fresh pitcher of Miller Lite and a clean mug in just her right hand, her other hand on her hip.

"Sounds wonderful." Cheryl smiled. She placed the fresh pitcher of beer on Bud's table and put a clean glass beer stein on the table. Bud stood up to greet her, and Cheryl leaned in and hugged him and after pouring his beer.

Bud returned the affection. *Man, she gives the best hugs.*

Backing away slightly, Cheryl grabbed Bud's hand and gently pulled it.

"You got a minute?" Cheryl said, nodding her head toward a corner.

"Uh, okay."

Bud sheepishly looked at his friends at the table, each smiling back at him. Kenneth and Alejandro quickly refilled their beer mugs and focused their attention on the Texas Rangers game, sensing that Cheryl and Bud wanted a private conversation.

Cheryl took bud to a two-top table in the back of the restaurant, close to the restrooms and out of proximity of any patrons. Cheryl sat down and Bud joined her.

"So, how's your day been?" she asked.

"Better now that you're here."

Cheryl blushed and brushed away her blond hair. "Oh really? Isn't that what you say to all your *other* girls?" And with this the verbal and nonverbal flirting began.

"What do you mean by that?"

"Oh, I heard things about *you,* Bud Garza."

Bud looked at Cheryl's face and smiled. "Did *they* mention anything else?"

"No. But I have a question."

Bud gazed at Cheryl. The color of her eyes were ethereal, sparkling with blue and silver. "What's that?" he asked in a low voice.

"Why is it that all the times that you've come in here you have not asked me out?"

Bud bought some time for his response. "What did you say?"

"You heard me, mister. Every time you come in here, you request me as your waitress. Most of the time you're lucky, because you or your friends almost always sit in my section. And you never come here with a date. So what gives? Do you think I'm ugly or something?"

"I do not," Bud said. "The opposite, in fact."

Bud reached over to the bottom-left edge of his chair and pulled himself closer to Cheryl. Cheryl creased her lower lip over her upper, and with an impatient look blew a small blast of air upward toward her forehead, fluttering a few locks of hair dangling in her face. "So, what's it gonna be?"

Bud leaned over and tilted Cheryl's lips toward his. She offered no resistance. He kissed her softly. Surprised, but receptive to Bud's sudden gesture, she returned his kiss.

After another moment, Bud pulled away.

"You are right," he said. "So, when's your next night off?"

"Friday," Cheryl whispered.

"How does seven o'clock work?"

"Perfect."

Bud leaned in a bit and whispered into Cheryl's ear, "So, where do you live?"

Cheryl pulled her order pad from her work apron and wrote down an address.

"My roommate gets back from her international studies in Spain in a few weeks and she and I are in between apartments right now," she said. "So I'm crashing at my folk's house for the time being."

Cheryl smiled again, ripped off the top sheet of the order pad and handed it Bud. "It's the smaller house on the left."

"But I'll probably see you tomorrow anyway?"

"Probably. I might pick up a late shift tomorrow night for the game."

"I may or may not swing by." Bud half grinned.

"I call bullshit. You better be here. It's game seven of the Stanley Cup Finals. You probably know as much about hockey as I do, but I bet you will be here, along with every die-hard hockey fan in West Texas."

"There are probably more people here now than all the hockey fans in Lubbock."

Cheryl slapped Bud's stomach with the back of her right hand.

"Hey smartass, you know what I mean. I'm leaving you now, Bud Garza. Shift's been over for the past fifteen minutes."

Cheryl reached around her back to untie her work apron, wrapped the tie strings around and held the apron in her hand. She walked to the back room of the bar and placed her apron in one of the vacant cubbyholes and promptly left the restaurant. Bud's eyes followed her the whole way. Before she walked through the front door, she glanced back and smiled at Bud one last time. Bud returned a grin of his own.

I probably look like an old hound dog sniffing a scent, Bud thought. *But I don't care.*

Once she was gone, Bud walked back to his table where Kenneth and Alejandro were still watching the Texas Rangers game. Bud picked up his mug of Miller Lite, pulled the glass close to his lips and drank.

With his eyes still staring at the elevated television, Kenneth said, "Looks like you finally asked her out?"

"Yep."

"And did she say yes?"

"Friday night. Picking her up at her house."

Alejandro then chimed in, his eyes remaining fixated on the baseball game as well. "About time. I thought for a minute there y'all were going to need to get a room." He took a tug from his beer. "Where is her house, anyway?"

Bud reached into his pocket and read from the slip of paper Cheryl handed him. "5110 Ninety-First Street. A block behind York Place."

"Ninety-First Street and York Place? That can't be her house."

Bud handed the piece of paper to Alejandro. "That's what she wrote down."

"She lives next to Lake Shore Country Club? That's moneyland. If I remember, that house is somewhere between the sixteenth and seventeenth hole."

"It's her folk's house. She said something about her roommate being in Spain until July, and they were going to get a new place."

Kenneth lowered his eyes from the TV as the game went to commercials. He looked at Bud with a mock-serious expression. "You know what that means? You will probably have to meet dear old Dad."

"And you better hope he is not cleaning his shotgun or some other large firearm," Alejandro added as he poured himself another beer.

"Hey, it's Cheryl. We all know her. Why are y'all giving me shit?"

"Because it's *Cheryl.*" Alejandro placed his hands in front of his chest and pretended to grasp imaginary and breasts in his open hands. "The goddess of Conference Café!"

Kenneth pushed Alejandro's hands down and spoke more seriously—really seriously this time. "We've been busting Bud's balls for weeks on when he would finally ask Cheryl out. Now that he has, we got to show him some support, right?"

Bud grinned and smiled at his fraternity brother. "Thanks, Ken."

"Now, when talking *support*, Bud, we need to confirm whether that means a B-cup or C-cup," replied Kenneth.

Bud lowered his head in his hands as both of his good friends roared in laughter.

Sports. Wine. Friendship. And now a date with the prettiest girl in West Texas.

21

Monday, June 13, 1994
10:00 p.m. CDT
Lubbock, Texas

Across West Texas, televisions set to the local news broadcasts joined the rest of the nation as they reported that the bodies of Nicole Brown Simpson and Ron Goldman were found near the steps of former NFL superstar O.J. Simpson's home in Brentwood Estates in southern California.

People from all over the country watched as O.J. Simpson left the Los Angeles City police department, with no comment to reporters. His lawyer, Robert Kardashian, reported that his client "is extremely depressed and . . . under the care of a physician to help him during this difficult time of grieving."

22

Tuesday, June 14, 1994
12:24 a.m. CDT
US Highway 87, six miles north of Tahoka, Texas

Traegar Jackson's body fell backward to the ground.

Silence returned to the abandoned farmstead across from South Plains Cellars. Then the sounds of distant cars traveling on US Highway 87 gradually returned, along with the wind in the cottonwoods. Roberto unscrewed the silencer on his pistol and placed his handgun in his front waist, just above and to the left of his belt buckle. The silencer he tucked into the back right pocket of his jeans. Looking for instructions on his next step, Roberto stood next to the old man and waited.

"Señor Zavala?"

Santiago Zavala's anger diminished from his face, and he turned off the flashlight. Darkness returned. He turned toward Roberto and spoke softly.

"Listen to me very carefully, Roberto. Gather all this man's personal effects from his vehicle and on his body and make sure you get every film canister, used or not used. I want to see what pictures this man took from here."

Roberto nodded his head in agreement.

"Next, call Esteban and have him bring over one of the large blue tarps we have in storage at the winery, several rolls of gray duct tape and a few of the red throw rugs we have in the barrel-room closet. You and Esteban will need to wrap this body as quickly as possible, with at least two layers of blue tarp surrounding it. Then, wrap the duct tape around the tarp. Use as much duct tape as possible and seal every space you see in the tarp. Then roll the throw rugs around the blue tarp. We need to make this man's body look like a giant roll of red carpet."

Zavala then moved closer to Roberto and continued.

"Last and most important. Once you have all the personal effects removed from his vehicle and the body wrapped, place it in the back of his vehicle. I want you and Esteban to drive straight to El Paso. *Tonight.* This poor bastard will start to smell soon. Try to leave in the next hour, as it is a six-hour drive to El Paso. Once you reach the border, drive into Juárez and head over to the Ciudad Juárez de Castillo Landfill. Once you approach the front gate, ask for a man named Guillermo. And give him this."

Zavala handed over five one-hundred-dollar bills.

"Tell him Señor Santiago Zavala needs to make a deposit. Guillermo will know what to do from there. Then leave the car, with the body, and give Guillermo the keys. And here—" Zavala pulled another four one-hundred-dollar bills from his pocket and gave them to Roberto. "Walk back across the border and grab a cab to the El Paso International Airport. Use this money to purchase airfare for you and Esteban and return back here. Do not speed when driving tonight. I have a feeling that this man may have a few friends that will come looking for him in the next few days, and for his Chevy."

Zavala then flipped on his flashlight and pointed it at Jackson's body. Blood slowly oozed from the back of the former DEA agent's head and pooled on the ground.

"And finally, clean up the blood here. Esteban will know what to do. Nobody must know what happened here tonight. Nobody."

Zavala glared at Roberto.

An almost exasperated Roberto responded, "Señor Zavala, I understand. Who do you think he worked for? He's didn't act like the local *policia*."

Zavala muddled over Roberto's inquiry. He walked over to Jackson's body and turned off his flashlight. Even with their concealment behind the grove of cottonwood trees, Zavala still took precautions. He looked down the road in both directions, double-checking for any cars driving from either direction.

"Help me roll his body over."

Roberto placed his hands on the right hip and midsection of the dead man and flipped him over. The man's shattered knee flopped oddly sideways when he did so.

The dead man's wide-open eyes now stared toward the ground. Zavala fished his hand into the man's back-right pocket. Finding nothing, he then turned his attention to the left pocket and pulled out a black leather wallet. He turned on his flashlight, opened the wallet and shined the light on the contents. He cursed to himself when he saw Jackson's badge and three large, black letters, spelling out the acronym DEA.

This man does not have a few friends, he has many friends, Zavala thought.

This was not good.

He reflected on the dead man's last words, "You will regret this."

I have to make sure that those words do not become a prophecy, he thought.

"Who does he work for?" Roberto inquired.

Zavala snapped the wallet closed and gave Roberto the flashlight with a stern look.

"Never mind. You need to move quickly; but first, I have something else for you to do."

23

Tuesday, June 14, 1994
12:51 a.m. CDT
South Plains Cellars

Bill Masterson placed the last stack of money inside his duffel bag and said nothing else. With the duffel bag strap over his shoulder, he and Armando walked back to the Freightliner. Once outside and on the crush pad, the large garage door to the red wine room closed.

Masterson noticed the shadow of two men in the distance, approaching from behind the Freightliner. He recognized the older bald man walking toward him as Santiago Zavala. He didn't recognize the other man, but did respect the man's large athletic build.

Masterson whispered to Armando in the darkness, "Armando, do you recognize Zavala's new *caballero*?"

"No, Señor. I never seen him before," Armando whispered back.

"Zavala must have hired a new guy. Bigger than the last one."

Before reaching Masterson and Armando, Zavala grabbed a small, black walkie-talkie in his pocket and spoke.

"Hector, please open the garage door."

The two came inside.

"Mister Zavala, to what do we owe the pleasure?" Masterson said.

Zavala ignored Masterson's question.

"Hector, please close the door."

Masterson did not like to have his questions ignored. But there was also something menacing about the old man that made him hesitate to express his displeasure. Masterson reached into his back pocket and grabbed a can of Skoal Straight dipping snuff. With the skill of someone who had dipped tobacco for many years, he thumped the top of the can with his right index finger three times, compressing the tobacco to one side. Masterson then pried open the can's lid, took a pinch of tobacco, opened his mouth slightly, and placed the tobacco between his right check and lower gumline.

Damn, he'd overestimated the amount of Skoal in his nervousness. He couldn't put the extra back in the can; that would ruin the rest.

Now, where was he going to spit it out?

Masterson's eyes lit upon the drainage grates that surrounded each of the winery's concrete tank pads. He walked to the closest drainage grate to spit the extra tobacco when Zavala followed up angrily.

"Now, Roberto!"

Just as Masterson spit into the grate, Roberto quickly moved to Masterson, thrust his large and strong hand around Masterson's neck and squeezed. Masterson coughed violently as tobacco and spit came out of his mouth. Zavala's normal soft-spoken demeanor was now nowhere to be seen.

"How many times have I told you not to spit that shit in my winery?"

Confused and surprised, Masterson tried to pull his neck and body away from the large man's grasp, but Roberto's grip on his neck was tight.

Coughing, Masterson replied, "Zavala—what—the hell—is going on? And—who the hell—*is* this guy?"

Roberto increased the pressure of his grip on Masterson's neck, pushing his hand and Masterson's body toward the ground. Masterson complied with Roberto's direction and crouched until the right side of his face was on the cold concrete floor, his straw cowboy hat shifted cockeyed over his head. Zavala walked over and knelt behind Masterson. Roberto kept his hand firmly around Masterson's neck.

Zavala spoke into Masterson's left ear. "And how many times have I asked that you off-load your product using the two-inch metal supply lines near the back of the winery and not through the garage door?" Zavala stood up and walked around Masterson's head so he could look at Masterson's face. Masterson turned his scared eyes upward and to the left toward Zavala until he was looking directly at the old man.

"It . . . it takes twice as . . . twice as long . . . if we use . . . use those small metal supply lines. . . . The four-inch line is . . . is much quicker. . . ." Masterson began to lose his vision, and his body slowly swayed back and forth, just skipping the surface of unconsciousness.

"Stop!" Zavala barked.

Roberto released his death grip on Masterson's neck, who started to cough violently in a confusion of saliva and tobacco as he rolled onto his back and heaved oxygen unevenly back into his lungs.

Zavala's anger did not cease. "It takes twice as long? I don't care if it takes all fucking day! Do you know what happens when you open this garage door at night and use the four-inch hose line, instead of the smaller ones in the back? *Anyone* can see what we are doing! Do you know how bright the lights are in this place?

"It's . . . it's the middle of the night," stammered Masterson.

"Yes, yes, it is! Exactly. What do you think happens when you open this garage door? The entire West Texas sky is lit up. You might as well hang a giant fucking banner that states 'Drug off-loading site' with big, bold letters!"

Armando and Hector said nothing, both of their heads staying lowered. With a fresh supply of oxygen, Masterson continued to cough but began to gain his bearings and raised his body to a sitting position on the winery floor, his hands and arms supporting him.

Zavala's anger seethed on. "Roberto, it is Señor Hector's turn."

Roberto approached Hector, extended his arm around Hector's neck and pulled it and him toward the winery garage door, applying extensive pressure. Hector gasped and raised his hands to try to remove Roberto's headlock, but to no avail.

Zavala then reared back his right foot sheathed in an alligator-skinned boot and kicked Masterson in his backside, barking, "Get up, you stupid hick! Armando, get your amigo on the crush pad, now!"

Zavala glared at Armando, who didn't need any prompting.

Still coughing and wincing from Zavala's violent blow, Masterson took Armando's hand and stood up painfully. Armando then helped his friend walk toward the winery's garage door.

Zavala punched the green button and the garage door opened again.

Walking awkwardly backwards in Roberto's grip and gasping for air, Hector was soon on the crush pad, both feet dragging, moving further and further away from the winery. Masterson continued to limp behind with Armando's help, only then thinking to refit his hat square over his head.

Hector, finally released, took a large breath, coughed, and collapsed on the ground. Armando and Masterson remained close.

Zavala shouted, "Now look around. Look! Do you see how fucking bright it is out here?"

Hector rolled over, his lungs still burning.

"Yes, Mr. Zavala. It won't happen again."

"You're damn right this won't happen again, and not for the next few months as well!"

Hector, Masterson and Armando shared glances, gauging each other's reactions to Zavala's last comment.

Masterson, still coughing, managed to speak. "Mr. Zavala, what do you mean by not for the next few months?"

"Because, you idiot, look what I found just over there!"

Zavala produced Traegar Jackson's wallet and opened it up. The large, black letters of "DEA" sent a shock of fear into Zavala's audience on the crush pad.

"And guess what DEA Senior Special Agent Traegar Jackson was doing until about ten minutes ago?"

Again, no responses from the men on the crush pad.

"Taking pictures of all of you! And what fucking great lighting he had for his pictures, too!"

Zavala's eyes glared at each of the men as he spoke. After an uncomfortable ten seconds eclipsed with no one speaking, Masterson broke the silence, his coughing having subsided.

"Santiago, where is Agent Jackson?"

Zavala did not reply. Instead, he stared directly at Masterson. His eyes said enough.

Masterson looked at both Hector and Armando, who said nothing. The quicker he and Armando could get out of here the better. Let Zavala deal with this DEA mess. The less he knew, the better. Masterson adjusted his Resistol hat again and spoke in a conciliatory tone.

"Señor Zavala, we realized we fucked up here tonight. You have our word that this won't happen again. When do you want us to resume our deliveries?"

"End of September. Get rid of that damn rig tonight and get a different one with a different color. No one will know what happened here tonight. It will remain that way. We can't afford to have another 'Kiki' situation."

Zavala glared at the men in front of him. All three nodded in affirmation.

"Roberto, go and get Esteban and follow my instructions. Remember, it should look as if nothing happened."

Masterson and Armando walked back to the Freightliner and jumped into the cab. Once inside, Masterson suggested they drive to Amarillo, Texas, about a two hour's drive north of Lubbock. With its proximity to Interstate 40, the market would be higher for the resale of the Freightliner, along with the selection of new semitruck rigs as a replacement.

24

Tuesday, June 14, 1994
1:34 a.m. CDT
Interstate 27, just north of Lubbock, Texas

Once inside the cab of the Freightliner, Armando and Masterson did not speak to each other for the next ten minutes of their drive north. Armando was the first to break the silence.

"Señor Bill, I have a question. What did Señor Zavala mean by 'Kiki situation'?"

Masterson, still sore from the boot kick from Zavala, shifted his weight in his seat to minimize the pressure of the truck's seat against his bruised back. He turned his gaze from the interstate to Armando.

"Back in 1985, the leader of the Guadalajara drug cartel, a man named Miguel Ángel Félix Gallardo, known as "El Padrino," or Godfather, had full reign over Mexico's drug business. This guy was pulling in millions every month and had a deadly reputation. Several of his lieutenants, including a young El Astuto at the time, called him the 'Don Corleone of the Narcos.'"

"Don Corleone?" queried Armando.

Masterson looked at Armando, "From *The Godfather*?"

"*No lo recuerdo, señor.*"

"Anyway, this El Padrino used to be a street cop in Mexico. He then became a bodyguard and ended up as one of the most powerful narcos in all of Mexico. El Padrino used his contacts in the police department and bribed police commanders, mayors, politicians, governors, you name it. He was the drug lord you couldn't fuck with or arrest. However, all this power went to El

Padrino's head, and he went a step too far. Just like tonight, the DEA came poking into El Padrino's business but on a much larger and sophisticated scale. They scored this huge drug bust and found El Padrino's biggest marijuana field, over a thousand acres in the high desert of Zacatecas. And you know what they did? They torched it."

"*Dios mio*, a thousand acres?" said Armando.

"Yep. Five thousand metric tons of marijuana burned to the ground. Anyway, one of the DEA agents who discovered the field was this guy named Enrique "Kiki" Camarena. He was later murdered by El Padrino's men. After that, the DEA came down hard on El Padrino and his gang. It eventually led to El Padrino's fall, along with several of his close associates. From then on, no drug cartel ever tried to kill a DEA agent."

"I never heard about this Kiki." Armando let out a small yawn as he drove the truck.

"Shit, if word gets back to El Astuto about what we know happened tonight, we are all fucked. I just hope Zavala and his guys can clean up the mess. One thing those DEA guys are good at is finding shit. If word gets out that one of their own got snuffed out, we may have to leave the country, my friend."

Armando shrugged. Masterson unbuckled his seat belt and carefully crawled into the sleeper cabin of the Freightliner. "Now where did you say that bottle of Windex was?"

"Lower left corner, under my seat."

Masterson located the Windex then grabbed the cloth rag lying next to it. Working methodically, he sprayed the back of the cab and started cleaning everything around him, wiping each area with purpose. Neither man spoke until they reached a Motel 6 on the outskirts of Amarillo, Texas.

25

Tuesday, June 14, 1994
7:19 a.m. MDT
Drug Enforcement Agency El Paso Intelligence Center, El Paso, Texas

Brian Harris arrived in his office at the DEA El Paso Intelligence Center, nicknamed EPIC, off Ssg Sims Street on the southeast corner of Biggs Army Airfield, on the federal reservation grounds of Fort Bliss. Entering the salmon-colored brick building, he ventured down the first-floor hallway to his office. For ten years he'd been an SAC, a DEA Special Agent in Charge, working hard to earn that rank over the last twenty-six years since graduating from Sam Houston University in Huntsville, Texas, with a major in criminal justice. Huntsville was known more for its notorious penitentiary complexes, rather than for hosting one of the top universities in the country for his major.

A creature of habit, Harris opened the door to his office, placed his work bag behind his fifteen-year-old government desk and grabbed his large coffee mug. In the ten years since taking over his division, Harris's team's reputation was one of the best in the country. El Paso was considered the "Super Bowl" for illegal drug trafficking in the U.S., which helped his department's arrest record tremendously. But, as Harris knew, the narcos didn't walk into jail on their own. You had to arrest them. And to do that, you had to build a case.

Harris himself worked for the office director, Phil Colangelo, who was no pushover. Limits of the law were pushed when it came to a first-year-law-student interpretation of the Bill of Rights, but within that gray area came a high rate of convictions. It also helped having a very friendly ally at the judicial level. Within the U.S. Western District of Texas and based in El Paso was U.S. District Federal Judge Louis Lawrence, quietly nicknamed "Judge Loose" by the DEA agents at the EPIC office. Judge Lawrence approved warrants and authorized wire taps with what might have been considered the slightest appearance of malfeasance. Almost ninety-five percent of the warrants and wire taps issued resulted in a bust, a rate envied by the other twenty domestic field offices of the Drug Enforcement Agency.

Harris enjoyed the first thirty minutes of his workday, unencumbered by the daily interruptions that would arrive thirty minutes later. After the initial brew of fresh coffee reached the two-cup line painted on the large glass carafe, Harris poured himself what he considered the most important food group of the day into his large mug, then walked back to his office and settled into his office chair. He called the overnight recording service used by his team of agents in the field, gave his six-digit identification and listened. Only one message was on the service. The familiar female computer voice spoke first.

"Monday, June thirteenth, nineteen ninety-four, eleven oh four p.m. Message . . ."

An audible click, then Harris heard a familiar voice.

"Hey Brian, Traegar here. I hope you can hear me; I don't know how great the cellular coverage is out here. So: after making a pit stop in Big Spring, Texas, our two suspects drove north on US Highway 87 just south of Lubbock, Texas. The Freightliner pulled up at South Plains Cellars, off County Road 7600 and Highway 87 just before midnight. I pulled over about a hundred yards away, and I'm seeing some activity from inside. I smell something sweet in the air, like . . ."

The voicemail audio then garbled something unrecognizable before continuing with words that sounded like *elches ape oose*. A few seconds passed with only a faint background hum, then Jackson's voice again: "Lights, camera, action."

The recorded voice of Traegar Jackson ended. Then, the familiar female voice came to life.

"End of message."

Harris mused at Jackson's movie-set expression. He knew that Jackson took multiple pictures when he was on surveillance. The man was a fanatic for photography. Jackson went so far as to disregard the Canon camera the DEA issued him and instead opted for the more expensive Nikon. FM2 something, Harris remembered. He'd expect Jackson to call his office at 8 a.m. for his daily morning check-in. Hopefully everything could be cleared up, including his exact location.

Harris was not overly concerned. Jackson always checked in on schedule. He was as regular as clockwork.

Glancing at his watch, Harris picked up his morning copy of the *El Paso Times* and started to read. The O.J. Simpson article caught his eye first.

26

Tuesday, June 14, 1994
7:59 a.m. MDT
Ysleta–Zaragoza International Bridge, El Paso, Texas

Esteban opened his mouth, yawned, and looked at his watch. He'd forgotten to set it back an hour when they arrived in Mountain Daylight Time. Roberto was fast asleep in the back passenger seat of the black Chevrolet Tahoe. Esteban had not worked with Roberto that long. The guy didn't say much. Esteban did like that Roberto had memorized every request from Zavala concerning the disposal of the DEA agent, along with the agent's vehicle and all his personal effects. Roberto and his strong muscles were especially helpful in getting the agent's body wrapped in the blue tarp and rolling the corpse into the red carpet.

As both men arrived at Ysleta–Zaragoza International Bridge, the wait time driving across the bridge into Mexico was minimal. However, the bridge with incoming traffic from Mexico into the United States was already backed up. Once the men crossed the border, Esteban stopped at a nearby market and purchased a map of Ciudad Juárez. He had no idea where the Ciudad Juárez de Castillo Landfill resided, and Zavala had failed to give him Guillermo's telephone number.

"Typical Zavala," Esteban muttered. "Always making you figure out your own problems after his are solved." He glanced at his watch and added an hour in his head. This was going to take some time.

After Harris's daily newspaper reading ended around 8 a.m., his assistant Judith Longsworth arrived, along with the bulk of the office and support staff at EPIC. Harris reviewed his team's progress reports and the phone calls started to pour in. Twenty-one minutes later, he looked at the clock on his wall: 8:21 a.m. All his agents in the field reported to him that morning, except for Traegar Jackson. Jackson was typically the first to call in to his boss.

Harris pulled the receiver off the cradle of his office phone then looked at his Rolodex. Seeking the guide letter J, he flipped through the Rolodex's cards as they tumbled in a circular motion around their axis; at J he flipped twice more to stop at Jackson's card. He referred to the cellular phone number on the card and dialed. The customary ringing on the other end of the line did not occur. Instead, Harris heard another familiar female voice . . .

"You have reached the voicemail of . . ."

Then a pause, and the words of Traegar Jackson sounded.

"Traegar Jackson."

Then another pause . . .

"Please leave a message at the beep."

And another brief pause, followed by an audible *beep*. Confused, Brian Harris placed his finger on top of the Radio Shack push-button tone office phone, disconnecting the call. He punched in Jackson's cellular phone number again, putting the receiver to his ear. There was the same response from the female voice, along with Jackson's. Harris slowly lowered the phone's receiver into the cradle on top.

He glanced at his Rolodex again and placed a phone call to Jackson's apartment on the north side of El Paso. The phone rang and rang, but no one answered.

"Well, that's not good."

Most of the time, DEA agents worked in pairs, so as to avoid the situation Harris currently faced. However, with multiple investigations taken on by his team over the past few months, Harris allowed more experienced agents to work solo on their investigations if they kept up with their routine calls to the office.

Harris walked over to the Intelligence Division office, a large room filled with mainframe computers, switchboards and monitors. He zeroed in on his overweight target, Paul Hagen, who was currently doing his best to consume a sugar-coated donut without the sugar crumbs falling on his well-worn tie.

"Morning, Paul. You know the glazed donuts don't crumble as bad as the sugar-coated ones."

Paul responded with something completely unintelligible.

"Might want to finish what you have in your mouth before ya speak, Paul."

Paul shrugged and swallowed. "They don't taste as good as the sugar ones," he replied.

"Good point." Harris pointed his index finger on Paul's sweetened tie. "Bit of sugar there."

Paul looked down. "Ah, shit." He quickly brushed off the donut particles. Then: "What do you need, Brian?"

"I'm missing an agent."

"An *agent*? Those guys don't go missing. He's probably hiding from you or got lucky last night."

"Not this one."

Paul Hagen finished cleaning his tie and looked up at a Harris. "So, who has gone off the ranch?"

"Traegar Jackson."

"The wunderkind, huh? Maybe he did get lucky last night."

"His last message to me was from the field last night, just south of Lubbock."

"Lubbock? There's nothing up there except fields of cotton and all those gentlemen's clubs off Highway 84. You can't screw a cotton boll, and he's too cheap to go to a strip club."

Paul laughed at his own joke, and walked over to another workstation, with a much larger monitor.

"If he's anywhere, we will find him," Paul said. He punched his keyboard and activated the DEA's newest toy, the LoJack, a locator system for missing automobiles.

When they became available, the U.S. government began to install LoJack systems within the law enforcement community and other agencies of the federal government, drug enforcement included. The DEA went a step further and requested their vehicles include both tracking devices and transponders. The thought was that each of the twenty-one divisions of the

DEA could track their agents in the field, not only to monitor their field investigations, but to offer support in case a surveillance situation went wrong or a vehicle was stolen.

Paul Hagen's monitor came to life. After a few more keystrokes, his screen displayed the National Crime Information Center's Missing Vehicle Report. Before Paul could ask his first question, Harris shoved a piece of paper in front of him. Paul started typing on his keyboard:

VIN Number: 1GNEC13R5XJ334096

Owner: Traegar David Jackson

Type of Vehicle: 1993 Chevrolet Tahoe

License Plate: LTZ 578

State: Texas

Address: 11339 SSG Sims Street

City: Fort Bliss

Zip: 79918

Badge Number: DEA Senior Special Agent 86304

Time: 08:29 AM

City/State of Last Known location: Lubbock, TX

After Paul double-checked his entries on the screen versus the paper Harris gave him, he hit the keyboard button marked ENTER. Almost immediately, the LoJack tracking device hidden in the chassis under the rear left wheel of Traegar Jackson's Chevrolet Tahoe turned on. This technology never ceased to impress Paul. Extremely powerful, the uniquely coded radio-frequency signal from a LoJack tracking device had enough strength to penetrate concrete, metal and even the dense woods of a forest.

Paul then entered "Lubbock," Jackson's last known location. Several LoJack transponders were activated in multiple city of Lubbock police cars, giving the description of Traegar Jackson's vehicle, along with the special note "DEA." After ten minutes, Paul received a phone call from a sergeant at the Lubbock Police Department. Paul punched the speaker button on his office phone, and a man with a strong West Texas accent immediately began to speak.

"Yeah, this is Sergeant Hightower with the Lubbock Police Department. Our boys received your LoJack signal about ten minutes ago and nothing is pinging back. Are you sure you got the last known location for this stolen vehicle?"

"Yes, Sergeant Hightower. This is DEA Special Agent in Charge Brian Harris, El Paso Division. We are missing one of our agents; his last called-in position was just south of your city."

"Wish we could help y'all, but as I said, we've got nothing to report. I suggest you draw a circle around Lubbock and start pinging cities outside that radius. I bet you'll find him soon."

Harris walked over to the large State of Texas map, mounted on the office wall adjacent to Paul's workstation.

Paul, noticing Harris's absence from the phone, spoke up. "Thank you, Sergeant Hightower. We will call you if we need anything else."

"All right, you DEA boys, have a good day in El Paso."

The phone went dead, and Paul walked over to where Harris was staring at the large map of Texas.

"Paul, please grab your notepad and write these names down."

Harris glided his pointer finger straight up the map and paused on the city of Lubbock. He then targeted the immediate cities and towns around Lubbock and started to rattle off names, starting northwest and going clockwise.

Paul walked back to his terminal and activated the LoJack system and pinged each of the designated cities. As Paul worked on his computer terminal, Harris sat across and grabbed the piece of paper that had Jackson's vehicle information. He flipped the paper to its blank side and started writing numbers and his analysis.

Harris began to speculate: "If someone stole Traegar's Chevrolet Tahoe, they couldn't have gotten that far. Traegar's last message was time-stamped eleven ten p.m. MDT, which was twelve ten a.m. CDT just south of Lubbock. If he or the person that stole his vehicle were to drive sixty-five miles per hour in any direction from Lubbock, they could be as far as . . ."

Harris wrote down the number 65 and looked at his watch. It was almost 8:43 a.m. MDT. After some quick calculation, he settled on a five-hundred-mile radius, then went back to the large map of Texas hanging on the wall and wrote down more names of cities.

Twenty-two minutes later, Paul Hagen and Harris received phone calls on separate extensions from all the cities Harris had listed off. No luck and no tracking signal for Jackson's Tahoe. Harris turned his attention to his map and rattled off more cities, which Paul wrote down.

Nineteen minutes later, all the town sheriffs and police in the targeted cities came up empty.

Harris continued, "Amarillo. Big Spring. Midland. Odessa. Abilene." Twenty more minutes elapsed, and phone calls poured in again.

Nothing.

Harris looked at the Texas map again. Beyond the scope of those bigger cities in West Texas, there was not much out there in terms of major population or towns. And other than the occasional rancher, cotton farmer or roughneck working on an isolated oil rig, there were no big population centers or towns big enough to warrant a police department, let alone a LoJack system. And the small towns dotted across the vast plains and deserts of West Texas were lucky to have a town sheriff, let alone a county sheriff.

Paul shrugged. "Brian, what do you think? Should we go further west and ping some of the bigger cities in New Mexico, Colorado, or go east and try Oklahoma?"

A thought then popped in Harris's head. He was ignoring the most obvious possibility.

"Paul, ping El Paso."

"El Paso? But you said you called Jackson's apartment and there was no answer. Are you sure?"

"Yes. Do it."

27

Tuesday, June 14, 1994
9:37 a.m. MDT
Drug Enforcement Agency, El Paso Intelligence Center, El Paso, Texas

Paul punched Agent Traegar Jackson's vehicle information on his keyboard and pinged the El Paso Police Department. Meanwhile, Brian Harris placed a call to a friend there, Captain Stuart Campinero. Both men had known each other for many years back from the time Harris's and Stuart's sons played on the same youth soccer team.

"Stu, *mi amigo*. How's Maria and the kids?"

"Very good, Agent Harris, thanks for asking. How are yours?"

"Growing up too fast. Is Daniel going to play soccer in the fall? I believe the upcoming U14 season is the last time the boys will be together again."

"He sure is. Too bad our boys will attend different high schools next year. How about Robbie—is he playing this upcoming season?"

"He's chomping at the bit for mid-August to start again."

"What can I do for you, Brian? You need some help from us local boys again?" Stuart chuckled to himself.

Harris paused. "We're missing an agent."

"Missing an agent?" Stuart regretted his chuckle of laughter.

Harris could sense Stuart's eyebrows furrowing on the other end. "Yeah. Senior Special Agent Traegar Jackson. He's gone off the grid. No response to cellular phone calls and nothing from his apartment. Paul Hagen just pinged the LoJack system for El Paso. Can you give us a heads-up if your boys get a signal?"

"Will do." Stuart hung up his phone and the line went dead. Harris walked over to the map on the wall and stared at it again.

Where did you go, Agent Jackson?

Roberto munched on a street taco, sitting in the passenger seat inside the DEA-owned black Tahoe. Next to him, Esteban studied his map. A bright red light flashed on the dashboard of the Tahoe and a small screen just below the car's radio came to life. The display flashed, and the LoJack logo appeared. Puzzled, both men stared at the small flashing red light and the LoJack image on the screen.

"What did you do?" barked Esteban.

"Esteban, I touched nothing. It just came on by itself."

"Shit! We need to find this landfill fast!"

Esteban slammed the transmission into drive.

"As soon as you see somebody, ask them where the hell Ciudad Juárez de Castillo Landfill is, because it is not on this fucking map!"

After driving the streets of Ciudad Juárez for a few minutes and looking for street signs, Esteban's eyes wandered to the Tahoe's front console and he slammed on the brakes, staring directly at the small monitor mounted on the dashboard.

"What's wrong, Esteban?" asked a perplexed Roberto.

Esteban pointed toward the small video screen.

"That is what's wrong."

28

Tuesday, June 14, 1994
10:12 a.m. MDT
Near Ysleta–Zaragoza International Bridge, El Paso, TX

Fifteen-year veteran Sergeant James Gilmore and his new partner, rookie Dwane Lopez of the El Paso Police Department, sat in their police-issued Chevrolet Caprice vehicle parked less than two hundred yards from the Ysleta–Zaragoza International Bridge. Both officers were drinking coffee, a short respite as they entered their third hour of duty watching the dual flow of people and goods crossing the border. Suddenly, the vehicle's LoJack responder activated, with a signal indicating the preliminary location of a missing vehicle. Sergeant Gilmore clicked a switch, and the tiny Toshiba TV screen came to life. The same message that Esteban just saw a few miles west appeared.

VIN Number: 1GNEC13R5XJ334096

Owner: Traegar David Jackson

Type of Vehicle: 1993 Chevrolet Tahoe

License Plate: LTZ 578

State: Texas

Address: 11339 SSG Sims Street

City: Fort Bliss

Zip: 79918

Badge Number: DEA Senior Special Agent 86304

Time: 08:29 AM

City/State of Last Known location: Lubbock, TX

DEA?

Holy shit, thought Lopez.

Sergeant Gilmore quickly read the gray-colored text that flashed on the monochrome screen. He paused and then reread the message. Lopez did the same and then gave his boss an anxious look.

Sergeant Gilmore turned to his partner and spoke. "Go ahead, Dwane, call it in."

Lopez picked up the car's transmitter microphone. "This is unit four one four. We have a positive LoJack signal on DEA Senior Special Agent Traegar David Jackson's vehicle, license plate Lima, Tango, Zulu, five, seven, eight." Officer Lopez repeated the message and released the transmit button, and both men waited on the reply, which came a few seconds later.

"Copy that, unit four one four. Please advise on your transponder's distance and proximity."

Officer Lopez then looked at the bottom of the screen and replied.

"Looks like three miles directly west, inside Ciudad Juárez, Mexico."

"Roger. Standby."

Officer Lopez then looked at his partner. "James, what do we do now?"

Sergeant Gilmore scratched his salt-and-pepper hair. He turned his eyes toward the border at the Ysleta–Zaragoza International Bridge.

"We don't have the authority to cross into Mexico. All we can do is wait here and give the department updates."

Perplexed, Dwane pressed the issue. "We can't go after the vehicle? It would be hot pursuit, wouldn't it?"

James faced his new rookie partner. "Dwane, that car is in *Mexico*. We have no authority to continue this pursuit. For now, we just sit here and give updates to headquarters as needed."

"But it's a DEA agent's vehicle!"

"And I'm sure the DEA boys will get the info. So just relax and keep watching that screen for any updates."

Sergeant Gilmore took a sip of his coffee and stared at the Ysleta–Zaragoza International Bridge and shared his thoughts. "I bet the guy went across the border for some late-night entertainment and forgot to lock his car. Let the DEA handle this one."

29

Tuesday, June 14, 1994
10:42 a.m. MDT
Ciudad Juárez de Castillo Landfill, Ciudad Juárez

Directly three miles west of Gilmore and Lopez's police issued Chevrolet Lumina, a now very nervous Esteban and Roberto finally arrived at Ciudad Juárez de Castillo Landfill, despite the poor cartography of the city map. The vehicle's LoJack system and constant pinging noise elevated the anxiety of its passengers, both of whom were very concerned that local law enforcement, or worse yet, other DEA agents would discover the stolen Tahoe and the dead agent in the back. Esteban breathed a sigh of relief when the well-worn sign spelling out the name of the landfill grew closer. Quickly, he parked the Tahoe to the left of the landfill's entrance.

As Esteban and Roberto exited the SUV, the stench of the outside air overwhelmed them. Each raised a hand to pinch his nose. Large garbage trucks lumbered one by one past their parked vehicle into the entrance, each with the task of depositing the city's refuse.

"God, this place stinks," said Esteban.

Roberto nodded his head in agreement, then asked, "What is the name of the man again?"

"Guillermo."

Esteban double-checked his wallet for the five hundred dollars and waited for another passing garage truck to drive through the entrance. Immediately, both men walked inside the entrance and noticed a very small building that sat elevated four feet above the ground on the right side of the entrance driveway. Surrounded by three sides of glass, the building had just enough space for one unlucky soul whose job was to wave through each garbage truck. Esteban waited for the garbage truck in front of them to drive past this checkpoint. He then approached the building, walked up the few steps behind the small edifice and knocked on the door.

Seconds later, a short, squatty man of at least sixty years opened the door. His white shirt looked as if it had not been washed in months, and small letters embroidered on the left of his chest spelled out the name Mateo.

"What do you want?" an irritated Mateo gruffly replied to his unexpected visitor.

"I'm here to see Guillermo. Señor Zavala needs to make a *deposit*."

Mateo's disposition completely changed, his eyes widening as he snapped to attention.

"One moment, Señor, please."

The man then closed the door, grabbed the telephone at his small workstation, dialed several numbers on the phone's antiquated rotary dial, and spoke briefly.

Esteban could not make out most of the words, but he heard "Guillermo" and "Zavala." An elevated voice spoke quickly in Spanish, and then Esteban heard yelling, from both the short squatty man named Mateo and whoever was on the other line. Mateo hung up the phone and opened the door again. He looked outside, nervously moving his head from left to right, and then he spoke.

"Where is your car?"

"Out front."

"We must move quickly, gentlemen. Follow me."

Mateo waddled down the steps and quickly walked to the parked SUV. Both Esteban and Roberto were surprised at the old man's speedy gait, especially given his rotund body.

Mateo turned his head around and barked, "Quickly now, we must hurry!"

Esteban and Roberto jumped in the driver's and passenger's front seat, and the old man opened the right rear door and sat in the Tahoe's large back seat.

"Drive now, hurry. I will tell you where to go. We must go now, quickly."

Esteban yanked the transmission into reverse, and after moving several feet backwards, dropped the transmission into drive and drove through the landfill entrance and past the small checkpoint building.

"Keep going and the road will split two ways. Turn left." Mateo extended his arm and hand in the negative space between Esteban and Roberto, pointing his finger toward the upcoming fork in the road.

Impatiently, the fat back-seat stranger spoke again. "Please, mister, you must drive faster."

Esteban turned his head toward their newest passenger. "Why are we driving so fast?"

The old man turned his head and looked out the back windshield. "The police are on their way."

Esteban and Roberto looked at each other. They both shrugged. Esteban depressed the gas pedal further down. The SUV roared down the landfill road, driving past the small mountains of trash and garbage which reeked of stench and filth.

30

Tuesday, June 14, 1994
10:14 a.m. MDT
Drug Enforcement Agency, El Paso Intelligence Center

After Officer Dwane Lopez of unit 414 reported on the LoJack signal of DEA Senior Special Agent Traegar Jackson's vehicle, El Paso City Police Captain Stuart Campinero received the news from his dispatch officer. Stuart immediately called Harris, and the two men spoke briefly. Harris hung up the phone and immediately called DEA Supervising Special Agent Easton Derderian, who was wrapping up the paperwork on a drug bust near Pecos, Texas.

"Easton, it's Brian. I need your help. We found Jackson's vehicle across the border in Juárez. Grab your tactical gear, and we'll cross. Meet you up front."

By now the news of missing Senior Special Agent Traegar Jackson had filtered through the entire building at the El Paso Intelligence Center.

Derderian simply replied, "Yes sir," grabbed his duffel bag of tactical gear and met Harris at the building's entrance. Both men quickly walked to Harris's car, a black 1990 Chevrolet Suburban. Derderian threw his duffel bag in the back seat.

DEA Supervising Special Agent Easton Derderian was built like a football tight end with wide shoulders and a small waist. Originally from Annapolis, Maryland, and a graduate of the United States Naval Academy, Derderian successfully passed the SEAL Physical Screening Test and enrolled at the Naval Special Warfare Preparatory School in Great Lakes, Illinois. Eight weeks later, Derderian arrived in Coronado, California, to begin twenty-four weeks of training at Basic Underwater Demolition/ SEAL (BUD/S) school.

The day after successfully passing Hell Week, Derderian reported to medical for pain in his lower back. Subsequent examination discovered Derderian had a hairline fracture in the lumbar region. Unable to finish his SEAL training, the Navy reassigned Derderian to Pearl Harbor, where upon his back healed in the tropical paradise. After finishing his naval service, but with his dreams of being a Navy SEAL gone, Derderian applied for work with the Drug Enforcement Agency. Phil and Harris took a quick interest in Derderian and immediately hired the former naval officer. Derderian moved up quickly, reaching the rank of DEA Supervising Special Agent in just four years.

Derderian arrived at Harris's office wearing his tactical gear under a black jacket with "DEA" emblazed on the back in yellow letters. Harris was listening to his office phone when he came in.

"Brian, I have Capitan Díaz from Juárez Police Department on the other line," said a voice on the other end. After a couple of audible clicks, another voice, this one accented, joined the conversation.

"Señor Harris, a pleasure to speak to you again."

Harris grinned. He could just picture Captain Díaz coolly grooming his thin mustache with his thumb and index finger while speaking,

"Captain Díaz, how are you and that very handsome mustache doing?"

In perfect English, but with a strong Oaxacan accent, Díaz replied, "Fine, fine. Captain Stuart tells me that one of your DEA agent's vehicles is here in our fine city of Juárez, but that this agent of yours is not responding to any of your calls."

"Indeed, Captain. I'm getting ready to head over to the border right now. The vehicle's LoJack signal is coming near the intersection of Isla Cerdeña and Zacatenco on the northwest side of town. Do you know that part of town?"

"Not much is there, a few warehouses, and the city landf . . ." Captain Díaz's voiced trailed off.

"Just a moment, gentlemen," Captain Díaz held his hand to cover the receiver and spoke at his young dispatch officer in Spanish. Harris's Spanish was not the best, but he was able to make out what Díaz was saying.

"Diego, please send an all-points bulletin to any officer near the Ciudad Juárez de Castillo Landfill. Have the closest units move in and converge. We need to find the location of a missing black Chevrolet Tahoe."

888

Meanwhile, in a parked trailer situated eleven blocks away from the Ciudad Juárez de Castillo Landfill, Guillermo Badillo sat in his office, reading the morning edition of the newspaper *Norte de Ciudad Juárez* and drinking his third cup of coffee. Suddenly, Guillermo's tuned police scanner picked up Diego's all-points bulletin over the airwaves. Guillermo's coffee mug descended and crashed on the trailer's floor when the words "Ciudad Juárez de Castillo Landfill" arrived. He started shouting out expletives to himself.

Guillermo reached for his telephone receiver to call Mateo at the front gate when the phone magically rang. Surprised, Guillermo picked up the receiver when Mateo relayed the message of a "deposit" on behalf of Señor Zavala and the arrival of a black Chevrolet Tahoe. If these strangers had not mentioned Señor Zavala's name, he would have told Mateo to tell these men to fuck off. Not only was Guillermo in danger of being arrested for disposing of a vehicle and possibly a dead body, his other and more profitable illegal operation could be exposed as well.

Guillermo barked at Mateo through the phone and instructed him to show these men to the "nest." He slammed the receiver handset on the phone, quickly exited his office trailer and jumped in his 1993 white Jeep Grand Cherokee. He drove to a small, gray warehouse on the western edge of the landfill. The warehouse looked like any ordinary edifice in Juárez, Chihuahua, Mexico. Above the garage door a small sign in red letters said Badillo Auto Repair.

Behind the small warehouse building, eight feet of chain-link fence extended both south and north, the property line of the landfill. The steady beeping noises as garbage trucks dumped their payload could be heard in the distance.

Guillermo approached the warehouse; he pressed a button on the black garage door opener clasped on the inside of the passenger overhead visor. The garage door opened, and Guillermo drove into the warehouse. Once his car was fully enclosed in the small building, he clicked the garage door button again and the large door shut behind him. Darkness surrounded Guillermo's vehicle.

The small building had no windows and no furniture. The only structures were two large yellow steel cylinders, each about twenty-four inches in width and eighteen feet high, almost touching the interlocking metal cross frame supporting the warehouse's roof. Each cylinder sat poised on either side of Guillermo's Jeep. Immediately below the Grand Cherokee's tires was a large, rectangular steel plate, with forged grooves meant to give tension to the car's tires. Guillermo pressed another button on the garage door opener. Two overhead lights turned on, illuminating the windowless building. The sound of metal on metal clanged as the large steel plate came to life. Inverted panels of metal, about eight inches in height, began to rise at each end of Guillermo's car to prevent it from moving forward or backward.

After the metal panels stopped moving, the distinct hissing sound of pneumatic pressure pipes and hoses filled the small building, and a small red light, much like those of old police sirens, flashed in circles between the two overhead lights as Guillermo and his Jeep Cherokee slowly descended into the earth below.

Twenty seconds later and nineteen feet below the ground, the pneumatic hissing ceased as the large plate of steel reached its stopping point on the concrete floor. The sound of screeching metal returned as the inverted panels lowered into place. Another small red light, this one mounted to the left of the yellow cylinder and lighting up the word ALTO, flashed off and was immediately replaced by the green word VAMOS. Guillermo turned on his Jeep's headlamps and pressed the third button on his special garage opener. A path of lights reminiscent of an airport landing strip at night turned on in the upper corners of the tunnel in twenty-meter segments, lighting the four-by-four-meter space.

Guillermo depressed the Jeep's brake pedal with his foot, moved the transmission lever into drive, and eased slowly off the large rectangle steel plate. Another light, this one mounted on the tunnel's wood crossbeam about nineteen feet in front of the industrial car riser, sparked to life, lighting up the red word ALTO again. Guillermo pressed the second garage opener button again and the car lift repeated the process, this time with no vehicle on the steel plate. Once the large steel plate reached ground level, the red words ALTO flashed off and the green word VAMOS displayed overhead.

Guillermo found himself in a drivable tunnel under the landfill. He headed into the darkness.

31

Tuesday, June 14, 1994
10:27 a.m. MDT
Ciudad Juárez, Chihuahua, Mexico

Brian Harris and Easton Derderian raced across the Bridge of the Americas, one of the four main bridges into Mexico and the closest crossing from EPIC headquarters. Instead of following the commercial lane of traffic where they could be stuck for close to an hour, Captain Díaz had called ahead, requesting the Mexican customs authority at the bridge to provide speedy passage for the agents. The customs personnel closed off one of the many entrances on the bridge with a set of orange cones and made a lane for them.

"I'm still amazed at the *power* of orange cones," quipped Harris as he drove his Suburban to a stop.

Derderian, his nerves jangled, couldn't believe how calm Harris was at this moment. They had sped through the streets of El Paso, running stoplights, dodging cars and sailing recklessly through all the twists and turns of roads and thoroughfares. But Harris seemed unfazed.

"Orange cones," repeated Harris. "Hell of a thing."

Derderian nodded and let out his held breath. "You know, you're right," he said. "Now I know what to get you for Christmas."

Harris laughed as he rolled down his window. A Mexican customs agent approached his driver's side window and Harris flashed his DEA badge and a pleasant smile.

"Good morning, sir. I believe Captain Díaz said we were coming."

888

After inching forward for about eight more minutes, Guillermo reached a large garage door and stopped. He reached into his driver's side console and pulled out another garage door opener that offered two side-by-side buttons; he depressed the button on the left.

Immediately, the garage door opened, and a large, cavernous workspace revealed itself, encased in darkness. He then clicked the button on the right of the remote and large overhead lights turned on, illuminating the entire space.

Originally, the long tunnel carved into the earth that Guillermo traversed was meant to be a public works project, envisioned by Ciudad Juárez city leaders in the mid-1960s. Inspired by the irrigation canals of Phoenix, Arizona, and meant to increase water supplies for the growing populace, workers started digging the canals in the fall of 1970. More canals were dug from other areas outside the city with the intention of connecting all canals toward the city's public waterworks supply distribution plant. Unfortunately, corruption and kickbacks plagued the construction, which delayed the vast project. By the late 1970s, just after work started on the SOP JKL-049 west canal, the project was abandoned. All that remained was a four-kilometer ditch that started nowhere and ended nowhere, west of the city. By 1987, city leaders annexed more land to the west to increase the capacity of their rapidly filling landfills. At that time, a twenty-nine-year-old grease monkey and car thief named Guillermo Badillo started to make a name for himself by stealing vehicles from gringo tourists visiting Juárez.

Instead of waiting until the cover of darkness or minimal surrounding foot traffic of city pedestrians, Guillermo blatantly stole cars in broad daylight, smashing unoccupied car windows, jamming screwdrivers into the key ignition ports to start the vehicle, and speeding off. Guillermo became so successful that his problem was not getting caught by the local authorities (whom he bribed when necessary) but a storage issue. Other car thieves like Guillermo roamed the city, sometimes stealing Guillermo's prizes from undisclosed warehouse locations scattered through the city. After losing a sweet 1992 white Toyota Lexus from a rich American gringo, a frustrated Guillermo had hit upon a solution: the long, diagonal trench just on the outskirts of the landfill.

Guillermo had no idea why the landfill would have a trench dug so precisely on its perimeter. But his imagination took off as he began to envision a solution to his storage problem. The stench alone would be a formidable barrier to the noses of his competition.

Driving back to his apartment, Guillermo made a phone call. Soon his idea traveled up the ranks of the Sinaloa Cartel and came to the attention of Señor Santiago Zavala. Zavala knew about the high profits of selling stolen cars, and with the immense cross-border traffic between El Paso, Texas, and Ciudad de Juárez, he would have an endless supply of product, and that product would increase in the coming years. In just a matter of weeks after his phone call, Guillermo's storage solution came to fruition. He didn't even mind that he would owe fifty percent of all profits to Santiago Zavala and the Sinaloa Cartel in perpetuity.

Included in the deal somehow was Zavala's arrangement for Guillermo to be appointed directing manager of the Ciudad Juárez de Castillo Landfill.

Inside Guillermo's chop shop were dozens and dozens of automobiles, ranging from American made to high-end German and Japanese imports, all late models. Amongst the vehicles were workbenches, tool chests, machine lathes and other standard equipment you would expect to see at a typical automobile repair shop. Dozens and dozens of Glade air fresheners used and new were scattered on the work benches, along with small pine-tree scented deodorizers dangling on each of the vehicles' rearview mirrors. Near each workstation, industrial-sized fans sat motionless. Guillermo drove quickly forward, passing through the garage door and the dozens of automobiles. He crossed the distance of the large workshop and pulled to a stop. Directly in front of him stood a large wall, complete with tin metal sheeting, a few mounted shelves and pictures of the latest Playboy Playmates taped to the wall.

Guillermo made sure to stop his vehicle a good ten meters from the wall. He grabbed his keys, jumped out of the Jeep and quickly walked over to the left end of the wall, where a small metal box was mounted about one and half meters high. With his left hand holding the set of keys, he found the correct key and inserted it with his right hand into a small wafer lock on the right side of the box. Turning his hand counterclockwise, the front metal panel opened and a red-and-black lock handle of a non-fusible disconnect switch appeared, positioned downward in its OFF setting. He tucked his keys into his front left pocket and waited.

32

Tuesday, June 14, 1994
10:33 a.m. MDT
Ciudad Juárez de Castillo Landfill

"What do you mean *stop*? I thought you said the police were coming?"

"Trust me. You are going to see something you have never seen before."

Stunned, Esteban looked at Roberto, who raised his shoulders, indicating he had no idea what the fat, old man in back was talking about. Esteban noticed a cream-colored Volkswagen on his right. It looked as if someone had driven the car up the base of another large mountain of trash. Esteban then noticed how small the road he was driving on was, diminishing in size as he etched closer to the Volkswagen. In just a few more meters the road completely vanished, with nothing but mounds of trash and refuse on all three corners of the men in the stolen Tahoe.

Esteban slammed both his feet on the brake pedal, stopping the vehicle in its tracks, dust and rocks surrounding the Tahoe in a mist of dirt and grime. He turned around to face Mateo.

"Now what? We are sitting ducks here for the police."

Mateo smiled, saying nothing, and he pointed his finger toward the front windshield. The hissing sound of hydraulics and compressed air filled the immediate area around the Tahoe as directly in front of them a large mound of trash began to shift inward in a single plane before beginning to recede into the lower edge of the mountain of trash above it. This trash-covered door, close to four meters high and three meters wide, raised inward slowly, and after about twenty seconds, it stopped.

Mateo spoke, "Quickly, please drive in!"

Stunned by the wall of trash's transformation, Esteban drove the Tahoe into the mountain.

Roberto said nothing, his mouth still agape and eyes wide open at the entire spectacle himself.

Once through the entrance, Esteban noticed a man inside signaling him where to go.

Esteban obeyed. The man then raised his hand, flashed his right palm upward and shouted, "¡Alto!"

Then just as quickly the man sprinted to the right side of the SUV and disappeared. Before Esteban spoke, he heard the hissing sound of hydraulics again and the door of trash began to close. In about twenty seconds, Guillermo, Esteban, Roberto, Mateo, the Tahoe and the dead body of Traegar Jackson were safely inside.

Corporal Nicolas Suarez and Officer Emiliano Velez of the Ciudad Juárez de Castillo Police drove past the small checkpoint building at the entrance of the Ciudad Juárez de Castillo Landfill. Velez watched as large garbage trucks lumbered through the gate and on to their monotonous delivery work route.

Velez kept driving when he reached a fork in the landfill road and spoke. "Which way?"

Corporal Suarez looked to his left and to his right and shrugged.

"I said, which way, Suarez?"

"I don't know, Sergeant!"

Suarez opened his door and looked at the ground below him. It had rained that morning, albeit for a short time. To his right, the road showed wide tire impressions, deep in the ground, formed by vehicles transporting enormous weight. He walked over to Officer Velez's side of the car and looked down at the road on the left, noticing just one set of tire tracks, not so deeply compressed in the ground and not so wide. He got back in his police car and rolled the dice.

"Left, Velez."

Wasting no time, Officer Velez pressed the gas pedal and turned his police car toward the left road.

Just as Suarez and Velez departed the forked landfill road to the left, Harris and Derderian arrived at the entrance of Ciudad Juárez de Castillo Landfill, pulling up behind one of the city's garbage trucks, which lumbered past the checkpoint and the still raised crossarm. He, too, stopped his vehicle when they reached the same forked road in the landfill. The large garbage truck in front of them turned right. Easton Derderian was staring intently at the LoJack monitor.

"Well?"

"Turn left here—this signal is pinging like crazy," said Derderian. "Less than a mile away."

Wasting no time, Harris spun left and sped his Chevrolet Suburban down the road.

33

Tuesday, June 14, 1994
10:46 a.m. MDT
Inside the Ciudad Juárez de Castillo Landfill

After the large door closed and the pneumatic compressor stopped hissing, an eerie silence descended. Mateo immediately opened the back passenger door and exited the vehicle, leaving his door open, and walked briskly to one of the workshop tables. There was a knocking sound on Roberto's passenger window. Roberto lowered the automatic window and the man spoke, with his index finger raised over his mouth, indicating silence.

"Both of you, exit the car now, but keep the keys in the ignition and the car still running, and keep quiet," Guillermo spoke softly. "Not a sound, and don't close the doors."

Both Esteban and Roberto did as they were told.

"Mateo, where are you with that wireless RF detector?"

Mateo quickly walked back to the Tahoe, holding a device no bigger than a standard house brick, with a rubber antenna extending upwards. He gave the device to Guillermo.

"Now, gentlemen, please stand back and remember, no sounds."

Esteban and Roberto walked backwards from the Tahoe and watched Guillermo.

Guillermo turned on the RF detector. A small, green LED screen lit up and the device started to ping with a loud beep. Guillermo cursed to himself while he fumbled to find the volume button, lowering the pinging sound.

Esteban spoke. "That sounds like the same sound we heard . . ."

Guillermo glared at Esteban and cut him off with a violent shush.

Embarrassed, Esteban's face flushed; he lowered his head and stepped back a few steps further away from the Tahoe.

Confirming that the Chevrolet Tahoe possessed a LoJack system, Guillermo quickly walked over to the driver's side and gazed underneath the dashboard looking for the vehicle's sixteen-pin trapezoid-shaped onboard diagnostics port, which was usually located under the dashboard, beneath the steering wheel column.

Harris and Derderian sped along the road twisting through the landfill's high piles of refuse. Despite rolling the windows up and the Suburban's climate system closed off, Harris's car reeked of foul smell and stench.

"Less than a hundred yards," Derderian reported, his eyes glued to the small video screen.

Harris depressed the gas pedal further, moving his car at an even higher speed.

Guillermo didn't see the OBD-II port below the Tahoe's steering wheel, but he did see it on the left side, underneath, close to the driver's side door. A small, black box covered the port, with a small, red LED light flashing. Using his right hand, he pulled, and the small, plastic black box popped off the port. The red LED light stopped flashing. Guillermo then sat in the driver's seat, pressed the brake and shifted the transmission to neutral. Just as quickly, he pulled the vehicle's hood release. Guillermo turned off the Tahoe's ignition.

"Remove those battery cables!"

Both Esteban and Roberto, fascinated at watching Guillermo work, had completely lost sight of Mateo, who stood at the ready in front of the car, with a small wrench and a pair of pliers. Mateo raised the hood and located the battery and the connected battery cables. He quickly removed the positive and negative cables connected to the Tahoe's battery—and then nothing but silence followed.

Guillermo breathed a sigh of relief.

❒ ❒ ❒

"The signal. It's gone!"

"Can't be," answered Harris. "You just said we were less than a hundred yards away."

"I'm telling you, the signal's gone."

"Then it has to be close."

Derderian scanned the area with his eyes. "Other than the shit tons of trash everywhere, the only car I see is what looks like Mexican police and a Volks . . . Oh shit, Brian, slow down!"

Harris saw the same thing Derderian did—a very sharp curve ahead on the landfill road—and he slammed on the brakes, stopping his Suburban about thirty feet from a parked car with POLICIA on its side. Harris and Derderian looked at their immediate surroundings. Just beyond the Cuidad Juárez police car, the road had reached a dead end. Mountains of trash stood on all three sides and the only three vehicles were Harris's Suburban, the police, and a beat-up, cream-colored Volkswagen.

"It has to be here!"

"Brian, I just told you. It's gone off the scope."

"A six-thousand-pound vehicle can't just disappear."

"Maybe the LoJack system went bust for some reason," Derderian suggested. "Let me power it down and power it up again." He turned off the LoJack monitor, hit a few buttons. The screen went dark and then powered up again.

Harris looked around his surroundings again and stepped out of the Suburban to get a better view, leaving the car running and his driver's side door open.

At the same time, Corporal Nicolas Suarez and Officer Emiliano Velez got out of their vehicle and slowly walked to Harris's car.

Ah, shit, Harris thought. They looked like they were in the mood for a confab. This would take some time. Time that Harris knew he didn't have.

34

Tuesday, June 14, 1994
10:58 a.m. MDT
Inside the Ciudad Juárez de Castillo Landfill

Demanding silence still with his index finger pressed against his mouth, Guillermo pointed to the left side of the large door that recently closed behind the group. All three men obliged. Near the left edge of the door was a table upon which sat a large black rectangular box with a bank of electronics and a few switches and dials on its face. On top of the box rested a large thirty-nine-inch cathode ray Panasonic television set. Guillermo flipped a few switches on the black box and the television came to life.

The television screen showed colored images in crystal-clear quality. Mounted high above on the workshop's roof and obscured by the trash and debris was a Sony HDCE-100 high-definition camera, which fed the images below. Guillermo did not recognize the men on his television screen, but he suspected all four of these men were looking for the Chevrolet Tahoe. Two of the men were local police, easily indicated by their Ciudad de Juárez police uniforms. The other two men were gringos from across the border, but not in uniforms. Guillermo paused a moment, studying the gringos' images and movements on the screen as he tried to determine who these men were. Easton Derderian then turned his back to the camera, and Guillermo saw the large yellow letters of "DEA" on his windbreaker.

Guillermo swore to himself. His "deposit" was hotter than he realized.

Guillermo turned in the direction of Esteban and Roberto, who were themselves watching the TV screen with great interest.

"You two. Do you recognize these gringos? One, if not both, work for the United States Drug Enforcement Agency."

Roberto shrugged his shoulders, saying nothing.

"Look, like we told the fat man," Esteban said, "Señor Santiago Zavala told us to drop off this vehicle here and make a 'deposit.' Nothing else. We got no idea who these gringos are."

Esteban reached into his wallet and pulled out the five hundred-dollar bills that Zavala gave Roberto almost twelve hours ago. He handed the money to Guillermo.

Guillermo looked at the money and thought for a moment. Five hundred dollars was a pittance to what Guillermo would make stripping the late-model black Chevrolet Tahoe and selling it again on the black market. But a request from Señor Santiago Zavala was never questioned, especially since he was Guillermo's original benefactor for his entire operation. Guillermo shoved the money in his front pocket and motioned both men to step closer.

"Listen to me," he said in a low voice. "You need to do exactly what I say, with no questions. Understand?"

Esteban and Roberto nodded. Guillermo continued in a hushed tone.

"Grab any of your belongings that are in the Tahoe and meet me next to that Jeep over there. Mateo will handle things here."

Guillermo reached into his pocket, pulled out a single hundred-dollar bill and handed the money to Mateo. He whispered for a few seconds into Mateo's right ear, and the fat man nodded his head.

"Yes, Señor. Consider it done."

Esteban and Roberto performed a quick once-over inside the Tahoe and grabbed their few belongings. Each man then climbed into Guillermo's Jeep. Guillermo cranked the Jeep, turned it around, and drove back down the tunnel.

After the garage door to the chop shop closed behind them, Guillermo stopped the Jeep, faced his passengers in the back seat, and extended his right hand. With a raised voice, he spoke.

"I forgot to introduce myself earlier. My name is Guillermo Badillo."

Esteban looked surprised, slowly extending his hand to shake Guillermo's.

"Esteban. I thought you told us to speak quietly?"

"We are okay now. The walls of the shop are tin sheet metal. Even with all the trash glued to the outside of the walls, sound still travels. Now that we are underground, there is no issue with sound." Guillermo shifted his gaze to Roberto. "And you?"

Roberto extended his hand, and Guillermo shook it. "Roberto."

"Nice to meet you," Guillermo said, addressing them both.

"I will drive you south of the city. I take it that you both are headed back to the border, no? I will show you a less known path that will allow for a quicker crossing."

They drove onward through the tunnel.

35

Tuesday, June 14, 1994
11:14 a.m. MDT
Ciudad Juárez de Castillo Landfill

After five wasted minutes given over to persuasion, Brian Harris got hold of Captain Díaz on Suarez and Velez's radio, and Díaz explained the situation.

Harris walked back to his Suburban, opened the driver's side door, sat in the driver's seat, and turned to Derderian.

Harris spoke in an exasperated tone. "You *get* anything?"

Frowning, Derderian replied, "Nothing. I restarted the LoJack system twice in this car and we got nothing. And while you were dealing with our two new friends from Juárez, I was able to speak with both Paul Hagen at EPIC and Stuart Campinero. There is nothing on either of their systems either."

"Shit." Harris cranked up the Suburban's engine.

"What do you want to do, Brian?"

"We can't do anything. Even if we got a warrant, the city of Juárez is not going to dig through all these mountains of trash to find a black Chevrolet Tahoe." Harris reversed the Suburban and drove back the way they came in.

"Can't we file a stolen vehicle report with the Mexicans?"

"Sure we will. And we both know it'll be a waste of time." Harris winced as he drove through the mountains of trash, his nose still not adjusting to the fetid air. He looked around everywhere. Just more garbage.

"I can't *fucking* think with this shitty smell around us. Let's get back to the office."

Derderian nodded his head and neither man spoke again until they reached the Bridge of the Americas. While Harris drove, flashbacks of when he heard the news about the murder of DEA Agent Enrique "Kiki" Camarena crossed his mind repeatedly.

That was supposed to never happen again.

If it had, the DEA was going to have to send a message that would never be forgotten.

8 8 8

A few miles south of the Ciudad Juárez city limits, Guillermo, along with Esteban and Roberto, arrived at a small building on the left side of Highway 2. Indicating years of abuse from the sun's light, the faded blue letters of PAN DE JUAN looked as if they were almost a hundred years old. About one hundred feet behind the small building rose the vertical poles of border fencing, closely spaced and nearly ten meters in height. Immediately behind the vast steel fence, the Rio Grande River ran its course south. Beyond the river lay the Las Pampas Number 2 Colonia, part of the U.S. city of San Elizario, Texas.

Guillermo opened the glove box in his Jeep and retrieved a beige-colored remote. He pressed the button, and the garage door opened. Once the door fully opened, Guillermo drove his Jeep inside, shut off the car's engine, and pressed the remote again. Sunlight coming through one window in the building revealed a sparse interior featuring a single large, brown throw rug on the floor near the front of Guillermo's parked Jeep.

"Okay, gentlemen, grab your stuff, as this is where you will cross back into the United States."

Guillermo then reached back into his glove box and retrieved a small flashlight.

Esteban exchanged the same look of confusion as Roberto, and both looked back at Guillermo. Esteban spoke first.

"What do you mean? Where do we go from here?"

Guillermo smiled. "Follow me, and I will show you."

Guillermo exited the vehicle, placed the small flashlight in his pocket, and walked to the front of his Jeep. He took a few steps toward the throw rug. With both of his hands, he grabbed the rug and swept it aside, revealing a square wooden door in the floor just a few meters in diameter. Guillermo pulled a black iron ring on the left side of the door, pulling the wooden aperture to the right side. When fully opened, the door revealed a narrow passage below a sharply descending stairwell.

"Who do you think built that tunnel we used to escape your friends at the landfill? Señor Zavala has many tunnels like this, north and south of the city. They are not used as much anymore since Mexico and the United States signed the NAFTA treaty."

"What do you mean?" inquired Esteban.

"Ever since that treaty was signed, in a few years Juárez will be the top industrial city in all of Mexico, especially with all of the *maquiladoras* owned by our gringo friends across the river. Automobiles, washing machines, airplanes, textiles, you name it. The Americans want all of these products made here so they can make more money when we ship the final goods across the border."

Guillermo motioned them toward the entrance in the floor as he continued speaking.

"With all of that increased commercial traffic, you are seeing more and more tractor-trailers crossing the border each day. You can move more 'product' hidden in those trailers in a day than you can using dozens of mules through hidden tunnels like this."

Esteban nodded his head. What Guillermo said made sense.

"Good. The staircase is steep and narrow, so watch your step. It's about thirteen meters down, with no lighting."

Guillermo then pulled out the flashlight from his pocket and handed it to Esteban.

"Use this flashlight. Once you get to the bottom, you will see the tunnel. It is made of large irrigation pipe. Unfortunately, you will have to bend down a bit as you walk since the height is only one and a half meters. Once you reach the end of the tunnel, there will be a small ladder. Go up the ladder, and you will see a square door like this one. Turn the iron ring on the right side of the door and push hard. Once you open the door, you will be in a building like this. Unlock the only door from the inside, and you will be back in *los Estados Unidos*."

Guillermo started to lift the wooden door off the floor.

Esteban stopped and caught Guillermo's attention.

"Hey, will there be anybody to pick us up to take us to the airport?"

Guillermo peered his face over the door and smiled.

"You boys look strong and healthy. There is a Best Western hotel a few miles down the road, off Interstate 10. Take a cab."

Guillermo then promptly closed the wooden door.

Esteban and Roberto were encapsulated in darkness. Both men could hear Guillermo moving the large rug over the wooden door and then silence. Esteban turned on the flashlight and both men descended the stairwell.

36

Tuesday, June 14, 1994
2:02 p.m. CDT
Lubbock, Texas

Steve Worthington opened the front door of his house and placed his keys on the small table in the entry. He immediately walked over to the kitchen and poured himself a very large glass of ice water. Worthington's current girlfriend Tracey was curled up on his couch, wearing a pair of his pajamas, watching television and eating a bowl of cereal.

With her eyes on the television screen, she spoke. "How was your run?"

"Good." Worthington took a big gulp of the ice-cold water. He could feel the coolness hit the inside of his body with a shock. "What are you watching?"

"Oh my gosh. It's been on the news all morning. The police in Los Angeles found the body of O.J. Simpson's ex-wife—Nicole—along with another, something Goldman. And they found them in front of O.J.'s house!"

Intrigued, Worthington walked to his couch and joined Tracey, grabbing the television remote and raising the volume.

Thirty minutes later and having taken in all he could about O.J. Simpson's wife and who he assumed was her boyfriend, Worthington flipped the channel to ESPN.

"I was still watching that," frowned Tracey.

"There's another TV in this house. I've got to get my sports fix."

Irritated, Tracey stood up and walked to the backyard patio, where another TV hung under its pergola. She turned it on and flipped back to her news channel.

Meanwhile, Worthington settled in to get the latest in the sports world.

"This is Charley Steiner, and you are watching SportsCenter. The Vancouver Canucks arrived at Madison Square Garden today in what will be an exciting game seven against the New York Rangers to see which team will hoist Lord Stanley's Cup tonight. For more on the story we go to . . ."

Worthington melted into the couch, oblivious to anything besides the television announcer's voice.

37

Tuesday, June 14, 1994
11:03 p.m. CDT
Conference Café

"Well, that was a helluva game," Bud Garza said as he took another drink of beer.

"What was it, first time since 1940?" Alejandro queried.

"Yeah, fifty-four years. But not as long the city of Houston has suffered," quipped a laughing Kenneth. Bud started to chuckle as well.

"Very funny. You just wait. My Rockets are up two games to one against the Knicks," Alejandro replied.

All three Sigma brothers stared at the television screen, watching postgame interviews and footage of the celebrations occurring at Madison Square Garden as the New York Rangers defeated the Vancouver Canucks 3–2, winning the Stanley Cup Finals. New York Rangers captain Mark John Douglas Messier hoisted Lord Stanley's Cup over his head while his teammates, along with close to eighteen thousand New York Rangers fans, screamed with delight. Coverage then moved almost three thousand miles west, where disgruntled Vancouver Canuck fans rioted in the streets of Vancouver, British Columbia.

"Look at those crazy Canadians. Aren't they supposed to be *nice*?" exclaimed Alejandro.

"They love their hockey," observed Kenneth.

"Shit. It's their national pastime," said Bud.

"Are those fireworks they're shooting off?" asked Alejandro.

"Sure looks like it," Bud replied.

"Hey, speaking of fireworks, are we still going to *Fandango* on the fourth?" said Kenneth.

"You bet. Heath Crawford is the lead this year. Says it's going to be the best one yet," Alejandro put in.

"Where?" asked Bud.

"Heath mentioned Wolfforth," said Alejandro.

Bud and Kenneth nodded their heads in approval and spoke in unison: "Cool."

"So, whaddaya think of this shit with O.J.'s wife and that boyfriend of hers?" asked Alejandro.

Bud didn't answer and looked at Kenneth instead, who wasted no time in answering Alejandro's question.

"Oh, I know he killed her and that Ron guy. I guarantee it. A good-looking woman like that. Didn't the news say that O.J. and Nicole were separated? How much you wanna bet that when her and Ron arrived back at O.J.'s house, O.J. saw them kissing outside his house and he just freaked out. I heard that guy has got a serious temper."

"Yeah, but it's O.J. Simpson," argued Alejandro. "I mean, he won the Heisman Trophy. He got inducted in the NFL Hall of Fame, even though he played most of his career on all those shitty Bills teams. He did all those Hertz commercials and was in those *Naked Gun* movies. I can't believe he would kill her and her boyfriend."

"I'm sure the cops in L.A. will find out who did it," Bud added. "I don't know who killed them, but it doesn't look good having two dead bodies on your front porch, one being your wife and another man."

"True that, Bud," agreed Kenneth.

Alejandro changed the subject. "You know, guys, we got one helluva sports lineup these next few days. The Houston Rockets are playing the New York Knicks tomorrow night for game four; the World Cup starts this Friday in Chicago; and the 94th U.S. Open starts this Thursday—"

"You know Alejandro will be glued to the Golf Channel Thursday morning," Kenneth interrupted.

"I can't watch the first-grouping tee-off since I have eight a.m. class, but I got my VCR set to record so when I finish at eleven, I can make it home to watch it."

"Where's it being held again?" Bud queried.

Alejandro stared at his friends with a dismal look. "I can't believe y'all don't know where the U.S. Open is this year." Both of his friends stared back with no response. A few seconds of silence hung in the air, and Alejandro explained, "Oakmont Country Club. Oakmont, Pennsylvania?"

Bud and Kenneth shrugged.

"It has a 77.5 USGA course rating, with over two hundred bunkers—it's regarded one of the most difficult golf courses in the United States. It's where Johnny Miller shot a final round of sixty-three and set the record lowest score in U.S. Open history back in '73."

"Didn't know that."

Kenneth echoed Bud's comment. "I didn't either. Dude, that's why you know all the sports questions when we play Trivia, remember?"

"You guys are killing me." Disgruntled, Alejandro took a drink of beer and continued. "Plus, rumor has it that this's maybe Arnold Palmer's last time to play in the U.S. Open."

"Now *that* guy I know. He's 'The King,'" confirmed Bud. "My dad watched him play at Colonial back in the sixties and seventies. Every now and then on Saturdays, I'd catch my dad watching golf. Next to Lee Trevino, Arnold Palmer was his favorite."

Alejandro shook his head, "Both of you guys are sports idiots."

Kenneth raised his glass in a mock toast. "Obi-Wan Kenobi, teach us the ways of the Force and golf."

Bud clinked Kenneth's beer mug with his and said, lowering his voice, "Obi-Wan never told you what happened to your father . . ."

Kenneth followed suit. "He told me enough. He told me you killed him."

"No, Luke. I am your father."

Kenneth then finished the impromptu *Empire Strikes Back* scene from when Luke Skywalker learns that his father is Darth Vader.

A loud "*Noooooooooo!*" erupted from Kenneth, finishing the scene, while Bud joined his two friends in laughter.

Alejandro shook his head, trying his best to not laugh as well.

38

Wednesday, June 15, 1994
6:03 a.m. MDT
El Paso International Airport, El Paso, Texas

Brian Harris yawned and stretched out his arms. He hadn't slept well the previous night, his mind analyzing his current experience from the day before. The missing DEA Senior Special Agent. The agent's Chevy Tahoe and the LoJack signals that appeared in the middle of a Mexican landfill . . . and the next moment vanished. Easton Derderian yawned in return as both men sat in chairs on the upper-level concourse near Southwest Airlines gate B4. Near the entry gate and Jetway, an elevated video screen indicated departure time to Lubbock at 6:45 a.m.

Harris looked out the window toward the Jetway tarmac; there was no plane. He walked to the gate agent and asked the young lady a question.

"Is Southwest flight five in the glide path yet?"

The young lady looked at her monitor, smiled and replied, "Yes, we show touchdown and gate arrival in about twelve minutes."

"Thanks," Harris said, then turned around and addressed Derderian back at his seat. "Easton, you want a coffee?"

Derderian, who'd been staring ahead either sleepily or contemplatively into the middle distance, registered Harris's voice after a slight delay, turned his head abruptly in Harris's direction and answered, "Yes, black. No sugar, no cream."

Harris walked to the closest coffee vendor at the El Paso airport and recalled the previous day when they'd left empty-handed from the landfill.

888

The day before, Harris had gone through the timeline of events that were known about Traegar's activities again and again. Agent Derderian sat across the office desk as Harris pulled up his notepad marked CONFIDENTIAL and started with his first written entry on Thursday, June 9, 1994, 9 a.m. He read out loud his shorthand notes from his first conversation with Jackson in Marfa, Texas.

"Green garbage truck. Suspect driving Hispanic male. Witnesses claim same green garbage truck arrives Fort Stockton every month. But Fort Stockton uses blue garbage trucks. Green garbage truck reminds locals of same garbage truck seen in Big Bend National Park."

Harris flipped the page for his next entry for Sunday, June 12, 1994, 8:00 p.m.

"Followed green garbage truck Marfa to Big Bend National Park. Suspect parked near Rio Grande Village Camping Market. Emptied visitor center trash bin in green garbage truck. Suspect stayed in vehicle. Later confirm w/ park rangers green garbage trucks dump at Sanderson Landfill. One hundred miles to east. Why same green garbage truck one hundred miles west in Marfa, Texas? Why same garbage truck showing up one hundred miles north in Fort Stockton? Suspect drove to Rio Grande Village Campground. Did not leave vehicle all night. Drug smuggling or human trafficking suspected."

He continued to read notes for Monday, June 13, 1994.

"Several mules seen arriving green garbage truck early morning. Prob illegals, each with large backpacks. All mules plus backpack seen entering inside garbage truck through door on right side. Followed green garbage truck to Fort Stockton. Multiple pickup trucks and large tractor trailer—looks like milk truck. Freightliner tanker truck with Texas license plate LFD eight two six."

Harris then looked at his last entry, which had the initials "V.M." He hadn't had time to transpose the voicemail from Jackson Monday night. Wasn't there something about Lubbock and a winery?

He pressed the speaker button on his office phone, and after hearing the phone's dial tone, punched several digits, then selected the last voice message from Traegar Jackson. Derderian remained silent and Harris pressed the number 7 on his phone.

Jackson's last words came to life.

"Hey Brian, Traegar here. I hope you can hear me, I don't know how great the cellular coverage is out here. So: after making a pit stop in Big Spring, Texas, our two suspects drove north on US Highway 87 just south of Lubbock, Texas. The Freightliner pulled up at South Plains Cellars, off County Road 7600 and Highway 87 just before midnight. I pulled over about a hundred yards away, and I'm seeing some activity from inside. I smell something sweet in the air, like . . ." The audio message garbled a few seconds, followed by what sounded like the words "elches ape oose" and then Jackson made his closing remark: "Lights, camera, action."

An automated female voice then asked if the message needed to be replayed again. Harris pressed the button to indicate "Save Message."

"Something happened at or near that winery," Derderian said to Harris. "I think someone or somebody snuck up on Traegar and discovered what he was doing."

"Go on."

"We've got to get to Lubbock. Find this winery and try to determine where Traegar parked his Tahoe. We ask around, see if anybody saw Traegar or the Chevy."

Derderian then sensed someone behind him, and he spun around.

"Sorry, sir, I didn't know you were there."

"No worries, Easton," said DEA Office Director Colangelo. "I didn't want to interrupt your thought process."

Colangelo then looked at Harris.

"What do you think, Agent Harris?"

"I think Easton is right."

39

Wednesday, June 15, 1994
8:48 a.m. CDT
Lubbock International Airport, Lubbock, Texas

As the first two passengers to exit Southwest Airline flight 5, Brian Harris and Easton Derderian walked up the jet ramp.

"You say you've got a good friend that lives in Lubbock?" inquired Derderian.

"Yeah, we both went to college at Sam Houston State," Harris replied. "Studied criminal justice together. He decided to go the lawyer route and I cut my teeth on the street, taking down bad guys."

"What's his name?"

"Vernon Truett. Good guy, has a few connections with the local police, albeit he has his own private practice. Let's head out to South Plains Cellars first and if we have time, I'll introduce you to Vernon."

"Wait. How do you know where South Plains Cellars is located?" asked Derderian.

"Look there." Harris pointed his finger to a large South Plains Cellars poster, mounted on a load-bearing column in the middle of the airport. Other business posters hung on the column as well, along with a Lubbock Tourism and Convention Bureau poster.

"Looks like an easy drive from here. South down I-27 and then take a left on CR 7600."

Derderian yawned again. "Cool, you drive."

Ten and half minutes later, the last two passengers of Southwest Airlines flight 5 walked down the same ramp. Cautious not to bring attention to themselves, Esteban and Roberto had made a concerted effort to sit in the back seats of the plane.

"I need to change clothes," whispered Roberto.

"Same here. I didn't expect to wear the same clothes for three days." Esteban believed both men were fortunate, since their flight was only half filled with people. He could smell his own body odor through his blue shirt. Roberto's brown shirt smelled worse.

When both men exited the Jetway, Esteban suddenly stopped in his tracks.

"Follow me."

Roberto followed Esteban as he turned left and walked the airport concourse. After passing another Southwest Airlines gate and the Delta Airlines gate, he took them past two more gates, all empty and with no airline designation.

"Why are we walking this way?" asked Roberto, looking back. "Our exit is the other way."

"Let's give the people on our flight a few more minutes to get their luggage."

After walking past all five gates at Lubbock International Airport, Roberto and Esteban went through the security exit, past the luggage claim, and then outside to the taxi stand. Only one taxi was available, and a cheerful taxi driver hopped out and opened both doors for the men, happy to finally land his first fare of the day.

"Good morning, gentlemen. No luggage?"

Esteban was the only one of the two who spoke English, albeit with a heavy Spanish accent, "No. Please drive us to South Plains Cellars."

Both men entered the taxi, and as the taxi driver closed the last door, he thought to himself that at least his first fare was going to be good—at least for a small town like Lubbock. South Plains Cellars was seventeen miles away.

40

Wednesday, June 15, 1994
9:37 a.m. CDT
County Road 7600, close to South Plains Cellars

The DEA agents made it to the Avis Car Rental desk ahead of any other passengers looking to rent a vehicle at Lubbock International Airport. Since both men had brought only carry-on luggage, they quickly obtained a 1993 cigarette-smoke-reeking blue Monte Carlo and drove to the winery. In less than twenty minutes, they drove past the front road entrance of South Plains Cellars. Slowing down, Harris and Derderian looked at the winery and the surrounding vineyards. Both men noticed the cottonwood grove along the road and Harris drove the vehicle toward the trees and parked the rental a bit further east, concealing the car even more.

"It's a pretty place," Derderian commented.

"Yep," Harris replied.

The wind blew from the south, which gave relief to an already eighty-five-degree and partly cloudy day. The agents exited the rental, gladly inhaled the fresh air outside and walked alongside the road toward the cottonwood trees. Both men kept their eyes toward the ground looking for anything unusual.

Ten feet below South Plains Cellars was a fifty-by-thirty-foot room with walls of cinder blocks painted white. While not uncommon in Lubbock due to tornado threats in spring and early summer, basements in this part of the country required sump pumps to remove excess water that occasionally seeped in the walls. Most homeowners with basements in Lubbock had at least one sump pump to address the issue of water seepage. This facility had four sump pumps so as to avoid any issue with moisture leaking into the room.

On one of the walls, laboratory coats and N95 masks rested on pegs. Santiago Zavala set high standards for his heroin production and expected his workers to dress appropriately.

To the right of the cutting room, another room with windows elevated by two feet overlooked the entire production. Here there were over a dozen nineteen-inch Sony cathode ray television sets surrounding the three windowless walls, each providing a live feed of video from all parts of the winery, including sections outside. A separate air conditioner was installed to keep the room cool, since the television monitors ran twenty-four hours each day, seven days a week. The only man viewing the monitors at the moment was Jaime Sáenz. He spun in his office chair and reached over for his fresh mug of coffee.

Sáenz witnessed the efficiency of his surveillance operation and smiled. He remembered when Santiago Zavala approached him two years ago. The native Bolivian had grown up with an active interest in the outdoors, chemistry and electronics, the latter subject his wealthy Bolivian parents supported from an early age. Young Jaime hiked the deep canyon trails and spent time with his parents and friends camping on the hilltop to viewpoints such as Cerro Corazón de Jesús and Cerro de la Cruz overlooking his Bolivian hometown. After graduating at the top of his class in high school, young Jaime was accepted by Universidad San Francisco Xavier, historically known as University of Charcas, a top public university based in Sucre, Bolivia. There, young Jaime focused his studies on biochemistry, electrical engineering and mechanics. During his time at USFX, Sáenz first became fascinated with security systems, including cameras, televisions and audio/video surveillance equipment. Graduating almost a year early, Sáenz was recruited by a large Mexican-based security company, Seguridad del Paladín (Paladin Security), and he was moved to the company's headquarters in Mexico City.

Paladin Security built a reputation as the "go-to" company for high-quality security and surveillance systems in the mid-1980s. Legitimate and illegitimate companies alike purchased surveillance equipment and installation services from Seguridad del Paladín, and Sáenz's reputation quickly rose amongst the ranks of the narcos in Mexico. That is where he gained the eye and attention of Gustavo del Victorio Herrencia, "El Astuto," and his top lieutenant Santiago Zavala.

Zavala took the young Jaime to dinner one night and explained his security needs for a new operation in West Texas. Zavala's comment of a "blank check" to build a system from the ground up caught Sáenz's attention quickly. After dinner, along with several snifters of twenty-year-old Torres Brandy, Jaime expressed his displeasure at living in Mexico City. The extreme air pollution, the sixteen million inhabitants jammed on top of each other surviving on a former lakebed, along with the hundreds of shanty towns of poor people and the fetid smells of the streets were beginning to take their toll. He missed hiking and camping near his peaceful hometown surrounded by the desolate beauty of the badlands of desert and rocky hills. He came from the land where Butch Cassidy and the Sundance Kid lived out their final days, and the city, Tupiza, where they met their ends. Perhaps a bit of their outlaw nature had gotten into Sáenz himself.

"What if I were to introduce you to an area, near our operation in West Texas, which is very similar to your homeland in Bolivia?"

Intrigued by the prospect of living in the United States in a place that felt familiar, and a bit tipsy from the snifters of old vintage brandy, Jaime Sáenz agreed. His only condition was that he would be able to visit the area first, before accepting the job.

The very next day, Santiago Zavala and Jaime Sáenz flew El Astuto's private jet from Mexico City direct to Amarillo, Texas. When both men arrived at Corporate Aviation at Rick Husband Amarillo International Airport, Esteban pulled up in what looked like a brand-new black Suburban, complete with fresh dealer paper tags. All three men drove thirty minutes south and just east of Canyon, Texas. From there Esteban drove the two men to a small terracotta house on the southern outskirts of Palo Duro Canyon State Park, the second-largest canyon in the United States. As soon as Jaime Sáenz laid his eyes on Palo Duro Canyon, he knew he wasn't going back to Mexico City.

Sáenz didn't mind the hour-and-forty-minute commute from his new home to Zavala's operation south of Lubbock. Anything to get him out of

Mexico City worked in his favor and it was an extra bonus that this part of Texas reminded him so much of Tupiza.

Sáenz looked at his wrist. The Baume & Mercier watch dial showed 9:41 a.m. He had a few more hours before he switched out all fourteen videocassette recorder tapes that would have documented all activity from every security camera at the winery from the previous day.

Suddenly, a bright red light flickered, joined by the beeping of an alarm from a videocassette recorder labeled with the number 13. Sáenz spun in his chair to face the room's left wall, and his attention focused on the live feed from security camera 13. Sáenz saw two men walking from a distance near the cottonwood grove along County Road 7600.

He picked up a small black box with a black joystick and a wire tethered to another machine. He punched the numbers 1 and 3 on the machine's ten-digit keyboard next to where the joystick's wire ended. Next, he pushed the joystick up and well-concealed security camera 13 zoomed in toward the two men. Sáenz then flipped another switch on the machine with the blinking red light. A parabolic microphone mounted next to the security camera activated, filling the security room with sounds from outside.

Sáenz twisted a small black dial next to the joystick, bringing the images of the two men into sharper focus. He made sure that VCR 13 was still in record mode. He watched and listened diligently.

8 8 8

Derderian looked at the ground again. He saw nothing that would pinpoint Senior Special Agent Traegar Jackson's vehicle's position to this location a few days ago. No tire tracks, no footsteps in the reddish-brown, sandy clay loam soil, no depressed grasses, nothing. Either they were in the wrong spot or whoever abducted Jackson and his Tahoe did a heck of a job cleaning up the scene.

"Are you sure he said *cottonwood grove*, Brian?"

Harris grunted. "Yeah, he did. Any luck?"

"Nothing. I mean literally nothing. It doesn't look like anybody has been here in months. No footprints, no tires tracks, nothing."

Harris looked at his surroundings again and walked toward the largest cottonwood tree. He set his eyes toward the winery, clearly seeing a large concrete pad and equipment. The only activity he saw was a man spraying a large water hose on the ground. Out of the corner of his right eye, he watched a yellow taxi pull up to the crush gate. Keeping his eyes on the taxi, Harris watched as it pulled up to the crush pad and stopped. Two Hispanic males exited from the back.

"Easton, do you have your binoculars?"

Derderian handed his small 10 × 25 Bushnell binoculars to Harris.

"Something about those two men look familiar?" Harris looked again and handed the binoculars to Derderian.

Derderian adjusted the binoculars to his vision settings. "I see 'em. The guy in the blue shirt and the larger one in a brown shirt. There is definitely something familiar about those guys."

"If they work there, why would they be taking a taxicab to work?"

"Kind of expensive for a couple working Joes to take a cab. Makes more sense to drive your own car to work. You're right, that is strange."

"I know I have seen those guys before."

Derderian watched as both men entered through the large winery door and disappeared.

Harris stepped away from his current perch. He closed his eyes and pictured himself in Jackson's previous position two nights previous. *If I had been Traegar, I would've parked my car over there, concealing my vehicle as much as possible.*

Harris opened his eyes, turned to his left and walked where he envisioned Jackson doing the same. After a few yards, he crouched and examined the ground closer. A minute later, something caught his eye. He walked closer and the object came into better focus. Depressed in the ground, the colors of green and white appeared. Harris reached into his pocket and pulled out a small, silver telescopic rod. He extended the rod and picked at the green-and-white object. With very little resistance, the ground released its grasp of a canister of Fuji 1000-speed film. Using the silver rod as a probe, Harris rolled the film canister over the ground and he saw the black initials of "TJ" inscribed on the canister.

"Easton, come over here. I found something."

Derderian walked over and watched Harris grab a small Ziploc bag from his other pocket. Harris whipped his wrist, forcing the bag to break its soft seal and open. He laid the open bag on the ground next to the film canister. He then pushed the film canister into the bag with his telescopic pointer. With the film canister completely inside the bag, Harris stood up, sealed the bag and collapsed his pointer. Harris handed the evidence to Derderian.

"See the initials?"

Derderian grabbed the bag gently and confirmed Harris's question. "TJ."

"He was here."

"My God."

"Let's get this canister over to the Lubbock Police Department. We need to confirm the fingerprints on here."

"Brian, you know its Traegar's. Who else would put their initials "TJ" on a Fuji 1000 film canister? He hates Kodak."

"We know Traegar's penchant for Fuji film, but we need confirmation. Unfortunately, it only tells us that Traegar was here taking pictures. It doesn't tell us what happened to him. In the meantime, we need to learn everything about South Plains Cellars, along with the owner of this home next to the winery. I know it looks abandoned, but we need to check it out as well."

Harris and Derderian walked back to their parked Monte Carlo and drove down the road to the Town & Country convenience store. Using the closest pay phone, Harris made a call while Derderian remained in the rental car. In a few moments Harris was connected to Detective Raymond of the Lubbock Police Department.

***

Sáenz watched this scene play out with increasing alarm. He listened to the entire conversation up until both men entered their car, zooming the security camera as far as he could, making note of the license plate on the Monte Carlo. He flipped off the switch of the parabolic microphone and walked over to the office phone mounted on the wall, closest to the door of the security room. He punched thirteen digits on the phone. After a five-second delay, there were a few audible clicks and, nine hundred miles to the south, a phone rang.

***

One of the guards at El Astuto's Tamazula Valley hacienda picked up the patio phone and answered. A minute later that same guard silently approached Santiago Zavala, informing him of the phone call. Zavala walked over to the phone and spoke.

"Bueno."

"Mister Zavala, Sáenz here. We have a situation here at South Plains Cellars that needs your immediate attention."

Santiago Zavala covered his mouth as he whispered, "Mister Sáenz, do you realize that I'm at least three hours by plane away from you and the winery?"

"Yes, I do, and I apologize. But as I said, we have an urgent situation that needs your attention."

Santiago's instinct immediately told him something was very wrong. He stood up and spoke.

"Don Herrencia, forgive me for a moment. I must take this phone call."

El Astuto, sitting at a large table beside his pool, waved his hand toward Santiago as he continued his conversation with three other gentlemen sitting at the table.

Santiago stepped away from the table and walked to the edge of the pool.

"*What is wrong?*" he hissed like a viper into the phone.

Sáenz gave Santiago a brief recap of what had just occurred outside the winery with the two men. After Sáenz finished his summary, Santiago wanted to slam the phone's receiver into the table. He then took a deep breath and coolly replied, "I will be there first thing in the morning." Santiago hung up the phone.

"Problems, my friend?" Santiago looked back toward El Astuto's voice.

"No problem I cannot handle, El Astuto. A minor issue with production equipment."

El Astuto nodded his head in acknowledgment. He was about to ask Santiago to explain what the "minor issue" was when a beautiful woman adorned in a white bikini approached El Astuto with a plate of fresh fruit and pastries.

"Are you ready for breakfast, El Astuto?"

El Astuto's eyes looked upon the gorgeous and barely clad young woman holding a plate of food, and his mind immediately focused on the present task at hand.

"Gentlemen, let's eat!"

Santiago Zavala breathed a sigh of relief. It wasn't the first time he had lied to his boss, but his current string of successes in El Astuto's eyes was unbroken so far, and he meant to keep it that way. He punched up another number on the phone and spoke quickly with a person on the other end. In a few hours, he would be in a car, driving from this mountaintop hacienda into the Tamazula Valley and toward Aeropuerto Internacional de Culiacán.

41

Wednesday, June 15, 1994
10:07 a.m. CDT
Lubbock, Texas

"Take the Nineteenth Street exit, then drive four blocks west to Texas Avenue," Harris instructed Derderian. "Then hang a right, and once we pass Broadway Street, the Lubbock Police Department is two blocks on the left, the northwest corner of Tenth Street."

"Got it," replied Derderian. "From what you just said, sounds like Detective Raymond was going to help us."

"He mentioned his uncle was retired DEA living in Mesa, Arizona. Told us he would offer any resources we needed for our investigation."

"That's cool." Derderian turned the Monte Carlo left on Nineteenth Street.

"So, let's say that the fingerprints on the Fuji film canister match Traegar's. That only tells us that Traegar was there. We know somebody drove his Tahoe to a trash dump in Juárez, but we still don't know what happened to Traegar. What does your gut tell you?"

Harris looked at Derderian and shook his head. "Texas Avenue is coming up on your right. But to answer your question, I think Traegar saw something he wasn't supposed to see, and he got popped."

Derderian gave Harris a look of shock. "Do really think Traegar is dead?"

"Unfortunately, I do. If he was still alive, we would have heard something by now. Ransom offer, a phone call, something. Whoever did this wanted Traegar erased from the scene and has ties to Mexico. Why else would we lose Traegar's vehicle inside a Mexican landfill?"

"It couldn't be the Mexicans. Thought they learned their lesson from the "Kiki" thing. DEA guys are supposed to be hands-off. Plus, what Mexican cartel would be operating here in Lubbock, Texas? That's way beyond their reach."

"That's what I thought at first. No, there is something going on at that winery. Ever since Traegar filed his first report to me when he was in Marfa back on Thursday, he was tracking what he suspected to be both illegal immigration and drug smuggling." Harris grabbed his notebook titled CONFIDENTIAL, reviewed his notes and continued.

"Monday morning Traegar reported a Freightliner tanker truck with Texas license plate LFD eight two six, which we know he followed here to South Plains Cellars in Lubbock. We know from his last voicemail that the Freightliner pulled up at the winery and he witnessed something with his 'lights, camera, action' comment. So, what do tanker trucks do? They transport liquid or gas from one place to the next. Whatever Traegar saw, that tanker truck was off-loading something, probably liquid, at the winery. But tell me, what illegal drugs do you know that are liquid in form?"

"Methamphetamine, for one," replied Derderian.

"Correct. That's what I first thought, but all the ingredients for illegal methamphetamine production can be sourced locally—hell, even in this city. Why would a suspected Freightliner tanker truck, first identified near Fort Stockton, drive north all the way to Lubbock with a load for making crystal meth?"

"Yeah, that doesn't make any sense. Meth is mainly a California problem, at least from what I've read in last month's update. How about the rest of the guys?"

"Nope," answered Harris. "Nothing has hit the radar in our EPIC sector. There's no market for meth here in Texas, at least not yet." He returned to his original question: "So, what illegal drug, if any, comes in the form of a liquid?"

Derderian scratched at his day-old beard with his left hand as he drove. "I don't know."

"Neither do I."

Harris looked ahead. "The police department is coming up on your left. Once we get there, Detective Raymond and I will work on the fingerprints on the film canister, and I'm going to place a call to headquarters in Arlington. I'm curious if anybody there can tell us if there are any other illegal drugs in liquid form. Meanwhile, start making calls to find this Freightliner with license plate LFD eight two six."

Derderian nodded as he drove north on Texas Avenue. Soon he performed a quick U-turn, parking the Monte Carlo in the first available parking slot in front of the Lubbock Police Department.

42

Wednesday, June 15, 1994
1:31 p.m. CDT
Lubbock Police Department

"Here you go, gentlemen. The best breakfast burritos in town, albeit for lunch."

Detective Tim Raymond arrived with six foiled-wrapped bacon, egg, potato and cheese burritos in flour tortillas, along with three large Styrofoam cups filled with unsweetened iced tea. Raymond handed Harris's credit card and lunch receipt back to him. "Always a pleasure when the government picks up lunch."

"Thanks, Detective Raymond." Harris put his credit card back in his wallet and placed the lunch receipt in his notebook. He began to unwrap the foil around his burrito and Derderian did the same.

"And here is the best part, the hot sauce."

Detective Raymond held up three small clear plastic Solo cups with sealed lids, each containing red salsa. "But be careful, just use a little. That sauce packs a punch."

When they arrived at the Lubbock Police Department, Detective Raymond led his visitors to his office. As they approached the large room accommodating all of the detectives' offices, Harris noticed the picturesque sign above the door welcoming incomers to PRAIRIE DOG TOWN. He immediately recognized the metaphoric symbolism and laughed to himself.

Harris pointed out the sign to Derderian, who didn't get it.

"Detective Raymond, why do y'all call this room Prairie Dog Town?"

"Just about two miles northeast of here and next to Mackenzie Park, there is a public attraction called 'Prairie Dog Town.' It's popular with the locals and for folks who have never been to Lubbock. Sure enough, it's filled with wild prairie dogs. Every now and then, you can go out there and soon you'll start seeing these little guys popping their heads up and down out of the ground.

"So, several years ago, before I came aboard, the story goes that all the detectives on the Lubbock Police Department were here early on a Monday morning for a big meeting with the newly elected Lubbock County District Attorney, Neal Hutchinson. Each of the detectives spent time socializing, catching up on the latest cases, personal family stories and so on, while waiting for DA Hutchinson to arrive. Almost fifteen minutes later and still a no-show, the detectives each made their way to their own office and started catching up on their cases, all the time waiting for the DA to show up."

Detective Raymond then lowered his voice and whispered, "Apparently Hutchinson shows our detectives the same amount of respect he shows for arriving on time for events."

Raymond continued at a normal volume, "About hour later, DA Hutchinson finally gets here, and Chief Decatur escorts our new district attorney to this room. He sees no one at their desk. Embarrassed, Chief Decatur starts screaming off the names of different detectives. Slowly, each detective's head pops up above each of the partitions. Chief Decatur then mouths off, 'What are y'all, a bunch of fucking prairie dogs? Get your asses out of your office and come meet our new district attorney!' After that, the name stuck."

Each of the men concentrated on finishing his lunch. Derderian made the mistake of pouring too much hot sauce on his burrito and after a second bite his tongue was burning, and he was breaking out in a sweat. Derderian quickly grabbed a few napkins and patted his face.

"Wow, you weren't kidding. This stuff is hot, but it tastes great."

Detective Raymond chuckled and handed Derderian a few paper towels. "I told ya, just use a *little*."

After Harris finished and swallowed his last bite, he took a sip from his iced tea and wiped his hands clean with a paper towel. Looking up, he noticed Derderian seemed to be engaged in an brainstorm.

"Brian," Derderian suddenly said, "can we listen to Traegar's last voicemail again?"

Harris looked to Detective Raymond. "Detective, I need to use your phone again."

Raymond nodded.

Harris picked up the phone receiver, listened for a dial tone, pressed the number 9 on the keypad, waited to hear for a dial tone again and called the EPIC message service. He then pressed the SPK button on the phone speaker box extension. All three men listened intently.

"Monday, June thirteenth, nineteen ninety-four, eleven oh four p.m. Message . . ."

"Hey Brian, Traegar here. I hope you can hear me, I don't know how great the cellular coverage is out here. So: after making a pit stop in Big Spring, Texas, our two suspects drove north on US Highway 87 just south of Lubbock, Texas. The Freightliner pulled up at South Plains Cellars, off County Road 7600 and Highway 87 just before midnight. I pulled over about a hundred yards away, and I'm seeing some activity from inside. I smell something sweet in the air, like . . ." Again, the audio message garbled something and then continued: ". . . elches ape oose."

A few seconds of silence again and then Jackson's last words played: "Lights, camera, action."

"End of message."

After listening to Agent Jackson's voicemail a third time, Harris pressed the number 9, which saved the voicemail. He then pressed the SPK button and hung up the phone.

Both Derderian and Detective Raymond transcribed in shorthand Jackson's last words. Both men read their handwriting, and then they blurted out in unison: "What is 'elches ape oose'?"

"I don't know," Harris replied. "That's the part right after Traegar's message gets garbled and before his 'lights, camera, action' comment." Harris looked at his watch, which read 1:53 p.m. "All right, let's review what we know so far. We received confirmation that the fingerprints on the Fuji film canister are an exact match to Traegar Jackson's. And Easton, your search of the Freightliner tanker truck, license plate LFD eight two six, ended in a successful find in a truck resale lot in Amarillo.

"I already spoke to Thomas Chapman at our DEA office in Amarillo. He's bringing a fingerprint kit so he can dust that entire Freightliner, along with everything about that truck, including previous ownership and any descriptions of the suspects who sold it. How payment was made, seller info, anything. He is also going to check the inside of the tanker for any remaining liquid residue. There's got to be a fingerprint of some sort on that vehicle."

"So, what's next, boss?" asked Derderian.

"Easton, I need to you to go scout that abandoned farmhouse and get it set up for surveillance."

Harris looked at Raymond. "You're not going to give us a hard time for trespassing on private property?"

"Our records indicate it's abandoned; shouldn't be an issue. Just don't bust the door down."

Derderian smiled.

"Good. Once you've secured the farmhouse, get an inexpensive hotel room to spend the night. I'll plan on seeing you at the farmhouse early in the morning."

"Okay, but where are you going?" Derderian asked Harris.

"I'm staying here. I'm waiting on a call from DEA headquarters about other "liquid-based" illegal drugs. Plus, we may need to get a few more agents to assist from the Amarillo office. I'm waiting for approval on that request. And I want to know more about this South Plains Cellars."

Detective Raymond chimed in next, "That's a nice place, that South Plains Cellars. I was there a few months ago. Only problem was, it was for the wrong reason. The DA held a fundraiser there back in April before his reelection this past May."

Harris squinted at Raymond. "I got the impression you didn't like the Lubbock County District Attorney."

"He's an asshole. But Chief Decatur 'volunteered' a few of us to attend the fundraiser at the winery, had us dress in our police best so Hutchinson could show us off, tell everybody there how much he backs the blue, etcetera. It was all bullshit, but I got a free meal out of the gig and drinks were free, too. I'm not much of a wine drinker, but what I had tasted pretty good."

"Detective, are you okay giving me a lift this afternoon to a friend's house?" Harris asked. "He lives off Ninety-First Street."

"Sure. About what time?"

"Say, about four p.m.?"

"No problem."

Derderian extended his hand to Detective Raymond, "Pleasure meeting you, Tim. Good call on those burritos."

"Remember, Easton, just a little bit of hot sauce next time." Both men smiled.

Detective Raymond stood up from the table, patted his stomach, and said, "I'll be in my office."

"How long are we going to stay here in Lubbock?" Derderian asked Harris as they walked back to their rental outside.

"A few days."

"And who are you meeting with again?"

"Vernon Truett."

"That's right, your buddy from Sam Houston State? The lawyer?"

"Yep, the lawyer. He left the Lubbock County District Attorney's office awhile back and now has his own practice."

"Ambulance chaser?" Derderian snickered.

"No, he's doing probate, wills and the like."

Both men approached the blue Monte Carlo, and Harris followed Derderian to the trunk, where Derderian inserted the key and turned it clockwise to pop it open. Harris reached in and grabbed his carry-on luggage while Derderian walked around the car, hopped into the driver's seat, turned the car on and rolled down his window.

Harris closed the trunk and walked around to Derderian, who shook Harris's hand through the window. Harris briefly watched Derderian pull out of his parking spot and start his drive back to the abandoned farmhouse, and then he headed back into the Lubbock Police Department.

43

Wednesday, June 15, 1994
4:22 p.m. CDT
Lubbock, Texas

Detective Tim Raymond slowly drove his Lubbock PD–issued white 1991 Caprice Classic and stopped at 5110 Ninety-First Street.

"Big house," commented Raymond.

Not as big as this car, Harris thought. "Thanks, Detective Raymond, you've been a great help."

"I know this is a DEA investigation, but if you need anything else from us on the local end, happy to help."

"You will be the first I call." Harris smiled and Detective Raymond returned the gesture.

Harris exited the car and opened the right rear passenger door and grabbed his luggage. As soon as he closed both doors, Detective Raymond drove slowly away.

Harris then heard a familiar and very loud voice speaking in his direction.

"You not here less than a day, and the Lubbock Police Department is already dropping your ass on my front lawn. What, is the city lockup full?"

Harris spun around and replied, "Apparently someone wrote on the jailhouse wall, 'For a Cheap Defense Lawyer and a Good Time, call Vernon Truett.'"

A boisterous laugh exited Vernon Truett's gut, and he walked down the sidewalk toward his old friend. Both men embraced in a strong hug. Vernon's six-foot-three frame and barrel-chested body squeezed his friend in a strong embrace; Harris winced slightly in pain. He'd forgotten just how strong Vernon was.

"Good to see you, Brian. What has it been, at least eight years?"

Harris meekly replied, "At least."

Vernon removed his arms around his childhood friend and patted him on the back, "Here, let me help you with your stuff." Both men walked toward the front entrance of Vernon's home and Harris took in the elevation of the homestead in front of him.

"You've got a beautiful home, Vernon."

"Trish picked it out about seven years ago. She was dead set on making sure Cheryl attended Coronado High School, just like she did."

"How is Trish?"

"She's dying to see you. She's in the kitchen getting dinner ready. You remember her chicken and dumplings?"

Trish Truett's chicken and dumplings were some of the best Harris had ever eaten. "Oh, yes."

Vernon opened the eight-foot-high wooden front door and both men entered. Vernon's law practice obviously paid well, and the home was beautifully decorated in a Western theme of dark woods, frontier-inspired decorations, and tan marble features, with hand-scraped wood floors. As the men entered the foyer, another voice beckoned.

"Is that *Brian Harris*?" A well-tanned woman appeared, still as thin as Harris remembered from eight years ago, with only a slight gray mixed in with her originally blond hair.

"Trish, good to see you." Harris opened his arms, and Trish gave him a hug almost as strong as Vernon's.

"How long are you in town?"

"A few days. Thanks for letting me crash at your place."

"Anytime. You know that you are welcome to stay here for as long as you want. How is Stacey?"

"Stacey's great; she says I work too much."

"And what about Robbie? Fourteen, right? Still playing soccer?"

"Good memory, Trish. Yes, Robbie is still playing soccer, getting ready to play U14 this August. He's also super excited about the World Cup starting on Friday. He's got a bunch of his buddies from the team coming over to the house for the weekend."

Vernon Truett chimed in to the conversation. "That's right. First time the United States will host a World Cup."

"And how's Cheryl doing?" Harris asked. "Almost twenty-two? My goodness."

Trish smiled. "Cheryl is doing great. She's staying here at the house for a few weeks, until her roommate gets back from a Tech study abroad program in Spain. She'll then move into her new apartment right off Third Street. Super close to campus. She should be home tonight, albeit late in the evening. I know she'll be happy to see you."

"What is she now, a junior?"

"Yes, she should graduate next year."

"And I finally get a pay raise," smirked Vernon.

Trish looked back toward the kitchen. "Okay, you two get to catching up. I've got to finish the dumplings before they overcook." Trish then hustled toward the kitchen and Vernon patted his friend on the back and led him to the Truett study.

Vernon's study was walled with an impressive display of law books and other scholarly pursuits. In front of the mahogany wood desk sat two leather chairs. Vernon went to a small bar in a corner, complete with a brown granite countertop and sink. Above the sink were two glass cabinets, displaying an impressive arrangement of top-shelf spirits. Underneath the granite countertop was an open-faced wine rack with almost every wine slot filled with various red and white wines, all lying horizontally

"Bourbon or scotch?"

"I'll take the bourbon."

Vernon opened the cabinet and gazed at his selections of Bourbon. "Here, I had someone at Doc's recommend this one. A bit pricey; cost me thirty bucks, but it's incredible."

Vernon opened an adjacent opaque cabinet and pulled two rocks glasses off the shelf. He dropped a few ice cubes in each glass, poured a few ounces of the bourbon into each and handed the first one to Harris.

Harris swirled the glass, sniffed the aromatics, and took a small sip.

"Damn, this is good. What's it called?"

Vernon took a sip of his drink, then grabbed the bowling-ball-shaped bottle and handed it to Harris. "Blanton's," he explained. "Single-barrel bourbon from Kentucky."

Harris noticed the bottle's slightly raised ridges that gave it the distinctive look of a small barrel. He turned the bottle around and examined the rest of the label. He then examined the horse-and-jockey miniature that crested the top of the bottle's corked cap.

"Yeah. The guy at Doc's says that one day, bourbon like this will be hard to find."

"Shit, bourbon is an old school drink. That's all my old man and his dad ever drank."

"Yeah, but they drank the cheap stuff. This one is different. Plus, all the kids nowadays drink vodka with cranberry juice. Not many folks these days drink bourbon."

"Well, less for them and more for us." Harris raised his glass. Vernon returned the gesture, and both men clinked their glasses and each took a sip. Then they sat in their respective leather chairs.

"So, whatcha investigating?" Vernon asked.

"You mean an old friend can't just come over for a visit?"

"Nope. Brian, I've known you for too long. If you were coming to visit, you'd've brought Stacey and Robbie."

"Well, truth be told, I am conducting an investigation. What do you know about South Plains Cellars?"

"South Plains Cellars? The winery outside of town?" Vernon paused, thinking. "Well, not that much. I know they make pretty good wine."

Vernon stood up and walked over to his wine cabinet and pulled out a bottle, which he handed to Harris. Harris placed his drink down on Vernon's desk and grabbed the bottle.

"South Plains Cellars 1990 Nathan Vineyards Reserve Cabernet Sauvignon," said Vernon.

Harris spun the bottle around and read the back label.

"Probably the best Texas wine I've ever had. I think Trish and I have about six bottles left."

After examining the label and the bottle of red wine overall, Harris placed it next to his drink on Vernon's desk and grabbed his bourbon. "What else do you know?"

"Well, I do recall that a few years ago there was some commotion out there. They reneged on paying several grape growers, and those good old boys got super angry. The winery almost filed for bankruptcy. Lubbock police sent a couple units over to calm things down. No arrests, but it was the talk of the town for a few weeks."

"Did they call you to investigate?"

"Nah. I left the DA's office well before that. And after Neal Hutchinson got elected as Lubbock County District Attorney, I was glad I left. Something about that guy—I don't like him."

"You know, today I met somebody else who feels the way you do. He mentioned that DA Hutchinson is not that well-liked by the police department."

"Oh, the city council and all the money families in Lubbock love him. But he treats his people like shit. I wasn't the only assistant DA to quit. There were several of us who left. But it was a good move for me. Private practice is much more lucrative than helping put away bad guys."

"Yes, I can see that all around me," Harris said with a smile.

Vernon finished his glass of Blanton's and stood up. "Want another?"

Harris gave the empty rocks glass back to Vernon. "Hell yes, that is some good bourbon."

Vernon poured a few ounces more in each glass and as he sat back down handed one to Harris.

"So, why is South Plains Cellar the subject of a DEA investigation?"

Harris leaned forward in his chair. "How about I tell you and Trish over dinner? That way I've only got to say it once. Because if I just tell you, you know Trish is going to ask me the same thing over supper."

Vernon grinned. "Good point." Both men settled in their chairs and sipped their bourbon.

A couple of hours later and after the best chicken and dumplings he had eaten in a long time, Harris brought Trish and Vernon up to speed with his investigation.

"Still doesn't make sense," Vernon said, looking perplexed. "A DEA agent and his vehicle goes missing in Mexico. And this all started at a winery here in Lubbock?"

Trish chimed in. "I know there are illegal drugs here, just like any city across America with a major university. But do really think there's an illegal drug operation going on at South Plains Cellars? That's crazy. I was just there last month for a beautiful wedding. Vernon, you remember Will's daughter? She got married and had her reception there. Beautiful place."

"I don't know for sure, but I plan on bringing a few more agents to start our surveillance. They should be here tomorrow morning."

"So how long do you plan to stay?" asked Trish.

"A few days, enough time to get the surveillance team set up and for us to do some more research on South Plains Cellars."

"Well, you are welcome to stay here as a long as you want." Trish stretched her arms out and stood up. "Now that we're done talking shop, do you mind going to the fridge and bringing me another bottle of KJ Chardonnay? You've got to bring me up to speed with Stacey and Robbie." Trish then stepped out of the dining room.

Vernon looked at his empty wineglass and spoke. "Well, enough wine for me today. I'm going to pull a quick tug of that Blanton's again. Brian, you want anything?"

"That Kendall-Jackson Chardonnay was good, and I'm normally not a Chardonnay guy. I'll stick with that."

"All right, suit yourself."

Vernon exited the dining room as well. Harris got up and walked toward the fridge. He opened the refrigerator door and scanned the contents, looking for the bottle of Chardonnay sporting the latest wine industry trend—no foil capsule on top of the bottle. Instead, the bottle had an Italian flange of glass on the top of the bottle, with a paraffin wax seal over the cork. He spotted the bottle and pulled it out, then stopped up short. Behind where the bottle of wine had stood rested an unopened plastic bottle of Welch's grape juice.

Harris took in a sharp breath.

Couldn't be, he thought.

But then he recalled Traegar Jackson's garbled voicemail. "I smell something sweet in the air, like . . . elches ape oose."

"Son of a bitch," muttered Harris.

44

Wednesday, June 15, 1994
7:54 p.m. CDT
Lubbock International Airport

After touching down at Lubbock International Airport, one of the three Gulfstream IV airplanes owned by El Astuto's Panama-based offshore holding company taxied toward the corporate aviation hangar north of the airport. The Gulfstream pulled to a smooth stop inside the hangar. The pilot, whose name was Alberto, turned off the engines and began his post-flight procedures. Santiago Zavala, one of the plane's two passengers, planned on spending the night, so there was no need to prepare for a quick turnaround.

Roberto opened the Gulfstream IV door and was the first to exit the plane. Zavala followed immediately behind Roberto and descended the stairs. As if on cue, Esteban pulled up in a white Toyota Landcruiser and pulled his vehicle close to the Gulfstream IV. Roberto stopped walking and held up his right hand. Zavala waited. Roberto then scanned the entire area from his left to right. The only people in the hangar were himself, Zavala, Esteban, and the pilot still in the cockpit of the plane. Roberto dropped his hand, indicating all clear, and both men entered the Toyota Landcruiser. Zavala got into the back seat, while Roberto hopped in the front passenger seat. Zavala barked out four words.

"South Plains Cellars, now!"

Esteban shifted the automatic transmission to drive and sped the Landcruiser out of the hangar.

Sixteen minutes later the three men pulled up on the crush pad at South Plains Cellars. Only one of the pad's halogen lights was on, partially illuminating the space. The remaining outside lights were off. No workers were in the immediate area.

Esteban parked the car near the large garage door and was the first to get out. Roberto exited next and then scanned the area again. After seeing no signs of danger, he walked toward the back of the Landcruiser and opened the door. Zavala jumped out of the car and walked toward the winery. Esteban pressed the green button, and the large garage door began to open. Zavala immediately dipped down and walked under the rising door. Roberto and Esteban followed.

In the security room, Jaime Sáenz watched Zavala's arrival from the television camera's live feed of images of the crush pad. He already prepped the videotape cassette that had recorded the outside events of this morning. All he had to do was hit the play button.

Walking past the winery's large tanks, Zavala progressed to the back portion of the building. Just beyond the last stainless steel wine storage tank were two large stainless steel doors about twenty feet apart, each with a large metal handle positioned vertically. For anyone seeing the structure for the first time, the room looked like a large walk-in cooler of a type popular in many restaurants, hotels and commissaries for the purpose of food storage at very cold temperatures. The top of the cooler, nestled in the southeast corner of the winery, stood only eight feet tall. The roof squared off and adjoined the south corner and east corner of the facility. On top of the roof sat equipment used in the production of wine, as well as extra water hoses and various plastic jugs of chemicals and cleaning liquids used to sterilize the equipment. To the left of the first large stainless steel door, a series of metal pegs stuck out from the east wall. Each peg held different-sized stainless steel hose clamps. In addition to the clamps, rubber O-rings of different sizes were on the remaining pegs. Below these pegs stood a wooden pallet, stacked with ninety-pound bags of citric acid.

On the opposite side of the cooler, the other stainless steel door looked just like its counterpart; however, this door was different. A ten-digit numeric keypad was mounted immediately to the right of its vertical handle. Zavala quickly punched in a six-digit code. An audible clicking sound occurred, and the lock securing the door released. Zavala pulled the door open, entered the room, and descended a well-lit metal stairwell. After sixteen steps, Zavala opened another door and entered a larger room.

To Zavala's right stood another room accessible by another large steel door. Yet instead of being obscured by more opaque walls of concrete blocks, the room was made visible through a wall of slanted floor-to-ceiling glass windows. Behind the glass windows stood an array of audiovisual equipment, complete with banks of television sets lining the back wall.

To Zavala's left was a large worktable around which were ten workers wearing goggles and N95 masks above white laboratory coats with no pockets lined up in assembly fashion. All ten of the workers were illegals, mostly from Chihuahua, with a few as far south as Tegucigalpa, Honduras.

On the far left of the room, a large stainless steel vessel stood, with two stainless steel pipes connected via shutoff valves. At the opposite end, another stainless steel vessel stood, about half the size of the other. The first vessel refined the opium from the initial processing inside the winery. From there, proper amounts of acetic anhydride and benzene were added to the opium inside the second vessel, which created 99.7 percent pure heroin.

Zavala insisted on the best equipment and processing in the manufacture of his heroin, free of acetylcodeine, papaverine, monoacetylmorphine and morphine. Unlike other drug manufacturers, Zavala, with Jaime Sáenz's management of his skilled workers, insisted on strict safety protocols, especially with the use of benzene and acetic anhydride. Zavala witnessed many illicit drug factories in Mexico where amateur chemists either blew themselves up by the sloppy use of acetic anhydride or succumbed to the poisonous fumes of benzene.

The end product was carefully measured, cut with confectioners' sugar, weighed, and packaged in small one-gram, blue wax envelopes. At any given time, Zavala's sophisticated drug lab would be housing one to five million dollars' worth of heroin, street value.

Drug-lab production hours at South Plains Cellars began at eight o'clock at night. The current ten-man shift of workers labored into the small hours of the morning, departing the winery at well before 5 a.m. Zavala preferred this arrangement, separating the legal business of the winery during the day from his heroin production at night. The only people employed at the winery who didn't know about the drug lab was the tour guide staff, except for one tour guide, whom Zavala knew was a drug mule that Jaime Sáenz hired for the Austin run.

Zavala entered the same room as Sáenz and spoke with a stern voice.

"Let's see what you have, now."

Sáenz pressed the play button on the videocassette recorder. Both men watched and listened as two men exited a Monte Carlo and began walking around the grounds near South Plains Cellars. Sáenz raised the volume on the video footage. As Zavala watched each frame of footage, he became more furious by the minute.

After watching and listening to the recorded footage of the two men, silence entered the security room as the two men being recorded walked back to their car. Zavala exploded with anger and rage. He picked up Sáenz's phone on his desk, pressed the asterisk button, the pound sign button, the number 4 button two times and screamed.

"Roberto and Esteban! Get to the lab now!" Zavala's voice projected over the entire speaker system of the winery.

Zavala slammed the phone's receiver back into its cradle, a crash that echoed over the speaker system across the entire winery as well.

Sáenz took a few steps back, saying nothing and slightly lowering his head. He had seen Zavala angry before, but not at this level. Zavala glared at Sáenz and barked a command.

"Rewind the tape!"

Sáenz stepped toward the VCR, hit the rewind button, and hit the stop button once he got the specified marker of time on the television screen.

Less than a minute later, both Roberto and Esteban quickly walked into the drug lab and entered the security room. Zavala stared at Roberto and Esteban and with his back to Sáenz, barked another command: "Watch."

Sáenz pressed play on the VCR again and all four men watched the security footage. Once the men on camera entered their car and drove off, Sáenz pressed the pause button. After watching the footage again, Zavala's temper boiled over.

"Looks like you men failed to do your job. I thought you said the entire area was clear, but we know that is not the case because these two men found a *film canister* with the man's initials on it! Explain yourselves."

Roberto and Esteban, still in shock from watching the video, did not speak.

Zavala leaned in closer, his face inches away from Roberto and Esteban, and continued screaming.

"We know these men don't work for the Lubbock Police Department, which means they are probably agents from the DEA! Your failure to do your job will cause the DEA to start investigating my operation here!"

Both men stood silent and continued to receive the tongue-lashing from Zavala.

"We have to stop this entire production so as to give both of these men nothing to investigate! And you know what that means! No more product! No more money! No more *salary*!"

Zavala wheeled around and quickly gut-punched both Roberto and Esteban, causing the two men to fall to their knees.

"Get the fuck out of my sight, both of you."

Roberto and Esteban groaned in pain, each slowly raising themselves from the floor and exiting the drug lab. Zavala took a deep breath, closed his eyes briefly and recomposed himself. He turned and spoke to Sáenz.

"How much product do we have left to process?"

"Between thirty to forty-five days' worth," replied Sáenz.

Zavala looked at his watch with its date window showing the number 15; he raised his index finger, pointing at the workers processing the raw opium.

"Fine. Make sure they get as much of our product ready for deliveries. Tonight will be their last shift. Afterwards, get them paid and tell them that we will restart production near the end of September. I don't want to see any of them arriving here to work after tonight."

Sáenz memorized Zavala's instructions and nodded his head.

Sáenz then hustled out of the drug laboratory to speak with the workers on the floor, leaving Zavala alone. For his next step, he needed to plan carefully. How to inform El Astuto of the situation and why he had to take one of his most profitable operations off-line for the next three months? That was not going to be easy.

888

Later that evening in Los Angeles, the latest news broadcast informed the American public that O.J. Simpson's attorney had already had discussions with the Los Angeles Police Department regarding arrangements to turn himself in should charges be filed.

And a short hour afterwards, the New York Knicks defeated the Houston Rockets 91– 82, tying the NBA Finals series, two games apiece.

The following morning, Thursday, June 16, round one of the 94th U.S. Open at Oakmont Country Club in Oakmont, Pennsylvania, commenced, heralded by the announcement that a former U.S. coastguard yeoman from Latrobe, Pennsylvania, Arnold Daniel Palmer, the King of Golf, would be playing his last tournament.

45

Thursday, June 16, 1994
10:30 a.m. CDT
South Plains Cellars

South Plains Cellars general manager Hank Evans was the last one to sit down at the head of the conference room table. Evans never liked the room and thought the amount of money spent furnishing it was a waste.

Jerry Campbell sat on Evans's left, drinking a glass of water.

"Where the fuck is Drew?" Evans spoke as he opened a large black notebook.

"He knows about the meeting. I saw him chatting with Gaspar Ramirez outside the winery lab," replied Campbell.

Seconds later the conference room door opened, and South Plains Cellars winemaker Drew Dalton entered.

"Sorry, Hank. I had to get a work order cut for Gaspar. The tank holding eleven thousand gallons of Regal de Cabernet is not stabilized yet, and we plan to bottle that wine in the next two weeks."

"Have we got enough bentonite for the job?"

"Plenty."

Upon bottling, most white, blush or rosé wines are stored at either room temperature or chilled in a refrigerator, since most of these types of wines are chilled before serving. Therefore, white wines need to be both heat and cold stable at a wide range of surrounding temperatures. A white wine that is not heat-stabilized will look cloudy and hazy due to the excess of proteins remaining in the wine after fermentation. Consequently, a white wine that is not cold-stabilized will produce excess tartaric crystals or simply cream of tartar. While tasteless, the obvious appearance of crystals inside a bottle discourages a purchase. Drew Dalton, like most winemakers, preferred to both heat- and cold-stabilize his white wines, starting with the use of bentonite.

Originally named after the town of Fort Benton, Wyoming, bentonite binds quickly to any floating particulates in wine, which fall to the bottom of the tank. The white wine is racked and pumped into another tank.

After the wine has been "fined" with bentonite, the wine is chilled to twenty-eight degrees and held in place for at least a week. The tartrate precipitates into crystals, which fall to the bottom of the tank. The wine is racked again. The rack valve, a protruding valve about six to eight inches in length and a few feet above the bottom of the stainless steel tank, provides the winemaker an easy method to transfer the clarified wine to another stainless steel tank. The remaining gallons of wine below the rack valve are then filtered to remove the remaining bentonite and tartrate lees.

"Well, after today, we are buying more bentonite," Evans replied.

"Hank, I just said we have plenty."

"I know what you said, Drew. But we've got to move another half a million by the end of the month. So, I want both of you to review your department's invoice ledgers. I need a punch list of items this winery needs to purchase by end of business next Friday."

Campbell shook his head. "Hank, we are starting to run out of space. We've got fifty cases of brand-new Riedel stemware that has not even been used."

Evans snapped back, "Then put it in the dumpster."

Campbell nodded his head silently.

Hank then looked at Dalton and spoke. "Drew, I need you to reach out to our sales rep at Scott Labs and start shopping for the latest in crusher-destemmers."

"Hank, the Demoisy we have now is not even two years old yet."

"I don't care. A big-ticket item like that is going to help us meet our invoice goal at the end of the month."

"What do you want me to do with the one we have now?"

"Not my problem. See if the Scott Labs guy can find us a buyer or start calling your winemaker friends out west. Tell them you'll settle for ten cents on the dollar and arrange transportation as well. Just make sure you run the original invoice amount to me first."

Dalton cursed to himself silently.

"That will do it, gentlemen," Evans said before standing up, grabbing his notebook, and exiting the conference room.

Campbell and Dalton followed, both with their shoulders slumped.

46

Thursday, June 16, 1994
11:34 a.m. CDT
Abandoned farmhouse across from South Plains Cellars

Steve Worthington pulled his car into the South Plain Cellars parking lot and parked in his usual spot. Nearby, someone was watching.

"White BMW 325i convertible. License plate FJF zero four five."

Agent Harris wrote down the information relayed to him by Derderian, who was peering through binoculars. Standing beside Harris and Derderian was Special Agent Randall Jones from the Amarillo DEA branch, who relayed the car and plate information from his portable CB radio transponder to Detective Tim Raymond, who punched the license plate into the Texas Department of Vehicles database from his location at the Lubbock Police Department.

Detective Raymond's orange monochrome screen filled with information associated with the license plate. He read back the information over radio.

"License plate FJF zero four five belongs to Steve Jackson Worthington. Age twenty-four. Lives in Lubbock. Texas's driver's license three six seven one four six one three. No violations, clean record. I bet he's a college student."

Agent Jones snorted. "A rich college student. That Beemer *must* have cost at least forty K."

"Indeed," noted Harris. "Where did he park?"

Agent Jones looked with his binoculars again. "Looks like he parked on the side and away from the front."

"Next to the beat-up gold Honda, the blue Corolla and the early model black Ford F-150 pickup?"

"Yep."

"How much you want to bet, Randall, that young Steve Worthington works there as well?"

Earlier that morning, the DEA surveillance team had run the license plate tags for all the cars parked at the winery. The names of Jill Hatten, Jason Rector and Doug Webster were the only ones under the age of twenty-five. The rest of the cars were owned by men, all of whom were over the age of forty. Hank Evans, Jerry Campbell, Drew Dalton and Gaspar Ramirez. Each of those men were currently being investigated by Supervising Special Agent Easton Derderian.

"Makes sense. If he was a customer or a tourist, he would have parked up front."

"He sure does drive a nice car, though. So, tell me, Randall: Why would a rich college student, and as you indicated, one driving a forty-thousand-dollar vehicle, be working as a tour guide at this winery? Look at the other cars next to his. Early models all of them, working-class college students, all with clean records. Hell, if you sold all those used cars, they wouldn't even sniff the value of Worthington's BMW. Something doesn't make sense. Let's keep an eye on him.

Agent Jones nodded. "Got it."

Worthington entered the back door of South Plains Cellars and circumvented the kitchen behind the tasting room, mainly to avoid talking with any of the tour guides working there. Once in the white wine room, he walked back to the winery's walk-in cooler. Looking over his shoulder as he passed the last large stainless steel tank, Worthington double-checked once more that no one else was around him. Two stainless steel doors stood, and Worthington walked toward the door on his right with the ten-digit keypad. He knocked on the door three times.

Inside, Sáenz grabbed a large sixty-four-ounce 7-Eleven cup full of the latest batch of processed heroin, each packed in one-gram blue wax envelopes. Once Sáenz reached the top of the stairs, he opened the door and spoke first.

"Here. Your timing is good." Sáenz handed Worthington the large cup.

"Jaime, when are you going to give me the code to this place? You know it would be easier if I could just come down to you, than the other way around."

"No. We have security protocols."

"Fine." Worthington paused. "Wait. What did you mean by my timing being good?"

"This will be your last run for a while. Come see me again the last Saturday of September, the twenty-fourth."

"Wait, what's going on?"

"Nothing for you to worry about. See you in September." Sáenz exited back into the cooler, pulling shut the large stainless steel door, which did not fully latch on first attempt. Sáenz pulled the door again, this time harder, resulting in an audible click.

Surprised at his temporary furlough as a high-paid drug mule, Worthington retraced his steps, exited the winery's back door and hustled to his car, his large 7-Eleven Double Gulp cup in his left hand. He began to contemplate getting through the next few months with considerably less income. Once his car cranked up, he sped out to the parking lot and headed toward the airport.

8 8 8

"Someone's in one helluva hurry," said Agent Jones, watching Steve Worthington speed away.

"And what's with the 7-Eleven cup? I don't remember him bringing *anything* into the winery."

Harris paused. "What? Rewind the tape and let's take another look."

Jones hit pause on the videocassette recorder and rewound to when Worthington parked his car at the winery. Jones then pressed play and both men watched the small television set of the recorded footage.

"See, no cup."

"You're right."

"A fancy winery doesn't seem to be the place to order a Double Gulp, does it?"

"No, it doesn't," replied Harris, writing down this observation in his notebook, as Jones did the same.

One hundred and twenty-five yards away, Jaime Sáenz had already returned to his workstation and listened to and recorded the ongoing conversation between Detective Raymond and the DEA agents. Unbeknownst to the DEA surveillance team, late on Wednesday night Sáenz had installed three remote microphones, well hidden inside the farmhouse. He correctly guessed the agents would spend most of their time in the kitchen, as this offered the best vantage point to observe the winery.

Sáenz then hit the stop button on his tape recorder, punched the eject button and withdrew the cassette tape. He quickly inserted a new blank cassette tape into the tape recorder and pressed the red-colored record button and the black play button at the same time.

Sáenz walked to the other side of the security room, inserted the latest cassette tape with the freshly recorded audio footage of Detective Raymond and the DEA agents and hit the rewind button. After listening again to the entire conversation, he rewound the tape. His watch read 2:02 p.m. He immediately called Santiago Zavala, who was staying at the Doubletree Hotel in Lubbock.

Two minutes later, Sáenz held the phone's receiver to the tape recorder's speaker and broadcast the latest findings by the Lubbock Police Department and the DEA. Zavala listened to the entire conversation.

"What do you want me to do next?" questioned Sáenz.

"Nothing. I will handle it from here. Tonight, our friends at the DEA will no longer have the help of the Lubbock Police Department or the use of that abandoned farmhouse."

Zavala hung up his phone. He picked up his small, black address book and found the name he needed and dialed the 806 area code.

47

Thursday, June 16, 1994
5:31 p.m. CDT
Lubbock Police Department

Detective Raymond brought Lubbock Chief of Police T. Charles Decatur up to speed with his part of the investigation into the disappearance of DEA Senior Special Agent Traegar Jackson. Decatur was a no-nonsense police officer, born and raised in the small West Texas town of Shallowater, Texas, and had put in almost thirty-three years of his life in law enforcement. His sixty-fifth birthday was next week, and he already privately confided with the mayor and city manager that he intended to retire at the end of the year.

Detective Raymond completed his recap, having no idea of what was coming next.

"Good, Raymond. Appreciate the recap and your assistance with the folks from the DEA, but you are going to have to shut down your part of the investigation."

"What?" Raymond was incredulous.

"According to District Attorney Neal Hutchinson, we don't have the budget or the resources to assist the Drug Enforcement Agency on this case."

"Wait"—Raymond stood up to emphasize his statement—"why is DA Hutchinson involved in this case? How does he even know?"

Chief Decatur remained in his office chair. "You heard me, Detective. You are no longer to investigate this case. The DEA needs to handle it from here."

"Chief, you didn't answer my question. Why is DA Hutchinson involved?"

This time Chief Decatur stood up and raised his voice.

"Detective Raymond, need I remind you that District Attorney Neal Hutchinson is involved in *every* case that this department investigates. It is his office that handles the prosecutions of *all* the cases we bring to him and his team."

Detective Raymond tried to retort again, but Chief Decatur cut him off by raising his hand.

"Detective Raymond, I don't need to remind you of whom you are talking to. I am your boss, and when the boss tells you to do something, you do it. No questions asked. Are we clear?"

Detective Raymond stood silently and nodded his head in affirmation. Chief Decatur sat back in his office chair, took a deep breath, and continued.

"And finally, your new friends with the DEA are technically trespassing, using that abandoned farmhouse as a surveillance location."

"Nobody remotely associated with property will ever know what's going on there; you know that."

"Doesn't matter. If the DEA wants to use that property for surveillance, it is up to the federal government to request permission from the probate court, not us looking the other way. Now, you will shut down your investigation, and if I hear or see you doing anything remotely associated with South Plains Cellars, I will suspend your ass for two weeks? Do you understand?"

Detective Raymond said nothing.

Chief Decatur walked close to Detective Raymond and repeated himself, "Do you understand?"

Raymond nodded, silently walked out of Decatur's office and went back to his cubicle. He felt dejected and now had to share the bad news. He dreaded the twenty-minute drive back to the farmhouse.

"Detective Raymond!" Derderian greeted the dejected detective as he entered the farmhouse. "I'm going to make a dinner run to that taco place we ate at the other day. Did you want something to eat?"

Tim Raymond said nothing and walked toward Brian Harris.

Harris noticed Tim's somber face. "Okay, what's wrong?"

"I've got some bad news, fellas. I've just been informed by Chief Decatur, my boss, that I and everyone else at the Lubbock Police Department can no longer provide any more assistance into the disappearance of Agent Traegar."

"What?" Harris's faced dropped in disbelief.

"Yes, and according to Lubbock District Attorney Neal Hutchinson, the DEA can no longer use the abandoned farmhouse for any future surveillance. The federal government is trespassing on private property and must remove itself and all surveillance equipment by tomorrow morning."

"Wait, why is the Lubbock District Attorney involved in our investigation?"

"I asked much the same question. According to Chief Decatur, all criminal cases eventually land on the district attorney's desk. Sorry."

Harris swore under his breath. "Tim, nobody knows we are here, except for you, Chief Decatur and now DA Hutchinson. They can't give us any leeway?"

"Nope. Chief Decatur was very specific."

Harris paused and thought about his next steps. After a few seconds of silence, he spoke.

"Okay. Please inform Chief Decatur we understand his request and will abide."

48

Thursday, June 16, 1994
6:21 p.m. CDT
Abandoned farmhouse across from South Plains Cellars

Agent Harris assessed his current situation. They had, at the most, thirteen more hours of using the abandoned farmhouse as a surveillance site. All the parked vehicles at South Plains Cellars were gone and the parking lot was empty. Agent Jones and Derderian had the first watch until 12 a.m. Harris would take the last shift until 8 a.m. He wanted his team and their equipment gone by the end of his shift.

Harris looked at his watch and yawned. "Easton, Randall, I will see y'all here in about six hours." He then walked out the back door of the farmhouse and drove his rental car back to Vernon and Trish's house.

As Harris drove off, Agent Jones opened a small duffel bag, pulled out a ten-inch Sony Trinitron color television set and flipped the AUX setting to VHF. He extended the television's telescopic antenna and turned the channel knob to the number 11. Jones moved the antenna to garner the best video-screen reception. He sat down and started watching the latest developments with O.J. Simpson.

"What are you doing?" asked Derderian.

"Now don't you worry, Easton. We've got three other cameras recording all that is going on next door. In fact, I brought too much surveillance equipment for this investigation. Aren't you the least bit curious at what's going on with O.J.?"

Derderian paused briefly in consideration, then nodded. "Good call on the extra TV set."

Derderian grabbed a bag of Tostitos, opened the Styrofoam cooler next to him, retrieved a cold can of Coors Banquet and both men watched the news coverage intently.

888

After listening to the latest conversation between the DEA agents next door, Jaime Sáenz made another call, this time a well-placed contact who worked with *Policía Judicial Federal*, the Federal Judicial Police in Mexico City. At the time, the Federal Judicial Police was considered the equivalent of the United States Federal Bureau of Investigation in Mexico.

"I need anything you can get me on the following people," Sáenz demanded, then rattled off the names of three DEA agents, including Lubbock Police Detective Timothy Raymond.

The voice on the other end replied, "The Drug Enforcement agents will be harder to ascertain. The United States government keeps their personnel records well-guarded."

"Like I said, anything you can get. Whatever you can find will help us and the businesses of El Astuto."

"Give me a few days and I will call you back." The contact ended the call.

What Saenz wouldn't know is that eight years later, in 2002, the Mexican government under the presidential administration of a right-wing populist, President Vicente Fox Quesada, would shut down the Federal Judicial Police due to rampant corruption within the department. Almost a quarter of its workforce, close to thirteen hundred members, were arrested due to connections to several Mexican drug cartels.

49

Friday, June 17, 1994
6:48 p.m. CDT
Lubbock, Texas

Bud Garza slowly drove his Ford Explorer east down Ninety-First Street, looking at the painted address numbers on the curbs in front of each house. Cheryl mentioned her home was *the smaller house on the left*. By the look of the homes Bud drove past, they were twice the size of the modest four-bed, three-bath home Bud grew up in back home. Eventually, Bud looked over his left shoulder and saw the address "5110" and the very large home behind it.

"Smallest house, my ass," Bud muttered to himself with a smile.

Bud hopped out of his car, walked toward the house, pressed the doorbell and stepped back a few paces. Almost immediately, a smiling Cheryl Truett opened the door. Gone was the usual ponytail, replaced with a mid-length coif hairstyle. She wore a black blouse, along with designer jeans, and looked stunning.

"Hey, Bud, come on in."

"Hey, you look great. Never seen you without your ponytail."

Cheryl beamed a smile. "Thanks! C'mon, let me show you around. By the way, where are we going tonight?"

"How does Jazz Café sound?" Bud did his homework ahead of time.

"Oh God, I love Jazz Café. Great Cajun food." Cheryl stopped in her tracks. "Wait, how did you know I love Jazz Café? Did Johanna or any of the other girls tell you that?"

"I'm not in a position to reveal my sources, but rumor has it that it is one of your favorites."

"I feel like a foregone conclusion."

"Nope. I may have one or two more surprises tonight." Bud smiled.

"Surprises, huh?" Cheryl walked closer to Bud and whispered in his ear, "They better involve you." Then she backed away and said in a normal volume, "I want you to meet my folks. They're in the kitchen. Along with Uncle Brian. He's not my real uncle, but he's my godfather, and I've always called him my uncle. My dad and Brian went to college together. Dad is the taller one."

Bud followed Cheryl into the kitchen. To the right of the kitchen was a living room and a large projection television set, displaying the latest news about O.J. Simpson, but the sound was muted. In the kitchen, Bud saw a woman and two men sitting around a large table, each drinking a glass of white wine and engaged in conversation.

No shotguns found in this room, thought Bud, and his face showed an awkward grin.

"Mom, Dad, Uncle Brian, this is Bud Garza."

All three people stood up from the table to greet Cheryl's date.

Bud extended his right hand toward Cheryl's mother first. "Mrs. Truett, nice to meet you."

Smiling, Trish extended her hand and replied, "Nice to meet you, Bud."

Bud greeted the tall, large man standing next to Trish. "Mr. Truett, Bud Garza. Nice to meet you." Bud extended his hand and gave Vernon an extra-hard handshake. Bud's hand almost disappeared in Vernon's large paw as the two men shook hands.

"Bud, nice to meet you as well."

"And I'm Brian Harris, Cheryl's not-really uncle. Nice to meet you, Bud." The two men shook.

"Nice to meet you, Mr. Harris," said Bud.

"So, why were you smiling to yourself right before we met?"

Harris's sudden spoken observation caused everyone to stop what they were doing. An awkward silence settled in the Truett kitchen.

With no one speaking and with Harris waiting for an answer, Bud replied as truthfully and quickly as he could.

"Honestly, one of my buddies said that if Mr. Truett were cleaning a shotgun, that I needed to leave the house right away."

The silence ended as Vernon roared in laughter, along with everyone else in the room.

"Bud, do you drink wine? I just opened a bottle of Kendall-Jackson Chardonnay."

Bud looked at Cheryl, who mouthed the word "yes" to her mother's question.

"Sure."

"Cheryl, honey, let me get you a glass as well." Trish walked over to a wineglass rack next to the refrigerator and grabbed two glasses.

Both Cheryl and Bud sat down next to each other and joined everyone at the kitchen table. Trish poured a glass of wine for both Cheryl and Bud. Bud pulled his glass toward him and started to swirl it at the base of the stem, just as Jerry Campbell showed him four days ago. Bud lifted the wineglass toward his nose; he took a deep breath, taking in the aromatics of orange blossoms, lemon, and other citrus fruits. Bud still had no idea of what fruits he was smelling, but they smelled good. He took a sip of wine, inhaling air as the wine hit his palate, and swallowed. Everyone at the table stared in silence as Bud performed his first wine tasting away from the winery.

Intrigued, Trish leaned in and spoke first. "Bud, do you know about wine?"

"Just a little. I got a job as a tour guide at South Plains Cellars a few days ago."

Everyone at the kitchen table except for Cheryl and Bud turned their heads and looked directly at Harris.

A few seconds passed and Harris spoke. "Bud, did you say South Plains Cellars?"

"Yes sir. My first day was this past Monday."

Trish and Vernon kept staring at Harris in silence, curious as to his next response.

Harris continued, "Good for you. I heard they make good wine there."

"That's what I've been told, but then again I just started there a few days ago. I've still got a bunch of books to read and videos to watch before I can start giving tours."

"Well, it looks like you are a fast learner," complimented Trish.

Cheryl couldn't believe her good luck. She could tell that her mother liked Bud but didn't know about her father yet. She didn't want to push her luck by having Bud interrogated by her parents and Uncle Brian for the next thirty minutes. Cheryl looked at her watch, stood up and spoke.

"Mom, Dad, we've got to go." She turned and glanced at Bud.

Bud stood up as well and placed his wineglass back on the kitchen table.

"That's a good Chardonnay. Thanks for the wine, Mrs. Truett. Mr. Truett." Bud nodded his head toward the couple. He then shifted his gaze to Agent Harris. "Nice to meet you, Mr. Harris." Harris only kindly nodded to Bud in response.

Everyone at the kitchen table stood up and followed Cheryl and Bud as the young couple walked toward the front door. Trish asked one more question.

"Oh, where are y'all going to eat tonight?"

Cheryl turned her head toward her mother, grinned and replied, "Jazz Café."

"Your favorite, nice. Well, have a good time."

Once Bud and Cheryl reached the front door, Bud opened the door and waited. Cheryl said her goodbyes and hugged her Uncle Brian. Bud held the front door open for Cheryl and closed the door behind her.

Vernon spoke first.

"Looks like South Plains Cellars has become a popular place this week."

Harris nodded his head. "You are right."

Harris then went over to Truett's living room window and caught a glimpse of Bud's license plate. He made a mental note of the plate number and planned to reach out to the surveillance team at the abandoned farmhouse to do a quick background check on Bud Garza as well, just in case.

Once the young couple reached Bud's Ford Explorer, he opened the passenger side door.

"Well, thank you." Cheryl said and slid into the passenger seat of the car.

"No problem."

Bud quickly hustled around the back of his car, fished his keys from this pocket, opened his door and started the engine.

"You have a nice car, Bud," said Cheryl.

"Thanks. My folks originally saved money for me to go to college, but when I got my scholarship, they spent some of the money on this car."

"I didn't know you got a scholarship. What sport are you playing at Tech?"

"Not that kind of scholarship," Bud replied with a half grin.

Embarrassed, Cheryl shrugged, "Oh, I'm sorry."

"No need to be sorry. Not a lot of people know, just my parents, my sister, Kenneth and Alejandro. But now you know too."

Ten minutes later, Bud parked his Ford Explorer in the hospital parking lot behind Jazz Café. Bud opened the car door for Cheryl and the couple entered the restaurant. Hootie & the Blowfish's "I Go Blind" was playing on the speakers overhead.

Like most restaurants across the United States, on Friday nights Jazz Café would be packed with patrons, but tonight the restaurant was only half-filled. The hostess grabbed two menus and led Bud and Cheryl to their table.

"Where is everybody tonight?" inquired Cheryl.

"Probably at home watching the O.J. coverage."

"Do you think he did it?"

"I don't know. But from what I've heard, it doesn't look good."

"The latest I heard was that O.J. was supposed to show up at the Los Angeles Police Department a few hours ago, but he still hasn't shown up."

"I heard the same thing. If he didn't do it, then why has he not shown up yet?"

Bud finished his survey of his surroundings. From Bud and Cheryl's table, a large forty-six-inch television was flush-mounted above the bar, with the channel tuned directly to NBC's coverage of Game 5 of the NBA Finals between the Houston Rockets and the New York Knicks.

"Oh good, we can watch Game 5 while we eat," remarked Cheryl.

Bud figured Cheryl knew her sports, which made her that much more attractive. "Yeah, this is a good spot."

"Who're you pulling for?"

"Neither. Unfortunately, I'm a Mavericks fan."

"Oh God, your poor soul," said Cheryl, smiling. "I'm a Bulls fan, so I'm like you, I couldn't care less who wins. I just want to watch a good game."

Bud looked at his watch, which displayed 7:14 p.m. A waitress then walked up and asked for orders.

Cheryl leaned over and spoke to Bud. "Do you trust me?"

Intrigued by her question and putting his menu down, Bud confirmed with a sly tone, "Impeccably."

Cheryl faced the waitress and spoke. "We need a pitcher of Miller Lite, two mugs, please. An order of Cajun hush puppies and two orders of red beans and rice."

Cheryl looked at Bud, who was nodding his approval. He'd rather enjoyed Cheryl ordering for him. He shook his head and said nothing.

"Great. I'll take your menus."

"They have the best red beans and rice in Lubbock," mentioned Cheryl as the waitress left the table.

"Looking forward to it," grinned Bud.

Bud had never had red beans and rice before in his life. A minute later, a cold pitcher of Miller Lite arrived, along with two frosted glass mugs. The waitress expertly filled the mugs to the top of each glass and went about her business at the other tables in her section.

Cheryl picked up where she left off during their drive to the restaurant, asking more questions about Bud. Eight minutes later, the food arrived all at once. In between hush puppies and red beans and rice, the only time Bud and Cheryl stopped talking was right before the start of game five, when the lead bartender suddenly flipped all the televisions in the restaurant to Channel 11, the local NBC affiliate in Lubbock, in anticipation of the night's big game.

What happened next caused everyone in the restaurant to stop speaking as they found themselves watching and intently listening to the latest developments about O.J. Simpson, delivered by NBC news and sports personality Bob Costas, who had suddenly cut into the pregame program.

Costas revealed that Simpson was confirmed to be riding *away* from the courthouse in a white Ford Bronco, with his good friend Al Cowlings at the wheel.

Bud and Cheryl, along with everyone inside Jazz Café, proceeded to watch one of the most infamous—and slowest—live broadcast police car chases. The immense news coverage, in fact, resulted in microwave signals causing television reports to give the effect of quick-changing channels.

Several minutes later, the atmosphere in the restaurant rebalanced somewhat when the news cut back to the game.

At halftime, however, with the New York Knicks leading 48–37 over the Houston Rockets, Bob Costas cut away to converse with NBC's national news broadcaster Tom Brokaw, who was reporting on the still-developing Simpson story.

"Bob, we are witnessing tonight a modern tragedy and drama of Shakespearean proportion being played out live on television, and you can probably believe this in our modern, popular television culture: People are going to the freeway, parking their cars and waving at O.J., we're told, as they drive by."

Tom Brokaw was correct. People lined up by the hundreds on bridges, freeways, and streets in Los Angeles. ABC's national news broadcaster Peter Jennings referred to the crowds' waving signs in support of O.J. Simpson an "utterly macabre scene."

When the game resumed, Bud and Cheryl silently ate dinner, watching the split screens on the television showing the O.J. Simpson car chase on the left and the game on the right.

Local Los Angeles ABC affiliate Channel 7 reported on the statements made by criminal lawyer and clinical psychologist Rex Beaber, who spoke during the car chase.

"For an innocent man to engage in this conduct would be bizarre. So unfortunately, however much the public would like to keep alive a hero, his conduct here suggests that his psyche has surrendered to the truth that he has committed a homicide. Death is the ultimate way to close your eyes to the truth."

O.J. Simpson and Al Cowlings's car chase ended at Simpson's home in Brentwood, California, where police spent the next hour trying to coax him safely out of his white Ford Bronco. Ninety-five million people watched this unfolding drama live and on television, in addition to the hundreds of Simpson's fans that lined the streets that day.

At 8:15 p.m. Tom Brokaw ended his final report and Bud and Cheryl watched as the split screens reverted back to full with the announcement, "The score now 65–61 Houston, we are in the fourth quarter . . . Here are Marv Albert, Matt Goukas and Ahmad Rashad."

At 9:17 p.m. O.J. Simpson, carrying a family picture, finally surrendered to the police, where he was placed under arrest and taken into custody. The New York Knicks ended up beating the Houston Rockets 91–84.

Bud looked at his watch. He and Cheryl just spent the past hour and forty-five minutes watching television, and it felt as if they had arrived at the restaurant twenty minutes ago. The waitress dropped off the check and Bud paid the tab.

Cheryl spoke first. "Did we just watch history?"

"I think we just did," Bud replied.

50

Tuesday, June 28, 1994
5:04 p.m. CDT
Lubbock, Texas

Detective Tim Raymond reached into the back pocket of his slacks and retrieved a fresh new can of Copenhagen mint snuff. An empty Coke can sat inside his car's cupholder, which served as an excellent spittoon. He didn't mind his thirty-minute work commute from Lubbock to Ralls, Texas. All his work colleagues lived in Lubbock, but Raymond still enjoyed living in his hometown. He kept in touch with his friends from high school, many of whom he had known since his early elementary days. Shortly after Raymond joined the police department, both his parents died in a car crash at the hands of a drunk driver going the wrong way on US Highway 62 just west of Idalou, Texas. He had no brothers or sisters, and Raymond inherited all his parent's possessions, including his childhood home and two hundred and sixty acres of neighboring land.

Just as Raymond's father had done, he continued to lease the family acreage for cotton production. Each of the two 130-acre blocks were irrigated by a center pivot mechanical irrigation system, which ran one quarter mile long. Raymond's land looked like the hundreds of similar-looking 130-acre squares that dotted the entire landscape around Lubbock County and the surrounding nine counties.

With the rising sun in the morning and the setting sun in the evening always in his rearview mirror, Raymond's commute gave him time to think, collect his thoughts, analyze current investigations and reflect on his day.

Pulling to a full stop on East Farm Market Road 40, Raymond turned on his directional signal and turned left on Farm Market Road 789. The only car in sight was in his rearview mirror, a black F-150 pickup truck about a quarter mile behind his vehicle. Raymond noticed it earlier, after he left the Lubbock Police Department on Texas Avenue.

Raymond's eyes went back to the road in front of him. Thirty seconds later, he glanced quickly back to the rearview mirror with the same large black truck growing bigger in size. Raymond turned his head to get a better look at the vehicle barreling toward him and suddenly his world turned upside down.

The black truck sped toward Detective Raymond's police cruiser's right side and clipped his bumper from behind. Instantly, Detective Raymond's Caprice Classic careened right and spun clockwise. All four wheels of the police cruiser, previously rolling north at fifty-five miles per hour, now suddenly pointed east. The inertia of the cruiser's speed caused the left side of the vehicle to elevate off the ground and it went into a violent spin, flipping over seven times and ending up on its roof between the right shoulder of the road and a field of sorghum.

Having just barely avoided crashing into the police cruiser, Esteban pulled up slowly to the toppled car on the side of the road. Roberto opened the truck's passenger door and walked toward the police cruiser. Tim Raymond remained in the vehicle, upside down and his body supported by his seat belt harness. He suffered multiple lacerations on his face, caused in part by his driver's side window smashing against it. The Caprice Classic's air bags deployed, pressing against Raymond's mouth and nose. Unable to breathe, he turned his head to his left and he took a gasp of air. His chest burned in pain as his lungs expanded and inhaled the fresh air.

Bewildered, Raymond took another breath, and his eyes caught a large Hispanic male walking toward him, with what looked like a medical syringe in his hand. He tried to speak, but no words came out.

The man approached Raymond's passenger door, knelt one knee on the ground and spoke softly.

"*Vaya con Dios.*"

Raymond tried to speak again, but again no words came out of his mouth. He then felt a sharp pain in his neck.

Roberto pulled the needle quickly out of Detective Raymond's neck. The fifty milliliters of air injected into the police detective's neck quickly entered his carotid artery before dissolving into his bloodstream and making its way toward the right side of his heart. A small gas bubble formed inside his superior vena cava, decreasing the blood flow. Tim Raymond immediately began to experience a heart attack. His chest heaved with more pain. Seconds later, the remaining air formed a large gas bubble in his carotid artery, just below the brain. The gas bubble immediately halted all blood flow, causing a cerebral arterial gas embolism, giving the young and moderately healthy detective a stroke.

By the time Roberto quickly ran back toward the black truck and closed the passenger door, Detective Tim Raymond was dying. Esteban stepped on the truck's accelerator and continued north toward US Highway 62.

Ten minutes later, John Gravers, a cotton farmer on his way home from Lott's Farm Supply, noticed the white Caprice Classic Lubbock police cruiser upside down on the right side of Farm Market Road 789. He pulled his pickup truck to a stop on the side of the highway near Detective Raymond's vehicle and walked toward the now dead detective.

51

Wednesday, June 29, 1994
1:16 p.m. CDT
Lubbock, Texas

Vernon Truett opened the inside door to his garage and punched the garage door opener. The sixteen-foot door slowly opened. Once opened, Vernon hit the garage door button again, leaving the large door raised only about one foot. The current heat wave hitting the Hub City and the South Plains was almost unbearable.

Earlier in the day, Vernon read two important newspaper stories in the day's *Lubbock Avalanche-Journal.* One hundred and seventy-five miles south and west of Lubbock, the dusty West Texas town of Monahans tied the state's temperature record the day prior, reaching one hundred twenty degrees. The other story on the front page was the reason for his calling his friend Brian Harris.

"He's *dead*?" replied Harris, sitting up suddenly in his desk chair. "How?"

"A single car accident, just south of Idalou. According to the paper, Raymond was driving north on FM 789. Sheriff's report says he lost control of his vehicle, and his police cruiser flipped several times. By the time the ambulance got there with the paramedics, Raymond had died."

Harris shook his head. "Doesn't make any sense. Last month I rode with Raymond several times. He never drove his car in an aggressive manner. In fact, he drove slower than Morgan Freeman in *Driving Miss Daisy*."

"Funny you mentioned that. That Lubbock police chief Decatur and I spoke earlier today. He said just about the same thing. Tim Raymond had a clean driving record his entire life. No speeding tickets or accidents. I could tell in his voice that Decatur was disturbed by the whole thing. Raymond was a popular detective with his staff."

"When will they perform an autopsy?" Harris asked, slowly reclining back into his seat.

"They could, but they probably won't. When the deceased is associated with police action, an autopsy is mandatory in the state of Texas. But since Detective Raymond was finished for the day and on his way home, I don't know how they'll interpret that. He has no immediate family, and both of his parents died several years ago. So no family is pushing to find out what happened."

Harris looked up to see his boss Phil Colangelo standing in his office doorway. He nodded in acknowledgment of Director Colangelo and said into the phone, "Thanks for the call, Vernon, I'll be in touch," then placed the phone back in the cradle.

"Whose autopsy?" Colangelo asked.

"Lubbock Detective Timothy Raymond died yesterday. Single car accident. His car flipped several times, and he was pronounced dead on the scene."

"Wasn't he the detective that helped you and the team with the initial investigation at that winery in Lubbock?"

"Same guy."

"And did the Lubbock Police Department determine it was an accident during police action?"

"Nope. It happened after Detective Raymond's shift was over and he was on his way home. Right now, they are ruling it as an accident."

"That sucks. Any other information?"

"Yeah." Harris shuffled through a few pages and found Derderian's notes.

"Remember how we reviewed all the names of the people working at South Plains Cellars? Derderian was able to find out more information on the managers and winemaking staff, in particular these gentlemen here." Harris shuffled the printout of reports. "Easton was even able to get their exact positions and job responsibilities at the winery."

Agent Harris handed his boss the four reports, each containing an enlarged photocopy of a Texas driver's license.

"That is Hank Evans; he's general manager at the winery. He's been involved with the winery since day one. In addition, when the winery faced bankruptcy, he was able to secure a new round of investments capital. His office is at Tanrock Capital Bank in downtown Lubbock."

Director Colangelo looked at Evans's picture and Texas driver's license information, making note of Evans's birthdate.

"Next is Jerry Campbell. He's the hospitality director who runs the tasting room, tours, along with private events and catering. Like Hank Evans, he is a day-one guy at South Plains Cellars."

Colangelo took the piece of paper with Evans's driver's license and placed it behind the three other sheets of paper. This time he examined Jerry Campbell's photograph and driver's license information.

"Then there's Drew Dalton," Harris continued, "South Plains Cellars' winemaker, also started day one. Spent some time in California at several wineries in Napa Valley before coming out to West Texas. Which leaves us with Gaspar Ramirez, who works as the assistant cellar master, helping Dalton in wine production. Agent Derderian has been unable to obtain any background on Gaspar at this time."

Colangelo looked at the last two pieces of paper. "Interesting. Both Hank Evans and Jerry Campbell have the same birth year."

"They do?"

"Yep. Both were born in 1949. Look." Colangelo held Evans's picture in his right hand and Jerry's picture in his left.

Colangelo restacked the papers and handed them back to Harris. He leaned back slightly in the doorframe. "You're thinking about going to Lubbock again, aren't you?"

"Yep. I think we should pay a personal visit to all of them: Evans, Campbell and Dalton. Since these men work in two different places, we can hit them with surprise visits. I can pay a visit to Jerry Campbell and Drew Dalton at the winery and Easton can visit Hank Evans at the same time."

"Why aren't you visiting Hank Evans?"

"I have a hunch he will be the first to shut down any conversation concerning South Plains Cellars and Traegar's disappearance. I'm betting he will be the guy who says, 'I need my lawyer before I continue any more questioning.' Since Campbell and Drew work for Evans, I have a feeling I might be able to get more from either man."

"Sounds good. When do y'all plan to leave?"

"Figure Easton and I will fly up to Lubbock this Monday morning and plan our surprise visits right at ten thirty a.m."

"Brian, this Monday is July fourth. You may want to rethink that date."

Harris shrugged and looked at his desk calendar. "Shit, you're right."

Harris scanned to the next available Monday. Monday, July eleventh was a no-go as his family was scheduled to go on a family vacation to Montana. His wife had planned the family outing for months. The week of July eighteenth was out also, as that was when twenty-one DEA divisions conducted their biannual review meeting with all department heads present.

Harris looked at the next available Monday and circled July 25.

52

Monday, July 4, 1994
9:07 p.m. CDT
Wolfforth, Texas

Bud finished his can of Miller Lite and grabbed another one from his cooler. Kenneth and Alejandro sat on the edge of Bud's open tailgate of his Ford Explorer, each drinking the same. Seven other vehicles were parked in a semicircle around Bud's vehicle, located on the northwest corner of Wolfforth Cemetery, fourteen miles southwest of Lubbock. Sixteen other Sigma fraternity brothers were doing the same—drinking beer, talking and waiting.

"When the hell is Heath getting here?" asked Kenneth. "He told us he'd meet us right here around nine o'clock."

"I'm sure he's on his way," replied Alejandro.

"He will be here. Tradition is tradition. Heath respects that," added Bud.

Kenneth finished his beer and grabbed another one from Bud's cooler. Headlights appeared in the distance, driving north on Research Boulevard and toward the group. The distinctive headlights of a 1989 Ford F-150 appeared, along with the distant sound of AC/DC's "You Shook Me All Night Long."

Alejandro and Bud said in unison, "There's Heath!"

Once Heath Crawford's F-150 passed Fifth Street, the paved road ended, and dirt from the caliche road kicked up in the air. Heath slammed his brakes, stopping just before reaching the other vehicles. A cloud of dust and dirt enveloped his truck. Heath called out his arrival to the group with a familiar cry.

"Gentlemen! Are we ready to *Fandango*, or what?"

Several of the Sigmas cheered at Heath's arrival and approached his truck. Alejandro was the first to arrive. Heath hopped out and gave Alejandro a bear hug.

"About time you showed up amigo," said Alejandro.

"*¡Mi hermano pecaño!*" exclaimed Heath.

"Your Spanish still sucks, big brother. You just called me 'my *sinful* brother.' It's *mi hermano pequeño.* My little brother."

"Hey, 'sinful,' 'little,' who cares? Means the same when I'm seeing you," chuckled Heath. Alejandro shook his head and laughed.

One of the Sigmas called out, "What took you so long, Heath?"

Heath responded to no one in particular. "You can't *believe* the line at the fireworks stand just south of Wolfforth. I think the entire town decided to buy fireworks today. Y'all want to check it out?"

Heath walked to the back of his truck and lowered his tailgate. Dozens and dozens of cardboard boxes labeled Roman Candles and about just about as many firework mortar tube shells appeared.

"Holy shit! How many did you buy, Heath?"

"Apparently the Roman candles were not selling as fast as last year, so the guy at the stand cut me a deal. And he threw in a bunch of multiple firework mortar tubes as well. Super cheap."

Another Sigma spoke up. "We're not going to have enough time to shoot all this shit off. The max time we have is about ten minutes, at least before the folks around here get wise and report us to the cops. Remember what happened last time at that cemetery south of town?"

"I remember," replied Heath. "But I also remember we all got away, eventually."

Any Sigmas attending summer school would do their best to keep the "Fandango tradition" alive on the night of every July fourth. Sometimes there were as many as thirty brothers, and other years were leaner. The unofficial Fireworks Committee Chair would pick a new cemetery located around the Lubbock area to keep the law at bay and purchase fireworks ahead of time, using monies remaining in the social budget from the spring semester.

Bud didn't know the exact date of *when* this "tradition" started, but it had to be after the 1985 movie *Fandango* came out. In one of the scenes, Gardner

Barnes, played by Kevin Costner, and Phil Hicks, played by Judd Nelson, and some friends decide to shoot Roman candles at each other in a privately held graveyard.

No current active Sigma knew *why* this summer tradition started. Like anything, it was probably a couple of Sigma brothers watching that movie one summer night and remarking how cool it would be to do the same thing.

Heath counted the number of actives in front of him. He then handed out materials to each Sigma and reminded the brothers of the rules.

"Okay, gentlemen. Each of you gets fifteen Roman candles, one pair of safety goggles and one brand-new BIC lighter. There are twenty of us, so ten on the east side of the graveyard and ten on the west side of the graveyard. And remember, no shooting in the face. We'll have about ten minutes before the neighbors get wise and call Johnny Law. I'll shout out a countdown for the start. And then after ten minutes, I'm going to blow this whistle." Heath showed his whistle to the group. "Once I blow this whistle, make sure you don't leave any used candles in the graveyard. Pick up all your shit, head back to your cars and get the fuck out of here. Everybody understand?"

Some of the young men nodded their heads in agreement, others voiced a verbal "Yes" and one active burped out loud in acknowledgment. Several Sigmas immediately laughed uproariously at this. After Bud, Kenneth and Alejandro received their Roman candles, lighters and safety goggles, the three decided to head to the west side of the graveyard. A few minutes later, seven other Sigmas joined, and each began to spread out, taking cover behind the gravestones.

Moments later, Heath shouted out the countdown, "Three, two, one . . . Light 'em up!"

Each active quickly struck his lighter and lit the wick of his first Roman candle. A few Sigmas lit two wicks at once. The West Texas night of Wolfforth radiated as dozens and dozens of Roman candles ignited at once. Screams of laughter, taunting and bravado complemented the sounds of exploding fireworks, with young men running between gravestones, shooting at each other.

Ten minutes later, Heath blew his whistle. All the Sigmas picked up their used fireworks and each raced back to their respective cars.

Bud was the first to reach his Ford Explorer, and he started his vehicle immediately. Kenneth and Alejandro jumped in afterwards. Bud departed quickly, traveling south down Research Boulevard to US Highway 62 and then headed northeast. The three didn't see any police cars headed toward their direction at any time.

In less than twelve minutes, they reached the outskirts of Lubbock. High fives were exchanged. Each began to tell their story of the night's event and celebrated no causalities in this year's "Fandango tradition."

53

Wednesday, July 20, 1994
7:08 p.m. CDT
Lubbock, Texas

Lisa Wellington carefully applied a fresh streak of lipstick, which at the time proved quite difficult. Usually, there weren't eight other women trying to do the same thing in the crowded women's bathroom at Shark Cove Bar & Restaurant.

Cheryl Truett waited behind the woman to Lisa's left. As soon as she departed, Cheryl squeezed into the vacant space next to her best friend, pulled out her small purse, and removed her lipstick tube.

"So, what do you think of Bud?" asked Cheryl.

"He reminds me of a some of the guys I met in Spain, but his skin is not as dark, his hair is not as long, he's not as tall, his smile is way too big, and he is not that charming." Lisa's tone of voice was dismissive.

"Are you serious?"

"Easy, Cheryl, I'm totally *fucking* with you. Yes, your new beau is hot. And funny. And charming. And smart. Congratulations. And yes, I'm totally fucking jealous. Where did you snag him, some *GQ* casting call?"

"Conference Café. He and some of his fraternity brothers are there almost every night. He just happened to sit in my station a bunch of times."

"Did *he* ask you out or did you ask *him* out?"

"Kinda both. You know how a guy likes you and how he acts? Bud sorta did the same thing."

"You know who Bud reminds me of, don't you?"

"Who?"

"Don't hate me."

"Who?"

"Steve Worthington."

"Ugh. Not him."

"I'm telling you, Cheryl, if they don't look like brothers, they sure look like cousins."

"Oh, God, I can't stand Steve Worthington anymore."

"Does Bud know that y'all dated?"

"I haven't had a chance to tell Bud the story."

"Well, as your best friend, I will advise you to tell him soon about you and Worthington and get that unpleasantness over with. And then you better hold onto Bud with both hands and hold on tight. When he walked in here, I think I saw almost a half dozen girls nearly crack their necks looking after him when he walked by. And I'm sure at least a couple were getting wet in their jeans."

Cheryl raised her right hand and playfully swatted her best friend's left shoulder. "Lisa Wellington, if your mother could hear you!"

"She can't since she is too busy drinking another bottle of Chardonnay with your mother."

Cheryl blurted out a snort of laughter. Lisa chuckled as well. Both friends continued to talk as Cheryl finished applying her lipstick. They exited the packed women's bathroom and made their way back to their table into a much more crowded and very loud bar, with the Smithereens's "A Girl Like You" blaring through the ceiling-mounted speakers.

Less than six months after its opening date, Shark Cove Bar & Restaurant had quickly turned into another popular college bar and eatery, rivaling the Conference Café. And on Wednesday, they offered half-price beer schooners. The bar was three deep with young men and women ordering drinks, and the waitstaff struggled to navigate plates of foods and large schooners of beer around the mass of bodies. Cheryl and Lisa finally found Bud, who was sitting down with his back toward them.

Bud was chatting with an attractive, long-haired brunette, who was purposely leaning over to expose her cleavage. Lisa tapped Cheryl's shoulder, pointed, and mouthed the words, "I told you." Cheryl came up behind Bud and put her left hand over his eyes while cupping her right hand around Bud's right ear.

"You know, if you stare at her tits long enough, I'll call my uncle and get you busted for voyeurism," she said in a low, mocking voice.

As the attractive brunette began to stand back up, Bud raised his hands and replied to Cheryl, "Guilty as charged. I guess that means I don't have to pay my tab tonight, right?"

Cheryl laughed and then grabbed Bud's face just under his chin and planted a big kiss on his lips. Cheryl then extended her right hand to the attractive brunette.

"Hi, I'm Cheryl. What's your name?"

"Alisha. Alisha Baker."

Bud, still grinning, interjected, "Alisha and I had the same International Economics class this past spring. We were just catching up."

Lisa, meanwhile, had moved to Bud's left and in squeezing toward her seat gently nudged Alisha away from Bud and the table.

"Hi, Alisha, I'm Lisa Wellington." Lisa extended her hand and the two shook.

Alisha quickly took in her surroundings, with two very beautiful women bookending Bud.

"I'm sorry, Alisha, I didn't mean to interrupt y'all's conversation." Cheryl took her seat right next to Bud and purposely moved her chair closer to his.

"Oh, no worries. See you later, Bud. Nice to meet y'all."

Alisha turned and walked away.

Lisa leaned over to Cheryl. "Way to mark your territory, girl," she whispered. "Do we piss in a big old circle around him next?" Cheryl tried but couldn't suppress a laugh.

"Am I missing something?" Bud asked.

"Oh, nothing," said Cheryl with a smile.

Lisa put in, "You know, when I was in Spain, people don't start eating dinner until after ten o'clock at night."

"Yeah, Cheryl mentioned you just got back from there. How was it?"

Lisa spent the next twenty minutes discussing her six weeks studying abroad. Cheryl kept her chair close to Bud's as they listened.

When Lisa finished her latest Spain story, it was Bud's turn to go to the bathroom. As soon as Bud left, a familiar face to Cheryl appeared three tables over.

"Oh shit. Speak of the devil."

"What?"

"Steve Worthington. He's sitting three tables to our right. And damn it, he just saw me looking at him."

888

Worthington noticed his ex-girlfriend Cheryl Truett sitting a few tables over. He leaned over to his current girlfriend Tracey and spoke quickly in her ear, then stood up, grabbed his schooner of beer and walked over toward Cheryl and Lisa's table.

"Well, looks like you get to tell Bud a lot sooner than you thought."

"He's coming over, isn't he."

Worthington paced nonchalantly up to the table and beamed, "Cheryl. Lisa. How are y'all doing tonight?"

Cheryl replied dismissively, "Great, Steve. How are you?"

"I'm great. You look amazing. And you look good too, Lisa." Lisa's eyes rolled back in her head.

"Hey, can I buy y'all some beer?" Cheryl and Lisa looked at their half-filled schooners next to a freshly filled pitcher, and Cheryl pointed her hands toward the filled container.

"No, we're good."

Worthington pulled Bud's empty chair toward him, spun the chair backwards and straddled the chair.

"You still working at Conference Café?"

"Yes."

"Do you still miss me? Because I sure miss seeing you." Worthington ran his hand through his locks of hair.

"What about the girl at your table?"

"Oh, Tracey, she's all right. But nothing like you." Worthington picked up his chair and moved it closer to Cheryl.

Lisa, meanwhile, was glancing away, eventually finding what she was looking for.

"Bud is on his way back to rescue you," she said with a smile.

Cheryl nodded and smiled back.

"You are smiling, so I guess that means you still miss me," said Worthington, oblivious to the exchange between the two women.

Then, sensing someone behind him, Worthington whirled around in his chair and stood up as Bud Garza approached. "Bud, what's up, brother?"

Bud's happy disposition changed immediately. "Hey, Steve. What's up?"

"All good, brother. Just hanging out with Tracey and a few other friends, and I noticed Cheryl and Lisa sitting over here, all by themselves. Thought I'd say hello and catch up on old times."

"Old times?"

"Yeah, Cheryl and I used to go out. She's one cool lady."

Lisa whispered in Cheryl's ear, "Well, so much for *you* telling Bud about Steve."

Embarrassed by the whole situation, Cheryl stood up and asserted herself.

"So, to answer your question Steve—and I want you to pay real close attention . . ."

Cheryl walked in between Bud and Worthington and planted a big kiss on Bud's lips. After five seconds, Cheryl continued to kiss Bud more passionately. Bud seemed surprised but delighted by this turn of events.

Meanwhile, Worthington looked away uncomfortably, and Lisa tried to keep her laughter to herself.

Cheryl finally finished kissing Bud and looked directly at Worthington.

"All right, I get it. I get it. Good luck, Garza. She packs one helluva punch." Worthington then walked back toward his table with Tracey and their friends.

Both Cheryl and Bud returned to their seats. Lisa whispered again in Cheryl's ear. "That's twice you've marked your territory. You'd better squat and piss just to finish the job."

Cheryl laughed. Bud realized Lisa said something funny, but probably figured he was better off not knowing what it was. Cheryl took the reins of the conversation.

"So, I didn't get a chance to tell you yet, Bud, but Steve Worthington and I did go out. Last fall semester. It only lasted a couple of months."

"What happened?"

"She found out that he is an asshole," Lisa put in.

"Yes, it did take me two months to figure that out. But it's over."

"So what did Steve mean by you packing 'one helluva punch'?"

"I'll tell you later."

"Well, if we are talking about past relationships with Steve Worthington, then I have my own."

"Oh, God, please don't tell me you're homosexual," said Lisa. "We were so hoping you were straight."

Bud shook his head with a chuckle. "If I were, Steve sure as hell wouldn't be my type. No, Steve and I used to be roommates. We had a falling out."

Both young women looked at each other in silence and then back toward Bud.

"And?" queried Cheryl.

Bud scanned the restaurant with his head left to right and pulled his chair closer to Cheryl and Lisa.

"Back in high school, my senior year, my best friend Chad Gallagher died from a cocaine overdose. I was with him in the ambulance when he passed away. Now, I never did *any kind* of drugs in high school, nor have I done them here in college. Not my thing. I guess you could say I listened when Nancy Reagan said, 'Just Say No' and have been following it since. Of course, lots of people do at Tech, and some of my fraternity brothers will smoke weed on occasion and whatnot, but I can't stand the shit. Whenever I'm at a party and I get just a whiff of that shit, makes my stomach turn and I feel like puking. Excuse my language, but I can't stand that shit. Any of it. Especially after what happened to Chad."

Bud's eyes got moist as he remembered sitting in the back of the ambulance, holding Chad's limp hand. Cheryl reached for Bud's arm to snuggle closer, and Bud let her pull him toward her.

"So, two years ago when Steve and I were roommates, he hosted a big end-of-semester blowout party at his house. The place was packed, with almost everybody outside and around Steve's pool partying. I had to go to the restroom. Somebody was using my bathroom, so I went to Steve's side of the house to use his. When I got there, there were three lines of white powder on a small mirror. Now, Steve had assured me he didn't do such stuff. He knew I wouldn't have stayed as roommates if he did. So, at first, I thought it belonged to somebody else at the party. But just as I'm washing my hands, Steve comes barging in with some girl. He gave me a high five and introduced me to his latest. I nodded and left. But I hung around the door a moment. There were no sounds of discovery or surprise, let me tell you. Just the sound of laughing and snorting. It didn't take a genius to figure out what was going on. So, I went to my room and packed. That night, I crashed at Kenneth's house. The next day I borrowed Alejandro's truck, and I moved the rest of my stuff out."

"What did Steve say?" asked Cheryl.

"I made up some story that I had to get on home to my folks' house back in Aledo for summer break, which was true. I stayed at Kenneth's apartment for a few more days and then did head to Aledo. Right before the fall semester, I came back to Lubbock early and got the same apartment I have now, right off Fourth Street. I thought I could avoid Steve Worthington for the rest of college, but unfortunately, we now work *together* at South Plains."

Bud shifted uncomfortably in his seat. "Steve knew how I felt. He knew my best friend died from addiction. But he used our place to do coke anyway. So, I'm not a Steve Worthington fan."

"Well, for what it's worth, I'm with you on the drug thing," Cheryl said. "I can't stand the shit. Give me a pitcher of margaritas and I'm happy as a clam."

Lisa was more to the point. "Fuck Steve Worthington."

More drinks of half-priced beer hit their table. Before they knew it, the assistant general manager at Shark Cove flipped on the lights inside the restaurant at 1:45 a.m., announcing the last call, with The Call's "Everywhere I Go" playing overhead on cue.

"Wow, it's nearly two. Time flies," Bud observed.

"It's times like this I wish I was back in Spain," Lisa said with a sigh. "They'll go until at least four in the morning."

Cheryl, who'd gotten quite tipsy, pouted dramatically. "I don't want to *gooo!* Is there *somewaa*—place we can still drink?"

Lisa shook her head, "Cheryl, honey, I think you've had enough tonight."

Cheryl then turned her head left toward Bud's face and planted a big kiss on his lips. Bud did what came naturally but then noticed Lisa's slight displeasure at her best friend's overly public display. He gently pulled his face away.

"I think Lisa's right. Let's pick this up at another time," Bud said, simultaneously noticing their waiter and raising his hand for the bill.

"You see, Lisa, I told you he is such a gentle-*muuun* . . ." Cheryl proclaimed, then stood up quickly and announced to no one in particular, "I have to pee." She then walked straight to the bathroom.

After Cheryl was gone, Lisa shook her head ruefully.

Bud sported a big smile. "You okay to drive her home?" he asked.

"Yes. Our apartment won't be ready until this Friday, so it looks like I'll be crashing at her folks' place tonight."

"Not *your* folks?"

"Oh, no. Cheryl's house is like a second home to me, anyway. I guarantee you that my mom and Cheryl's mom are fast asleep after drinking nothing but Chardonnay since six p.m. By the time I get Cheryl home, I'll grab a spot on the couch." Lisa reached in her purse for a small vial of lip gloss, which she began to apply.

"So how long have you known Cheryl?" Bud asked.

"Since kindergarten. Best friends since."

"That's cool. Rare, but cool."

Lisa took advantage of Cheryl's absence and spoke directly with Bud.

"She likes you, Bud. I like you. So many other guys I know would try and drive her back to their place right now. But Cheryl is right, you are a gentleman." Lisa finished putting on a fresh layer of lip gloss.

Bud smiled sheepishly. "Well, thank you, ma'am."

Their waiter dropped off the check and Bud reached for his wallet and attempted to grab the tab, but Lisa beat Bud to the punch.

"No way, Bud Garza. I've got this one."

"C'mon, at least let me split it with you," Bud said.

"Nope. It's my treat, you earned it tonight. Cheryl was nervous about telling you about her and Steve. You handled it like a man. Besides, you can pick up the next one."

"Sounds fair. Thanks again."

Bud put his wallet back in his back pocket and Lisa slipped her Visa credit card next to the check.

"So, Bud, what have you got going on this Friday?"

"Just a morning class, Advanced Latin."

"Do you have work afterwards?"

"Nope. I've got to work this weekend, though. From what I've learned, weekends are busy at the winery, lots of visitors looking to do something. Next to the Buddy Holly museum, we are one of the most popular things for tourists to visit while they're in Lubbock."

"Good. You can help Cheryl and me move into our apartment after you're done with your Latin class."

Normally, Bud hated moving. He'd had his share of moving not only his stuff from apartment to apartment during his time in college, but also helping Alejandro Rojas, Kenneth Snead and countless other Sigmas. But this time he'd be helping Cheryl and could be spending more time with her.

"I can help, *maybe*. I normally charge my friends fifteen bucks an hour. Otherwise, it's thirty."

"Are you kidding?"

"Nope." Bud's face did not flinch. "It's a rule us Sigmas have. Part of the swearing-in ceremony."

Lisa stammered and couldn't think of a reply, but then Bud cracked a smile.

"I'm messing with ya, Lisa. Happy to help y'all, but it is true that I can't just do this for free."

Lisa smiled and replied, "How about a case of beer?"

"Miller Lite?"

"Sure." Lisa smiled and winked.

"Smart lady. I see why you are Cheryl's best friend."

The waiter appeared again with Lisa's ticket and Visa. Lisa looked at the bill, put in a twenty-percent tip and signed the receipt.

Cheryl returned from the restroom and stood behind Lisa's chair. "So, what are both of y'all talking about?"

"Bud's going to help us move this Friday."

"Aw, that is *soooo sweeeet!*"

Cheryl leaned over and kissed Bud again. Lisa stood up and grabbed her drunk friend's hand and pulled her away from Bud.

"See, I told you Lisa, he's *sooooo sweeeet . . .*"

"Yes, Cheryl, honey, we know how '*sweeeet*' he is," Lisa replied. "Now you and I are going home."

They all exited together, Cheryl unsteady on her feet, and headed to the parking lot. Bud walked them to Cheryl's car.

"Let me see your purse, sweetie," Lisa said. "I need your keys."

Cheryl leaned over to rummage in her purse and began to fall backward. Bud quickly moved behind her and caught her.

"Oh Bud, where did you come from?" she asked, smiling.

She turned around inside Bud's arms and began to kiss him again, this time more passionately.

"Okay, you two. Either you can stay here in the parking lot or go get a room."

Bud pulled back gently and opened the passenger door.

"Here we go, Cheryl, time to get you home," he said.

Cheryl then flopped into the front seat and both Bud and Lisa helped her put on her seat belt.

"Good times tonight, Cheryl," Bud said. "I'll call you later."

Cheryl pouted. "You better call me, missstttteeeer."

Bud closed the door and spoke. "Lisa, nice meeting you tonight. See y'all this Friday."

"What's going on thiiisss Fridaaaay?" asked Cheryl. Bud was about to answer, but Cheryl had lowered her head and fallen fast asleep.

54

Saturday, July 23, 1994
11:52 p.m. CDT
South Plains Cellars

Close to twelve o'clock in the morning, Jill loaded another set of wineglasses in the dishwasher. Bud stood next to her drying and polishing the previous load of clean glasses. The catering staff left about an hour prior, so it was just the two tour guides and Campbell remaining.

"Tonight was crazy," Jerry said. "We had a ton of people here, more than expected, and with a limited catering staff, I asked a bunch of y'all. You went above and beyond the normal call of duty. Great job tonight."

"Thanks, Jerry," replied Jill.

"Yeah, thanks, Jerry," added Bud. "I got a question, though."

"What do you need, Bud?"

"We are out of citric acid and we have one more load of glasses to wash."

"Do you know where the walk-in fridge cooler is? It's in the white wine room, behind the bigger fermentation tanks, on the southeast corner of the winery. You will see on the corner of the east wall, just in front and on the left side of the walk-in cooler, a bunch of metal pegs sticking out with metal hose clamps and black O-rings. Just below that are the extra citric acid bags. Be careful. They are heavy, ninety pounds each. Don't try to carry 'em. You'll want to grab the dolly behind the barrels over there first."

Campbell pointed to the back of the barrel room before the entrance to the bottling room and to the right.

Bud replied, "Got it. I'll be right back."

Bud hustled over to the dolly's location and pulled it behind him while opening the barrel room doors. He walked past the bottling room, pushed away the large, clear insulating straps and entered the white wine room and made his way toward the rear. Between the two rows of large stainless steel tanks, he came upon several wine hoses and wine pumps laid out in front of him, which made walking with a dolly somewhat precarious. But sure enough, and just as Campbell described it, there was the walk-in cooler with the metal pegs on the east wall, bags of citric acid below them.

After loading one of the heavy, lumpy bags of citric acid onto the dolly truck, Bud glanced down at the ground and noticed a very small, light-blue envelope. It seemed out of place. Nothing else like that around, he thought. He picked it up and examined it. There was a small fold, and the envelope appeared to be empty. He started to peel the envelope open when a loud voice spoke."

"Bud, what are doing?"

Startled, Bud almost dropped the envelope. Campbell was standing in front of him.

"Sorry, Jerry. I found this on the floor, next to the pallet of citric acid. Looks like somebody dropped it by accident."

Campbell frowned and walked closer. "That's a pH indicator strip that Drew uses to test the wine. Give it to me and get your ass back up front. Jill is waiting for that bag of citric acid. Now c'mon, hurry."

Bud did as he was told and hustled back to the tasting room.

∎∎∎

Campbell waited for Bud to exit the white wine room and walked over to the second door of the walk-in cooler. Before he could knock, the door opened and Jaime Sáenz appeared. He grabbed the light-blue envelope from Campbell.

"That was close. Good cover story on the pH indicator strip."

"Yeah, well get your shit under control. We can't have packets like this lying around here."

"Jerry, we haven't been producing anything for over a month. I don't know how it got here. Besides, its empty."

"Just fix it! And make sure none of these are lying around." Campbell glared at Jaime Sáenz and returned back to the tasting room.

Twenty minutes later and the final wineglass polished, Jill let out a yawn as she grabbed her timecard and slid it underneath the time clock.

"Someone's tired," remarked Bud.

"Exhausted," replied Jill. "Are you working tomorrow?"

"Yep. Jerry has got me on the clock at eleven thirty in the morning." Bud grabbed his timecard and followed Jill's steps.

Both tour guides walked out the back door and to their respective automobiles and said their goodbyes. After Bud started his vehicle, he let the car idle for a bit. After finally getting a moment to himself, he took a deep breath. The small blue envelope came to mind. He'd seen a few odd envelopes lying around his former roommate Steve's room, and this one reminded him of that. Then Campbell snatching it like that and having his sudden change of mood . . .

Very odd.

Something about the way Campbell explained it as pH indicator strip didn't make sense.

55

Monday, July 25, 1994
9:47 a.m. CDT
Lubbock International Airport

Supervising Special Agent Easton Derderian followed his boss up the jet ramp at Lubbock International Airport. He felt as if he had just been here, not over a month ago, but nearly yesterday. Perhaps that was because the trip had ended so abruptly and inexplicably. Both men walked briskly to the Avis rental car counter and each rented his own vehicle. Before they parted, Agent Harris motioned Derderian to a quiet corner.

"Okay, let's review," said Harris.

"I drive over to Tanrock Capital Bank and wait in the car until ten twenty-five a.m. I then call the main number at the bank and ask for Hank Evans, using a deep voice. I will either get transferred to his secretary or directly to him. If his secretary answers and confirms he is in his office, I hang up. Same goes if I get directly transferred to Evans and he answers. Once I know Evans is in his office, I will call you."

"Correct."

"After we get confirmation that Hank Evans is in his office, I wait five more minutes and at ten thirty a.m., I pay him a surprise visit. I flash my badge and ask that we speak for a few minutes privately in his office. After that, I start reading off these questions on my notepad. After that, who knows."

"Good. And if he pulls the lawyer card—"

"I politely tell him thanks for his time, and I leave his office."

"Right. And after I get confirmation from you that Evans is in his office, I will be at South Plains Cellars' parking lot, and I will ask to meet Jerry Campbell right at ten thirty a.m. I will ask Jerry Campbell the same questions."

"So, what do we do afterwards?"

"Let's grab some lunch. Last time I was here, Vernon mentioned a spot called Abuelo's as having good Tex-Mex. I think it's in the south part of town, somewhere near the intersection of Eighty-Second Street and Quaker. We can review our notes there and then plan our next steps."

"Got it."

Brian Harris took his time driving to South Plains Cellars, but still arrived a bit early, driving past the winery's entrance around 10:05 a.m. He pulled his rental car into the parking lot and waited.

56

Monday, July 25, 1994
10:07 a.m. CDT
South Plains Cellars

"So, y'all are from Michigan? Well, it's great having y'all here at South Plains Cellars, and great timing, too. Today we get to witness crush, which out here happens only about six to seven weeks a year. We are going to stop here, right behind this yellow line, for safety purposes." Bud pointed to the yellow-painted line on the concrete crush pad. His tour consisted of two older couples.

"Now, almost all our grapes are harvested at night and arrive early in the morning. When the grapes arrive by truck, like this one here, they first stop next to that small building there; that's our weigh station." Bud pointed to the very small building, adjacent to the crush pad.

"Our wine cellar workers will weigh the grapes and then start loading them into this receiving bin using this forklift." Bud gestured his right hand forward. "Once the grapes enter this large stainless steel hopper, a giant auger screw at the bottom will move the grapes into our crusher-destemmer machine. That machine does exactly what it is called: it de-stems all the grapes from their stems, leaving us only grape juice, skins, seeds and pulp, or what we call 'must.' What remains is what we call 'MOG,' material other than grapes, which we dispose of in the fields of our estate vineyard behind us. From there, it depends if the grapes are meant to become red wine or white wine. The grapes here today are for a red wine.

"Now, if these grapes were white wine grapes, like Chardonnay or Sauvignon Blanc grapes, as they leave the crusher-destemmer, the must moves into either one of these large pneumatic presses. Each of these German-made presses can hold up to twelve tons of grapes. Once the press is filled, a giant bag inside inflates with air and softly presses the must. The grapes' juice is then extracted from the must, where it gets pumped into one of several stainless steel fermentation tanks in our winery.

"Making a red wine, like Carignan, which we have here, the grapes leave the crusher-destemmer, the must is pumped directly into our stainless steel tanks, and we add yeast to start the fermentation process. We will get to that process later in the tour. Any questions?" Bud looked at the faces of his foursome tour group and everyone kept silent.

"All right, let's get inside and we'll continue our tour."

Bud led the group indoors, but just before he began to continue his instruction, Drew Dalton appeared from behind one of the tanks and walked toward Bud and his group.

"Oh, ladies and gentlemen, this is Drew Dalton, our winemaker."

Dalton stopped in his tracks, smiled and gestured to the group.

Bud seized the opportunity to ask Dalton a question.

"Drew, I had a question the other day from another group and I meant to ask you. It's kinda technical."

Dalton smiled again. Unlike some winemakers, he liked sharing his knowledge with tourists, even during the busy crush season.

"Sure, what's the question, Bud?"

"What do you use to determine the pH when making wine?"

"Oh, that's easy. A Hanna Wine pH Tester with an electrode. Here, I'll show y'all."

Dalton walked over to one of the large stainless steel tanks and retrieved the pH test meter, which was shaped like a large thermometer. He returned and gave a quick demonstration to Bud's tour group.

Bud followed up with another question. "I read that some wineries like to use pH indicator test strips."

"Yeah, but those are unreliable. We like to use the best and most accurate winemaking tools here at South Plains Cellars. Test meters like this are much better."

"Thanks, Drew. Unless anyone has any other questions, we will continue our tour."

888

Still inside his rental, Agent Harris glanced at his watch, which displayed 10:24 a.m.

About twelve miles north, Easton Derderian stood in front of the closest pay phone about a block from Tanrock Capital Bank. He reviewed the list of questions for Hank Evans on his notepad, at the same time checking his watch every few minutes. At precisely 10:25, Derderian deposited a quarter and dialed a ten-digit number.

"Tanrock Capital Bank. How may I direct your call?"

Derderian lowered his voice. "Hank Evans please."

"Of course, let me transfer you." After a few audible clicks another woman answered the phone.

"Hank Evan's office. May I help you?"

"Is Hank Evans available?" Agent Derderian said, keeping his voice low.

"He is on the other line. May I ask who's calling?"

Agent Derderian promptly hung up the pay phone and walked directly to Tanrock Capital Bank.

57

Monday, July 25, 1994
10:30 a.m. CDT
South Plains Cellars

Brian Harris pulled the large wooden handle on the entrance door and entered South Plains Cellars' tasting room. Before him he saw small Doric columns, a large wrought-iron chandelier above his head and a granite-slated floor beneath his feet. To his left, he noted an abundance of South Plains Cellars merchandise and on his right, a long granite stone bar, with multiple wine bottles stored inside wall-mounted bins. The large room was immaculate. His gaze turned toward the noise of French doors opening up at the end of the tasting room.

"That does it for our tour today. Would anyone be interested in tasting a few of the wines we make here at South Plains Cellars?"

Bud walked behind the tasting-room bar and began to pull five empty wineglasses off their rack and placed all five glasses on the bar. Bud's tour group quickly gathered around the bar and Bud opened a fresh bottle of Sauvignon Blanc.

Agent Harris did his best to avoid being recognized by Bud Garza and began walking around the tasting room. A young man, medium built with red hair, approached him. He was wearing a pair of tan khaki pants, with a navy blue soft-collared short-sleeve shirt with a South Plains Cellars logo embroidered on the left upper chest.

"Welcome to South Plains Cellars. Are you interested in a tour, or is there something you're looking for in particular?"

Harris looked at the young man in front of him and smiled.

"Is Jerry Campbell here?"

"Yes. Follow me."

Jason Rector led Harris to Jerry Campbell's office, near the front of the tasting room. Jason knocked on Campbell's closed office door.

"Jerry, its Jason."

"Come in, Jason."

Jason opened the door and saw Jerry Campbell sitting at his desk, typing an email on his Toshiba laptop. Campbell kept his focus on the keyboard and did not look up to face Jason.

"What is it?"

"This gentleman asked to see you."

Campbell stopped typing and looked up from his keyboard. Next to Jason stood a man just under six feet tall with a medium shoulder build, slightly balding forehead with deep brown, short hair, but in relatively good shape. The man walked past Jason and approached Campbell's desk. He carefully unfolded his wallet in front of him and flashed his DEA credentials in a conspicuous manner at waist level.

"Brian Harris. Do you mind if we speak for a few moments?"

At the sight of Agent Harris's DEA identification, Campbell stammered a bit and stood up too quickly, hitting the underside of his desk with his knee in the process.

"Ah, yes, Brian Harris, is it? Yes, yes, of course, please have a seat."

Campbell rubbed the injured knee with his right hand and motioned with his left hand for Harris to sit down on one of the two chairs in front of his desk.

"Thanks, Jason. Please close my door."

Jason obliged Campbell's request, walked out of the office and closed the door.

"If you could give me a moment, Agent Harris, I need to finish typing this email; it is somewhat urgent. Please make yourself comfortable.

"Special Agent in Charge Harris, but please, call me Brian. Of course."

Campbell nodded, then looked down and quickly typed six words in a subject heading on his email server and briefly reviewed the message-less email:

From: Campbell, Jerry <jerry.campbell@southplainscellars.com>

Sent: Monday, July 25, 1994, 10:32 a.m.

To: Evans, Hank <hank.evans@southplainscellars.com>

Subject: DEA just walked in my office

Campbell pressed the ENTER key.

Agent Harris sat in his designated chair and took in his surroundings, not saying a word. Nothing stood out, other than normal office accoutrements, along with an "ego wall" of plaques and awards, along with Jerry Campbell's college diploma from Texas Tech University and what looked like a picture of Campbell's fraternity chapter, Sigma Class of 1971, on the right wall facing him. Harris stood up and walked over to view the fraternity picture.

Nervous as hell and with his antiperspirant working overtime, Campbell stared at his computer screen, waiting for a reply from Hank Evans, while at the same time waiting for the DEA agent to reply first. Harris took his time and scanned the pictures of Campbell's fraternity brothers and the individual names below. He found Campbell's name near the top. As he scanned to his right, he noticed the name Henry Evans and the picture above it.

"Were you and Henry Evans fraternity brothers?"

"Oh, you mean Hank? Hank Evans? Yes, yes. I've known Hank since high school."

"Is that the same Hank Evans that works here at South Plains Cellars?"

"The same, but he doesn't have his office here."

"I see."

"Ah excuse me, Special Agent . . . I mean, Brian. What can I do for you today?"

"I'm conducting an investigation into the disappearance of one of our agents, Senior Special Agent Traegar Jackson."

"Okay, I'm not familiar with that name."

"His last reported location was just across the street from this winery, just over six weeks ago, the evening of Monday, June thirteenth."

"Well, I wasn't here that Monday night. Our tasting room closes at five p.m. It usually takes me a few minutes to lock up and then I went home for the evening." Campbell's computer let out a soft beep, indicating a new email had arrived.

"Oh, excuse me. I've got to answer this electronic mail message really quick." Campbell looked at his red monochrome screen on his laptop and read.

From: Evans, Hank <chank.evans@southplainscellars.com>

Sent: Monday, July 25, 1994, 10:35 a.m.

To: Campbell, Jerry <jerry.campbell@southplainscellars.com>

Subject: Same here. Call you in a few minutes.

Campbell closed his laptop and apologized again, "Sorry about that, Brian. What can I help you with today?"

"How long have you worked here at—" Harris was cut off by Jerry Campbell's office phone ringing.

"Oh, excuse me a moment." Relieved by the phone call, Campbell quickly picked up the receiver. "This is Jerry Campbell."

"Jerry, this Hank. I'm whispering for a reason. Is the DEA agent still in your office? If so, please say the words '*What* time?' very loud and in a surprised fashion, like a question."

Campbell responded, "*What time?!*"

"Okay. I just politely kicked out a DEA agent in my office. Now please do exactly what I say. Tell the agent that you have an important business meeting here at the bank. Then drive over to my office so we can talk. I'm calling Drew Dalton next."

"I'm on my way." Campbell hung up the phone and stood up. "I'm sorry, Special Agent Harris. I have an important business meeting I need to attend at our winery's bank."

"Oh, no worries."

Campbell grabbed his car keys off his credenza and his leather suitcase. "If you will excuse me, I've got to go."

"Of course."

Harris stepped aside as Campbell walked past the DEA agent and opened his office door. He briskly followed Campbell outside and watched as Campbell closed the door and locked it.

Campbell scanned the tasting room and noticed Jason folding shirts.

"Jason, please come over here."

Jason stopped what he was doing and approached Campbell.

"Hank called. I've got an important meeting at the bank. I'm going there now."

"OK, is there anything else I can do?"

"Just in case I don't make it back by closing time, please lock up the place." He handed two keys to Jason.

"Sure thing, Jerry."

Campbell walked through the front door and headed straight for his car. He began trembling and could hardly insert his car keys in the driver's side passenger door. He exited the parking lot and drove straight to Tanrock Capital Bank.

Agent Harris stared at Jason as he tucked the keys into his front pants pocket and went back to folding shirts. There he found himself standing otherwise alone in the tasting room, trying to comprehend what had just occurred.

"Thanks for coming and y'all have a great day," Harris then heard.

Harris turned to see Bud Garza closing the door on a cash register as four elderly guests made their way to the front entrance of the winery. He snapped out of his daze and approached Bud.

"You are Bud Garza, correct?"

"Yep. And you're Brian Harris. We met at Truett's house, about six weeks ago. You're Uncle Brian, but not really Cheryl's uncle. What brings you to South Plains Cellars, Mr. Harris?"

"Work."

"What kind of work do you do?"

"I work for the government."

Bud nodded his head.

"Are you and Cheryl still dating?"

"Yeah. I helped her and her roommate Lisa move into their apartment a few days ago. She's great."

"Well, between you and me, you made a good first impression with her folks, especially with Cheryl's mother. She went on and on about you after you left on your date."

"That's cool. I was a bit nervous meeting both Cheryl's parents that night. It was unexpected."

"What time is the next tour?"

Bud looked at his watch. "Not until eleven, but there's nobody here. Would you like a tour?"

"Sure."

Agent Harris listened as Bud started his narrative tour, explained the activity on the crush pad, and shortly afterwards, both men entered the red wine room. Harris noticed the large stainless steel tanks, resting on elevated concrete platforms. Bud quickly explained the red-wine-making process of Cabernet Sauvignon and walked toward the white wine room.

Bud then said, "Let's see if we can escape the heat in this room. This next room is much cooler. Watch your step." Bud motioned his hand to the large three-inch winery hose stretching across the floor.

Bud and Harris stepped over the wine hose and moved the large vertically dangling clear straps of insulating plastic, and both men entered the cool white wine room.

Harris stood for a moment, taking in everything immediately in front of him and noticing the much cooler temperature.

"This is a big room."

"Yeah, this is where we make all our white wines. White wines are the majority of the types of wines we make here at South Plains Cellars. Our winemaker, Drew Dalton, prefers . . ." And suddenly Bud Garza stopped talking. He noticed Drew walking fast toward them.

"Speaking of Drew Dalton," exclaimed Bud.

Dalton looked up and quickly said, "Hey, Bud," and continued walking past both men at an even faster pace.

"Was that the winemaker?" asked Harris.

"It is, or it was. Looks like he's in a big hurry to go somewhere."

Harris stopped walking with Bud and followed Drew Dalton instead. Bud said nothing and followed him.

Once he reached the crush pad, Harris stopped and watched Dalton cross the winery's parking lot and open the door of a white 1994 Ford F-150 pickup truck with a burgundy South Plains Cellars logo painted on both doors. Dalton backed up his truck quickly and sped out of the parking lot.

Harris turned around to Bud, who had walked back to the crush pad.

"Say, Bud, can we do this another time? I just got a beeper message concerning work." Harris handed the ten-dollar bill to Bud. "It was nice meeting you again."

Bud grabbed the bill. "Well, it was nice meeting you again, Mister Harris."

Harris ran quickly to his Oldsmobile rental, jumped in the front seat and, just like Drew Dalton, sped out of the parking lot.

Bud walked back to the winery's patio before the French doors and stood watching Agent Harris drive away.

What the heck?

Bud entered the tasting room and closed the French doors behind him. Jason was behind the tasting room bar reading the August 1994 magazine issue of the *Wine Spectator*.

"Man, that was the craziest thing."

"Plenty of that going on today."

"What do you mean?"

"That guy you took on your tour . . . Hey, wait a minute, why are you back *here* and where is the guy that wanted the quick tour?"

"He just ran off. I mean, *literally*, he just ran off. We were in the white wine room and we both saw Drew Dalton blow past us. He got into the winery truck and sped off. Then, the guy on my tour did the same thing and took off in his car."

"That was the same guy that just saw Jerry. Brian Harris, right?"

"Yep, that's his name."

"Weird. So right after I took him to meet Jerry, a few minutes later he tells me he has an important meeting at the bank and scrams. He even gave me the keys to the tasting room just in case he didn't make it back before closing."

"So, it's just you and me today?"

"Along with Gaspar and the other cellar rats. But those guys will be working in the winery until late tonight."

Bud thought for a moment. "You thirsty?"

Jason smiled. "Thought you'd never ask. Whatcha wanna drink?"

"Sauvignon Blanc. How about you?"

"Wait a minute. Are you hungry?"

"I could eat."

"Let's hold off on that Sauvignon Blanc. I'm going to Pedro's Tamales just down the highway and I'll grab us a couple dozen fresh pork tamales. Wait until you try those with Regal de Cabernet, it will knock your socks off."

"Here, this will help." Bud handed Jason the ten-dollar bill.

"Hey, thanks for the cash."

A smiling Jason Rector went into the back kitchen and grabbed his keys.

About twenty minutes later, Jason returned with two dozen hot, freshly made, pork tamales. Both tour guides sat at the tasting room bar and ate lunch, while drinking an entire bottle of Regal de Cabernet.

Nobody visited the winery for the remainder of the day.

58

Monday, July 25, 1994
2:47 p.m. CDT
Lubbock, Texas

Agent Harris grimaced and replied to the question posed to him over the phone by Director Colangelo.

"Sir, we did not harass either Hank Evans or Jerry Campbell."

"Well, not according to Assistant U.S. Attorney Justin Shamkin. It's the word of Lubbock District Attorney Neal Hutchinson that you and Derderian harassed both gentlemen with outrageous questioning and threatened each man with arrest."

"Wait, why is the U.S. Attorney's office involved in this investigation?"

"I asked Shamkin that same question. Apparently, he and Neal went to the same law school together. Either way, it doesn't matter. You need to wrap up whatever business you have in Lubbock and get both of y'all's asses back to El Paso. With Shamkin's involvement now, it's best to shut down for the time being."

"Does Shamkin know about Traegar Jackson's disappearance?"

"He does."

"And?"

"And until you get enough information to implicate either Hank Evans or Jerry Campbell with the disappearance of Senior Special Agent Traegar Jackson, and a subsequent arrest warrant, *you and nobody on your staff* will investigate or question either of these gentlemen, do you understand?"

Harris shrugged. "Yes sir."

The phone line went dead. Harris looked at Derderian, who was sitting on the reception couch inside the business conference room of their Fairfield Inn. Derderian blurted out his frustration first.

"Damn it. I know these guys are hiding something."

"I agree. And every instinct I have tells me they are somehow involved in Traegar Jackson's disappearance. But you heard Colangelo. We need to get you back to El Paso."

"*Me?* Aren't you coming, too?"

"I promised my friend Vernon I'd swing by his place for dinner tonight. I'll take the first plane to El Paso tomorrow morning."

"This sucks, sir."

"Safe flight home, Easton."

Harris extended his right hand and he and Derderian shook.

Derderian, saying nothing, exited the conference room and the hotel lobby, walking toward his blue Pontiac rental car in the parking lot.

Trish Truett opened her front door to Agent Brian Harris before he had a chance to ring or knock. She gave him a big bear hug.

"Good to see you, Brian. Vernon said you were in town."

"I'm sure he did." Harris picked up his overnight bag and walked into the Truett home.

"We got you in the same room as last time. There's fresh linens and towels. When you're done putting your stuff up, come join us in the kitchen."

"We need to start charging this guy room and board," bellowed Vernon, who appeared around the corner of the living room. Both men hugged each other.

"You are right, so I figured this would help."

Harris opened his overnight bag and retrieved a bottle of Blanton's Bourbon whiskey and a bottle of Kendall-Jackson Chardonnay, handing each bottle respectively to the intended recipient.

Trish and Vernon's eyes lit up at the unexpected gifts of wine and spirits.

"Okay, you boys do your thing and I'm going to put this bottle of wine in the fridge. This will go great with the orange asparagus chicken I'm making for dinner tonight."

"How's Cheryl?"

"Oh, she's great. Cheryl and her new boyfriend Bud are coming over later tonight, in fact. She's picking up her stand-up jewelry armoire for the apartment. She completely forgot about it when she moved a few days ago, so now Bud's helping her with it."

Harris nodded and watched Trish walk toward the kitchen. Suddenly, something occurred to him. He drew in his breath sharply.

"Brian, you, okay?" asked Vernon.

Harris snapped back to attention. "What? I'm sorry, Vernon, what'd you say?"

"I said, you want to join me in the study?"

"Sorry, I just was thinking about something and my mind wandered off. Yes, of course."

"What were you thinking?"

"Nothing, really. Let's get that bottle of bourbon cracked open."

"Now that is a good idea." Both men made their way to the Truett study.

59

Monday, July 25, 1994
9:16 p.m. CDT
Truett home, Lubbock, Texas

"Mom! Dad! Bud and I are here!"

"We're in the back, honey!" replied Trish faintly.

Cheryl grabbed Bud's hand and led him to the Truett backyard. The house came complete with a large swimming pool surrounded by ornate landscaping decorations consisting of several large ceramic planters of multiple floral perennials. A large wood pergola shaded the area beginning at the back door and stretching toward the pool. Underneath the pergola a black ironwork table stood with six complementary ironwork chairs. Vernon Truett, Trish Truett and Brian Harris were sitting around the table, on which sat two bottles of Chardonnay, one bottle empty and the other half full. A half-full bottle of Blanton's Bourbon stood next to the bottles of Chardonnay.

Clearly some serious drinking had been going on. Cheryl and Bud caught Cheryl's dad in the middle of a story.

"And then Brian says, 'What do mean, officer, I'm just watering this tree!'"

Vernon, Trish, and Agent Harris all roared in laughter.

Cheryl whispered into Bud's ear, "My dad loves telling stories." She turned to the others at the table. "I hope we are not interrupting."

"Not at all, honey; you know your father and his stories." Trish regained her composure, stood up and hugged her daughter.

"You remember Bud." Cheryl gestured toward her boyfriend.

"Of course." Trish opened her arms and embraced Bud, who awkwardly hugged her back.

It was Vernon's turn to stand up and hug his daughter.

"Honey, good to see you."

Vernon offered his outstretched hand to Bud, which Bud shook firmly. "Good to see you as well, young man."

"Hi, Uncle Brian!" Cheryl walked around the table toward Harris, who was also standing now.

"Well, hello Cheryl."

Harris turned his gaze toward Bud. "And yes, good to see you again, Bud. Perhaps next time we can finish that tour." Harris smiled and extended his hand.

"Yes sir. Happy to make it up."

"Am I missing something?" Cheryl asked.

"Bud was giving me a tour at South Plains Cellars earlier today, but my pager went off and I had to address an issue for work."

"Oh, that's cool."

Cheryl turned her attention to Trish. "Mom, is my jewelry armoire in the garage?"

"Yes." Trish looked at Vernon. "Sweetheart, aren't you going to help your daughter?"

"Oh no, Dad, we got it. That's why Bud is here."

Vernon sat back down.

Harris remained standing. "Here, let me help Bud with loading up the armoire, it's the least I can do. Cheryl, please sit down here and catch up with your mom and dad. It shouldn't take too long." Harris paused. "What's the best way to the garage from here?"

"The garage door is just next to the fridge in the kitchen," replied Trish.

Harris excused himself and walked toward the kitchen, Bud following right behind. Opening the door and looking past the two parked vehicles, there was no mistaking Cheryl's stand-up jewelry armoire standing all by itself in the narrower end of the three-car garage. Harris figured if there was ever a good time to ask Bud for his help, this was going to be it.

"How do you like working at South Plains, Bud?"

"It's cool. I'm learning a bunch about wine."

"You know, I just realized this. I never told you my job. I work with the Drug Enforcement Agency as Special Agent in Charge, EPIC Division, El Paso, Texas." Harris grabbed his wallet and showed Bud his DEA badge and identification card.

Bud looked over Harris's wallet of credentials and nodded in acknowledgment. Harris noticed that Bud seemed a little alarmed.

"Bud, you ever see anybody or anything *unusual* at South Plains Cellars?"

Bud froze. "Yeah, in fact, I did."

"What did you see that was so unusual?"

"Before I answer that, what's a DEA agent who works in the El Paso office doing all the way out here in Lubbock? I mean, doesn't the DEA have its own office here in Lubbock?"

"You could say that. And yes, the DEA does have an office out here, but it's in Amarillo, not Lubbock."

"Oh. Okay."

"So, what did you see that was *unusual*?" Harris reached into his back pocket and pulled out a small notebook and a black ballpoint pen, which he clicked on the top to open.

"Is this between us? I mean, you just grabbed your pen and notebook. I don't want to say anything that gets me in trouble."

"Just between us," reassured Harris.

Bud took a deep breath and recalled his memory about the small blue envelope and the pH test strip story that Campbell had told him. "And then earlier today, our winemaker told me that he doesn't use pH test strips. He prefers using an electronic pH test meter."

Listening intently, Harris jotted notes as quickly as his shorthand skills allowed.

"Anything else, other than the envelope? Was it about the size of your thumb? Was it dark blue, or lighter blue with a waxy appearance? Anything inside the envelope? Any residue or off-putting smell?"

"Yeah, it was very little. About the size of my thumb. It was lighter blue and yes, a waxy appearance. Nothing was inside and no smell. It felt empty."

Harris finished writing his notes and shoved the pen and notepad back into his pocket. Both men regarded the jewelry armoire.

"Ready?"

"Yep," replied Bud.

The men then lowered their posture and grabbed the armoire on each side, just above the legs, and raised it to waist level. The armoire was light in weight, but bulky. They took it to Bud's Ford Explorer and carefully lowered it lengthwise onto its back into the vehicle. Bud closed the tailgate and swung the spare-tire triangle support back in place.

"I'll be honest with you, Bud," Harris put in. "The small light-blue envelope you described to me is something I've seen with several drug busts here in the state."

"Really?"

Harris walked closer to Bud and added, "Last month, one of our DEA agents busted a heroin dealer in the Austin area. We caught him with a bunch of small blue envelopes, just like you described, filled with heroin."

"*What?* You're kidding, right?"

"I wish I was."

"Shit. I fucking *hate* drugs."

"You don't have to appease me, Bud."

Bud's tone of voice rose. "I'm not trying to *appease* you, Agent Harris. It's . . . it's a thing with me."

Harris raised his voice in reply, "Look, Bud, there's no reason to get worked up."

"*I fucking hate drugs!*" Bud growled, ignoring Harris's advice.

Bud raised a hand toward his face and wiped away the tears that had swelled up there unbidden. His mind was on the memory of vomit and spit Chad had choked on as a result of a binge and an overdose.

"Hey, Bud, I didn't mean to snap at you. I guess I touched a nerve."

"No, it's not that," Bud replied. "I lost my best friend to a drug overdose in high school. Chad Gallagher. He died in the back of an ambulance. I was with him. Couldn't do a thing but watch him die. We were in Little League together. Rode bikes. Started a lawn-mowing business together one summer. And then that shit . . . it just *got* him."

Harris put a hand on Bud's shoulder. "Sorry, son."

"It was heroin mixed with cocaine, they said. He wasn't used to that. I mean it. I hate the fucking shit. Anytime I go to a party with my friends, the moment I see or smell anybody doing that crap, I turn around and leave."

Bud said no more, but the look in his eyes told Harris he was still far away in memories.

Agent Brian Harris could not believe his good fortune. He pitied Bud, but this was a perfect opportunity.

"Sorry to get so emotional, Agent Harris. I still miss the guy. We were going to always be, you know, friends, no matter what happened."

"Like Vernon and I are," Harris said softly.

"Yes, I guess so."

"Come over here, Bud. I want to talk to you a second."

Bud and Agent Harris returned to the lighted garage bay.

"Look, we barely know each other," Harris began, "so I'm going to give it to you up front. I'm not going to try to make you feel better because I don't know you and I certainly don't know your deceased best friend. And I'm not going to pretend I know him. What I do know is that I've been working for the DEA for many years. I've seen what drugs can do to people. I hate them just as much as you."

Bud nodded his head, acknowledging Harris's words, but said nothing.

"I'm going to be straight with you, and this stays between the two of us. That means anything I say *does not* get repeated. Not to Cheryl or any of your friends. Nobody."

"Okay."

"Last month, one of our DEA agents, a man named Traegar Jackson, was conducting a surveillance operation at South Plains Cellars and went missing. The next day, his vehicle was reported in a landfill in Juárez, Mexico.

"We tracked Senior Special Agent Jackson's vehicle within the city limits of Juárez, Mexico, but we lost the vehicle's LoJack signal just as me and my partner were closing in on its location. Immediately after that, we started our investigation from the last time we heard Agent Traegar's voice."

"South Plains Cellars," Bud replied. It wasn't a question.

"Exactly. And right now, we have nothing but our suspicions. However, what you told me tonight tells me that we are on the right track. Unless it's a pharmacy or a stamp collector, people don't leave little cellophane envelopes lying around, you know."

"Okay."

"I believe there is illegal activity at South Plains. I don't know what yet, and I can't prove anything at this point."

"So, what do you want me from me?"

"Would you be willing to get me some pictures inside the winery?"

"*Pictures?* Are you crazy? What happens if I get caught? Not only will I lose my job, but who knows who else I'll piss off?"

Harris knew that Bud was right. His request would put this young man in jeopardy.

"So, you told me that this just happened last Saturday night. What was going on at the winery that normally closes at five p.m.?"

"Oh, District Attorney Neal Hutchinson was hosting a fundraiser in memory of the Lubbock Detective who passed away in that car accident last month. Timothy Raymond."

"That's quite a good memory, Bud. So, how often does the winery host events like this?"

"I don't know. That was my first event. But from what I learned from the other tour guides, the winery hosts similar events like this quite a bit."

"Bud, if you can find out when the next after-hours event will be at South Plains Cellars, do you think you can make your way to the back of the winery again?"

"I think so. But what do you want me to do? Take pictures?"

"Yes."

"But what am I supposed to take pictures of?"

"You're a smart guy. Take pictures of anything that looks unusual. Anything that doesn't look like it belongs in a winery."

"That could be a bunch of pictures. I've only been working there for about six weeks."

"You'll do fine."

Suddenly, both men heard Cheryl's voice.

"Bud? Uncle Brian? Are you guys still out here?"

Harris spoke first, "Yes, Cheryl, we just finished up. We'll meet you in the backyard in just a minute."

"Okay," she responded.

"Bud, let's continue this conversation later. What's your schedule like tomorrow morning?"

"I've got Advanced Logic class that starts at ten a.m. Then nothing else the rest of the day."

"Good. I'm on the eight forty-five morning flight to El Paso on Southwest Airlines, so let's meet at Lubbock International Airport in the morning, say eight a.m.? I'll meet you next to the Southwest ticket counter, just outside security."

Bud groaned. "That's *kind of* early."

"Trust me, kid. You will be interested in what I have to show you. Now c'mon, let's head over to the Truett's backyard before they begin to wonder where we are."

888

At 7:50 the next morning, Bud pulled his car into the Lubbock International Airport parking lot, which was loosely scattered with parked cars.

Near the Southwest Airlines ticket desk, Bud saw Agent Harris sitting in a terminal chair. Harris stood up as Bud approached, smiled, and extended his right hand. The two shook. Before he could help it, Bud yawned widely.

"Thanks for coming, Bud. Did you stay up late last night?"

"Not really, just not used to getting up this early."

"Did you want some coffee?"

"No, thanks. I had a Diet Coke on the way over."

Harris sat down and Bud joined him.

Harris then handed Bud what looked like the rectangular Kodak Star 110 camera. But this version was much smaller and silver in color.

"I've never seen a camera like this," Bud cautiously whispered.

"This camera is not the kind you can purchase at a Montgomery Ward or Sears. It is made by the same folks at Kodak but is strictly sold to a few government agencies. It uses a special kind of film as well." Harris fished out four small film cartridges, the same dimensions that the Kodak Star 110 used, but much smaller.

"Here, I'll show you how to load a film cartridge."

When Harris completed the demonstration of loading new film in the small camera, he walked Bud through activating and deactivating the flash, and he showed him the button to depress to take a picture and the small slider to advance the film.

"So how am I going to take these pictures without getting caught?"

"Use your best judgment. Just like how you discovered the envelope. Look for things that don't belong. Make sense?"

"Well, yeah. But this could be dangerous. If what we both think is going on there, then the people associated with that line of business are not going to like me taking pictures."

"Pick a time when people are not working at the winery. You said yourself the winery likes to host parties in the evening. I'd start your surveillance then."

Harris looked at his watch and stood up. "I've got a flight to catch. When you finish off your first roll of film, call me at this number." He handed Bud his business card. "My office number is on the front and my home number is on the back. I will give you instructions on how to send me the used roll of film. Which reminds me," Harris said, bending down, "what's your phone number?" Harris dug into his work bag and pulled out his notebook and clicked the top of his ballpoint pen.

Bud rattled off his phone number at his apartment. Harris wrote the number down, put away his pen and notebook, stood up and extended his hand. Bud shook the DEA agent's hand in return.

"Good luck," he told Bud. "I will call around this same time next week to check in. Don't worry if you don't see anything or have anything to report. Investigations like this take time. And you are doing me and your government a huge favor. Also, I think, Traegar Jackson as well. It's one that will not be forgotten."

Bud smiled meekly in acknowledgment.

"Oh, and one more thing. This is very important. I know I told you last night, but as a reminder, keep this between you and me. No one else needs to know what you are doing."

Bud nodded his head and watched as DEA Agent Brian Harris walked toward the security gate. He then slipped the small camera into his front shorts pocket, along with the three rolls of film, and walked outside to his car.

"What the hell did I get myself into?" he muttered to himself.

60

Monday, August 8, 1994
1:04 p.m. CDT
Canyon, Texas

Jaime Sáenz's house phone rang. There were only two people who called this particular phone, both of whom wasted no time for small talk. Sáenz lifted the phone receiver and spoke.

"Hello?"

"How soon can we get operations at South Plains Cellars back up and running?"

Immediately Sáenz recognized the voice of Santiago Zavala. He cleared his throat and replied.

"Mr. Zavala, when we last spoke, I thought you wanted us to wait until late September due to what happened in June."

"Plans changed. El Astuto wants us to start immediately. Will that be a problem?" Zavala's question held more of the tone of a threat. Sáenz knew better than to challenge the man on the other end of the line. It was best to accommodate Zavala's request immediately. He looked at the date on his watch.

"Mister Zavala, it will only take a few days to recall our lab workers. The real challenge will be getting the first load of product from Mr. Bill and from our warehouse in Chihuahua City. It will take him some time to get it over the border and some time to arrange the juice mix. The soonest he can make it here will by September twenty-third."

Sáenz then pulled the phone slightly away from his ear, knowing what Zavala's response would be.

"That is unacceptable. It must be sooner!" barked Zavala.

Sáenz's brain began to search for solutions.

"The only other suggestion we have will cost us more and poses a much higher risk."

Zavala paused a few seconds and said nothing. He then replied. "I'm listening."

"Mister Gonzalez in Juárez is shutting down his operation temporarily. His team received a tip that the United States DEA along with the Mexican Marines were getting ready to move in. His team started the process of splitting up product in various safe houses across Juárez."

"Go on."

"We get a milk tanker truck and gather the product from each of Gonzalez's safe houses. We then fill the tanker with a minimal amount of water. Once we make it across the border into the United States, our truck makes its way to Fort Stockton, and we get the required amount of wine-grape juice. From there, the tanker will drive to our facility.

"The downside is that we don't have a tanker truck at this moment, and we run the risk of getting caught at the border. And Gonzalez is not going to sell his product to us at a discount. Just because he had to temporarily shut down his operations is not enough incentive for him to sell us his product at a lower price. He will want top dollar."

"How much more will this cost us?"

"Please give me a moment to run some numbers, Mr. Zavala."

Sáenz grabbed a calculator from his desk and started punching numbers. In a few moments, he spoke.

"I estimate we will make less than one million U.S. dollars on this production run. That does *not include* our truck getting confiscated by the United States federal agents at the border, which may happen if things go poorly."

Zavala mulled over Sáenz's plan. He knew the organization could easily cover the added expense, but he had to spread that cost over a period of months so as to not bring it to the attention of El Astuto.

"Start immediately. Then call me when the first batch of product arrives at the winery." Zavala hung up the phone and Sáenz placed the phone back into the cradle.

Sáenz looked at his Rolodex on his office desk and started making phone calls.

By that evening, Jaime Sáenz secured the men he needed to steal the milk tanker truck, albeit unknown to the owners of Compañía de Leche Fresca de Juárez, the Juárez Fresh Milk Company. In addition, after some considerable back-and-forth with Gonzalez, Sáenz purchased the opium which Gonzalez had separated into three different warehouses in the Granjero district, just east of the Juárez airport. Gonzalez was especially intrigued as to why his people needed to repackage the kilos of opium in corn husks before pickup by Sáenz's crew. Sáenz was able to convince Gonzalez the corn husks were needed to avoid detection from the U.S. *federales*. And finally, the general manager at the winery in Fort Stockton was more than pleased to sell two hundred gallons of unsold Sauvignon Blanc juice.

Now all Saenz had to do was wait for everything to come together and hope for a smooth border crossing.

Monday, August 8, 1994
7:28 p.m. CDT
Alpine, Texas

Two hundred and eighty-nine miles to the south, Bill Masterson sat on his living room couch, encapsulated in its dark brown leather, drinking a lowball glass of Jack Daniel's Tennessee Whiskey, with a few ice cubes. His on-and-off-again girlfriend Ashlee invited him to eat at Rope & Spur, a new high-end steakhouse that just opened in Alpine, Texas. Ashlee had called and informed Masterson that she would be at his house to pick him up in about twenty minutes, close to 7:50 p.m. Masterson took another sip of his charcoal-maple-filtered whiskey. Suddenly, his house phone rang. He immediately recognized the voice on the other end.

"We need your first delivery on the night of September twentieth. Can you make that happen?"

"Jaime, we can make that happen. Same time as usual?"

"No, Zavala is anxious to get restarted. Make it eight o'clock."

"And no problem with the mules?"

"No, other than they are getting more expensive."

Sáenz dismissed Masterson's concerns. "That's your problem. Not ours."

"Understood. We will see you the night of Tuesday, September twentieth."

"Good," Sáenz hung up his phone and the line went dead.

Masterson punched in Armando's phone number. After a couple of clicks followed by the familiar monotone rings associated with international calls, a voice answered.

"Hello."

"Armando, are you ready for another run?"

"Yes, Mr. Bill. Where and when do you want to meet?"

"Let's meet this Wednesday morning in Rio Grande Village. We can cross over the border to Boquillas. Any luck with more mules interested in a new life in America?"

"Yes. One of the coal factories near Nueva Rosita shut down last month. Plenty of mules lined up."

"Good. Please set aside a private section of The Parrot Bar in Boquillas so I can talk to each of these new prospects privately."

"Consider it done, Mr. Bill."

"Thanks, Armando."

Masterson hung up his phone. Looking through his living room windows, he noticed the headlights of Ashlee's Range Rover pulling up to his house. He finished off the remaining Jack Daniel's in his glass in one big gulp, placed his empty glass on the coffee table, stood up, grabbed his Resistol hat and walked toward his front door.

62

Wednesday, August 17, 1994
7:03 p.m. CDT
Lubbock, Texas

Bud pulled into the South Plains Cellars parking lot, which was completely full of parked cars. He had never experienced this lack of parking spaces at the winery, which made sense as he was always at the winery *before* an evening event. This time, Bud drove around the parking lot again and then exited down the tree-lined driveway entrance toward the highway. More parked cars lined the shoulder of CR 7600, with vehicles on both sides of the winery's entrance. Bud drove his car east and parked his vehicle at the next available space, just under a grove of cottonwood trees.

He turned off his ignition, removed his keys, leaned over toward his vehicle's glove box and retrieved the small camera that Brian Harris gave him a few weeks ago. He slipped the camera into the right front pocket of his khaki pants. He then grabbed his Ray-Ban sunglasses and slipped them into his front left pocket.

A few minutes later, Bud walked to the back entrance of the winery and into the kitchen. Both Jason and Jill were standing near the dishwasher with their backs to Bud. Jason was talking.

". . . and he asked me, how long does our Chardonnay go through malolactic fermentation?"

"And what did you say?"

"Four weeks, which is about standard, or least that's what Drew told me. Then the same guy asks me—" Jill turned her head and noticed Bud near the back and stopped Jason in his tracks. Her smile grew wide and she shot Bud a smile.

"Bud! What are you doing here?" she asked.

Jill gave Bud a big hug, pressing her chest hard against his own.

"You working tonight?" asked Jason.

"Nah. I think I left my sunglasses in the back of the winery while I was giving a tour the other day." Bud paused, gestured to the outside. "This place is packed, at least from all the cars in the parking lot and parked off the road. Why are y'all back here?"

Both Jason and Jill spoke in unison. "Rotary Club."

Bud furrowed his eyebrows. "What does that mean?"

Jill responded first. "The Lubbock Rotary Club has a bunch of members, but since many of the same folks are also active members of their respective Baptist churches, they tend to not drink much, especially in front of other rotary members."

"Then why do they hold their meeting here?"

Jason spoke next and lowered his tone of voice. "I heard the president and a majority of the executive officers are either Catholic or Episcopalian. They like to get their fill of wine when they can."

"Ha!" replied Bud.

Jason pulled Bud aside and asked another question. "If you left your sunglasses in the winery somewhere in the back, do you mind grabbing a couple bags of citric acid? We are down to less than one bag and that will help us as the weekend approaches."

Bud half-grinned at the opportunity. "Haul a hundred eighty pounds for no pay? Sure. Nah, happy to do it. Is Dalton or any other of the cellar rats working in the back tonight?"

"Nope. Just me and Jill tonight," Jason replied.

"What about Jerry?"

"Nah. He left about two hours ago."

Jason grabbed a bottle of South Plains Cellars Cabernet Sauvignon and said, "I'm going to see if the rotary execs need some more wine."

"I'll help," replied Jill.

Both tour guides left the kitchen and Bud headed for the back of winery, quietly walking through the French doors that opened into the large barrel room.

He worked his way behind the large group of people, grabbed the two-wheel dolly parked behind a stack of barrels and strolled down the hallway and opened the French doors quietly. He left the barrel room and passed the bottling room on his right. Bud moved away the large plastic flaps that separated the hallway from the white wine room and entered the much cooler and larger room, which was completely dark. The heavy smell of fermenting wine filled the place.

Bud turned on the lights and after a few seconds, the large halogen lights overhead flickered on, and the entire room was immersed in bright white light. Bud navigated his way to the back and toward the storage station which held the bags of citric acid. He parked the dolly upright and grabbed the first bag, and with some considerable effort and arm strength lifted the bag and placed it on the dolly.

Bud went to retrieve another bag—

Suddenly the other large stainless steel door in the cooler—the door that was *always* locked—opened.

A bespectacled Hispanic man emerged. He noticed what Bud was doing and in an irritated voice asked, "Who are you?"

"Bud Garza. I'm a tour guide. I work here."

"Did you turn the lights on in this room? They are supposed to be kept off during nonbusiness hours!" the man said sharply.

"Sorry, but who are you?"

"Jaime Sáenz, director of security and operations. Mister Sáenz to you."

"Well Mister Sáenz, this place is pitch black when the lights are turned off and the tasting room needs a few more bags of citric acid to help clean all the wineglasses from the visiting tourists. I didn't want to trip or fall on any of the hoses or equipment bringing these bags up to the tasting room."

The man got even more irritated and walked closer to Bud.

"Listen to me, *Bud Garza*. Someone from Mr. Dalton's staff is supposed to bring these bags up to the tasting room during regular business hours. Get what you need, get back to the tasting room, and turn the lights off when you leave. *Now!*"

Bud regarded the man cooly. He didn't like being barked at but now was not the time to lose his cool. With just one bag of citric acid on his dolly, he pulled the cart around and faced Jaime Sáenz. He carefully slipped his right hand in the front pocket of his Old Navy pleated khakis and gently pulled up the small camera to just below the edge of the pocket. If he could respectfully talk back to Jaime Sáenz and engage in conversation, perhaps he could distract him enough to snap his picture with his camera.

"Well, what are you waiting for?" barked Sáenz.

"Mr. Sáenz. Please accept my apology for turning on the lights in this room. I've only been working as a tour guide here for a few months, and I was only doing my best to help my coworkers up front. I understand that Mr. Dalton's team is responsible for getting us the citric acid bags we need. However, for this time tonight, that didn't happen as planned. I only wanted to do what was best for the winery and our valued guests. As you can see"—Bud pointed his left index finger toward the walkway between the large stainless steel tanks, strewn with winery hoses on the floor—"it's hard to walk past those hoses and winery equipment on the floor." Sáenz moved his eyes away from Bud and followed his index finger and the direction Bud pointed. Bud saw his chance and quickly lifted the small camera halfway out of his pocket and prepared to click the shutter button.

Suddenly Bud raised his left hand to his mouth and coughed loudly—and simultaneously clicked the camera shutter button.

"Excuse me, Mister Sáenz."

Relieved at his correct guess that his cough would sufficiently conceal the sound of the camera shutter, Bud quickly retrieved his left hand from his mouth as he released the camera from his right hand back into his pocket. Sáenz turned his attention back to Bud, who continued his fake coughing routine for a few more seconds, then finally composed himself.

Sáenz continued to look at him as if he were some kind of nuisance.

"My apologies, Mister Sáenz. I think I got a whiff of sulfur dioxide." Bud produced some more fake coughs and stepped away from Sáenz, at the same time pulling the dolly with the lone bag of citric acid back toward the tasting room. In between coughs, Bud spoke.

"Sorry, Mister Sáenz. I just learned that sulfur dioxide gas can cause the lungs to not function properly. I think I may have gotten"—Bud coughed—"a whiff of it. My apologies. As soon as I get to the bottling room, I will turn off the lights. Sorry."

Jaime Sáenz didn't say a word but only stared after Bud, watching him pull the dolly and the bag of citric acid away. Even after Bud turned the corner on the walkway and went out of view, Sáenz stayed in place, making sure all was secure. A few seconds later, Bud flipped off the light switches and the entire white wine room went dark.

Sáenz then made his way to the red wine room and outside to the crush pad. He threw on the master switch to the outside lights and the entire crush pad illuminated. He then looked at his watch, which displayed 7:54 p.m. The first tanker truck from Eagle Pass, Texas, was due in the next few minutes.

Meanwhile, Bud arrived in the barrel room and deftly navigated the dolly with the heavy bag of citric acid behind the rows and rows of people, still listening, this time to another Lubbock Rotary Club official. He worked his way toward the tasting room and made his way to the kitchen. Jason smiled and assisted Bud in unloading the heavy bag of citric acid upright next to the dishwasher.

Jill came into the kitchen.

"Hey Bud, did you find your sunglasses?"

Bud put his left hand in his front left pocket and pulled out his sunglasses, "Found 'em."

"Oh great. Where were they?"

"Right as you enter the white wine room from the red wine room, on the corner of the tank pad, next to the big ten-thousand-gallon tank." Before Jill could respond, Bud added quickly, "Hey, do either y'all know a guy named Jaime Sáenz? I bumped into him getting this bag of citric acid."

Jason and Jill looked at each other and said nothing.

"Who is he?"

"Jaime Sáenz is kind of a mystery guy around here," Jason offered. "He's in charge of security and operations here at the winery, but we rarely see him."

"And if we do, we do our best to avoid him," added Jill.

"I've never seen or met him until tonight. But he sure chewed my ass off."

Jill nodded. "Sounds like him. So what happened, Bud?"

Bud considered staying longer, maybe making up some tale about Sáenz, but it felt like a quick exit would be the safer course.

"Nothing. I left," he said. "Hey, are y'all working this weekend?"

Both tour guides nodded their heads.

"Good, see y'all then." Bud spun around and headed toward the exit. Jill and Jason looked at each other.

Three minutes later Bud walked toward his black Ford Explorer, which without the bright flood lights on the crush pad would have been very difficult to locate in the darkness of this area of the South Plains. Just as Bud inserted his keys into his vehicle's door lock, he heard a loud voice speaking Spanish.

"Is the hose connected?"

"Yes sir. Go ahead and open the main valve." After a pause of a few seconds, the voice returned.

"Is the juice moving?"

"Yes, it is."

Bud stopped attempting to unlock the door to his vehicle and walked closer to the sound of voices on the crush pad. In the distance, he noticed a large stainless steel tanker truck on the pad with the words COMPAÑÍA DE LECHE FRESCA DE JUÁREZ written on one side of the tanker. One man stood near the winery and another at the rear end of the tanker truck. Bud quickly pulled the little camera out. He took several photographs right away, but didn't know if the images would be useful. His heart almost stopped when he heard a very familiar voice, also speaking in Spanish.

"Are we good? Very well. Lights off."

Bud continued to click and advance a few more pictures, and when the lens of the camera centered on the man who had spoken, Jaime Sáenz came front and center in the view finder.

Suddenly the lights were killed and everything went black. Bud stepped back a few paces as his eyes adjusted to his surroundings without the bright crush pad lights. He quickly moved behind the road-facing side of his Explorer to avoid anyone seeing him. He unlocked his car door, jumped in the front seat, inserted the key into the ignition and cranked his vehicle to life. He flipped on his headlights and was on his way back home.

So, how does a guy open a stainless steel freezer door and not show any signs of being cold? Bud thought as he drove. *And anyway, I was told that door was always locked.*

Bud drove a little further. He remembered that there might be deer out tonight and slowed his pace a bit. The last thing he wanted to do was mess up his car on a West Texas deer. And the deer wouldn't like it much, either.

Bud shook his head as more thoughts came unbidden.

What is that same guy who's in charge of security and operations doing working on a winery crush pad at night while a milk tanker truck is unloading juice?

When he got back to his apartment, he'd convinced himself to call Brian Harris. He went over to his couch's side table and picked up the receiver of his Clear Trimline Style Metrolight phone. Harris's business card waited beside the phone. Looking down at the card, Bud dialed Agent Harris's number.

Agent Harris picked up on the second ring.

"Harris here."

"Mr. Harris, it's Bud. Bud Garza in Lubbock."

"Yes?"

"Not too late to call you, is it?"

"No, it's close to seven p.m. here."

"Seven p.m.?" Bud glanced at his watch, which displayed ten till eight.

"Bud, El Paso is on Mountain Daylight Time."

"That's right, my bad. Well, good. I've got some pictures for ya."

"Good. Can you tell me what you found out?"

On the other end Bud could hear shuffling and the sound of Harris clicking his ball point pen.

"First, I met some guy named Jaime Sáenz. Found out he oversees security and operations at the winery."

"Okay." Harris scribbled down the name and started taking shorthand notes.

"I bumped into him near the stainless steel freezer, while I was getting a bag of citric acid, and he immediately started chewing my ass out."

"Why?"

"He got pissed that I came to get the bag myself, instead of having one of the cellar rats bring a bag up during business hours."

"Cellar rats?"

"It's slang for a worker who helps in the winemaking process."

"Interesting. What else?"

"I kept my cool and apologized. I think I got a good picture of him without him knowing. Once I made it back up front with the citric acid, I left and walked back to my car."

"What else?'

"Well, he walked out of the freezer through a door that is always locked. But he didn't look like a guy who had been in a freezer. How can I say it? There was nothing *cold* on him. He had on short sleeves. I mean, it's that he didn't look like a guy that just exited a freezer. Does that make sense?"

"I get it. What else?"

"Right before I was about to leave, I noticed that same guy on the crush pad, barking out orders to a few guys on the pad where there was a milk tanker truck."

"A milk tanker truck? What's a milk tanker truck doing at a winery?"

"Don't know."

"Did you get any pictures?"

"Sure did. Now keep in mind, I was taking the pictures from near my car, behind some cottonwood trees, on the side of the road. I don't know how well the pictures will look."

Harris smiled to himself. Maybe he was finally going to be able to see what Jackson was observing several months ago.

"Anything else, Bud?"

"Nah. That was it."

"Good. Tomorrow morning, I need you to take that used roll of camera film and head over the closest Federal Express office."

"What time in the morning?"

"Take your time and shoot for nine o'clock. Have the Federal Express clerk call my office number, and I will give them our mailing address here in El Paso, along with the EPIC department's Federal Express number. That way the shipping charges get billed to our account. Just ask for a large mailing envelope and make sure it gets sent priority overnight."

Bud made a mental note of the Agent Harris's instructions and replied, "Okay."

"Thanks, Bud." Then the line went dead.

Bud hung up. He stood staring blankly into the middle distance, letting the memory of his day pass vaguely through his mind. A short time after he suddenly snapped back to consciousness and decided to go to bed.

Sleep was not easy in coming that evening, and he tossed and turned before finally dropping off to dream of mysterious voices, and someone chasing him in a cold, dark place.

63

Wednesday, August 17, 1994
8:16 p.m. CDT
South Plains Cellars

Jaime Sáenz sat at his workstation in the basement of South Plains Cellars viewing the images on the television screens. The first screen on his left showed the off-loading of grape juice from the tanker truck parked on the crush pad. Sáenz shook his head as the giant letters that spelled "Compañía de Leche Fresca de Juárez" still remained on the side of the milk tanker truck, even though he instructed his drivers to remove the letters once they crossed the border.

What a colossal fuckup.

This is what came from too much hurry.

The next screen to the right from camera 9 displayed a four-thousand-gallon, open-topped stainless steel tank. At the top of the tank were two steel I beams, mounted and suspended from the ceiling in a crisscross fashion above the opening. At the intersection where the beams crossed, two stainless steel spigots spun in a clockwise fashion, spraying grape juice into the tank below. The juice inside the tank bubbled as fresh juice entered it. Inside the tank, the extract from El Astuto's biochemistry doctor went to work, courtesy of Investigación Biomédica y Científica Incorporada. The process of removing the raw opium from the mixture of opium, grape juice, water and dissolved corn husks started. A tan-colored foam containing dissolved corn husks floated and bubbled in the top of the tank, mixed with a light-green olive color of the dissolved opium.

Sáenz turned his head right and set his gaze on the next television screen. Two men stood on the floor of the winery beside the same stainless steel tank. One man operated a large wine pump, which pulled the mixture from the tank's rack valve. Subsequently, the mixture entered the next machine, which any experienced winemaker would recognize as a hydraulic plate and frame filter press, commonly used in wine production for filtration purposes.

After a slurry of bentonite and wine is pumped into a holding tank for removal of solids before bottling, the mixture is pumped into the hydraulic plate and frame filter via the corner hole of each plate. Each of the twelve filter plates are squeezed together in a tight seal between all the plates, via a large corkscrew turn handle and hydraulic ram. The bentonite-wine slurry flows into each frame, allowing solid particles captured by the bentonite to accumulate on the filter cloths, which line each plate. The remaining filtered wine then moves to a drainage port in the flush plate and into a corner hole that is not being used for feeding the bentonite-wine mixture. The filtered wine then travels to another stainless steel tank for the next step in the production process. Soon after, the wine pump is turned off, and the filter press is ready to open. Each frame contains a filter of bentonite cake, which is the end result of the solids forming on the filter cloths. The hydraulic ram is then released, allowing the filter plates to separate. Each cloth filter on the frames is filled with solids, or bentonite filter cakes, which are scraped out of the frames using a spatula and fall into the stainless steel cake hopper resting below the press.

However, the hydraulic plate and frame filter press at South Plains Cellars was much larger than those used by wineries across the country, almost twelve square meters in size. And instead of bentonite, the cake mixture in the hopper consisted of opium and very minute particles of dissolved corn husk.

The first hydraulic plate and frame filter filled with the grape juice–opium mixture, and a second hydraulic plate and frame filter was in the open position, exposing each filter plate. The man not operating the wine pump carefully scraped the opium and corn husk into the cake hopper. That same man then used a small stainless steel shovel and transferred the mixture into five-gallon plastic buckets, which was then carried by another man toward the drug laboratory.

Spinning around in his chair toward the control room windows, Jaime Sáenz watched as the man carried the buckets of mixture through the large stainless steel door of the freezer and descend down the steps into the basement. His eyebrows furrowed with disappointment.

The man walked past Sáenz's angry stare and stopped. He placed the buckets on the ground and pulled up his N95 mask over his face, which was previously around his neck, and walked toward the large worktable in the drug laboratory. He then raised his right foot and ascended a small step stool that stood next to what looked like a large pressure cooker, almost five feet in height, with an open top. The man carefully poured the cake mixture into the large vessel. He repeated the same step with the second bucket. Once both buckets were empty, he returned upstairs to the winery cellar to start the process again.

Sáenz looked at the television screen above his head and watched as another man wearing a N95 mask and a white lab coat closed the lid on the large pressure cooker and secure the clamps on the outside of the lid. The worker flipped a few switches, and the pressure cooker started to slowly heat the cake mixture of opium and corn husks. In a few minutes the opium liquified and the heavier particles of corn husks succumbed to gravity, falling to the bottom of the pressure cooker. A green indicator light turned on and the man then opened a one-inch-diameter rack valve about a foot and half from the bottom of the pressure cooker. Connected to the small rack valve, a one-inch stainless steel tube, angled at ten degrees toward the floor, carried the liquefied opium to another similar-looking pressure cooker, only half the size as the first pressure cooker. However, this smaller vessel had a stainless steel dimpled cooling jacket surrounding the entire outside. Chilled propylene glycol flowed inside the stainless steel jacket and lowered the temperature of the liquified opium. At the same time, a small, red, curlicued hose with brass nozzles attached to a large cylindrical gas tank of benzene gas pumped the required amount of gas into the mixture.

A few minutes later, a blue-colored plastic hose with brass nozzles on either end pumped the required amount of acetic anhydride. This part of the manufacturing process always made Sáenz nervous. He repeatedly instructed his workers to always keep the special cooling/dehydrator system running in the small room that stored the large acetic anhydride storage tank, located in the far corner of the drug lab. Tan in color and made of high-density cross-linked polyethylene, safe storage of acetic anhydride required a secured closed container, with plenty of ventilation and always away from metal and moisture, in order to avoid a potential fire or explosion. While the use of benzene gas posed a danger, the deployment of acetic anhydride gave Sáenz fits of anxiety.

Fifteen minutes later, a green indicator light flashed on the smaller pressure cooker, indicating the vessel was safe to open. A worker released the clamps from the top of the vessel and opened the lid. He picked up a large measuring cup and scooped out heroin into six one-gallon buckets. Six workers, each three sitting abreast and all wearing white lab coats, safety goggles and N95 face masks, sat at the large worktable and waited. Dozens of small, light-blue wax envelopes rested on the table next to each worker. Measuring scales, spoons, knives and other utensils stood at the ready as well. Two large, clear plastic containers in the middle of the worktable each held pounds of confectioners' sugar. The worker then brought a gallon bucket of heroin to each of his colleagues seated at the table. Immediately, each worker started the process of cutting the pure heroin with sugar and packaging one-gram amounts into each of the small, light-blue wax envelopes.

Bautista De Soto was one of those men. He went about his task packaging his heroin inside the small light-blue wax envelopes with diligence. Originally from Villaldama, Mexico, Bautista used to work at the Jahuey Engine Plant, just south of Saltillo, Mexico, providing automobile engines for the Ford Motor Company. After a few months, he grew tired of the meager wages for his work and made his way north for a better opportunity. Crossing the Rio Grande at night, just north of the Anzalduas International Bridge and into McAllen, Texas, Bautista found temporary work harvesting Texas Rio Star red grapefruits in the Lower Rio Grande Valley. After the harvest season ended, Bautista made his way north, working as a day worker. Each of his day jobs took him further north and a year later, Jaime Sáenz met Bautista, sitting in the corner of a Town & Country Food Store, located on the corner of FM 1585 and US Highway 87.

An hour previously, Bautista was the lone day worker remaining after fourteen other men were picked out for a range of jobs earlier that morning. But what Bautista thought was the start of an unlucky day quickly reversed.

A morning conversation over fresh coffee between Sáenz and Bautista took place, along with a lucrative recruitment and employment pitch from Sáenz. The very next night, Bautista received his first training session in drug production.

Bautista tended to the job in front of him and was indifferent to his current employer. Three months ago, he was thrilled with his new job at the winery. His work hours were much shorter and more pleasant at his workstation than the hot days working in the grapefruit orchards or with construction outfits in West Texas. His income was five times greater than what he used to earn. But when Sáenz announced the shuttering of the drug lab in early June, Bautista's income froze. A month later, his money ran out. He leaned on a few of his fellow lab workers, borrowing what he could. By the time September arrived, he owed well over three thousand dollars, plus interest. He figured he would have to work at least a month straight to repay his debts, and that didn't leave any money left over for rent or food. Bautista took in his predicament and came up with a solution that would get him through this rough patch, but the plan came with high risk.

Bautista remembered his first day of work and the words Jaime Sáenz spoke to him that night.

"Listen to me Bautista, and listen well, as I'm only going to say this once. There will be absolutely no stealing of our product. If I or anyone else catches you stealing anything in this laboratory, you will be fired on the spot. We will then notify agents of the United States Immigration and Naturalization Service, who will promptly deport you back to Mexico. Do you understand?"

Bautista remembered having only nodded silently.

"And keep in mind, we are watching you. From the moment you walk in and until you depart, these cameras run the entire time." Sáenz had pointed his finger upwards and Bautista had recognized several cameras positioned in the basement ceiling.

Bautista had nodded his head again in agreement. At the time he wouldn't have even considered stealing anything. In fact, Bautista had quickly become the model employee. Always showing up on time and one of the last to leave in the early morning hours.

But now, staring down the hole of a tremendous debt, Bautista created what he thought a simple and foolproof way to steal several packets of heroin from the winery. He knew of at least two drug dealers that would pay top money for his merchandise. By his calculations, he only needed to steal a few one-gram envelopes during each of his shifts. In a short amount of time, Bautista could quickly pay off his debts and no one would even know what happened.

Then he would go back to being a model employee. It was a good job, after all.

Before arriving to work that evening, and with the few remaining dollars in his pocket, Bautista purchased a small roll of double-sided carpet tape. In his efficiency apartment, he pulled down one of his few shirts in his closet, a tan button down. He opened the shirt up and laid it on his bed. Next, he peeled a strip of double-sided carpet tape from the roll and removed the shiny brown paper that prevented the tape from adhering on both sides. He discarded the tape and kept the section of shiny brown paper. He placed the shiny brown paper on the inside right portion of his shirt. Bautista then grabbed a roll of duct tape and taped all four edges of the brown shiny paper down to the shirt. He then put on his shirt, leaving it unbuttoned. Next, Bautista peeled a smaller section of carpet tape and this time slowly and carefully positioned the tape directly on his skin, just below his right rib cage. He pressed his work shirt from the outside, ensuring that the brown-paper backing pressed over the entire length of carpet tape on his skin. Bautista then pulled the shirt away, confirming the carpet tape did not stick to the paper backing or the inside of his shirt. Satisfied with his work, Bautista quickly finished dressing to catch his ride to South Plain Cellars.

Jaime Sáenz stood up and watched the television sets at the far end of the room. Both images came from live camera feeds directed at the six workers, with one camera positioned behind three workers and the other camera in a similar and opposite position. This allowed anyone to quickly observe each worker cutting and packaging the heroin inside the light-blue wax envelopes. Along with the pocketless laboratory coats, the cameras also discouraged any theft of product.

A few hours later, Bautista turned his head as he heard the noise of Sáenz's surveillance room door open. Averting his eyes away from the office,

Bautista noticed from the corner of his eyes that Sáenz left the room and went up the basement stairs. Bautista seized his opportunity and, using his left hand, he quickly unbuttoned the bottom buttons of his laboratory coat and three lower buttons on his work shirt. He kept his right hand on top of the table and simulated the appearance of continuing his job so as to not alert his fellow coworkers, all of whom stayed busy with their own work.

Bautista grabbed two of the heroin-filled wax envelopes with his right hand and lowered them underneath the table. He then pulled his body closer to the table to obstruct any view from above his head. His left thumb and index finger grabbed the packaged heroin from his right hand. He carefully raised his right hand above the table and pretended to continue his work. He then angled his chest as close as he could to the table, simultaneously pushing his left hand and the two envelopes inside his lab coat and then inside his shirt. He pressed the envelopes on the double-sided carpet tape on his skin. Just as he'd hoped, the envelopes adhered to the carpet tape. A small grin appeared on Bautista's lips, concealed by his N95 mask. He leaned back from the table and quickly rebuttoned his work shirt and lab coat. Bautista finished his concealment by pressing and rubbing the outside of his laboratory coat over the tape and drugs to ensure a good seal.

Bautista returned to his small apartment in the early morning. He unbuttoned his shirt and observed the two small blue envelopes stuck to the tape on his body. Removing the carpet tape off his skin was much more painful than he expected, and a few pieces of adhesive remained, despite his best attempts to scrub it off with soap and water.

Either way, Bautista was elated. Once he sold these off, he planned to do the same thing tomorrow night. In a few weeks, he would be out of debt.

64

Monday, August 22, 1994
7:58 a.m. MDT
El Paso, Texas

Special Agent in Charge Brian Harris examined the large photographs on his desk, along with Supervising Special Agent Easton Derderian. Harris had expected the photographs Bud Garza took to reveal activity on South Plains Cellars' crush pad. However, there was one picture he didn't expect: a large closeup of a bespectacled man, Hispanic in origin, matching the image of a man seen on the crush pad. Derderian held the photograph up for a closer look and spoke.

"What did you say his name was again?"

"Jaime Sáenz."

"Well, this Bud kid got a great picture, especially close up, albeit at a ninety-degree angle. I wonder how he was able to snap this picture without this Jaime guy knowing?"

"Yeah, I wondered the same thing. The kid is deft at taking pictures."

Derderian studied the picture closer. "What did he say his name was again?"

"Sáenz, Jaime." Harris paused and grabbed his notepad. "Funny thing, there is no one with that name from the surveillance work we did from the farmhouse a few months ago." Harris paused briefly in thought. "Well, whoever he is, let's hope we can find out more about this Señor Jaime Sáenz. Judith is faxing that same picture to all our DEA stations in Mexico. Hopefully, we will get lucky and find out more about this guy."

Thinking of Mexico brought up another matter for Harris.

"So, how's the Gonzalez investigation going?"

"Better. We are waiting to hear from our informants in Juárez. Once we get what we need from them, we'll have enough for a warrant."

"Good."

Harris's phone rang. He picked up the receiver.

"Harris here."

"Brian, how was the weekend?"

Harris grinned. "Good, Vernon, how was yours?"

"Good."

"I'm glad you called. I've got some follow-up work planned in Lubbock in the next few weeks and for the life of me, I can't get a hotel room on Friday, September twenty-third or for the rest of the weekend, for that matter."

"Well, you know why? Don't ya?"

"No. What am I missing?"

"That's Tech homecoming weekend. They're playing Southern Methodist University that Saturday."

Harris completely forgot about one of the biggest sporting events on the South Plains, Texas Tech homecoming week. Hotel rooms in Lubbock during homecoming were booked months in advance and very difficult to obtain, especially on short notice. For those lucky ones that did land a hotel room, the room rates were exceedingly above normal market prices.

"Well, do you mind if I crash at your place that weekend then? Stacey is out of town that weekend as well, visiting her folks back home in The Colony. She's taking Robbie with her. She told me her parents have gone too many months without spoiling their grandson."

"Sure thing. What day are you coming over?"

"Flying in on Friday morning and then heading back to El Paso on that Monday."

"No problem. I'll tell Trish. She will be happy to see ya again."

"Thanks, Vernon. See you in a few weeks."

"See ya then, partner."

The line went dead, and Harris hung up the phone.

"So, you going back to Lubbock? Want me to join ya?"

Agent Harris looked at Derderian. "Maybe. But we may have trouble finding you a place to stay."

"Late September," Derderian said with a knowing nod. "Homecoming."

"How come everybody but me remembers that!"

65

Friday, September 9, 1994
10:31 a.m. MDT
El Paso, Texas

Agent Derderian approached Agent Harris's office holding several papers he had just retrieved from the facsimile machine. Harris's office door was open, and Derderian knocked on the inside door frame.

"Boss, you got a minute?"

Harris sat in his office chair, reviewing the latest investigations of his department. Keeping his eyes and head down, he replied, "Whatcha got, Easton?"

"A fax from our DEA station based in Insurgentes, Mexico. We got confirmation on Jaime Sáenz."

Harris raised his head quickly. "Read it."

Derderian read off the facsimile report, which began with a grainy black-and-white photograph of Sáenz at the top of the page. Harris listened intently as Derderian read Sáenz's known biography from his time in Bolivia to his career in surveillance. He continued to read how the team at the Insurgentes station provided information about Sáenz's associations with several Mexican drug gangs. The report concluded with the fact that Sáenz's last known whereabouts dated almost two years back and was last linked with Gustavo del Victorio Herrencia, better known as "El Astuto," and Santiago Zavala.

"Zavala? Santiago Zavala?"

Derderian doubled-checked the fax and confirmed, "Yep, Santiago Zavala."

"The DEA has been chasing that guy since the late eighties. His name appeared in multiple investigations over the years, but we've never been able to nab him."

"Should we tell the Insurgentes branch that we found Jaime Sáenz?"

"Not yet."

"Why not?"

"Information like that may end up on El Astuto's or Zavala's front doorstep. And if that happens, you can bet that Jaime Sáenz will be moving on somewhere else very quickly. No, we need to keep this between you and me."

Derderian nodded in agreement.

66

Saturday, September 10, 1994
4:07 a.m. CDT
South Plains Cellars

Bautista De Soto finished his work, packaging the last gram of heroin inside the small, blue wax envelope. Bautista looked around the table at his five fellow coworkers and spoke. The N95 mask over his mouth muffled his words.

"Does anyone need some help finishing up?"

All five coworkers shook their heads back and forth, and several whispered, "No."

"I'm finished," Bautista then said, this time much louder.

Sáenz heard Bautista's words and walked over to him.

"Bautista, you did good work here today. Wait for the others to finish. You all will receive your payment for this week; then, as always, you all can leave at the same time."

Sáenz walked back to his workstation behind the windows. With Sáenz's back to Bautista, he placed both of his hands just below his rib cage and made a circular motion on his belly, pressing down on his shirt. He wanted to double-check that the four small blue wax envelopes taped to his skin were secure. He even feigned his actions with a spoken comment.

"I'm starving. Can't wait to get something to eat."

Bautista cleaned up his workstation, stood up and walked toward the large windows of Sáenz's surveillance office. His fellow workers one by one finished their work and walked toward the glass, forming a line behind him. Sáenz waited until the last worker stood in line, sitting inside the surveillance room, with the bank of television sets, videocassette recorders and other audiovisual equipment behind him. Sáenz sat at his desk looking at each worker in front of him, all of whom were facing Sáenz's left. He pulled the stationary microphone next to his computer terminal and spoke.

"Turn toward me."

Each of the six workers did an about-face and turned left toward Jaime Sáenz.

"Now, remove your masks and goggles."

Each worker removed the N95 mask covering their face and the goggles. Several took a deep inhale of air.

"Now remove your laboratory coats and hang them up, along with your masks and goggles."

As instructed, all six men and women did as they were told. Sáenz got up from his workstation, exited his office and approached the group of workers. He walked past each worker, handing them each five hundred dollars.

"Okay, listen up. Our next load is scheduled to arrive in two weeks. There will be twice as much product to process with this load. For that reason, I want everyone to be here Saturday, September twenty-forth, at ten p.m., instead of the usual twelve p.m. And be prepared to work the next two weeks straight in a row."

A few of the workers grumbled in disappointment.

"You'll be paid. Remember Saturday, September twenty-forth, at ten p.m. Don't be late."

Bautista put the money in his pocket and waited as Sáenz walked in front of the line and toward the metal staircase. Sáenz ascended the staircase as Bautista and his five remaining coworkers followed behind. Once Sáenz reached the top, he pushed in the door handle and the large stainless steel door opened. The white wine room was completely dark, except for the faint green light emitting from the winery's stainless steel tank temperature LED gauges. Bautista failed to raise his right foot high enough to cross the doorsill and tripped. He fell forward, narrowly missing Sáenz, and crashed on the concrete floor.

"Bautista, are you okay?" exclaimed one of his coworkers who stepped closer to provide assistance.

His face red with embarrassment, Bautista quickly stood up and spoke.

"I'm fine. Thank you."

Unbeknownst to Bautista, one of the small, light-blue wax envelopes became dislodged from the carpet tape on his skin as his body hit the floor. As Bautista stood up, gravity took over and the wax envelope of heroin began its journey toward the earth. It slipped away and fell further down, clinging precariously to the inside and bottom of Bautista's untucked shirt. A remnant of adhesive from the carpet tape temporarily held the envelope in place on his shirt.

Bautista, more embarrassed than injured, instinctively patted himself with his hands in a downward fashion and toward the ends of his shirt. That action forced the light-blue envelope to release from inside the bottom of his shirt and fly unnoticed toward the wooden pallet supporting three bags of citric acid.

Wood pallets are made of continuous, longitudinal wood beams to support the decking components and contain four-way stringer notches, which allows a forklift and its metal tines to pick up the pallet from any direction. The blue wax envelope ended up near the pallet's front stringer notch and the concrete floor, mostly out of view. With the surrounding darkness and limited light, nobody noticed Bautista's stolen packet of heroin.

Thirty minutes later, Bautista arrived at his small efficiency apartment. Other than two large bruises, one on his right shoulder and another on his right knee, he was fine. His excitement over his latest score overruled the mild pain from his fall. He quickly unbuttoned his shirt and looked down at his belly. To his astonishment, he noticed only three light-blue wax envelopes stuck to the carpet tape on his skin. He looked at his shirt and examined the insides thoroughly. He removed his shoes and stuck his right hand inside each shoe. Next, he removed his pants and turned them inside out, frantically looking for the missing fourth wax envelope. All his efforts failed, and he sat down on the edge of his bed going through each motion of the evening. He absolutely knew he removed four wax envelopes and adhered them to the carpet tape on his belly. When his shift ended, he remembered feeling the four envelopes through his shirt when he rubbed his stomach in front of his coworkers, pretending to be hungry. Bautista's mind began to race with consequences.

67

Saturday, September 10, 1994
6:58 p.m. CDT
South Plains Cellars

"Ladies and gentlemen. I'm proud to announce the arrival of Mr. and Mrs. G. H. Williams!"

The entire room stood up and cheered as the bride and groom entered the barrel room. The announcer then introduced the maid of honor and best man, followed by each respective bridesmaid and groomsman, each pair entering the room together to cheering applause.

When Jill and Bud arrived, Worthington and Jason were both inside the kitchen, taking a quick break.

"I have never poured that much wine at one time," remarked Jason.

"Same here, and that was only the first round," added Worthington.

"Jason, how much wine did we pour so far?"

"Well, with two hundred people, each getting two eight-ounce glasses, that's sixteen ounces per person. . . . Hang on a minute." Jason left the kitchen and went to the tasting room. He walked up to the cashier register and grabbed a small LED calculator and walked back to the kitchen.

"We just poured close to eleven cases of wine."

"Wow!" said Jill. "And like Worthington said, that was just the first round."

"How much so far again?" bellowed Campbell as he entered the kitchen.

"Close to eleven cases so far, boss."

"Good. Now let's get back out there and see if anybody needs refills. And once the catering company starts removing plates to prep for the wedding cake, let's do our best to remove any glasses our guests stopped drinking from and get an early start on cleaning glassware. I don't want us here all night washing four hundred wineglasses."

Campbell walked over to the dishwasher and glanced at the plastic tub of citric acid.

"Jason, where are the extra bags of citric acid?"

"Don't know. I reminded Dalton before he left earlier today."

Campbell swore to himself. "And I reminded him earlier this afternoon as well."

"Bud, do you mind heading to the back and getting us a few more bags of citric acid?"

"Sure. But the last time I went back there I got my ass chewed out by some guy named Jaime Sáenz."

Campbell frowned. He and Jaime Sáenz did not get along at all. Drew Dalton despised Sáenz as well. Both men did their best to avoid Sáenz, a tough task when everyone worked in the same building.

"Well, don't worry about Jaime Sáenz. He's not working tonight. Besides, he took some vacation time and flew off to Bolivia to visit family. He'll be gone for the next two weeks."

"Good. I'll head on over now," Bud replied with a half-smile. At the same time, Bud made a mental note for Agent Brian Harris.

Bud worked his way as discreetly as possible from the kitchen to the barrel room and entered the white wine room, pulling the two-wheel dolly behind him. He reached the back wall and took a hard right and headed for the large walk-in cooler. He pulled the dolly to a stop and parked it upright.

He then turned his attention to the walk-in cooler with the two large stainless steel doors and looked right at the door where Sáenz appeared almost three weeks ago. He walked closer and upon further inspection, the door was slightly ajar and not fully closed. He paused, looked left and right to ensure no one was near, pulled the handle and opened the door. Bud entered the small room, descended the stairs and turned on the light switch. The entire basement was illuminated.

Bud stopped at the surveillance room with floor-to-ceiling glass windows, the array of audio and visual equipment and multiple television sets lining the right side of the room. Bud pulled out his camera and took multiple pictures. He then turned left and faced the large worktable, with a large stainless steel vessel on one side and another stainless steel vessel on the other. Stainless steel pipes, shutoff valves, and different-colored hoses connected these vessels. Standard cored concrete blocks lined the outside four walls and ran along the back wall. White laboratory coats hung on a peg board, along with face masks and goggles.

Bud snapped another dozen or so pictures. The small camera counter indicated "21."

Satisfied with the pictures he took, Bud exited the basement, turned off the light switch, ascended the stairs and reentered the white wine room. He closed the large stainless steel door behind him. He looked at his watch and turned his attention to the task at hand as he pulled the dolly next to the wood pallet of citric acid.

Worthington refilled a few wineglasses at one of the back tables in the barrel room. Campbell approached him and in a quiet tone asked, "Where's Bud with the citric acid?"

Worthington shrugged his shoulder, "Don't know."

"Well, he's been gone awhile. Do me a favor and when you're finished here, go see if he needs a hand."

"You got it, Jerry."

Bud grabbed the first bag and heaved it on top of the dolly's nose plate. He then repeated the same step, depositing the second bag on top of the first. This left only one bag of citric acid remaining on the pallet.

"Fuck it, let's get all three of 'em. Less to deal with later next week," Bud said to himself.

With his right foot on the winery's concrete floor and his left foot on the edge of the pallet, Bud leaned over to grab the final bag. Once Bud raised the ninety-pound bag, the pallet instantly became lighter and shifted away from Bud's left foot—which got caught in the gap between two longitudinal beams on the pallet deck, causing Bud to start to lose his balance. To avoid doing the splits, Bud quickly dropped the bag between his legs, which landed on the edge of the pallet closest to his right foot.

Bud silently cursed at himself. He wiggled his left foot free out of the pallet decking and closed his stance with both feet on the concrete floor. He carefully picked up the citric acid bag and laid it on top of the second bag. Satisfied the load on the dolly was balanced, he walked toward the skewed wood pallet with the intention of pushing it back in its original place.

Then something blue in color caught his attention. Bud knelt down and picked it up. It was the same kind of tiny light-blue waxy envelope he'd seen two months ago.

Bud carefully opened the envelope; inside was a white, powdery substance. He carefully folded the envelope back in place and put it back on the ground, near the pallet. He pulled out his camera and took a few pictures. Putting the camera back in his right front pocket, he picked up the light-blue envelope, intending to place it in his khakis' front left pocket.

"Bud, you back here amigo?!" shouted Worthington.

Startled, Bud accidentally dropped the envelope on the ground. He quickly scanned the ground before him. He looked behind him and he couldn't see Worthington, but based on the sound of his voice, he knew he only had a few seconds before Worthington would be there. He scanned the ground around him again, but he could not find the light-blue envelope.

"Bud, where are you?!" Worthington shouted again.

Time was closing in on Bud fast. Bud took a deep breath and exhaled.

"Back here, Worthington. Getting the last bag of citric acid," replied Bud.

Panic started to settle in, and Bud looked at the ground again, in desperate fashion. He then noticed something blue sticking from the folded hem at the bottom of the right leg of his khakis. Somehow, the tiny wax envelope had fallen into the hem of his pants. He bent his left knee on the ground and pretended to adjust his loafers, while at the same time extracting the envelope from the pocket of the folded hem. Worthington walked right behind him.

"Whatcha doing, brother?"

"I think I got a small rock or something in my shoe," replied Bud.

"That sucks. Did ya get it?"

"Yep. All good."

Bud carefully held the envelope in his right hand and slowly stood up, turning his body so his left side obstructed Worthington's view of his right side. He quickly inserted his right hand into his front right pocket. He then slowly pulled his hand out.

"Dude, are you okay? It's like fifty-eight degrees in here and you are sweating bullets."

Bud didn't notice his perspiration until he took his left hand to wipe the sweat from his forehead.

"I about busted my ass getting that last bag. The wood pallet shifted on me, and I almost lost my balance."

"You got to be careful next time, brother. Those bags are bulky and hard as hell to move. Here, let me haul that over for you," replied Worthington.

"Thanks, man."

Worthington grabbed the top frame handle of the dolly, lowered it at an angle and started to pull the bags of citric acid back to the tasting room. Bud followed.

"Damn, brother. You loaded this one with three bags?"

"Yeah. Figured one less trip for you and me next week."

"Uh-huh. Well, I think this is all the weight this dolly can carry. Look at the wheels and how they're bulging at the bottom." Worthington pointed toward the two pneumatic tires.

"That's my bad. Chalk this one up as another rookie mistake," shrugged Bud.

Bud parted the large clear vinyl straps and opened both sets of French doors in and out of the barrel room. Worthington carefully navigated behind Bud and pushed the dolly and the bags of citric acid back to the kitchen.

At nine o'clock that evening, the last of the wedding guests exited South Plains Cellars. The catering crew finished removing and loading all the catering equipment, along with the round tables and chairs. Inside the kitchen, Bud, Jill, Jason and Worthington wiped and polished clean a set of freshly washed Riedel glasses, while the dishwasher cleaned the last set of twenty wineglasses.

Campbell walked into the kitchen with a large smile on his face.

"I want to thank each of you for your work tonight. I'm starting my vacation tomorrow. Jason, you and Jill are in charge this week. I'll be back here Monday, September nineteenth. Have a good evening and again, great job tonight, each of you."

Campbell waited for the tour guides to leave the winery. After grabbing his things, he walked through the establishment's front door, locked it, got in his car, and drove home for the evening.

68

Sunday, September 11, 1994
8:58 a.m. CDT
Lubbock, Texas

Bud paced back and forth in his living room. When he came back to his apartment the previous night, he had carefully undressed from his work clothes and placed the small, light-blue wax envelope on his nightstand, next to his bed. Now he put on a pair of loose-fitting boxers and tried to sleep. His mind raced about the next steps to take. He decided he couldn't do anything at this late hour. Since it was Sunday, he decided to call Agent Harris around eight in the morning, his time. He pressed and held down the number 4, and the phone rang only once.

"Harris."

"I think I found something that will be useful for your investigation."

"What did you find, Bud? Can you describe it?"

"It is the same small, light-blue wax envelope, but it's not empty. It's filled with white powder."

"What does it smell like?"

"I don't know. Hang on a minute."

Bud placed the phone receiver down on his couch arm, walked to his bedroom, grabbed the small envelope and returned to his living room couch. He picked up the phone receiver and said, "Okay," bringing the envelope closer to his nose to take a quick sniff.

"Does it have a sweet, floral, or even chemical, aroma? An underlying metallic odor?" Harris asked.

"I don't smell anything."

"Well, that rules out cocaine. How about vinegar? Does it smell of vinegar?"

"Vinegar?"

"Some versions of heroin smell like vinegar, due to the chemical process of refining it from raw opium. The more vinegar the smell, the less pure and lesser the quality."

Bud took another quick sniff.

"I smell nothing."

"Is the texture like a dry powder?"

"Yep."

"I have a strong hunch what you have, Bud, is high-grade heroin. Is the envelope the same size you described to me earlier?"

"Yep, about the size of my thumb."

Harris thought for a moment about his next steps. "What else?"

"Remember the walk-in cooler and the right-side door that was always locked? It was open."

"And?"

Bud described his descent into the basement below the winery. He remembered the television monitors, VCR machines, array of audiovisual equipment, the large worktable, the large pressure cooker tank and the smaller one, and the stainless steel pipes, valves, wires and colored hoses. He then recalled the white laboratory coats, face masks and goggles hanging on the peg board.

"Anything else?"

"Nope. That was it."

"And you got pictures of all of it?"

"Yep."

"Bud, you just described the makings of a very sophisticated drug-manufacturing laboratory."

"Are you sure? I mean, it's inside a winery. Why would somebody put a drug lab in a winery in the middle of West Texas?"

"Best place for a drug lab, in my opinion."

"*Really?*"

"Why not? Who in their right mind would believe that a West Texas winery would be housing a drug lab? Makes perfect sense if you ask me. Low population density as compared to other cities. Anything else?"

"That Jaime Sáenz guy went on vacation for a while. Campbell mentioned he was visiting family in Bolivia."

"Bolivia, huh?" Harris wrote that note down immediately.

Bud went on to explain the citric acid and wood pallet story, and how he discovered the small, light-blue wax envelope.

"I also took a picture of where it was on the floor. Well, not exactly. I picked it up to look at it first, then I placed it back where I found it and took a few pictures."

"Smart."

"Thanks. So, Agent Harris, what do you want me to do next? That should give you what you need, right?"

"I hope so. Do you have a Ziploc bag and some aluminum foil in your apartment?"

"Yes."

"Listen carefully. Pull out a small sheet of aluminum foil, only about six inches long. Once you've ripped off the foil, place that small wax envelope in the middle of the foil. Then fold the foil in half, covering up the envelope. Then, just like wrapping a present, continue folding the foil on itself from each side until all you have is, like, a small foil box. Place that foil box in the Ziploc bag. Then head over to the Federal Express store first thing Monday morning and send me both your film cartridge and the Ziploc bag priority overnight. Got it?"

"Yes sir."

"Good job, Bud. When I get your package, I will reach out. It will probably be late afternoon, Tuesday the thirteenth. Will you be around?"

"I'll be around."

"Good." Harris hung up his home phone receiver.

Bud replaced the Trimline receiver into its cradle and leaned into his couch in relief.

"I sure hope this is the end," Bud said to himself.

69

Tuesday, September 13, 1994
1:08 p.m. MDT
Drug Enforcement Agency, El Paso Intelligence Center

Director Phil Colangelo, joined by Easton Derderian, sat on the opposite side of Brian Harris's desk. Colangelo picked up the last photograph from one of two piles on the desk and examined it. A few seconds later, he placed it on top of the pile of the other photographs.

"Impressive photographic work. You said your source works at the winery as a tour guide?"

"Yes sir," replied Harris.

"And what about the lab analysis on the drug sample?"

"The lab is finishing that up"—Harris looked at his watch—"should be very soon."

"You know I'm still pissed that you went around me, especially when I told you to stop your investigation."

"Phil, you said 'nobody on your staff' will investigate or question anyone at South Plains Cellars. Bud Garza is not on my staff."

Colangelo smirked at Harris's comment. "I think you need more evidence."

"What do you mean?"

"You've got pictures of what looks like a milk truck off-loading something liquid into the winery. And you have pictures of what many people in our line of work would consider a drug laboratory, complete with a high-tech surveillance system, and if your drug sample gets confirmed, the end product.

But what we don't have is the process in between. If your source, this Bud Garza, can get photographs of that, then we will have the complete picture."

"C'mon, Phil. You know we have enough for a warrant, especially since the winery falls inside Judge Lawrence's district. Judge Loose has approved multiple warrants for cases like this, with far less evidence."

Director Colangelo stood up and sternly replied, "Brian, I'm fully aware of how useful U.S. District Federal Judge Louis Lawrence is to our efforts with investigations. However, need I remind you of the ass-chewing I received less than two months ago from Assistant U.S. Attorney Justin Shamkin about this very investigation? We have to make sure our evidence and case against South Plains Cellars is tighter than a frog's ass. Do you understand?"

"Yes sir," replied Harris.

Nobody talked for a moment and silence entered the room. Then, there was a knock at the door. Colangelo opened it.

A petite blond woman, Gina Constance, the lead technician for the DEA Drug Analysis Office, walked inside. She approached Agent Harris and handed him a piece of green-and-white paper with small holes on each side.

"Brian, we got back your results for that sample you dropped off late this morning," she said in her heavy New Orleans accent. "Our analysis showed 80.7 percent pure heroin, with the remaining 19.3 percent C-twelve, H-twenty-two, O-eleven."

"What is that chemical compound?" Derderian asked.

"Why it's sugar, honey. But not a sweet as me," answered a smiling Gina.

"Definitely not as sweet as you, Gina," Harris agreed with a wink. "Thanks for rushing on this one."

"You are most welcome, Mr. Harris. Y'all have a good day." Gina Constance promptly left the office and closed the door behind her.

Harris whistled out loud, "Wow, eighty percent pure heroin. Easton, have you or the team run into anything that pure lately?"

"Nope. We call that *unicorn* heroin," replied Derderian.

"May I?" Colangelo gestured toward Harris for the drug analysis paperwork, which Harris immediately handed to him. Colangelo began reading the printout. "All right, Brian," he said, his eyes still scanning the page, "shoot me straight. Do you think this Bud Garza can get us what we need?"

"I think so. The young man has been super careful."

"Okay. Keep me informed, *daily*. Hopefully this college kid can get us the information we need. Once we get it, that will give me a better leg to stand on when I call Shamkin."

"After we get the warrant, right?"

"Correct, after we get the warrant."

70

Tuesday, September 20, 1994
8:03 p.m. CDT
South Plains Cellars

As the last two ladies from the Junior League of Lubbock wine-tasting event left the tasting room, Bud finished polishing the last Riedel glass. Campbell had dinner plans with his wife and Bud had agreed to stay behind to work solo, agreeing to lock up the tasting room for the evening.

Bud locked the front door, turned off the tasting-room lights, slid his timecard into the timecard machine and heard the machine's reliable *click-thump*. He grabbed his keys and did a quick double-check in his pockets. He walked back into the darkness of the tasting room and immediately noticed bright lights emitting from the crush pad. He walked toward the source of the light, viewing the crush pad from the French doors that led to the tasting room patio and heard the distinctive beeping sound of a large truck backing up. Bud watched and stared.

Bill Masterson looked at his watch and remarked, "You are slipping, Armando, three minutes late on delivery."

"Hey, it's not my fault. Too much highway construction."

Armando had done his best to make up time after hitting construction highway work on US Highway 87 just north of Tahoka.

"Do you think Jaime is going to be pissed?"

"Oh, you can count on it."

Armando drove the Freightliner in reverse and eased the tanker on the concrete crush pad, parking *away* from the winery's crusher-destemmer. Armando dropped the Freightliner's clutch into neutral, turned off the ignition and both men hopped out of the cab.

"Lights, please," shouted Sáenz over the loudspeaker.

The halogen lights illuminating the crush pad extinguished. The winery's large garage door opened and only one light emitted from the red wine room, nowhere near as bright.

Hector emerged from the red wine room and walked toward Masterson.

"Señor Bill, you are *tres minutos* late," Hector said, shaking his head.

"Hey, we're used to arriving at midnight. Jaime wanted us here four hours earlier."

"Let's hope Mr. Sáenz doesn't yell too much, my friend."

"I doubt it. Here you go." Masterson handed his set of keys to Hector.

Hector then turned around and shouted, "Boys, let's get started! Remember, the two-inch hoses, please."

Hector clapped his hands, and three men quickly went to work. A few moments later, Hector spoke again.

"Is tank four ready?"

Ten seconds later, a voice in the winery replied, albeit a bit faint, but easily heard.

"Tank four ready, Mr. Hector."

Hector turned the valve handle counterclockwise. The grape juice and opium mixture, along with dissolved cornstarch, guzzled into the winery. To the west of the winery, a large lightning bolt flashed and seven seconds later a large boom of thunder followed. A strong gust of cool wind hit the winery.

"We got some bad weather coming in, Hector," remarked Masterson.

"No worries, Mr. Bill. We should be done here in about twenty minutes."

8 8 8

Bud watched the men on the crush pad working in the darkness, the only light emitting from the red wine room. He remembered from his conversations with Drew Dalton that grape harvest and crush ended on the Texas High Plains in early August. Dalton mentioned something about "growing degree days," which are longer in cooler climates and shorter in hotter climates. He explained that in cooler-climate winemaking regions in California, Oregon and Washington, crush starts in late August and continues through October. In Texas, with a much hotter climate and shorter growing degree days, wine grapes reached maturation sooner. Harvested grapes in Texas arrive at wineries starting in late June and finish at the end of July and/or the first week of August.

Even if Dalton's winemaking team were working late, off-loading grape juice from another state, why would the lights of the crush pad be turned off? Bud remembered how he and others had been invited to work a weekend wedding event on a warm late-June night. Dalton had allowed Bud and a few interested wedding guests to watch him and his team crush Chardonnay grapes on the crush pad under the bright halogen lights.

Bud unlocked the front doors of the tasting room and quickly walked outside to his car and retrieved the special DEA camera and two extra rolls of film. He hustled back inside the winery, through the darkness of the tasting room, then through the barrel room and to the white wine room. With the lights out in the white wine room, the only light emitted came from the green liquid-crystal LED temperature displays on each tank. Bud carefully walked through the white wine room and approached the red wine room. The garage door between the white and red wine rooms was open and Bud began to hear voices. He carefully peeled away one of the clear vinyl straps near the right side of the garage door and entered the red wine room. Directly in front of him was an elevated concrete tank pad and a large stainless steel red wine tank. Just to the right of the large tank stood a stainless steel staircase. Bud quickly ascended the steps, carefully walking tiptoe to prevent the heels of his Cole Haan shoes from touching the steps and causing unwanted noise.

Now standing fifteen feet above the concrete tank pad and seventeen feet above the ground floor, Bud inched softly along the metal catwalk. The voices became louder and easier to understand. He picked a spot in the shadows behind one of the large red wine tanks and noticed two men conversing. One he recognized immediately as Jaime Sáenz, holding a black briefcase. He didn't recognize the taller, skinnier man with the cowboy hat.

Bud pulled his camera out of his pocket and took a couple pictures.

"You are late," said Sáenz.

"Yes, I know, Jaime. We can't control highway construction in Texas. Better late than never, and we should be just about done before this storm rolls in. By the looks of it, could be a nasty one."

"It better not happen next time," said Sáenz yawning. Twenty hours prior, Sáenz had boarded a plane from La Paz International Airport in Bolivia.

"It won't, I promise," lied Masterson.

Jaime Sáenz placed the black briefcase on top of the tank pad and waited. Another lightning flash and another boom of thunder filled the night sky. The storm was getting closer.

Hector then shouted, "All done! Pumps off! Now, boys, quickly get those hoses removed before this storm hits us."

Hector and the other men quickly went to work, removing the hoses, closing the tanker's lid and securing the valve cover over the tanker's spigot. In a few minutes all the men and equipment were safely inside but Armando, who drove the tanker truck under the protection of the crush pad awning and waited as rain began to pour in torrents.

Sáenz removed both clasps on the briefcase and opened the lid.

Masterson again saw his favorite founding father smiling back at him. He nodded and started placing the bundles of cash into his duffel bag. Once completed, Masterson lifted his right hand to his Stetson and tipped his hat.

"Thank you, gentlemen."

Sáenz replied, "Unless we say otherwise, we expect to see you again here in two weeks' time."

"You got it, Jaime. Pleasure doing business with you."

He quickly walked to his rig, opened the passenger door and hopped in. Armando drove the empty tanker truck slowly off the crush pad and into the pouring rain.

Bud crouched lower on the catwalk and took a minute to catch his breath. He could feel his heart thumping through his chest. He had never seen so much money in his life.

He watched as Sáenz looked at Hector, pointed his finger toward the large garage door that led out to the red wine room to the crush pad and barked out his next instructions.

"Close it up and start the extraction process. If you need me, I'll be in my office."

"Yes, Mr. Jaime."

Bud stayed in place and peered around the corner of the top of the red wine tank at Jaime Sáenz, carrying the empty briefcase and walking to the white wine room.

Bud then heard the loud splashing of liquid at the end of the catwalk, opposite from where he came. He then decided to investigate the sound, stood up in a crouching position and quietly walked along the catwalk. The splashing sound got louder.

He reached the end of the catwalk, before it took a hard left toward the large wine tank making the splashing sound. Two men stood near the bottom of the tank. One of the men walked over the adjoining concrete tank pad and turned on a radio. Spanish music began to play.

Bud looked at the top of the large wine tank, above which were two crisscrossed I beams. Unlike the other wine tanks, this tank, known by winemakers as an open-top fermentation tank, did not have a contained top with a manhole cover on its crescent. Above the tank spun clockwise two stainless steel spigots that sprayed liquid into the tank below.

Bud's nostrils filled with the confused scent of corn chips, grape juice, and the malodor of ammonia. He held his nose and breathed through his mouth as the stench of ammonia almost forced him to sneeze.

Inside the surveillance room, Jaime Sáenz sat in his chair. He was thoroughly exhausted, having failed to get any sleep on each leg of his flight home. He folded his arms, lowered his head, and closed his eyes. Minutes later, he was fast asleep.

Camera 9, active and recording, filled the television screen on Sáenz's left. A few minutes later, the image of a man crouching on the catwalk appeared from the bottom right. Nobody in the surveillance room noticed.

Bud walked closer to the open-top wine tank to get a picture of the contents inside, doing his best to inhale and exhale through his mouth only. Suddenly, he was engulfed in darkness, followed by the very loud sound of thunder.

Two miles east of South Plains Cellars, a lightning bolt struck the power line along CR 7600—and the power grid servicing the winery and the surrounding area went offline.

Immediately, South Plains Cellars' backup generators fired up, its main priority to provide power to cool the liquid propylene flowing inside the stainless steel wine tanks' propylene jackets. Without this control in place, the temperature of the wines inside each tank would slowly start to warm up and ruin hundreds of thousands of dollars' worth of wine.

Bud slightly startled at the sound of a woman's recorded voice speaking over the winery's intercom system.

"Emergency lighting activated."

A small amount of remaining power from the generators was then diverted to produce emergency low-level lighting in the white and red wine rooms.

The low illumination of the emergency lighting did little to improve vision in the red wine room. Hector stopped in his tracks and shouted.

"Boys, stop what you are doing and meet me in the white wine room. There's not enough light in here."

Bud heard the man shout, but he spoke too quickly for him to discern exactly what he said. As his eyes began to adjust to the low level of light in the vast room, Bud turned his head and noticed a brighter glow of light coming from the white wine room.

Bud began to retrace his steps along the catwalk back toward the white wine room. He then heard the ring of the wall-mounted phone in the white wine room and stopped.

Hector pressed the speaker button in the phone and spoke.

"Hello?"

"Hector, it's Drew."

"Señor Drew. Good you call. Electricity is no more. Everything out."

"Are the backup generators working? Are the tanks still cooling?"

"Yes, Señor Drew. Temperature good. No change."

"Good. Keep everybody in the white wine room for the time being. It's a bigger room and has more emergency lighting. Also, close the garage door between the white wine room and red wine room. We've got to keep that place chilled as best we can just in case the power doesn't come back online for a while. I will be at the winery in about ten minutes."

"Very good, Señor Drew." Hector hit the speaker button again to disconnect the call and manually closed the garage door, using the rope-and-pulley system on the door's right side. The garage door slammed shut and now Bud found himself alone in the giant red wine room.

Bud overheard Hector's side of the conversation with Dalton and could guess the rest. He seized his chance and quickly walked along the catwalk back to the tank. Pinching his nose with his left finger and thumb and holding the camera with his right hand, he walked to the open-top container and clicked his first picture. The entire tank, along with its contents, flashed with a bright light and then went dark. Bud's eyes began to see negative images in a purple hue of the picture he took as his retinas reacted to the bright light of the flash. Bud waited until his eyes adjusted back to the darkness. He repeated the same process three more times, this time closing his eyes before he snapped each picture.

After taking his pictures, Bud walked along the catwalk and toward the metal staircase, stopping close to the tank where he heard Dalton and the man named Hector speaking. He sat down and considered his options.

He could scale down from the catwalk, walk toward the crush pad garage door, open it and make his way back to the safety of the tasting room. But he worried that the power might kick on at any time and someone might see him in the red wine room or hear the crush pad garage door open. He decided to wait.

71

Tuesday, September 20, 1994
9:33 p.m. CDT
South Plains Cellars

Ten minutes later, Bud heard the crush pad door open. He looked around the large tank and saw Drew Dalton entering the red wine room carrying a bright flashlight. Dalton then manually opened the garage door to the white wine room, entered and let the door close behind him.

Jaime Sáenz, who woke up from his nap right after the power went out, was standing with Hector inside the white wine room.

"When can we start back up, Drew? We are in the middle of our extraction process, and I don't want any delays."

Despising Sáenz, Dalton tried to hold back his disdain. "Well, Jaime, good to see you tonight. Man, you look exhausted. Are you feeling all right?"

Sáenz's eyes were swollen around the sockets, and he let out a yawn.

"Don't worry about me. And you didn't answer my question."

"Can't do anything now, Jaime. It's in the hands of the folks at Lubbock Power & Light."

"There's no way you can divert any of the power from the generators?"

"And lose hundreds of thousands of gallons of wine? You're fucking kidding me, right?"

Sáenz wasn't used to people talking to him in such a manner.

"Listen to me, Drew, if you think you can tell me what to—"

"Tell you what?" Dalton cut Sáenz off. "You see all this?"

Dalton waved his hands toward all the chilled wine tanks in the white wine room.

"This is all my responsibility. That shit you are doing in the red wine room, that's your responsibility. Your shit doesn't have to be constantly chilled to keep it from going bad. My stuff does. And right now, my stuff has priority!"

Sáenz seethed with anger. Suddenly, the power kicked on and the white wine room's halogens began to glow brighter. The backup generator turned off, along with the emergency lighting.

"See? All better. Now if you will excuse me, I'm headed home."

Dalton made his way back to the crush pad. He pressed the white wine garage door, and the door immediately opened. Dalton smelled the strong stench of ammonia and shouted to Hector.

"Hector! Open this crush pad garage door and keep it open. And while you're at it, turn on all the exhaust fans in the red wine room. This place smells like shit."

"Yes sir, Señor Drew," replied Hector.

"Back to work!" shouted Sáenz.

A few minutes after the exhaust fans started up, Bud could breathe better. He walked as close as he could to the tank with the strong smell of ammonia. Domingo, one of Hector's assistants, and another man assembled the hydraulic plate and frame filter press near the tank, attaching the hoses and a pump.

Bud watched and took a few more pictures discreetly. After crouching for some time, he decided to sit down on the catwalk to give his legs some rest. The metal grate of the catwalk on his buttocks didn't feel much better. He shifted his weight to ease the pressure on his right side and almost fell off the catwalk. A quick grasp with his left hand on the catwalk support prevented him from falling to the wine tank pad fifteen feet below. Adrenaline kicked in and Bud decided to stand in a crouching position for the time being.

Thirty minutes later, the men turned off the hydraulic plate and frame filter press, unscrewed the ram and exposed the filter plates, scrapping a wet, powdered substance into a large holding tray below. One man scooped up the mixture and deposited it into two large five-gallon buckets. Another man then carried the buckets away. Bud walked carefully down the catwalk toward the white wine room and saw the same man carrying the buckets enter the room. He snapped two quick pictures and went back to his original perch, watching the same routine.

Two hours passed by as Bud observed maintenance activities and other interactions from his catwalk perch. Eventually, one of the workmen appeared with a water hose and began cleaning the individual plates off the hydraulic press. Bud began to hear more voices of several people entering the red wine room. He counted six new people below him.

After exchanging pleasantries, Hector and his team walked outside to the crush pad while the six new arrivals walked toward the white wine room. Hector killed the lights in the red wine room and closed the garage door to the crush pad and the garage door to the white wine room.

Bud knew he was alone again and decided it was time to leave. He carefully walked along the catwalk and descended the metal staircase.

At the crush pad garage door he waited for a few minutes, stretching his sore legs.

Hearing no more noises on the pad, he pressed the button, and the door opened. Once outside, he reached back inside and pressed the button again. The garage door came down.

Alone on the crush pad, Bud walked quickly back to the front doors of the tasting room, inserted the tasting room key and locked the door. Bud opened the keypad cover to the alarm, punched the code that Campbell gave him four and half hours prior and hit the ENTER button. He walked quickly to his car and drove home.

Twenty minutes later Bud was in his apartment. He didn't bother to take his wet clothes off. He fell on top of his bed and a short time later was fast asleep.

Bud woke up at 9:33 in the morning, missing his International Politics class. His legs and lower back were still sore from his extensive crouching the previous night. He removed his previous day's clothes and took a quick shower and got dressed.

Refreshed, Bud headed to his couch and picked up the receiver of his Trimline phone. He dialed Agent Harris. Harris did not pick up the phone, so Bud left a message informing Harris of the previous night's events, the power going out, his experience on the elevated catwalk and the film cartridges coming his way via Federal Express.

Bud then hung up and headed out for his remaining Wednesday classes.

72

Thursday, September 22, 1994
10:07 a.m. MDT
Drug Enforcement Agency, El Paso Intelligence Center

"Easton, meet me down at the photo lab," requested Agent Harris. "Latest pictures are done developing."

"Sure thing," replied Derderian.

Minutes later both men stared at the large photographs. The first two photographs featured a large tanker truck, like the one Traegar Jackson mentioned back in mid-June, and a man in a cowboy hat, speaking with someone who looked like Jaime Sáenz. The next two featured an open briefcase resting on a tank pad, with what looked for all the world like thousands of dollars. The next photographs were of men working around what Harris and Derderian guessed was a large filter machine, and a man carrying two buckets away from it.

What followed were flash photographs detailing a large tank and what appeared to be tan-colored foam on the top and inside of it.

"That must have been when the power went out," remarked Harris.

"How much you want to wager, Easton, that mixture is the raw opium, mixed with grape juice?"

"Yeah, I agree. But what is that tan-colored foam at the top?"

"I don't know."

Harris and Derderian finished their preliminary review of the photographs. Harris then placed a call to Director Phil Colangelo. Six minutes later, Colangelo arrived at the office's photo lab and reviewed the photographs.

"What's that beige stuff inside the tank?" Colangelo asked reviewing the flash photos.

Harris explained, "Our guy inside said the power went out and was able to get these pictures after all the workers went into another part of the winery. As for the tan-colored foam, we don't know."

Colangelo nodded his head and finished examining the photographs. Harris and Derderian said nothing and waited.

"All right, gentlemen, you've convinced me. Please proceed with obtaining a warrant."

Harris clapped his hands together in satisfaction. "Excellent. Thanks, Phil."

"When do you want to execute the search warrant?"

"As soon as we can," said Harris. "Easton and I can put together the affidavit and warrant application in the next few hours. We will detail *what* kind of illegal drugs we are looking for, *where* we think we will find these drugs and *why* we believe we will find them at South Plains Cellars."

"You know this already, Brian, but that warrant application better be as *detailed* as possible. And I want to review it before you present it to Judge Lawrence."

"Of course. When do you plan on calling Assistant U.S. Attorney Justin Shamkin?"

"Well, after you and Easton provide me with that detailed warrant application and we get it signed by our friendly 'neutral and detached magistrate,' then and only then will I call Shamkin."

"So, let's say we get everything you need," continued Harris, "and we get the judge's signature tomorrow, Friday morning. That will give us time to get a team to Lubbock and we can execute the search warrant, say this Saturday morning?"

"That sounds good. About how many agents will you need?"

"At a minimum, fifteen agents. Ten agents from El Paso and five from our Amarillo office."

"Fine. Good work here, gentlemen." Director Colangelo turned and left the lab.

Derderian gathered the photographs and he and Harris went back to Harris's office to start the warrant application.

Three hours and a great deal of back-and-forth later, Harris looked up from a large printout before him.

"Easton, this must be the most detailed warrant application I have ever read. Nicely done."

"Thanks, Brian."

"Okay, I've got a flight to catch. If all goes as planned, Phil will sign off on our warrant application today, and then tomorrow morning, you will pay a visit to U.S. District Federal Judge Louis Lawrence and get his signature. I will then see you and the El Paso agents I've listed here at Lubbock airport Saturday morning. Our Amarillo team will drive down that morning, with vehicles and armaments, fully loaded and at the ready."

"So, I guess we're flying commercial?" replied Derderian, disappointment in his voice.

"Yes, no need to fire up the Beechcrafts for this one."

The EPIC office was home to a small fleet of Beechcraft twin-turboprop King Air aircraft, which could carry up to ten passengers and was often deployed for elite-level DEA operations in Mexico and Central America.

Agent Brian Harris gathered his things and shook Derderian's hand firmly. "See you in a few days."

73

Thursday, September 22, 1994
6:58 p.m. CDT
Lubbock, Texas

Cheryl opened the passenger door of Bud's car and stepped out.

Bud reached around toward his back-seat floorboard and grabbed a brown paper bag. He then exited his car and met Cheryl at the hood, and from there they walked to the front door of Cheryl's house.

"So, what's in the bag?" inquired Cheryl at the door.

"A bottle of South Plains Cellars Chardonnay. Surprise for your mom."

"Well, aren't you sweet?"

Bud grinned back at Cheryl and said nothing. Jill Hatten previously mentioned to Bud that every now and then, Jerry Campbell encouraged the tour guides to take a bottle of South Plains Cellars wine home to sample and become more familiar with the chosen varietal.

The Truett home door opened, and Trish greeted them both.

"Cheryl, honey, so good to see you." Trish embraced her daughter at the doorstep with a big hug.

"You too, Mom."

Bud smiled and said, "Good evening, Mrs. Truett. I took the liberty of bringing you a bottle of Chardonnay. It's not Kendall-Jackson, but I think you will like it."

Trish smiled. "Aww, isn't that a nice gesture. Thank you, Bud." Trish took the bottle of wine and after a few awkward seconds said, "Well, just don't stand there, come on inside, both of you. Cheryl, your father and Brian are in the back near the pool."

"Uncle Brian is here? Cool!" exclaimed Cheryl.

Cheryl and Bud walked through the house and arrived at the Truett's back patio. Cheryl blurted out, "Hi, Daddy!"

Both Brian and Vernon stood up from the table and Cheryl quickly hugged Vernon. While Cheryl and Vernon embraced each other, Agent Harris smiled and nodded toward Bud, but said nothing.

"Daddy, you remember Bud Garza?"

"Yes, of course."

Vernon extended his right hand. Bud shook Vernon's hand with a firm grip.

"Mr. Truett, good to see you again, sir."

Vernon motioned his head toward Harris's direction. "I think you remember Brian Harris?"

Bud looked toward Harris and extended his right hand. "Yes sir, I remember. You helped me move Cheryl's armoire from the garage and into my Explorer about five weeks ago."

"That's right," Harris said shaking Bud's hand. "Bud, good to see you again."

Vernon decided to change the subject. "I read the other day that O.J. Simpson has already hired some of the most expensive defense attorneys money can buy. Can you believe that guy? I still can't believe O.J. Simpson did what he did. I know he killed his wife and that Ron guy. Why else did he drive all over creation in that white Bronco trying to avoid the L.A. police when he was supposed to turn himself in?"

"The media is already saying that it will be the trial of the century, bigger than the Lindbergh trial," added Harris.

"When do you think the trial will start, Daddy?" inquired Cheryl.

"Yeah, Counselor, that's a good question." said Harris.

"Well, with that *dream team* of lawyers that O.J. hired and how crowded the docket is for a major metropolitan area like Los Angeles, I bet that trial won't start until early next year. I can only imagine all the pre-court hearings that will occur, along with trying to get a jury of peers that have not been influenced by all the damn media coverage."

"Well, Bud and I are going to help Mom with dinner."

"Honey, don't be silly," Vernon said. "Bud, please sit down and *Cheryl and I* will help her mother get dinner ready."

Cheryl and Vernon returned inside the house and Bud sat down at the table. Harris pulled the empty chair next to Bud and sat down.

"So, looks like we have some time to ourselves," Harris spoke in hushed tone.

Bud looked over his shoulder as Cheryl and Vernon walked inside the house and whispered in reply, "Yeah, it looks like it."

"We can talk here, Bud."

"Okay, you're the boss."

"So, anything new since you sent me that last batch of photos?"

"New? I thought I was done!" exclaimed Bud. He pulled his chair closer to the DEA agent.

"My ass almost got caught this past Tuesday night. That last batch of photographs I sent you shows *everything*. I got pictures of the tanker truck, all the guys on the crush pad, one guy paying another guy a shit ton of cash in a briefcase, and the guys inside the winery processing the mixture."

Frustrated, Bud continued. "You know the power went out there for about fifteen minutes? I almost fell off an elevated catwalk seventeen feet above the ground getting your pictures. I was super close to one of the tanks. I smelled ground-up corn chips mixed with grape juice, but then I was almost knocked over by a strong smell of ammonia."

"That's the smell of raw opium," confirmed Harris.

"Cool, thanks for the aromatic tip, Agent Harris," Bud quipped.

Noticing that Bud had obviously reached his limit these past few weeks, Harris decided to back off with questions for now. Unlike so many other informants, Bud was helping him to just help him. It wasn't somebody looking for a cash payoff, to cut a deal with a prosecutor or seek a lesser prison sentence. Hell, Bud hadn't even *asked* to be paid. Harris changed his approach and spoke with compassion in his voice.

"Look, Bud, I want to personally thank you for everything you've done these past few weeks. What you provided us will help us nail these guys. It is essential."

"All right, so when do you guys go marching in with your guns, helicopters, tanks and a search warrant so I can retire from my second job as drug informant?"

"Helicopters? Tanks? You are thinking about our BATF friends and those knuckleheads in Waco."

Bud lowered his head and smiled.

"The search warrant should be forthcoming in the next few days."

"The next few days?"

"Bud, you said yourself nobody at the winery saw you. You will be fine."

"What happens if somebody *did* see me?"

"After Tuesday night, did you work at the winery the next day?"

"Yeah."

"Did anything happen?"

"No, it was just another day at the winery. Nothing exciting."

"Are you working this weekend?"

"Yeah, there is another wedding reception this Saturday up there. Almost one hundred fifty people coming. Campbell has all the tour guides on this one, all hands on deck.

"You will be fine. Just hang tight. Again, you did a great job."

"Who did a great job?" spoke a familiar voice.

Bud and Agent Harris turned around and saw Vernon Truett, looking down at them. Turns out Vernon's services were not needed to assist with dinner and almost as quickly as he left, he returned.

Harris replied, "Vernon, how long have you been listening to our conversation?"

"Since . . . well, 'the smell of raw opium,'" admitted Vernon.

"Shit," replied Harris.

Bud crossed his arms around his chest and slightly lowered his head, saying nothing.

"Vernon, I've got to trust you on this one. It's not standard protocol to discuss ongoing investigations with folks outside. And I'm sure I'm about to violate about a half dozen DEA rules and regulations."

"Brian Harris, shame on you. How long have we known each other?"

"Yes, I know. Since grade school. But this one we must keep strictly confidential."

"I'm a lawyer for Pete's sake. I know about confidentiality."

"Confidentiality? What's so confidential?" another familiar voice spoke.

All three men turned and saw Cheryl Truett standing near the back door. Harris sighed and mulled over the current predicament, made a quick judgment call, and replied to Cheryl's question.

"So *confidential* that we need to discuss it over dinner." Harris stood up. Bud quickly followed and Harris led the group into the house.

"Dinner is ready," announced Trish, who stood at one end of the dining table, closest to the chilled bottle of wine.

"Looks great, Mom," said Cheryl.

Bud chimed in next. "Mrs. Truett, this looks great."

"I can't wait to try the bottle of wine you brought us, Bud. Just need to give it about ten more minutes in the freezer. Oh, honey. Bud brought us over a nice bottle of wine."

"That's good," replied Vernon softly.

Noticing the apprehensiveness in the room, Trish appraised the situation. Everyone at the dining table just stared at Harris and said nothing.

"Did I miss something?" Trish asked.

A few seconds passed and Harris broke his silence, clearing his throat. "No, Trish, you didn't. First, dinner looks great."

Trish sensed something else was up. "And?"

"And second, what I'm about to tell you and everyone here tonight stays in this room. If word gets out, it could mean the end of my job, and for some people, it could be worse. It could put them in danger to life and limb."

Intrigued, Trish leaned in and said nothing.

"Vernon, I've known you since grade school. Trish, we've known each other since high school and Cheryl, I was there at your baptism."

"What about Bud?" Vernon quickly interrupted.

"Bud is a big part of this."

Cheryl turned her head left and looked at Bud, who said nothing.

"Cheryl, Bud didn't do anything wrong. Bud was only doing what I told him to do these past five weeks. In fact, he has helped us out a bunch. He kept his word by telling no one, at my request," Harris said.

"Okay—telling no one *what*?" Trish pressed.

For the next hour over dinner, Harris explained almost everything he knew about South Plains Cellars, starting with the disappearance of Senior Special Agent Traegar Jackson, the drug lab inside the basement of the winery and the discovery of the small, blue wax envelope of heroin. All the dinner guests ate in silence and listened intently as he spoke.

Harris did not share everything, such as Campbell and Evans's attempt to avoid questioning and his boss's initial request to close the investigation at the bequest of an assistant U.S. district attorney.

"That's about it so far," Harris concluded. "And like I said, please keep this amongst us."

Cheryl was the first to speak. "So how does this involve Bud?"

"Bud has been our best asset. Working at the winery on the *inside*, he helped us gather enough information and photographic evidence to obtain a search warrant."

"That sounds dangerous, especially with what you said happened to that Agent Traegar Jackson," said Cheryl.

"Bud has been very cautious, and his contributions are getting ready to pay off," reassured Harris.

"I'm being careful," Bud assured.

"But Bud, you don't know who these people are. If what Uncle Brian says is true, you could be in real danger."

"Danger of what? I'm just a tour guide. Nobody there knows what I'm doing. And I plan to keep it that way."

Vernon, who like Bud had kept his silence as well, finally spoke up.

"How far are you from getting a search warrant?" he asked his friend.

"We have a couple internal matters to settle first. Should be ready to execute in a few days."

Vernon nodded his head.

"So, I'm going to say this one more time to everyone at this dinner"—Harris looked at each person in the eye one by one—"I'm trusting each of you tonight to keep your word of confidentiality. Please under no circumstances share with a soul what I discussed tonight."

Everyone at the table nodded their head in agreement.

Bud and Cheryl remained silent during the ride back to Cheryl's apartment. Bud pulled his car to a full stop in her apartment parking lot. Cheryl spoke first.

"Bud, why are you doing this? You could get in real trouble, or worse."

Bud guessed correctly that Cheryl would be concerned and had time to prepare a response.

"You remember my story about my best friend Chad Gallagher, dying from of a drug overdose."

"Yes, I'm so sorry."

"Cheryl, I've told you this before and I'm going to say it again. I *fucking* hate drugs. I despise them and anybody who has anything to do with them. For example, Worthington does that shit and I do my best to avoid him as much as I can."

"Yeah, but you could be in actual danger. Like, your life could be in danger. Do you really think that there is a drug operation at the winery?"

"I know so."

"What about the other tour guides? Did you think they know?"

"I don't think so. We normally never get anywhere near the walk-in freezer and where the basement is located. All our tours are on the other side of the winery."

Bud walked Cheryl to her apartment, with neither person saying anything. Once they reached the apartment door, the young couple kissed each other. Cheryl embraced Bud with both arms around him and then moved her lips away from his and whispered in his ear.

"Please be careful."

Half smiling, Bud replied, "I'll be careful. Call ya later."

Cheryl inserted her apartment key in the lock of the front door, turned the key and pushed the door open. Bud stayed on the stoop outside until Cheryl closed the door behind her.

75

Thursday, September 22, 1994
11:20 p.m. CDT
South Plains Cellars

Jaime Sáenz sat in the basement, reviewing surveillance tapes from the week he was gone, while his team worked processing the latest batch of opium. Sáenz decided to review the footage from security camera 1. This camera viewed almost the entire drug laboratory. Again, Sáenz didn't expect to see anything as none of his workers worked in the laboratory the week he had gone on vacation. He punched the eject button on the videocassette recorder and the tape popped out of the machine. Something immediately caught his eye. The clear plastic view window on the top and right side of the videotape cassette showed a slight thickness of brown videotape on the take-up reel. Sáenz immediately recognized that security camera 1 recorded *something* while he was gone.

Sáenz took the videocassette tape, inserted it back into the VCR and hit the rewind button. Once the tape stopped, he pressed the play button. The television screen showed white block letters in the lower left of the screen and a set of numbers on the lower right screen, indicating the recording time.

P.M. 06:42
Sep 10 .1994 **00:00:00.10**

The screen went from darkness to becoming engulfed with light. Sáenz noticed an empty drug laboratory, indicating somebody had turned the lights on. He stared closer at the television screen and saw a man from his back as he walked toward the workstation table inside the laboratory. In his right hand, the man held what looked like a small handheld camera. Sáenz couldn't make out the man's face since the camera and the man's hands blocked it from clear view. The only image he did recognize was the white short-sleeved polo and an athletically toned forearm. Shocked, Sáenz continued to watch the black-and-white footage, straining to catch a better view of the man's face but unable to make it out exactly.

Less than a minute later, the man exited the security camera's line of vision, and shortly afterwards the screen went dark. Right before the footage stopped recording, the white numbers and letters flashed on the screen.

P.M. 06:44

Sep 10 .1994 00:00:01.52

Anger enveloped Sáenz and he pressed the rewind button and watched the same footage again four more times Sáenz. Someone was taking pictures where they had no business taking pictures. Sáenz immediately thought to review the security coverage of the white wine room to perhaps get a better view of who came into the laboratory but cursed out loud to himself. He had just *erased* all the security footage from the entire winery, including the video footage from the white wine room.

The next hour he sat in his office and hatched a plan to confirm this man's identity.

75

Friday, September 23, 1994
9:22 a.m. MDT
Drug Enforcement Agency, El Paso Intelligence Center

"Did you already get back from seeing Judge Lawrence?" asked Director Colangelo.

"Ah, no sir. According to Derderian, Judge Lawrence is sick today," replied Agent Harris.

"Out sick?"

"So, you don't have a signed warrant?" queried Colangelo.

"Nope."

"I just brought the Assistant U.S. Attorney Shamkin up to speed with all the new developments with our investigation at South Plains Cellars and gave us the go-ahead. How soon can we get that warrant application signed?"

"When Easton talked to the judge's assistant, she didn't believe he was that sick. So, hopefully by tomorrow."

"Shit. We are in a holding pattern until we get that warrant."

The team's plan to execute the warrant now depended on what time Saturday Derderian could obtain the signed warrant. And that, it seemed, was at the mercy of somebody's current gastrointestinal disorder.

76

Friday, September 23, 1994
11:19 a.m. CDT
Office of the Lubbock District Attorney

Sitting in his conference room, Lubbock District Attorney Neal Hutchinson quietly reviewed the Post-it note his assistant handed him earlier. His attention went back to the last morning brief from his staff of attorneys.

"All right, ladies and gentlemen. That will do for the day. Have a good weekend."

Hutchinson stood up and quickly left the conference room, avoiding any goodbye pleasantries with his team.

Hutchinson poked his head through his office door and spoke to Sarah Ferris, sitting at her desk.

"No phone call or interruptions please."

"Yes sir," replied Sarah.

Hutchinson closed his office door and punched a ten-digit number on his office phone.

"Hello," answered Jaime Sáenz.

"It's Neal. What's up?"

"Santiago is arriving tomorrow night. He wants the whole team at the winery."

Hutchinson cursed to himself. Seems Zavala didn't keep track of local football events, let alone people with dinner plans at the Cattle Baron Steakhouse on a Saturday night.

"What time?"

"Ten p.m."

Jaime Sáenz hung up his phone.

With the dial tone, Hutchinson hung up his office phone. At least he could keep his dinner plans with his wife. It was explaining why he had to go the winery late at night—*that* was going to be the next challenge. He grabbed his office phone and placed another phone call.

"Hank Evans."

"Hank, it's Neal. We need the entire team assembled at South Plains Cellars tomorrow night at ten o'clock."

"What? You know that's Homecoming weekend, right?"

"I'm very aware of that, Hank. The big man wants to see us all of us."

"Why? What's going on? We are on pace to double what we laundered last year."

"I don't know but call the rest of the team and make sure they're all there. Do we have any events at the winery tomorrow night?"

"Let me check." Evans paused and looked at his calendar book on his office deck. "We've got a wedding. One hundred and fifty guests."

"Who plans a wedding reception the same day as Homecoming?"

"I don't know. But they got the place booked from five to nine that night."

"That will be fine."

Hutchinson hung up his office phone. A face-to-face meeting with Santiago Zavala was never positive. Now he wanted everyone involved with South Plains Cellars to meet with him Saturday night. Hutchinson then placed a call to Lubbock Police Chief Decatur.

A long-awaited plan Hutchinson had been working on might just come to fruition.

77

Saturday, September 24, 1994
9:51 a.m. MDT
Drug Enforcement Agency, El Paso Intelligence Center

Sitting at his desk in the EPIC office since early that morning, Derderian shuffled through his reports. His office phone rang, and he picked it up immediately.

"Easton."

"Easton, it's Brian. I just got a phone call from our Insurgentes branch. They have strong intel that Santiago Zavala is on his way to Lubbock *today*. He should arrive sometime early this evening. Any news from Judge Lawrence or his assistant?"

"Nothing."

"Okay. Listen carefully. If you don't hear anything by three o'clock your time, I want you to drive directly over to Lawrence's house and get that warrant signed."

"Got it."

"Once I get word from you, I'll notify the Amarillo branch. The El Paso team won't have enough time to fly commercial for this one. Call EPIC flight ops and have them prep two Beechcrafts for early this evening. Destination Lubbock, Texas."

Derderian smiled.

"Yes sir."

78

Saturday, September 24, 1994
4:13 p.m. CDT
Lubbock, Texas

Cheryl drove her Honda Prelude east down Fourth Street, passing Jones Stadium. Bud and Cheryl noticed all the people in attendance at the football game. It seemed that the entire town of Lubbock was watching it.

"Thanks for giving me a lift to work. I have no idea what's wrong with my Explorer. The triple-A guy towed it to the dealer about an hour ago. Monday morning was the earliest he could expect to hear anything from the service department."

The young couple drove for another minute without saying anything. Finally, Cheryl broke the tension.

"Bud, I need to tell you something. I'm just really worried about what Uncle Brian told us Thursday night. Are you sure you're being careful?"

"I'm being very careful. I got Agent Harris all the information he needs, and nobody at the winery knows what I did. Remember all those pictures I took this past Tuesday? I went to work the next day, and nothing happened."

"I know but just promise me you'll be careful. I just have a bad feeling about tonight."

"A bad feeling? C'mon Cheryl. Everything will be fine."

Bud wanted to change the mood inside the car.

"Here, let's put on some music."

Bud turned on Cheryl's radio. The searing guitars of Sponge's "Plowed" filled the Prelude.

Cheryl smiled after the first few lyrics drove into the chorus. "Very appropriate song for you tonight."

Bud shrugged and didn't say anything.

Twelve minutes later, Cheryl drove down the tree-lined entrance of South Plains Cellars and entered the circular driveway. Multiple cars were already parked in the lot and more kept arriving.

"Oh my gosh, this place is beautiful."

"Yeah, I told ya the place is nice."

Cheryl pulled to a stop near the front entrance. "So, what time again?"

"The wedding reception starts in about thirty minutes and goes on until nine tonight. A party of this size usually takes us about thirty minutes to an hour to clean up. How about I call you around ten o'clock?"

"All right, mister, but you owe me. Can't believe we are missing the Homecoming game." Cheryl smiled.

Bud leaned closer toward Cheryl. "Fair enough." He extended his right hand and grasped the back of Cheryl's head and planted a big kiss on her lips. Cheryl almost melted in her driver's seat.

"Okay, you better go, or you're going to be late."

"Call ya soon."

Bud flashed his boyish grin and opened the passenger door.

Cheryl watched Bud approach the front doors of the winery and walk inside.

79

Saturday, September 24, 1994
6:37 p.m. MDT
University Medical Center of El Paso

Supervising Special Agent Derderian held a manila envelope in his hand while sitting in the waiting room at University Medical Center of El Paso, Texas. Next to him was Charlotte Lawrence, Judge Lawrence's wife. Both heard a woman speak out loud.

"I'm looking for the family of Louis Lawrence."

Charlotte Lawrence immediately stood up and walked toward the woman. "I'm Charlotte Lawrence, Louis Lawrence's wife."

The woman smiled and shook Charlotte's hand. "I'm Dr. Maria Montgomery. First, I want to say Louis is doing just fine. His heart is in good condition, and we observed no signs of a stroke."

"He complained about some abdominal pain and felt some nausea," replied Charlotte.

"His appendix is fine, and his white blood count is normal. We determined he has a bowel obstruction. We are currently treating this with a tube inside his nose to his stomach, which will help relieve his abdominal swelling. He is up and talking if you would like to see him."

"Thank you, Dr. Montgomery."

Charlotte walked back to where Derderian was now standing.

"Louis is fine. He has some bowel blockage, which they are treating with this tube-thing in his nose."

Shaking her head, she continued, "Louis never listens to me about his diet. Still eats the same food he did in college and law school. Hopefully, this little *incident* will finally kick those bad eating habits." Charlotte paused. "Please give me a few minutes alone with him. After I'm done, I'll come get you. I know how anxious you are to get my husband's signature. It should only be a few more minutes."

Eight minutes later, Judge Lawrence called Derderian in.

"This must be a first, Agent Derderian. I've never signed a search warrant application from a hospital bed with a tube up my nose."

"At least the tube is not up your ass, honey," cracked Charlotte.

Judge Lawrence gave his wife a look and Derderian did his best to not laugh, lowering his head.

Judge Lawrence finished signing the search warrant and handed off the paperwork, "Agent Derderian, I have one request."

"Yes sir?"

"Not a word to any of your any of colleagues at the DEA, including Brian Harris, about what you saw here today. Word gets about my current condition, and the story gets retold repeatedly, this tube currently in my nose could very well end up in my ass. I'm a U.S. federal judge, for Chrissake. Can't fight the war on drugs looking like that."

Derderian smiled. "Yes sir. Mum's the word."

Judge Lawrence smiled at Derderian and extended his hand. "Good luck, son."

"Thanks, Judge."

Derderian looked at Charlotte. "Mrs. Lawrence, thank you very much."

He then quickly exited the judge's hospital room. He fished out a small notebook in his front pocket and looked at the number for Brian Harris's cellular phone. Once he arrived at the nurse's admission desk, he politely asked the nurse on duty if he could borrow her phone. Minutes later, he brought Harris up to speed on the signed warrant.

80

Saturday, September 24, 1994
8:47 p.m. CDT
South Plains Cellars

A flash of lighting and the subsequent thunder crashed outside. Campbell escorted the last wedding guest to the front-door entrance.

"Thank for you coming tonight. Drive home safe."

Campbell waited as the last guest walked through the doors. He locked the doors and went to the tour guides behind the bar.

"Great job tonight, as always. Jason and Jill, y'all can go ahead and clock out."

"Yes!" Jason blurted out quickly and walked into the kitchen.

"What about all the wineglasses in the kitchen, Jerry?" asked Jill.

"Steve and Bud can handle those. Go ahead and go home, Jill. These guys will be able to finish up."

"Are you sure? I'm more than happy to help Bud and—"

"Jill, go home," he cut her off abruptly. "Good job tonight. The weather is getting bad, and we want you to get home safe."

With just Worthington and Bud remaining, Campbell spoke. "All right gentlemen, get those wineglasses cleaned up."

Campbell walked back to his office and closed the door. Bud and Worthington entered the kitchen, and both saw dozens and dozens of used wineglasses piled up.

"Can you believe this shit? There's got to be close to a hundred wineglasses back here and Jerry expects us to clean 'em all?" exclaimed Worthington.

"Yeah, not what I expected to do on a Saturday night. Hey, at least we've got plenty of citric acid."

Bud pointed to the tub of citric acid, with two ninety-pound bags sitting adjacent. Both fraternity brothers started loading the first set of twenty wineglasses in the dishwasher.

81

Saturday, September 24, 1994
7:52 p.m. MDT
Biggs Army Airfield, El Paso, Texas

Since 1989, Biggs Army Airfield was the home base to Joint Task Force Six. Its sole purpose was to help support and facilitate counter-drug missions. Originally, the airfield was built in 1916 and renamed Biggs Airfield, in honor of World War I pilot and El Paso native Lieutenant James B. "Buster" Biggs.

Sitting inside one of the two Beechcraft twin-turboprop King Air aircraft and dressed in full tactical gear, Agent Derderian looked at his watch. Four of his fellow DEA Agents dressed similarly, along with five other DEA agents waiting in the other Beechcraft. Derderian unbuckled his seat belt, walked to the cockpit and spoke to the pilots.

"What's the latest, gents? We got some bad guys we gotta bust."

The copilot responded first. "Nasty weather just flared up west of Lubbock. Tower says we got to wait this one out before we get our clearance to take off."

"How long?"

"Could be another ten or fifteen minutes. I've got another call to the tower here in about five minutes. I will give you and the team an update then."

"Roger."

Derderian walked back to his seat and informed his team of the current situation. Next, he grabbed his brick-like DynaTAC Motorola portable cellular telephone and pressed the orange SEND button again. Red digital numbers appeared at the top of the keypad as the phone redialed Brian Harris.

"Harris."

"Hey, boss."

"You take off yet?"

"Not yet. Bad weather is coming into Lubbock. We're stuck here for the next ten, fifteen minutes until we get the okay from the tower. Where are you?"

"Believe it or not, I'm in the drive-thru lane at Taco Bell."

"What?"

"Between getting you, the El Paso and Amarillo teams coordinated, I didn't get a chance to eat any dinner tonight. Tech played in its Homecoming game today so every restaurant in town is packed. I figured on heading over to Vernon's to eat a quick dinner. Right now, we are just waiting on you and your team's departure from El Paso. Once you and the team are airborne, the Amarillo team will drive down and we will all meet up at the Lubbock International Airport."

"Got it. Oh, boss, one more thing"—Derderian put on his best Spanish accent—"*yo quiero* Taco Bell!"

Ten minutes later, Agent Harris pulled his rental car up to the Truett house and his phone rang. He pressed the orange SEND button and held the large phone up to his ear.

"We got clearance, boss, and are getting ready to take off. Our pilot said our touchdown at Lubbock International Airport should be close to twelve thirty a.m."

"Twelve thirty a.m., got it."

"You still want to hit the winery around that time? Kinda late to execute a warrant."

"Let's make that decision when y'all land. You and the team may run into delays with this weather."

"You got it, boss."

The line went dead, and Harris called his Amarillo team leader next.

82

Saturday, September 24, 1994
9:59 p.m. CDT
South Plains Cellars

"Are you guys done?" Campbell asked.

"I just loaded the last tray in the dishwasher," replied Worthington.

"Good. I need your guys' help with one more thing and then you are good to go home. Follow me."

Campbell walked to the side door that led from the kitchen to the barrel room and held the door open. Both tour guides followed and soon both Worthington and Bud were walking to the white wine room.

"There's a gentleman I'd like y'all to meet. I've told him that both of y'all are my best tour guides and there may be an opportunity to get some special recognition for your hard work. I don't think you've had a chance to meet Hank Evans, our general manager. He is always working away from the winery."

"We are meeting Hank Evans *tonight*?" queried Bud.

"Like I said, Hank is a very busy man, and he came in earlier this evening for a meeting with Drew Dalton. Both are in the conference room above the laboratory."

Worthington and Bud looked at each other and said nothing. Campbell walked up to the entrance of the white wine room and stopped.

"Okay, wait here. I'm going upstairs and I'll come down when Hank is ready to see y'all."

Bud and Worthington did as Campbell said and waited.

8 8 8

Campbell parted the clear plastic flaps, walked into the white wine room and took a hard right. He then ascended the stairs to the second floor and walked to the conference room. He opened the door and entered.

"You are late!" a voice barked.

Campbell looked at his watch, which displayed 10:01 p.m.

"I'm sorry, Mister Zavala. I have no excuse."

Santiago Zavala sat at the head of the conference table. To his right was Jaime Sáenz, and next to Sáenz was Drew Dalton. Sitting on Zavala's left was Neal Hutchinson, flanked by Hank Evans. Behind Zavala was a black steel Safco adjustable audiovisual cart with three shelves. Perched on the top shelf was a large television set and on the second shelf a videocassette recorder. In the corners of the conference room stood two men. One of the men Campbell recognized. The other, larger man was unfamiliar.

"Sit!" yelled Zavala.

Campbell quickly grabbed a seat next to Hank Evans, who said nothing. Hutchinson spoke first,

"Okay, Zavala, you have us all here. You wanna tell us what's going on?"

Zavala looked at Roberto and then at Neal Hutchinson. Roberto approached Neal and punched him in his right jaw, hard. Hutchinson's body wheeled sideways from the blow, bumping into Hank Evans. If Evans had not been sitting next to him, Hutchinson would surely have been knocked out of his chair.

Hutchinson tried to gather his bearings and grasped his face with his right hand.

"I'm running this meeting, not you!" exclaimed Zavala.

Waiting a few seconds for effect, Zavala continued.

"Jaime, play the tape. Esteban, lights."

Saying nothing, Sáenz grabbed a small black remote and hit the tiny play button. Esteban walked over to the conference room's entrance and flicked off the light switch. The television screen came to life, showing the white block images of letters and numbers near the bottom of the screen.

P.M. 06:42

Sep 10 .1994 00:00:00.10

A black-and-white image of the basement drug laboratory appeared, along with a man walking toward the workstation table inside the laboratory. The man held what looked like a small, handheld camera. As before, it was difficult to distinguish the man's face as his hands and camera blocked it from view. Each of the men watched the footage. The only image they did recognize was the white short-sleeve polo and an athletic-toned forearm. The video played until the next images were solid black. Sáenz hit the stop button and Esteban turned on the lights.

Each man at the table looked at each and said nothing.

"That looks like one of the shirts we sell in the tasting room," remarked Hank Evans.

"Does anyone want to tell me *why* this man is taking pictures inside our basement?"

Dalton, Evans and Hutchinson said nothing, but all three men stared at Campbell, including Sáenz and Zavala.

"Señor Campbell?" said Zavala.

Campbell stammered, "Mister Zavala, this is the first time I've seen this video. The white polo shirt looks just like what our tour guides wear. Based on the images I've seen, it could be either Bud Garza or Steve Worthington."

"How do you know?"

"I spoke with Jaime Sáenz earlier this evening, I reviewed our time sheets for Saturday, September tenth. Both Bud Garza and Steve Worthington worked that evening."

"Do you know which one? Jaime informs me that Mr. Worthington helps us with our distribution. Do you think Mr. Worthington has been turned by the *federales* and is trying to obtain more information?"

Hank Evans saw where this was going and interjected.

"Okay, gentlemen, we know it was either Bud or Steve taking pictures. What do we do next once we get a confession? And we will get a confession?"

"We make sure that he is eliminated," replied Zavala.

Everyone in the conference room turned their heads toward Zavala. A few of the men gasped. This time Dalton spoke.

"Señor Zavala. There must be another way to deal with this problem. You just can't get rid of somebody like this."

"Why not?"

None of the men in the room responded.

"There's little to no *federales* presence here, thanks to Señor Hutchinson. And there is no need to worry about any local police getting involved as well. This is *el perfecto funcionamiento,* the perfect operation. We can continue to run it for many years to come as we see fit."

Zavala paused a second then continued.

"That is unless the young man who took those pictures somehow gets the *federales* involved. And if that happens, I will be more than happy to fly you to El Astuto's hacienda in Tamazula and you can tell him yourself why!"

Drew Dalton said nothing and lowered his head. A boom of thunder sounded outside the winery. Hutchinson, who up to this point remained quiet, double-checked the concealed bulge under his suit's left armpit and took a deep, nervous breath.

"Now that we all understand each other and the importance of keeping this operation running: Señor Campbell, please bring these tour guides to us so we may have a word with both of them."

Campbell immediately stood up and went downstairs to retrieve Bud Garza and Steve Worthington.

Once he reached the bottom of the stairs and approached Bud and Worthington, Campbell spoke.

"You guys ready?"

Both young men shook their heads in acknowledgment.

"Now Hank Evans is sitting on your right of the conference table. In addition, we have a few other gentlemen present. Don't worry about them, they are just on the Operating Committee of the winery. Like I said, y'all are both making a great impression. The only thing I ask is if one of them asks you a question, just be honest and answer."

"Sounds good," replied Worthington. Bud nodded his head, saying nothing.

Campbell led Bud and Steve up the stairs, followed by Worthington and then Bud. Campbell reached the conference room entrance first and opened the door. Worthington walked in first, followed by Bud. Another sound of thunder filled the winery. The storm was getting closer.

"Gentlemen, I'd like to introduce you to Steve Worthington and Bud Garza," said Campbell, announcing the arrival of the two young tour guides.

Hank Evans stood up and walked over to Worthington and Bud, with his right hand extended.

"Steve, Bud: Hank Evans. Nice to meet you both. Jerry tells me that you gentlemen are the best we have here at South Plains Cellars. On behalf of myself, Drew Dalton, our winemaker, and a few folks from the winery's Operating Committee, we want to thank each of you personally for your hard work and dedication."

Bud and Steve stood awkwardly glanced at each other and the men in front of them.

Evans continued, "We do have one question we'd like to ask you before we continue, so please take a seat and keep your eyes on the television set in front of you."

Evans sat down in his chair. "Do either one of you have any idea who this is on the television screen?"

Bud and Steve looked at each other bewildered by the question and both fixed their eyes on the television screen.

Campbell walked toward the door's entrance and stood at the ready near the light switch. Esteban walked toward the front of the room and stood near Roberto. Sáenz pressed the play button on the remote and the screen came to life.

Bud watched the video unfold, and his adrenaline level spiked.

Bud watched himself on the screen for another ten or so seconds as his mind began to seize in panic—but then a much louder crack of thunder enveloped the winery, and the entire conference room went dark, along with the television set and the bright halogen lights of the white wine room. Confusion filled the conference room in its darkness. Suddenly, the conference room door opened, and someone ran out of the room. Immediately, South Plains Cellars' backup generators fired up. The winery's intercom system sounded off with its programmed woman's voice.

"Emergency lighting activated."

The winery's emergency lighting system kicked on and small emergency lights dimly lit the conference room.

Bud Garza was nowhere to be seen.

"Get him, now!" yelled Zavala.

Roberto and Esteban hustled toward the conference room door.

83

Saturday, September 24, 1994
10:27 p.m. CDT
Cheryl and Lisa's apartment, Lubbock, Texas

Cheryl sat on her couch watching television while Lisa, her roommate, was out on her fourth date with Bud's friend Alejandro. She began to worry once more about Bud when her apartment phone rang.

"Hello, this is Cheryl."

Whispering, Bud spoke. "Cheryl, it's me, Bud."

Cheryl could hardly hear Bud's voice. "Hey, I was just thinking about you. Are you ready for me to pick you up? And why are you whispering?"

"Cheryl, please listen carefully. I don't have much time. The guys at the winery found me out."

Cheryl tried not to scream into her phone. "*What?*"

Bud pulled away the white wine room's wall-mounted phone receiver away from his ear.

"And please whisper. The bad guys might hear you."

Cheryl whispered in reply, "Sorry. Where are you? And what do mean by bad guys?"

"Inside the winery. Look, the power is out here and it's almost completely dark. I'm trying to hide from these guys. They caught me on a video taking pictures. Hold on."

Cheryl faintly heard the sound of Roberto and Esteban speaking Spanish in Bud's background as they searched for Bud.

"Gotta go," Bud suddenly said and hung up the phone.

Cheryl hung up her phone and thought for a moment.

She grabbed her car keys and approached the front door of her apartment when the door opened. Lisa and Alejandro stood in the entrance, returning from their date.

"What's wrong, Cheryl? You look like you just saw a ghost."

"Bud is in real trouble, and I need both of y'all's help."

Cheryl quickly brought Alejandro and Lisa up to speed on what Bud had been doing up to this point, including a quick recap of his working undercover for the DEA and all the pictures he took at South Plains Cellars. Several times Cheryl repeated the need to keep Bud's involvement with the DEA a strict secret. At first, Alejandro and Lisa thought Cheryl's story was too incredible to be real. But as Cheryl spoke, they could tell by her tone of voice that she was dead serious. It was clear Bud needed help immediately.

"Do you have any idea of what we can do?" asked Cheryl.

"You are telling me that Bud is stuck hiding somewhere inside that winery and people are looking for him," Alejandro said. "So, what if we could stop those people from looking for Bud, and instead focus their attention on us?"

"Yes, but I don't know what that means. How do we get people looking for Bud inside a winery to pay attention to us?"

"I've got something that just may work. Let me make a quick phone call first. In the meantime, meet me at the Sigma lodge in half an hour. Where's your phone?"

Cheryl pointed toward the small table next to the couch. Alejandro quickly walked over and grabbed Cheryl's Trimline phone and made his first phone call.

"Hello?"

"Heath, its Alejandro."

"Well, whatcha doing, my little *hermano*?"

84

Saturday, September 24, 1994
10:27 p.m. CDT
Truett home

Cheryl closed the passenger door on Lisa's Audi 80 and both women trotted to the door of the Truett home.

"Oh, thank God. I think he's here. There's a car I don't recognize in the driveway."

Cheryl dug in her purse for her set of house keys and opened the door.

"Uncle Brian?"

Brian Harris was in the kitchen just finishing his last taco. Cheryl's folks were out dining with friends that night, so it was just him inside.

"Cheryl? I'm back here in the kitchen."

Cheryl and Lisa ran toward his voice.

"Whoa, what's the hurry?"

"I just got a call from Bud. He's been discovered as the guy who took all those pictures."

"What?"

"Right now, he's hiding somewhere in that winery. And the power is out, which should help him for a while, he said. Lisa and I came over to tell you so we all could go over and help him get out safely."

"Cheryl, I can't let you do that. We don't know who or what is trying to find Bud inside that winery. It could be very dangerous."

"Are you kidding me? You are a DEA agent. Can't you go with me?"

"Cheryl, we don't have the search warrant yet. It's currently in the sky somewhere between here and El Paso."

"What do you mean?"

"If we go marching into that winery without a search warrant, all the work that Bud and my team did will go to waste. We will be unable to use any other information in a court of law."

"So, what do we do for *Bud*? He's in there by himself with guys trying to find him. Or worse, hurt him!"

"We wait. When my team lands at the airport, we will immediately head to the winery."

"That is ridiculous. Something could happen to him before you and your team arrive. Something bad."

"I'm sorry, Cheryl. It's the best we can do. You need to stay here with me."

"No, I can't believe this. I won't!"

"Cheryl, I know you want to help Bud, but the best thing we can do is wait till my guys arrive. I have close to thirty armed and trained people who are going to be available shortly."

"And Bud could be dead by then."

"So could you."

"That's bullshit! C'mon, Lisa."

Cheryl stormed off from the kitchen, with Lisa in tow.

"Cheryl, please understand. We can't go there now! We must wait for backup."

"Well, I'm going! I don't need a *fucking* warrant!"

"Cheryl, you could get hurt. Your parents will never forgive me."

"I'll never forgive myself if something happens to Bud," said Cheryl. "I . . . I think I'm falling in love with him."

Harris continued to protest, but Cheryl and Lisa were already out the door.

Damn it, he thought. *I can't let those girls go out there alone.*

He started to follow. Then an idea popped in his head. He could speed things up considerably. He picked up the Truett kitchen phone and pressed the number zero.

"Operator, how may I help you?"

"Yes, this is DEA Special Agent in Charge Brian Harris. Please connect me with late-night desk Lubbock International Airport."

A few minutes later, Harris was speaking with Kasey Dunn, the senior airport traffic controller on duty at Lubbock International Airport and one of the few women in her position across the country.

"Yes," Harris confirmed after laying out his requests to Dunn. "Please relay the message that our two teams need to fly as fast as possible. Please grant these two incoming Beechcrafts priority landing privilege."

Harris paused as Dunn requested he confirm the identifying information of the DEA Beechcrafts.

"Yes, N-numbers are 9941 Yankee and 1498 Lima. Thank you."

Agent Harris hung up the phone and quickly left the Truett home and got into his rental car.

85

Saturday, September 24, 1994
10:31 p.m. CDT
South Plains Cellars

After Bud had heard the Spanish-speaking voices and hung up on Cheryl, he had walked through the vinyl straps between the white wine room and entered the red wine room. His luck ran out when the garage door to the crush pad was closed. He then began to hear voices again in Spanish and he quickly scaled up the metal staircase. From there he quietly tiptoed along the elevated catwalk platform and stopped at the same large open top fermenter.

This was the second time in five days that he was hiding in the shadows of South Plains Cellars.

On the catwalk, Bud crouched against the large red wine tank, the furthest the elevated catwalk went before stopping at the east wall of the winery. He contemplated his next move as the events of the previous minutes streamed through his head. After seeing his image on the television screen and the power going out, he had bolted out of the conference room and descended the stairs as quickly as he could. With the illumination provided by the emergency lighting, he quickly ran the entire length of the white wine room and found the wall-mounted phone to call Cheryl.

Bud shook himself into the present and refocused on his next course of action.

After Roberto and Esteban started their foot chase to find Bud inside the winery, everyone else remained inside the darkened conference room. Zavala stood up and was fuming, arguing with Evans, Campbell and Dalton. Only Sáenz and Worthington remained silent. Ten minutes later, the electricity came back on and the conference room lit up.

"What are you people still doing here? Go and find this Garza and bring him here to me, now!" yelled Zavala.

Noticing that Zavala's bodyguards were nowhere to be seen, Hutchinson looked down at his right hand, flicked his right thumb against a few of his fingers, and spoke with a dismal tone.

"Zavala, why don't you look for him yourself?"

An incredulous expression hit Zavala face. "Why you *insolent bastard!* Nobody talks to me that way!"

Out of habit, Zavala looked for his familiar bodyguards, who were no longer in the room.

"I *will* talk to you that way, you son of a bitch!"

Hutchinson quickly stood up and punched Zavala hard in his gut. Zavala bellowed over in pain. Hutchinson then lifted his right knee quickly, squarely hitting Zavala in his face, causing his nose to bleed. Zavala crumbled backwards to the ground and Hutchinson kicked Zavala several times, with his M.L. Leddy's elephant-skin boots, all the while thinking that he was ruining two thousand dollars' worth of endangered leather.

Writhing on the ground in pain, Zavala tried to retrieve his Taurus 38 Special stainless-barrel handgun from his back hip holster, but Hutchinson kicked Zavala's hand and his gun scattered across the conference room floor. Hutchinson then reached inside his suit jacket and pulled out his Smith & Wesson Sigma nine-millimeter and pointed it directly at Zavala.

"Hank, grab that phone line, rip it out of the wall and bind this bastard's hands!"

Evans stood frozen in shock and didn't move.

"Now, Hank!"

Evans walked over and ripped out the phone cord from the wall.

Hutchinson began to loosen his necktie with his left hand, while pointing his gun toward Zavala with his right.

"Drew, stuff this tie in his mouth," he ordered. "We don't want *Señor Zavala* to say anything for a while."

After removing the tie off his neck, Hutchinson looked at the silk-woven tag on the inside of his tie, which spelled the words HERMÈS PARIS. "Well, that's a damn shame," muttered Hutchinson. He handed the tie to Dalton.

Campbell spoke up. "Neal, what the *fuck* are you doing?"

"Shut up, Jerry. I've been planning something like this for quite some time. A little coup. Take back our power. Seems your new tour guide helped us move things a lot quicker than I had originally planned."

Dalton was having difficulty putting Hutchinson's tie inside Zavala's mouth as he refused to open his jaws. Hutchinson pulled back the slide on top of his Sigma and placed the muzzle of the gun next to Zavala's right cheek.

"Zavala, did you know as district attorney in Texas, I'm allowed to legally carry a handgun? No shit, state law. Yeah, it feels good protecting the dear citizens of Lubbock with this baby. She's a real beauty. You'd be amazed how *big of a hole* a nine-millimeter shot at point-blank range makes." Hutchinson depressed the muzzle hard against Zavala's cheek.

Zavala looked up. Was that fear on his face? Yes, it was, Hutchinson decided.

"Now, open please."

Zavala did as requested and opened his mouth, and Dalton stuffed the expensive French-made tie into it.

Evans then pulled Zavala's hands behind his back and wrapped the phone cord around them several times and tied the cord with a double knot.

"Now, now, we can't keep Señor Zavala on the floor like that. Hank, Drew, help this man up and sit him in this chair," instructed Hutchinson.

Evans and Dalton picked up Santiago Zavala and positioned him in his original conference room chair. Zavala's bloody nose and body faced the conference room wall, turned away from the group of men.

"Okay, now what?" exclaimed Campbell.

"We wait," replied Hutchinson, who sat back in his chair.

"Wait? Wait for what? We are in a world of *shit* right now, Neal!" shouted Campbell.

"Señor Sáenz. Can you please show these gentlemen the video you showed me last night."

"Yes, Señor Hutchinson."

Jaime Sáenz walked over to the television and depressed the eject button on the videocassette recorder. He inserted a new videotape and pressed the play button. Hutchinson noticed that Zavala still had his back turned to the television set.

"Oh, you need to see this too, Santiago."

Hutchinson stood up and kicked the back of Zavala's upper right shoulder, causing his chair to spin leftward to face the television set. Zavala squinted hard, wincing from the impact. He reopened his eyes to see black-and-white security footage appearing on the screen with white time stamps below.

A.M. 02:31

Jun 14 .1994 00:00:12.33

A man captured from behind was kneeling down in the basement surveillance room next to a steel safe. The man spun the dials of the safe and opened the small door. Stacks upon stacks of money filled the inside of the safe. The man began pulling out the stacks and placing them in a small duffle bag. Once he finished, he closed the safe door and spun the dial. When he stood up to leave, his face came in complete focus.

The video concluded with Santiago Zavala leaving the surveillance room.

Sitting in his chair, Zavala's eyes grew wider.

"You know, I think you look better now, more than that image on TV," Hutchinson told Zavala. "And it's going to be a *damn* shame when a copy of that tape ends up at El Astuto's hacienda early next week."

Zavala grunted in anger, unable to speak.

"Oh, and just so El Astuto knows exactly how much you have stolen, Señor Sáenz included a note, detailing each day, time and the amount of money you have *stolen* from your employer. How much was it again, Jaime?"

"Over three million dollars U.S.," replied Sáenz.

Hutchinson whistled out loud. "Wow, three million dollars. That's a lot more than thirty pieces of silver, wouldn't you say, Santiago?"

Zavala grunted again and tried to loosen his bound hands.

"Now, rest easy, Zavala. You are not going anywhere. You've got a few more days to live. At least until El Astuto gets our videotape and note."

Hutchinson turned to Sáenz.

"Jaime, that copy of the tape we sent yesterday via DHL, how long do you think before it arrives at Señor Gustavo del Victorio Herrencia's residence in the Tamazula Valley?"

"Should be there by this Tuesday," replied Sáenz.

Hutchinson turned back to Zavala. "Excellent. So, I guess that gives you until this Wednesday, maybe Thursday at the latest, Santiago."

Zavala struggled again. Saliva and gasps of air were coming out of the sides of his mouth, along with muffled words. Campbell, Evans and Dalton sat in amazement at everything that had just unfolded before them.

Evans spoke next.

"So, what are we going to do with Santiago in the meantime? I mean, when his goons finally find Bud, they're going to bring him back here."

"Jaime will meet them at the bottom of the stairs and make up some story that Santiago requested they stay there for the time being and watch the kid."

Hutchinson looked at his watch, stood up and made his way to the conference room bar. He pulled out a bottle of 1992 South Plains Cellars Cabernet Sauvignon from the wine storage cabinet and grabbed several wineglasses. He retrieved a corkscrew and started to open the bottle.

"In the meantime, we've got a couple Lubbock black-and-whites that will arrive here around one a.m. They will arrest Señor Zavala and his goons and take all three of 'em to the Lubbock County Jail. None of these guys are U.S. citizens, so nobody is going to care about three illegals sitting in a Lubbock hoosegow. We will keep them in detention until Wednesday morning. By then, El Astuto will know what Señor Santiago Zavala has done. And we will release all three of them, probably drop them off somewhere outside of town, near the abandoned stockyards in Slaton. Of course, El Astuto will know ahead of time where to find Zavala and his men. Problem solved."

Hutchinson poured the red wine into his glass, walked over to his conference room chair, and sat down. He took a taste of the wine, looked at Dalton and spoke.

"This is good wine, Drew. Nice job."

An incredulous Dalton replied, "What about *here*, going forward?"

"Business as usual," replied Hutchinson. He looked to Steve Worthington, who had sat transfixed through all that had transpired. He was shaking like a leaf. "Wouldn't you agree, Mr. Worthington?"

"Y-yes sir, Mr. Hutchinson. Business as u-usual."

"That reminds me, Jaime, please get Mr. Worthington his package so he can leave for Austin in the morning. With this three-month hiatus, we need to get him and our other mules back on track."

Steve Worthington immediately felt calmer. Yes! Somehow, he was going to make it out of this fucked up evening just fine! He even had his old job—his real job—back.

Worthington and Jaime Sáenz left the conference room. A few minutes later, Worthington exited the white wine room with his usual sixty-four-ounce 7-Eleven cup and made his way to the kitchen. He punched his timecard and grabbed his car keys. A few minutes later, he was driving home.

86

Sunday, September 25, 1994
12:27 a.m. CDT
Sigma Lodge, Lubbock, Texas

Alejandro inserted his finger and thumb in his mouth and blared out a loud whistle. The room of thirty-nine Sigma actives became silent.

"Gentlemen, let's review this one more time so everyone is on the same page."

Alejandro pointed with a black Sharpie marker to the large sheet of paper hanging on one of the walls of the Sigma lodge. A large box was scrolled on the middle of the paper, with the words SOUTH PLAINS CELLARS written inside it. Written around the four corners of the box were four numbers: 1, 2, 3, 4, each with a circle surrounding each digit.

"Now remember, when you reach the winery entrance, kill your headlights and park your cars on the shoulder of the main road, near the entrance to the driveway of the winery. You will need to walk down the driveway with the trees lining it. Once you have reached your designated spot around the winery, get your gear set up. And make sure your walkie-talkie is on. Then wait. You will get a signal from me. Everyone understand?"

"Fuck yeah!" yelled an active.

"Let's do this!" shouted another. Several other Sigmas cheered with excitement.

Immediately afterwards, all the Sigmas exited the lodge and piled into several cars and trucks in the surrounding parking lot. Several Sigmas carried cans of beer with them. Alejandro was the last to leave the lodge, locking the front door.

"Well come on, my little Mexican buddy. We're waiting on your ass!" shouted Heath Crawford from his F-150 pickup.

"Give me a minute, Heath."

Alejandro ran across the street to Lisa's parked Audi 80 carrying a black walkie-talkie. Lisa rolled down the window and both her and Cheryl looked at Alejandro.

"We are going. Just follow me, Kenneth and Heath in his pickup."

"What if we lose you on the way?"

"You won't lose us. We will be the loudest truck on the road. We will see you at the South Plains Cellars winery entrance, just off the road," said Alejandro, smiling.

Alejandro ran back to Heath's truck and jumped into the back seat.

"About time, amigo," remarked Kenneth. "C'mon, we got a brother to save."

"How about some AC/DC, gentlemen?" asked Heath while turning on his truck's sound system.

"Crank that shit up, Heath," replied Alejandro. The intro guitar riff to "Highway to Hell" blasted from the truck's speakers, and the song was turned up louder as they drove.

87

Sunday, September 25, 1994
12:29 a.m. CDT
Lubbock International Airport

Agent Harris drove his rental car and met the DEA Amarillo team at the Corporate Aviation hangar, parking on the tarmac. A team member handed Harris a tactical vest and a dark blue jacket, with bright yellow DEA letters silk-screened on the back. Another team member handed him a Glock 17 handgun and a Remington 870 twelve-gauge shotgun. Other members of the Amarillo unit waited outside, next to three 1992 black Chevrolet Suburbans.

A minute later, two Beechcraft King Air turbo-prop planes taxied toward the group of DEA agents and stopped fifty yards away. Both doors opened and nine DEA agents from the El Paso team exited, with Easton Derderian the final one to deplane. Derderian located Harris and walked over to him.

"Got here as fast as we could, boss."

"Good. Got the warrant?"

Derderian nodded and flashed the warrant from his jacket pocket.

"Good, you're riding with me."

Derderian jumped into the back seat of one of the Suburbans and Harris opened the front passenger door. He waved his hand and arm in a circle and closed the door. Harris's driver turned on his light bar and siren and sped toward South Plains Cellars. The two other Suburbans did the same.

88

Sunday, September 25, 1994
12:32 a.m. CDT
South Plains Cellars

Hutchinson took another drink from his glass of Cabernet Sauvignon.

"But what do we do about this Garza kid?" asked Evans.

"Fire his ass, I don't care. He is no use to us anymore," replied Hutchinson.

"But what about the video and the pictures Bud took?"

"He probably wanted something for his scrapbook. Even if he didn't, what's a *tour guide* going to do with pictures of an empty laboratory?"

Campbell spoke next. "But what if Bud is working for somebody else, like the DEA?"

"I had Assistant U.S. Attorney Shamkin shut down that DEA investigation of this place almost two months ago. There is no DEA investigation. If there were, I or someone in my department would know about it."

All the men in the conference room remained silent.

Hutchinson looked at this watch. "Okay, it's almost one o'clock. Help me get this piece of shit outside so Lubbock's finest can haul his ass away."

Evans, Dalton and Campbell converged on Santiago Zavala, who struggled with his captors. The three men forced Zavala to the conference room door. With his hands bound, Zavala grabbed the inside door frame with his fingers, refusing to walk down the stairwell.

Hutchinson, still holding his gun in his hand, shook his head in disappointment.

"Drew, Jerry, hustle down these steps, quickly please."

The men did as they were told, and once they reached the bottom of the stairs, both men looked up.

Hutchinson then approached Zavala from behind, poking the barrel of his gun into Zavala's back and putting his mouth close to Zavala's left ear.

"Listen to me, you piece of shit. If you don't walk down these stairs, I'm going to tell these guys to *push* you downstairs." Hutchinson pointed to Hank Evans and Jaime Sáenz, both standing behind Zavala.

"You know, this far up, a man that falls down these stairs from this height will for sure risk breaking an arm, leg or worse, *a neck*."

Hutchinson tapped his right index finger on the back of Zavala's neck for extra emphasis.

Zavala's eyes raged with anger. More grunting sounds emerged from his mouth as Hutchinson's tie became soaked with more saliva.

Zavala then released his grip from the door frame and slowly descended the stairs. Hutchinson, Sáenz, and Evans followed. All five men surrounded Zavala at the bottom of the stairs, and together as a group they walked toward the crush pad.

89

Sunday, September 25, 1994
12:47 a.m. CDT
South Plains Cellars

With the lights back on inside the red wine room, it was much easier for Bud to see his surroundings. From his crouching position behind the red wine tank, he caught a glimpse of a large Hispanic man walking below and away from him on his right, looking around the edges of the red wine tanks. Bud then heard footsteps ascend a metal staircase—soon followed by slight vibrations indicating that someone was walking on the same catwalk that he was on.

Thinking fast, Bud grabbed the lower end of one of the catwalk support poles and lowered his body toward the base of the catwalk. The problem was, he was now hanging with arms stretched and with his feet dangling in the air, about nine feet above the concrete tank pad. The sound of footsteps on the catwalk came closer.

Bud let go.

His feet hit the concrete pad hard, but he managed to land square and absorb the impact with his legs, bending at his knees as much as possible, his buttocks nearly hitting the concrete. His toes and the top part of both of his feet were on fire. Bud grimaced in pain, but he remained silent. The impact of his landing had been muted in part by the soft leather soles of his Cole Haan shoes. Able to walk, Bud quietly scuttled behind another large red wine tank and lowered his body to the floor of the winery. He kept in shadows and out of sight from the man on the catwalk.

"Roberto, did you find him?" shouted Esteban from above.

"Nothing, Esteban."

"Well, keep looking. He has to be somewhere in here."

90

Sunday, September 25, 1994
12:51 a.m. CDT
South Plains Cellars

With their headlights out, eight passenger cars and two pickup trucks slowly pulled up near the driveway at the entrance of South Plains Cellars and parked on the shoulder of CR 7600. The only light source outside the winery was the ground-fixed spotlights under each tree of the winery's entrance. Light glowed from the red wine room from near the top of the crush pad garage door windows. The rest of the winery was completely dark, with the lights over the crush pad, the overhead lights above the tasting room and those inside the tasting room turned off. With the passing of the recent thunderstorm, the sky was clear and revealed by partial moonlight. Above was a gibbous moon.

As instructed, each of the Sigma fraternity brothers quietly exited their vehicles with many carrying duffel bags and flashlights. Each group walked carefully down the winery entrance road, in between the trees and then to their designated position outside the winery.

Heath Crawford pulled up to the driveway entrance of South Plains Cellars, his music having been turned to a low volume about a thousand feet back. He killed his headlights.

Lisa pulled her Audi just behind Heath's truck.

Alejandro opened Heath's passenger door and walked up to Lisa's car. Lisa rolled down her window, with Cheryl peering out from the passenger seat.

"Go ahead and park your car over there." Alejandro pointed to the side of the road, just past the entrance. Lisa followed Alejandro's instructions, and Alejandro made his way over to her parked car.

"Now come on. Y'all are joining us, right?"

"Join you for what?" questioned Lisa.

"I'm game!" exclaimed Cheryl, who quickly opened the passenger door. Lisa's eyes rolled in her head, and she did the same, quietly closing her driver's side door.

Both women followed Alejandro and got into in the front passenger seat of Heath's F-150. Kenneth walked out and met Alejandro near the driver's side. Heath, who already had his window rolled down, spoke first.

"Okay, little brother, this is your show," he said, handing Alejandro a black walkie-talkie. Alejandro turned it on, pressed the talk button and spoke.

"All wings report in."

"Red One, standing by," came the first voice.

"Red Two, standing by," another voice responded.

"Red Three, standing by," followed a third.

A loud burp and a few chuckles were heard next. "Red Four, standing by."

Heath and Kenneth started to laugh.

Heath then looked at Lisa and Cheryl and said in a low tone, "Alejandro just loves the movie *Star Wars*."

Alejandro depressed the talk button on his walkie-talkie, "Red Five, standing by."

Kenneth and Alejandro jumped into the cargo bed of Heath's truck, sitting in hardtop plastic seats that were bolted down opposite the cab window. With Kenneth and Alejandro's back to Heath, Cheryl and Lisa, both young men grabbed the lap seat belts on each chair and snapped the buckles in place.

Heath leaned back and with his right hand opened the sliding glass window in the back of the truck's cab. He then switched on his truck's stereo system, ejected the compact disc and then inserted a new one. Suddenly, the kaleidoscopic opening riff of AC/DC's "Thunderstruck" began to soar loudly from the truck's speakers.

Alejandro depressed the talk button on the walkie-talkie again and shouted, "Light 'em up, boys!"

Suddenly, the clear, quiet night sky became filled with the lights and sound of exploding fireworks, as dozens of Roman candles began shooting in the air from all four corners of the winery. Firework mortar tubes ignited next, with each shell shooting upwards into the sky, exploding with loud sounds and bright lights.

Heath dropped his transmission handle to D, turned on his headlights and raced down the winery's entrance driveway. He took a hard left and drove straight to the crush pad and began performing donuts on the concrete pad and adjacent area, kicking up dust and small stones from the caliche driveway. Kenneth and Alejandro began shooting Roman candles from the back of the cargo bed into the sky. Lisa and Cheryl held on to each other and screamed with excitement.

Zavala and his five captors arrived in the red wine room when the fireworks started. Whistles of Roman candles, explosive sounds of firework shells and the bright bursts of light lit up the entire area.

Hutchinson picked up his pace, walked ahead of the group to the crush pad garage door and punched the green OPEN button. As the crush pad garage door opened, Hutchinson, along with the other five men, stood in shock and amazement.

"What the fuck?" exclaimed Hutchinson out loud.

Bud Garza, doing his best to hide on the backside of red wine tank number 5, filled with Cabernet Sauvignon and an ice-covered propylene jacket, heard the sounds of fireworks first. The sounds didn't make any sense. His memory flashed back to those same sounds he remembered at a cemetery in Wolfforth, Texas, on July fourth.

Intrigued, Bud inched closer around the corner of the tank toward the edge of the concrete pad. Staring directly at him was Roberto, standing in front of the rack valve.

Bud quickly looked for an exit and noticed the rack valve lever on his right. Bud lifted the rack valve lever to the open position and red wine began bursting out of the valve. The strong pressure of the expelled wine blew Roberto forward several feet and knocked him down.

Bud doubled back across the concrete tank pad and toward the crush pad garage, which was now opened.

The sounds of fireworks became much louder. Bud saw Campbell, Evans, Dalton, Sáenz and one of the other men he remembered seeing in the conference room standing near the crush pad garage door.

Bud slowly walked toward while keeping behind the group of men, all of whom were staring at the commotion outside. Once he was a few yards away, he broke into a flat-out sprint and ran as fast as he could to the crush pad outside. He immediately recognized Heath Crawford's pickup truck and ran straight for the vehicle.

"Stop the truck, Heath! It's Bud!"

Heath hit the brakes, and Cheryl quickly unbuckled her seat belt and opened her door.

Bud immediately noticed and cried out, "Cheryl!"

Bud was only a few feet away from her when his legs went from underneath him and he crashed hard on the ground.

He looked up, and there was saw Zavala's man, Esteban, looking down on him.

Then came the soft sound of footpads behind Esteban.

Esteban felt a tapping on his shoulder.

"Hey. Mister."

Esteban whirled around just as Cheryl threw a right-handed haymaker squarely at his jaw. Esteban immediately collapsed to the ground.

Alejandro and Kenneth, still in the truck, stared with shock as they took in what had happened. Then, almost in unison, they cried out with excitement.

"Holy shit! One hit!"

"Damn, what a punch!"

Bud slowly pulled himself off the ground. Cheryl walked over and embraced him with a big hug.

"Now I know what Steve meant when he said you pack one *helluva* punch."

Cheryl smiled. "Like I said, I'll tell you the story later."

8 8 8

Sergeant Braxton Rawlings of the Lubbock Police Department noticed the fireworks display immediately as he slowed down his police cruiser to a stop at the entrance of South Plains Cellars. Following immediately behind him was Corporal Chance Wexton, who did the same. Rawlings picked up his radio and called his partner.

"Chance, are you seeing what I'm seeing?"

"Sure am, boss. Is the winery celebrating something?"

"I don't know. But fireworks are illegal this time of year. Light 'em up."

Both police cars turned on their sirens and light bars and drove into the entrance of the winery. In addition to the lights and sounds of fireworks, red, white and blue sirens added more cacophony to the mix.

With his clothes drenched in red wine, Roberto stumbled his way outside toward the crush pad in his pursuit of the runaway tour guide. He immediately noticed Zavala, with his hands bound and Hutchinson pointing a pistol at Zavala's back. Campbell, Evans and Dalton surrounded Zavala with their backs toward Roberto as they stared at the fireworks-filled sky.

Roberto's protective instincts took over and he sprinted toward Hutchinson, his shoulders lowered and tackled him to the ground. The force of the impact caused Hutchinson to drop his gun, which Roberto quickly retrieved from the ground. Roberto then stood by Zavala and, directing the pistol at the other men to keep them at bay, he used his free hand to remove the expensive silk tie from Zavala's mouth and then helped Zavala remove the phone cord around his wrists.

Zavala barked out loud, "Roberto, that man there. Get him up and keep your gun pointed at his head!"

Keeping the pistol pointed at Hutchinson's head with his right hand, Roberto pulled the district attorney up from the ground and wrapped his left arm around his neck.

"What the hell?" exclaimed Derderian. "Who's shooting these fireworks? And who called in the Lubbock Police Department?"

Agent Harris looked intently at the chaotic scene unfolding in front of him as he and his team of DEA agents pulled into the entrance of South Plains Cellars.

Harris pulled the radio microphone to his mouth and spoke.

"Stay focused, people. Once we reach the winery, I want guns hot and at the ready!"

Adrenaline levels rose and each DEA agent prepared for the unexpected. With flashing red and blue lights, Harris's Chevrolet Suburban followed the police cruisers toward the crush pad. The other two Suburbans full of DEA agents followed immediately behind.

A roaring chaos of men shouting with guns raised, onrushing vehicles with lights and sirens, and exploding fireworks all combined to shake the air and sky around South Plains Cellars.

91

Sunday, September 25, 1994
1:07 a.m. CDT
South Plains Cellars

Agent Harris was the first one to exit his vehicle. The remaining DEA agents filed out just as quickly, guns raised and barking out commands for everyone to remain in place, raise their hands and drop any weapons.

The Lubbock police officers, already having exited their cars, shouted back at the DEA agents. Angry cries flowed back and forth between the two groups.

Someone is going to get himself shot, Harris thought.

Elevating his shotgun, Harris discharged a round in the air. After the loud report of gunfire there was a stunned silence.

As if on cue, the last of the Roman candles and mortar shells stopped firing in the air as well.

Harris called out as loud as he could and still be understood.

"Ladies and gentlemen, I'm DEA Special Agent in Charge Brian Harris! My colleagues are here"—he paused and looked directly at the two Lubbock police officers—"under *federal* jurisdiction, to execute a search warrant of these entire premises!"

"I don't think so!" shouted Zavala.

Everyone stopped what they were doing and turned their heads and attention to Zavala. Beside him remained Roberto, who still had Hutchinson in a headlock with a gun pointed at his head.

"Unless you want your district attorney dead, you will do exactly as I say!"

The DEA agents and Lubbock police said nothing, looking at Harris for a reaction.

Harris raised his shotgun and pointed it at Zavala. But then he noticed Agent Derderian, shotgun at the ready, walking quietly behind Zavala and the large Hispanic man who had Hutchinson in a headlock. Needing to give his partner more time, Harris slowly lowered his shotgun.

"Santiago Zavala, am I right?" Harris said. "Look around you. Look at the firepower. The moment your man fires his gun you and your guy are dead where you stand."

Hutchinson started to scream in fear. "Do what he says, whoever the fuck you are—I'm the Lubbock district attorney for Chrissake!"

Zavala shouted back, "Nobody tells me what to do!"

Zavala's next intention was to instruct Roberto to kill the district attorney, but his words never came out of his mouth. Instead, he collapsed to the ground.

Behind Zavala stood Agent Derderian, who had struck Zavala behind his head just above the base of his neck with the butt end of his shotgun.

Before Roberto could react, Derderian quickly pointed the muzzle of his shotgun at his head.

"*¡Déjalo!*" barked Derderian, commanding Roberto to drop his weapon.

Seeing his employer lying on the ground, motionless, Roberto dropped his gun and released his headlock on Hutchinson.

Harris spoke next. "Everybody, please stand in place, with your hands raised. Jones, move your men in."

Amarillo Agent Randall Jones began barking commands to the other DEA agents, who started to round up everyone on the crush pad.

Hutchinson, after a few strong coughs, regained his composure and straightened his suit jacket. With a dejected look on his face, he raised his hands in the air. Campbell, Dalton and Evans followed suit.

"Harris! He's waking up," Derderian warned.

Harris walked toward his partner, who still had his shotgun pointed at a now kneeling Roberto.

Beginning to gather his bearings, a groggy Zavala pulled himself up, rubbing the back of his head and sitting on the ground.

Harris walked over toward Zavala, who stared up at him.

"Santiago Zavala, you are under arrest for the murder of Traegar Jackson."

Agent Harris handed his shotgun to Agent Jones, who in turn handed Harris a pair of handcuffs. Harris proceeded to read Zavala his Miranda rights while securing the handcuffs on his wrists. The other DEA agents followed Harris's lead and began handcuffing Jerry Campbell, Hank Evans and Drew Dalton, each of whom remained quiet and in shock. Neal Hutchinson complained the loudest, shouting back at the arresting DEA agent as he reminded him of who he was and how he wouldn't have a job the next day. The agent smirked, said nothing and led the handcuffed district attorney toward his Chevrolet Tahoe.

Another agent then approached Heath's truck with his shotgun raised and started yelling at the college students to move toward the crush pad.

"Agent Frida! These folks are with me," snapped Harris. "Why don't you put a pair of cuffs on this poor bastard"—he pointed to Esteban's motionless body still lying on the ground—"and go help out Agents Derderian and Jones over there when you're done here." Agent Frida did as he was told and approached Esteban.

Cheryl walked to Agent Harris and gave him a big hug.

"I told you to wait."

"Yeah, I know you did. I'm just glad you're here."

Bud walked up then, and Harris extended his hand.

"Thanks, Agent Harris."

"No, thank *you*, Bud." Harris paused and looked around. "So, who was shooting off all those fireworks?"

"Them." Bud pointed to his fellow Sigma brothers, who started walking toward the parked DEA and Lubbock vehicles on the winery's crush pad.

Harris muttered to himself and sighed. "Phil is going to love this report."

92

Sunday, September 25, 1994
11:02 a.m. CDT
Lubbock International Airport

Steve Worthington parked his white BMW in the airport parking lot. He grabbed his overnight Reebok athletic bag and removed the 7-Eleven Double Gulp cup from the vehicle's front passenger seat. He locked his car and walked into the airport entrance under the Southwest Airlines awning.

Once past the airport's automatic sliding doors, Worthington walked up the ramp entrance toward the Southwest Airlines ticket counter. Several people were ahead of him and Worthington took his place in the back of the line.

Suddenly, a man with wide shoulders approached him.

"Hey, whatcha drinking?"

Worthington was caught off guard by the man's question. "Who are you?"

"I said, whatcha drinking?"

Worthington became irritated. "Mr. Pibb," he answered with his fallback.

"Really? Nobody drinks that shit anymore."

Easton Derderian then reached into his pocket and flashed his DEA badge with his left hand, pulled out a handgun with his right and pointed it at Worthington. Out of nowhere, three other men descended around Worthington pointing their own guns at him.

A lady walking past the Southwest Airlines ticket gate screamed as the DEA agents quickly grabbed Steve Worthington and escorted him outside the airport.

With all the commotion, Worthington accidentally dropped his 7-Eleven cup on the ground. The lid popped off and several small light-blue envelopes scattered on the tile floor.

Harris, standing in a corner nearby, quickly scooped up the cup along with the scattered envelopes and followed his DEA agents outside.

Once outside, Derderian began to speak.

"Steve Worthington, you are under arrest for the unlawful distribution of narcotics, with the intent to sell. You have the right to remain silent. Anything you say can and will be used against you in a court of law. You have the right to a lawyer. If you cannot afford a lawyer, a lawyer will be provided to you by the court. If you decide to answer questions now without an attorney present, you will still have the right to stop answering at any time until you talk to an attorney."

The DEA agents yanked Worthington's arms behind him, and he felt the cold steel of handcuffs around his wrists. Saying nothing, Worthington began to weep.

A black Chevrolet Suburban pulled up quickly and stopped next to the curb. One of the agents opened the back passenger door, another agent got inside the car and Derderian shoved Steve Worthington into the back seat.

"Do you understand these rights I have just read to you?" Derderian continued. "With these rights in mind, do you wish to speak about the charges against you?"

Harris was the last man to enter the Suburban, opening the front passenger door and sitting down on the seat. He closed the door and turned around, handing the 7-Eleven cup to Derderian.

Derderian pried open the plastic lid and peered inside to gaze at the cluster of small blue wax envelopes.

"Sure doesn't look like Mr. Pibb to me, Mr. Worthington."

The black Suburban then sped off and away from the airport.

93

Thursday, September 29, 1994
5:07 p.m. CDT
Lubbock, Texas

Cheryl Truett sat on Bud's couch having just finished a beautiful and tasty meal. "The last time I had a man cook me dinner, he was a line cook named Tito, and he made me a cheeseburger."

"Well, my name is not Tito, and I think what you just had wasn't a cheeseburger."

"And what is this wine you are serving me? Are you trying to get me drunk, Bud Garza?"

Cheryl looked at the nearly empty bottle of Sauvignon Blanc. The wine Bud chose was very good. "And is there any more of this? It's good."

Bud replied from his kitchen, "Are *you* trying to get *me* drunk?"

Cheryl snorted out a laugh. "No, just a bit beyond the normal levels of moderation."

Bud flashed a smile back at Cheryl. "There's another bottle in the fridge."

Cheryl grabbed the chilled bottle of Llano Estacado Sauvignon Blanc, opened it, filled her wineglass and then walked to Bud's living room, while Bud stacked all the used plates, bowls and silverware and placed them in his kitchen sink. He figured he could clean the dishes tomorrow.

Bud's apartment phone rang. He walked over to his couch and answered it.

"Hello?"

"Bud, Brian Harris. You got a minute?"

Bud smiled. "Yes, I do. There's someone here you know quite well."

Bud sat on the couch and Cheryl sat next to him. He held the clear, see-through phone's receiver between both of them so they both could hear.

"Hi, Uncle Brian."

"Cheryl, oh good, I'm glad you're there."

"What's up, Agent Harris?" interjected Bud.

"Well, I have to say that what happened this early Sunday morning was a first in my career. Not only were we able to arrest a man the DEA has been looking for since Ronald Reagan was president, but you also helped us in breaking up one of the largest drug operations in West Texas history. On top of that, you helped us expose and arrest a corrupt district attorney. Our accounting team believes there has been some money laundering there as well. All in all, you made a real difference in helping your community in removing illegal drugs off the street."

Bud looked at Cheryl and smiled. "Well, thank you, Agent Harris. Now, if you don't mind, I have to go. I made a promise tonight. It's going to be just Cheryl and me for once. I hope you understand."

"Oh, of course. But there's one more thing I want to discuss with you when you *do* have a minute. What plans do you have after you graduate? I was talking to our director here in El Paso, who, by the way, expressed his appreciation for all your efforts. Have you ever given consideration to working in law enforcement, perhaps the Drug Enforcement Agency?"

Cheryl looked at Bud and raised her eyebrow.

"Agent Harris, may I call you later to discuss that opportunity?"

"Of course, Bud."

"Great. Have a good evening, Agent Harris."

"Bye, Uncle Brian."

Bud hung up his phone.

Cheryl looked at Bud with a mischievous smile. "Agent Garza?"

"Mmm . . . that does have a ring to it."

Bud rose from the couch and walked toward his entertainment center. He picked up his Zenith television remote, turned on his television set and his videocassette recorder. He pressed the VCR/TV button, pushed a videocassette tape inside the VCR and hit the play button.

"What are you doing, Agent Garza?"

Bud grinned at Cheryl's comment.

"Believe it or not, I remember you mentioning that you wanted to see that new series *Friends* a few weeks ago. So, I set my VCR to record the premiere last Thursday. And with everything that happened last week, I completely forgot about it. Now, after we watch the premiere, I figured we could watch the second episode live right after.

"Oh my gosh, I totally forgot that show was coming on last week. You *do* remember what I tell you." Cheryl leaned into Bud and kissed him.

The young couple then nestled into Bud's couch and began watching *Friends*.

Thirty minutes later Bud spoke.

"Well. Whaddaya think?"

"I liked it. It was funny. What did you think? Be honest."

"Okay, I'll be honest. The girls are hot," Bud said, smiling.

Cheryl thumped Bud on his chest with the back of her left hand.

Bud laughed. "What? You told me to be honest."

Cheryl chuckled at Bud's reply. "The boys are good looking, especially that Italian one, Joey."

Bud stood up and stretched. He picked up the TV remote, clicked the VCR/TV button to KCBD Channel 11, the NBC Lubbock affiliate, which was in the middle of a Taco Bell commercial.

"Great," commented Bud. "And as planned, it's just a few minutes before seven."

Cheryl's eyes were fixed on the commercial. "I like that Taco Bell chihuahua. He's cute."

"Yeah, he's cool."

"That chicken you made tasted great with this wine," she added, holding up her half-full glass.

"Thanks. The guy at Doc's said the lemon citrus of the Sauvignon Blanc matches the lemon juice and garlic of the chicken. Maybe I can get a job there." Bud rolled his eyes. "Or maybe I'm done with wine for a while."

Cheryl laughed. "Hmm. Let's review your current résumé, Bud Garza. Unemployed winery tour guide, formerly a lifeguard. Helped DEA take down one of the biggest illegal drug operations in West Texas and a corrupt district attorney along the way. Oh, and knows how to pair wine with food."

"I don't know about that. Someone did give me some good advice once when it comes to pairing food and wine. When in doubt about what food to pair with what wine, just read the back label on the wine bottle. Poor Jerry. It's going to be a while before he uses *that* skill again."

Cheryl laughed out loud.

With an empty wineglass in his left hand, Bud reached for the bottle of wine on the coffee table with his right and refilled Cheryl's glass, then his own.

The young couple watched the second episode of *Friends*. After the show was over, Bud returned to his entertainment center and inserted a new videocassette tape and hit play. He walked over to Cheryl on the couch and planted a big kiss on her lips.

"Well, about time you kissed me like that, mister."

Bud grunted, lowered his voice and spoke. "Mmm . . . First eat food. Watch magic box of small pretty women talking. Then kiss woman."

"Who is this? Caveman Bud?"

"Me like woman. Me kiss more."

Cheryl returned Bud's kiss but started to giggle.

"So, Mr. Neanderthal, what are we going to watch next?"

Bud grunted. "Mmm. Movie favorite of woman. *Tombstone*." Bud's television screen lit up and the voice of Robert Mitchum started narrating the beginning scene.

Cheryl smiled. "You are too good to me, Bud Garza. I just love Val Kilmer. He's so *damn* sexy."

"Mmm. Caveman like Dana Wheeler-Nicholson."

"Oh, you do, huh?"

"Me like her in *Fletch*. Wish she take off towel in water buffalo scene."

"So, do you want me to just wear a towel then while we watch?"

"Maybe after."

Bud grinned and kissed Cheryl again.

The pair sat on the couch and enjoyed the rest of the evening together.

Acknowledgments

In June of 1993, I entered the incredible world of the American wine industry as a novice tour guide at CapRock Winery in Lubbock, Texas. My knowledge of wine was as blank as a brand-new composition notebook, filled with nothing but empty pages. Through the years that book would fill to the brim with wine knowledge, and even thirty-two years later it continues to add new entries of wine information, facts, details, and other aspects. I would like to personally thank the following folks that helped fill that notebook. Kim McPherson, Greg Bruni, Mark Hyman, David Pearson, Melissa Bracken, Robert Hendrickson, Crawford Malone, Scott Hughes, Leon Cikota, Jenn Engel and Marian Leitner-Waldman.

This novel started on an American Airlines flight from DFW to SFO in mid-2017, and it took close to seven years to complete, with most of the writing done on various flights for work or late nights in hotel rooms when I couldn't stop writing in the small hours of the morning.

I would like to thank my wonderful wife, Stacey. Without her, this work would not be possible. My children Braxton and Charlotte are just plain awesome, and I love them very much.

Quick thanks to my parents, Judy and John Sanchez, who I know are looking down on me and smiling.

A quick shout-out to my only and favorite sister, Judith Hightower, my best roommate in college. And you are right, I was Mom and Dad's favorite child. ☺

A nod of thanks and appreciation to George Dunham, Craig Miller and Gordon Keith on *The Ticket* at 1310 AM/96.7 FM. I've been a proud

P1 (an avid *Ticket* listener) since late 1996, and I listened to "The Musers" every morning since. Y'all help start each morning with a good laugh, including the weekday bits at 8:40 a.m. and Fridays with the Emergency Brake of the Week.

Finally, to my new friends at Brown Books, including Milli Brown, Brittany Griffiths, Mary Winzer, Tony Daniel, Ben Davidoff, Laura Irizarry, Danny Whitworth, Amy Goppert, Krysta Herrera, and all the other great people there. Y'all are the best!

Notes on Current Events Featured in the Novel

On June 19, 1994, the Houston Rockets defeated the New York Knicks 86–84, tying the series to three games apiece. Three days later on June 22, 1994, the Houston Rockets closed out the series against the New York Knicks 90–84, becoming NBA Champions.

The New York Knicks blew their 3-2 lead and lost the series. They have not won a championship since 1973.

The New York Rangers 1994 Stanley Cup victory remains their only championship since 1940.

Brazil defeated Italy 3–2 to win the 1994 FIFA World Cup and become the first country to win four World Cup titles.

The 1994 Major League Baseball season ended prematurely when the players went on strike, and for the first time since 1904, no World Series was played.

Arnold Palmer would continue to play on the Senior Tour in the decade following 1994. He retired from tournament golf in 2006.

More than fifteen helicopters were following the O.J. Simpson car chase. The TV coverage achieved some of the highest-ever ratings. Ninety-five million people tuned in to watch as former NFL superstar O.J. Simpson led police on a low-speed, sixty-mile chase across Los Angeles that ended with "The Juice" in handcuffs. The dialogue between police, Al Cowlings and O.J. in the Bronco was later ruled inadmissible at his trial.

8 8 8

The timeline of events surrounding the O.J. murder and car chase as chronicled on Bud's first date with Cheryl Truett and the notes here can be credited to filmmaker Brett Morgen's experimental documentary *June 17th, 1994*, which debuted May 20, 2016, on ESPN's *30 for 30* television series. Morgen was quoted that the aim of his documentary was "to look at the soul of America."

While attending Texas Tech University in 1994 in graduate school, I was on a date at Jazz Café on Friday, June 17, and watched live on television the O.J. Simpson car chase and Game 5 of the NBA Finals at the same time. That personal experience, along with Brett Morgen's documentary, was one of the inspirations for this book. If you have not had the chance to enjoy Brett Morgen's documentary *June 17th, 1994*, I highly recommend it.

About the Author

Born in Fort Worth, Texas, Eric Sanchez is a fifth-generation Texan and happily married to his wife, Stacey. He's the proud father of his above-average children, Braxton and Charlotte. His family resides in Prosper, Texas.

Eric's career in the wine business started over thirty-two years ago when he became a tour guide and "cellar rat" at two wineries in West Texas while in graduate school at Texas Tech University. Upon graduation, Eric worked with several wine suppliers in sales and has since spent the majority of his career working with a major alcohol beverage wholesaler in Texas and the United States. This is his first book.